For all the women who have had to weather the storm.

Jenner and Evie's Playlist

▶ **Starts with Goodbye**
Carrie Underwood — 04:06

▶ **I'll Be Waiting**
Cian Ducrot — 02:52

▶ **Wishful Drinking**
Ingrid Andress & Sam Hunt — 03:14

▶ **Rest (with Sasha Alex Sloan)**
Dean Lewis & Sasha Alex Sloan — 03:13

▶ **You Are the Reason (Duet Version)**
Calum Scott & Leona Lewis — 03:11

▶ **My World**
Calum Scott — 03:23

▶ **Lighthouse**
Calum Scott — 03:10

▶ **I Choose You**
Forest Blakk — 03:00

▶ **Beautiful Things**
Benson Boone — 03:00

Prologue

Jenner

The distant rattling sound coming from the vicinity of our master bathroom dragged me from a deep sleep.

Groggy, I rolled over in bed, not ready to face the day. Reaching across the mattress, I expected to curl my arm around Evie and bring her warm body flush with mine. When my hand came up empty, it hit me that the noises in the bathroom must be her, and I sat bolt upright.

With my heart racing, I leapt out of bed, rushing to the bathroom door, not bothering to knock before entering.

I could only view her from the waist down, where she knelt on the ground, her upper half digging through the cabinet beneath the sink. There was a frantic energy in the room that didn't help to ease my panic.

"Evie?" I asked cautiously. We'd been through so much in the past few years, and I'd been forced to watch the woman I loved crumble one too many times.

"I know I have some stashed in here somewhere." Even though she spoke under her breath to herself, I could hear the high-pitched panic in her voice.

"Baby?" I stepped closer. "What are you looking for?"

Evie froze. "Go back to bed, Jenner. I'm fine."

Yeah, she sure as hell didn't look fine. Truth be told, she hadn't been "fine" in a very long time.

Rubbing a hand along my jaw, I drew nearer, doubling down. "Honey, let me help you. Just tell me what you're searching for."

Slowly, violet, red-rimmed eyes peeked over the edge of the cabinet door, and my heart twisted inside my chest. She didn't have to say the words to confirm what I already knew.

Almost as if she were ashamed, she broke my gaze, whispering, "Tampons. I threw them all out but thought maybe I'd missed some. I'd been so sure this time—" Her lower lip trembled, the implication of yet another failed attempt hitting her with full force.

I was on my knees in a flash, pulling her to my chest.

She finally shattered, her loud sobs echoing throughout the bathroom. Her chest heaved, and she choked out, "I'm s-so sorr-ry."

Evie's heart was breaking because our latest round of IVF had been a failure, but mine was breaking for her. I would find a way to live without us having a baby—my wife was all I would ever need—but for Evie, it had become a compulsion. Her focus had narrowed to achieving that singular goal of getting pregnant, regardless of the physical or emotional toll it took on her, on our marriage.

Stroking her hair, I held her tighter. "You have nothing to be sorry for."

Her sad words were muffled against my chest. "This isn't how this was supposed to go."

Fuck. There was no amount of money that could give my wife what she wanted most in this world. And I had more of it to spare than most. I would give it all up—the fame, the fortune, the ability to play a child's game for a living—if it meant I could end this living nightmare for us both.

The worst part was not knowing why. We'd been through the testing, but all the results came back negative. There was nothing physically wrong with either one of us. If only they'd found something. If the tests had revealed I had wonky sperm or Evie had some internal issue, the doctors could have developed a plan of action, using years of research to overcome our specific roadblocks. But unexplained infertility was a black hole of despair. Our bodies were simply failing us, and there was nothing we could do about it.

When she quieted enough that only the occasional sniffle remained, I eased Evie off the tiled bathroom floor. Keeping my arm around her waist, I led her to the walk-in shower, reaching my hand inside to turn on the hot water.

I kissed her temple. "You take a shower, and I'll run out to the 24-hour pharmacy to get what you need. Okay?"

She nodded, not bothering to look back at me as she shed her clothing and stepped inside.

I knew the second I was gone, she would fall apart again. It was a vicious cycle—one we'd been putting ourselves through for years—and I couldn't do it anymore.

I was done watching my wife suffer.

A tiny ding sounded as I passed through the pharmacy's sliding glass doors. I was a man on a mission, wasting no time in striding to the back of the store, where I knew the feminine hygiene products were shelved. After six years of marriage, there were no secrets between me and my wife. I knew her body as well as I knew my own, and I wasn't scared to walk into a store and buy a box—or three, in this case—of tampons.

But this morning was the first time it was painful to do so.

Standing in the aisle, I wondered what kind of sick fuck had thought it was a good idea to place the pregnancy tests right next to the period products. Didn't they have any sensitivity toward women struggling? Women like Evie? That seeing a brightly colored box featuring a smiling baby would rip their hearts out? Seemed like a cruel joke, if you asked me.

Eyeing the rows of tampons and pads, I determined that a man must be in charge of marketing these products to women. Most of them featured figures of sporty women, promoting some kind of female empowerment that just because they were on their period, it didn't have to slow them down. Had any of these fools ever encountered a woman on her period? I knew from experience that the last thing they wanted to do was work out. As soon as I got her situated, Evie would be curled up in bed for the following twenty-four hours minimum.

Sighing, knowing I couldn't waste any more time silently raging at strangers working at the tampon company, I grabbed three boxes of Evie's preferred brand in different absorbencies since she said she'd gotten rid of all of hers—she needed a full restock.

Stepping up to the checkout counter, I placed them down, grabbing an assortment of chocolate bars at the register on impulse.

The middle-aged woman working the counter rang me up. She peeked up at me when I set down the tampons, her smile growing when I added the candy.

"Must be some lucky lady to have you taking care of her like this," she mused, scanning each item and placing them into a bag.

If only she knew.

I forced a tight smile and nodded. "She's my whole world."

Her gaze dropped to my left hand, which was holding my credit card, my wedding band visible. "You take care of each other, you hear?"

Lord knows I'm trying.

Evie was tucked into bed, mindlessly watching trashy reality TV, but I couldn't keep my eyes off her. She was beautiful, the love of my life, but the light had dimmed from her unique violet eyes the longer we struggled to conceive—both naturally and with the help of medical interventions. What began as excitement over starting a family had quickly turned into dread of the constant treatments and the inevitable disappointment each time we were faced with failure.

She'd always put on a brave face—at least in public. Almost no one at the rink knew of our private struggles, and Evie kept a smile plastered on her face, playing the dutiful hockey wife at games and team events. Only my captain, Maddox Sterling, was privy to what went on behind closed doors, and only because I'd needed someone to talk to.

Evie had these online support groups filled with women dealing with infertility. She would hop on her phone or computer with anonymity to talk with complete strangers versus talking to me. So, I'd been forced to confide in my closest friend on my professional hockey team, the Indianapolis Speed, when the weight of my helplessness threatened to crush me.

Without family nearby, our only tangible support system came from my teammates and their significant others. But Evie was too ashamed to let anyone know that her body couldn't do the one thing it was designed to do—carry a baby.

"You know, I was thinking," she mused beside me. "I'm definitely going to try to lose some weight before our next round."

"No." The word came out sharp and fast, like a reflex.

Evie sighed. "I know you're always telling me you like me the way I am, but the doctors have told us since the beginning that my being overweight could be a potential hindrance."

My wife wasn't only beautiful; she had the most voluptuous curves. And damn, did she own it, which made her even sexier. Her soft body—featuring thick thighs, wide hips, belly rolls, and breasts so full they were nearly the size of my head—was the perfect complement to my hard planes of muscles, earned from years of working out to compete at the highest levels of professional sports.

Taking a deep breath, I braced for what I needed to say. "No, I meant I can't do another round."

There was a beat of silence, then came "You're giving up? I thought we both wanted this."

The rising pitch of her voice forced me to look at her after my admission. That was a mistake. The agony in her light, bluish-purple eyes was like a dagger to my heart. She blamed herself, and I could see she thought I blamed her too.

"Evie, listen." I reached for her, but she flinched away from my touch, scrambling out of bed to put space between us. "Baby, you know I will give you anything you ever ask for, but I think it's time to take a step back from the fertility treatments."

She sank her teeth into her lower lip as she fought back tears, and I hated myself for doing this to her.

Her voice was barely above a whisper as she said, "Jenner, I *need* this. More than anything."

I slung my legs over the edge of the bed closest to where she stood. "I know. But this isn't the end of the road. There are other options. We can look into surrogacy or even adoption. We can still have a family."

Evie's body shook, and I prepared to have her collapse into a sobbing mess for the second time in a few hours' time, but when she screamed, "No!" I realized she was shaking with rage. "You don't get it! How can I watch another woman carry *my* baby? I can't. Please don't ask me to."

"I can't watch you suffer anymore, babe. It's fucking killing me."

"You don't think it's killing me? That every time we try, we come up with nothing, and no one can tell me why? That the dreams I had of filling this big house with tiny redheaded replicas of the man I love are slowly slipping away with each failed attempt?"

Closing my eyes, I strengthened my resolve. I was putting an end to this for her sake. There was only so much she could take before she shattered completely. I couldn't watch that happen, not when I had the power to stop it.

"Evie, I'm sorry. I just can't anymore."

When I opened my eyes, she was gone.

"Evie?" I called out, standing from my perch on the bed.

The rustling of fabric reached my ears, and I strode into our walk-in closet to find her on her knees, throwing clothes into a suitcase.

"What are you doing?" I asked, even though the answer was clear.

"I have to get out of here," she muttered, seemingly to herself, as she stood to grab more garments.

As much as I hated spending time away from her—especially during the hockey season when I traveled constantly to away games—maybe it was good for her to take a breather, to calm down. Perhaps if she had the time and space to think through what I'd said, she'd see that there was a way for us to move forward in our quest to create a family. We weren't out of options yet.

Checking my watch, I groaned. "I've gotta head to practice." Stepping closer, I dropped a kiss atop the blonde hair at the crown of her head. "I love you. Take all the time you need, okay?"

She hummed but didn't acknowledge me with a verbal response.

Grabbing my sneakers from a shelf inside the closet, I headed downstairs and hopped into my car, ready to work out my frustration on the ice.

But as I drove away, I had no idea that would be the last time I saw my wife.

Chapter 1

Evie

Four Years Later

"I'm sorry, Ms. Grant, but at this time, we are unable to have your profile listed in our catalog for prospective birth mothers to choose adoptive parents for their babies."

Six.

That was the number of rejection calls I'd received from adoption agencies within the state.

Four years after leaving my life in Indianapolis behind, I was no closer to becoming a mother.

Tamping down the sinking feeling of defeat, I pinched the bridge of my nose as I replied, "May I ask why?"

If she was going to crush my dreams of parenthood, then I didn't care if my pushback made her uncomfortable.

There was a pause from the woman on the other end of the line. "Unfortunately, your living situation isn't quite as stable as we'd hope for when placing a child."

Translation: you're single and living with your parents, working in town as a bank teller.

On paper, I didn't hold a candle to those perfect couples applying for adoption alongside me, but what I lacked in terms of a partner, I made up for with heart. There wasn't a person alive who would love a baby like I would. I just needed someone to give me a chance.

Not giving up the fight yet, I pressed, "How so? I have a built-in support system where a child would grow up in the loving home of their grandparents. Not to mention, my brother is the town's family physician, so they would receive immediate access to proper medical care."

She sighed. "Be that as it may, at this time, our decision is final. Good luck in your quest, Ms. Grant."

It was times like these that I wished I still had a landline to slam down the receiver, a way to make my frustration known to the person on the other line. Pressing a button on a cellphone was far less satisfying, especially when the three beeps in my ear indicated the woman from the adoption agency had hung up first.

Elbows crossed on the kitchen table of my parents' home, I dropped my head to the wood.

My hometown of Rust Canyon, Oklahoma, was in the middle of the Bible Belt, but I'd given up on God a long time ago. How could I believe in a deity that would allow me to suffer for years, trying to conceive a child with a man I loved? Or one that would allow every adoption agency in this conservative area to block my applications? And I'd be damned if I set foot in a church where I was expected to believe there was a lesson to be learned from the difficulties I'd faced over the past seven years.

It drove my mother insane, but I wasn't budging.

Almost as if the thought conjured her presence, Maddie Grant entered the kitchen. Taking one look at my defeated posture, she tsked. "Elbows off the table, Evie."

I groaned but obeyed, lifting my head and facing my mother.

"I know I raised you better than that."

"Sorry, Mama," I mumbled.

She eyed my phone, discarded on the table. "Bad news?"

"Suppose it depends on who you're askin'," I said wryly, twisting my lips.

She threw both hands on her hips. "Was it not clear I was askin' you?"

With my eyes cast down in shame, I replied, "Just another judgmental adoption agency deeming me an unfit mother because I'm not married and live with my parents."

Mama let out a deep sigh, dropping onto the seat opposite me at the kitchen table.

I peered over at her, frustration finally taking hold. "I don't get it. There are thousands of unwed moms all over the world! But I'm not good enough to be one because I can't carry the baby myself? How is that fair?"

"I agree. It's not fair, darlin'." She grasped my hand over the table. "But the world isn't always fair."

"Tell me about it." If life were fair, I wouldn't be back living with my parents. I'd be in Indianapolis with my husband, surrounded by children we'd made together.

It would seem her mother's intuition was spot on because she remarked, "I know you won't want to hear it, but this whole process would have been easier if you hadn't left Jenner."

There it is.

My mom still hadn't gotten over the fact that I'd cut and run on my marriage when times got tough. To be fair, I had been hurting, reeling from yet another failed attempt at IVF, when Jenner suggested we stop trying. It had felt like the world was crumbling, like he was giving up on me because I couldn't get pregnant and give him a family that, to that point, I'd thought we both wanted. So, I'd packed my things and come back home—home being Oklahoma—with my tail between my legs.

The ultimate irony was that he had suggested exploring other options—like adoption—that day, and I'd shut it down. Now, here I was, four years later, trying and failing to go down that path alone.

If there was truly a God up there, I sure hoped he was having a good laugh. Someone might as well find humor in my misery.

When I remained silent, Mama said, "You know, most people would be thrilled about their children coming back home after they'd moved away. But you and your brother?" She shook her head with a sigh. "I wish neither of you had come back if it meant the both of you were still happy."

My younger brother Tucker's divorce had been finalized shortly after mine. He'd been working in Baltimore for a big-name research hospital but had given it up to practice family medicine in the town we grew up in.

We were both single by choice—a rarity in this town.

Once or twice, a handsome young cowboy had offered to buy me a drink, hopeful it would turn into something more, but I always declined, not wanting to lead them on.

Jenner had married me before we discovered I was broken. I couldn't in good conscience rob another man of a future family. That, and Jenner would always hold my heart, even if we weren't together anymore.

Tucker, on the other hand, was pining after a woman. But it just so happened that the woman was *not* his ex-wife. He had no regrets over his divorce as I did mine. His regrets ran deeper, further rooted in the past.

The Grant siblings were batting a thousand when it came to life and love, it would seem.

Mama stood, coming close to tuck a piece of my hair behind my ear. "I love you, darlin', but you're not living."

I squeezed my eyes shut. Her words were so accurate it hurt.

My world had been placed on pause, my heart frozen in time, when I walked out on Jenner.

But honestly, I'd stopped living a long time before that. The pressures of our infertility struggle had consumed me, stealing focus away from the happy life I had once shared with my husband. I hadn't been easy to live with during that steady stream of failed attempts at conceiving. It was no small miracle he hadn't left me before I left him.

But none of that mattered now because the ink had been dry on our divorce for four years. That chapter of my life was closed.

Summer was upon us, and every year, Rust Canyon hosted a celebration during the summer solstice that the entire town attended. Not like it was a huge town, but six hundred people in one spot sure made Main Street feel crowded.

It was one of the feature events of the year—the only real competition being the annual tree lighting during the holiday season—and the whole town shut down for music, dancing, and drinks in the middle of the street.

During these types of gatherings, I was often relegated to the company of the town's widows and spinsters. In this place, being single at thirty-one, I might as well be a spinster, and with my prospects of ever adopting a baby dwindling, that was the path I was headed toward.

Betsy Sullivan was on a familiar tirade about her grandson, Tripp, and how she was going to die before he made a move on the Atkins girl. I couldn't help but smile, not only at the meddling meemaw she was, but that she had those two nailed. Anyone with eyes could see there was a spark between Tripp and Penny. That girl had moon eyes for her best friend, but he always kept things respectable, never crossing the line of their friendship into something more, even though you could see the heat in his gaze when he stared at her when she wasn't looking.

Betsy grumbled, "If that boy keeps sitting on his hands, some other man is gonna swoop in and scoop that girl up. Then he'll be sorry."

"Youth is wasted on the young." Rose Crawford sighed. "What I wouldn't give to be that age again, being in love with a handsome young man who can heat your blood with nothing more than a look."

A sound that could only be described as a moan slipped past Betsy's lips. "You and me both. When my Milton was still alive, we tore up this town. It's a wonder no one ever caught us foolin' around."

Okay. The conversation had taken an unexpected and uncomfortable turn, and I needed to escape before they asked me about my past love life. Or worse, they decided to start playing matchmaker for me with a few of the eligible bachelors in town.

"Excuse me, ladies. I'm parched. I'm fixin' to get myself a drink."

Betsy elbowed Rose. "Listen to our girl. It took her a few years away from the city, but her twang has finally come back."

Heat rose to my cheeks; I was embarrassed that they might ever discover how hard I'd worked to lose it during my time away. The folks down here were proud of that accent, proud of where they came from.

Of course, I loved my hometown, but I'd been fortunate to have traveled the world, and I knew there was so much more out there.

My time away had given me perspective on the place I called home—both good and bad. It hadn't taken long to realize that I would never encounter a community as welcoming and supportive as the one I grew up in, where everyone knew everyone and neighbors helped each other without question. However, I'd learned quickly that people immediately judged me as uneducated when they heard my accent. It wasn't true—we had doctors and lawyers, the same as anywhere else—but city folks held tightly to their stereotypes about those of us from the country.

Leaving the ladies to their own devices, I walked to one of the vendors to snag a hard cider. I was about to pay for my drink when an arm reached around me, handing cash to the man behind the makeshift bar, accompanied by a deep male voice. "Drink's on me."

I rolled my eyes, ready to shut down whatever eager man had caught a glance of me in a sundress and cowgirl boots from behind, and decided to shoot his shot.

Spinning around, I was met with the smirking face of my baby brother. I shoved at his shoulder as he began to laugh. "You think you're funny, don't you?"

He shrugged, a twinkle in his eyes. "Seeing you all riled up is always worth it, Evie."

I tilted my bottle at him before taking a long pull. "Thanks for the drink."

"Looked like you needed it."

A wry laugh fell from my lips. "Oh, you know how it is. Betsy Sullivan and Rose Crawford are over there, reliving the good ole days. Had to get away from them before they got more graphic about their youthful adventures with their late husbands."

Tucker cringed. "Yikes."

"Yeah."

His gaze locked on something over my head; he was six feet tall and able to see over my five-four frame with ease. The color drained from his face, and he ducked down, trying to hide from whomever he'd seen behind me.

"Not sure I even wanna know," I mused on a laugh.

"It's Sarah Bowers," Tucker explained. "She's made it no secret she's interested. Keeps making appointments, trying to get alone time with me. Tried to tell my receptionist that she was due for a gynecological exam when she had one performed less than six months ago by my female partner."

I patted the top of his head with my free hand. "Aw, poor Tuck has the young town hussy chasing after him. Such a rough life you lead."

Peeking up at me, he rolled his eyes. "Not looking to lose my medical license, but glad you're amused."

A sugary-sweet voice came from behind. "Tucker? Tucker Grant, is that you?"

"Busted," I whispered to my brother.

He narrowed his eyes. "You're not my favorite sister anymore, you know that?"

I flipped my hair over my shoulder, popping one hip. "You know, I'd be more inclined to believe that if I weren't your *only* sister."

Spinning around, I came face-to-face with the barely twenty-one-year-old girl who had set her sights on the town doctor. She was thin and beautiful, with a luscious mane of chestnut brown hair. It curled over her breasts placed on full display this evening, but it was clear her mama had never told her that men wouldn't respect her if she gave up the goods for free. It was well known in Rust Canyon that if you were a guy looking for a good time, Sarah Bowers was your girl. She never turned down a night out—or a quick lay behind the bar, if the stories were to be believed.

Smiling at the young woman, I upheld my good manners, even if my brother wasn't in the mood to do so. "Sarah, mighty fine evening, isn't it?"

Sarah blushed, likely knowing I knew of her intentions with my brother. "Yes, ma'am. It's always a blessing when the whole town can come together."

The fabric at the back of my dress shifted. That, combined with Sarah's gaze traveling over my shoulder, signaled Tucker had stood from his hiding spot behind his big sissy.

Heat flared in Sarah's eyes. "Tucker. I thought that was you."

I peeked behind me at my brother, deciding to give him a much-needed helping hand when it came to fending off this girl. "Don't you mean, Dr. Grant?"

A pink tint rose up her neck and onto her cheeks at having been caught. She dipped her chin. "Of course, my apologies."

"Was there something we could do for you, honey?" I prompted.

She shuffled on her feet, toeing the ground. "I—uh—I was wondering if Dr. Grant would care to join me for a dance?"

"Well, aren't you sweet? Mighty courageous of you to come and ask a man for a dance." If there was one thing we country folk knew how to do well, it was disguising our digs to sound polite.

"U-uh—" Sarah stammered.

Tucker looped an arm around my waist, letting the girl down gently. "My apologies, Miss Bowers, but I promised my sister the next dance."

"Oh." Sarah's mouth dropped open, realizing she'd been shot down. "Of course. I'll—uh—see you around, I suppose."

When she turned and walked away, I had to hide my giggles behind my hand. Tucker pinched my side, and I squealed, trying to extract myself from his hold.

"Stop!" I cried. "You're gonna make me spill my drink!"

"Would serve you right."

I spun around to face him. "I don't know what you're complaining about. You should be thanking me. Doubt that girl will be making any 'appointments' anytime soon now that she knows people are onto her."

Tucker grumbled, "Thank you, Evie."

Patting his cheek, I smirked. "Now, was that so hard?"

Looking skyward, he blew out a breath before settling his gaze on me and extending his hand.

"What are you doing?"

"Taking my sister for a spin on the dance floor. I know you're not gonna make a liar outta me."

He knew he had me there.

Tucker had always been there for me, even though he was my younger brother. He was the one who had told me I'd be a fool not to follow Jenner to Indy when I still had two years left of college and considered hanging back. He was the one who had gotten us referrals to the best fertility specialists in the country when we needed them. And he'd been the one to help me pick up the broken pieces of my life when I'd shown up on my parents' doorstep in tears after I'd walked out on my marriage.

I owed him. So, if he needed me to join him for a dance in front of the entire town, it was hardly enough to repay him for his consistent unconditional love and support.

Placing my hand in his, I let him lead me onto the makeshift dancefloor set in the middle of Main Street near the band.

You didn't grow up in Rust Canyon and not learn how to two-step practically before you could walk. The moves were automatic, born from years of muscle memory, even after time spent away. Tucker pushed me around the dance floor with ease, and I tried to clear my mind.

Truth be told, I was exhausted. The weight of the rejections had settled heavily over my heart.

What if I never got the chance to hold a baby and call them my own, genetics be damned?

I was convinced that becoming a mother was the only thing that could thaw my frozen heart. The love of a child would melt the ice surrounding it, and I would become whole again. Or at least, that's what I hoped.

Tucker must've seen the faraway look in my eye and spun me around as he admitted, "Ma told me about the latest agency turning you down. I'm sorry."

A heavy sigh shook my chest. "I don't know what they want from me, Tuck. Is it really a sin worse than death to give a baby to a woman without a man by her side? Seems like a huge step back for feminism that they don't deem me 'worthy' because I don't have a husband."

"You know I'm on your side, sis." He let out a soft chuckle. "Maybe you and I should pretend to be hitched to get you a kid. We share a last name. Who would know the difference?"

He was only half kidding. Tucker would do anything to help me achieve my dream of becoming a mother.

Stopping him before he thought about it too much, I teased, "Way to lend credence to the stereotype that country folk are all inbred."

Tucker nodded. "You're right. It wasn't my best idea."

"Yeah, there's the little matter of them requiring a marriage certificate, regardless of us having the same name. Grant is a little too common."

But something about that tickled the back of my brain.

Marriage certificate. Same last name.

My mother's words from earlier came rushing back.

"This whole process would have been easier if you hadn't left Jenner."

I had a few documents that still held my married last name of Knight—my unexpired passport being one of them. Not taking anything in the divorce, I no longer had the means to travel, so it had been pointless to have my name changed on it. Adoption agencies would ask for a marriage certificate, which I had, but I would lay bets that they didn't go digging for four-year-old divorce decrees.

If I could pass off Jenner and me as still married and applied to a new agency closer to Indianapolis—where he still lived—then maybe there was a chance. Worst case, they'd reject my application. It wasn't worse than anything I'd been through already.

But best case . . .

There was no doubt this was a Hail Mary last-ditch effort, but I had to try.

Chapter 2
Jenner

"Dude, when are you getting up here? I know Bristol is the one known for having debilitating panic attacks, but I'm on the verge of a meltdown."

I rolled my eyes through the phone screen as I video-chatted with my best friend and now coach, Maddox Sterling. He'd always been known for being dramatic, and that hadn't changed since his playing days ended due to a career-ending injury.

"Is this the part where I'm supposed to coach you on your breathing? This isn't a fucking Lamaze class, man."

Maddox ran a hand through his thick, dark hair. "This ring is burning a hole in my pocket. I don't know how much more I can take."

"Why didn't you put it in the safe in the hotel room?" Seemed like the most logical place to hide an engagement ring from your hopefully soon-to-be fiancée.

He huffed out an annoyed sigh. "*Because* she wanted to stash stuff in there. So, I had to grab it back out of there before she could see it. Now, I'm walking around with it everywhere we go. I'm not going to make it until tomorrow at this rate. I need you to get your ass up here and distract me!"

Up here happened to be Minnesota, where our friend and my Indy Speed teammate, Braxton Slate, was getting married to his fiancée Dakota. Dakota was best friends with Maddox's girlfriend, Bristol, and they were all in cahoots, having planned out his proposal for during the reception.

Maddox had given me a lot of shit over the years about crying at my wedding when I'd watched my wife walk down the aisle, so I didn't feel the least bit bad for him that he was freaking out over asking the girl he loved to marry him. It was a little bit of karmic payback if you asked me.

"All right, buddy. Don't get your panties in a twist. The car I ordered to take me to the airport is on its way to my house now. I'll be there in a few hours. Try to calm down so you don't have a heart attack before I arrive, old man."

He was only four years older than me, but I loved to goad him over that fact. And it sure didn't help his case that his girlfriend was significantly younger, twelve years his junior.

"Just get here," Maddox snapped.

"First round's on me, okay? Feel better now? You won't have to dip into your retirement fund to cover alcohol this weekend."

Maddox grumbled, "You're an asshole."

I was pretty much the only man alive who was allowed to joke about his forced retirement and the fact that he was no longer paid as handsomely as the players.

Maddox wasn't hurting for cash. He'd played professionally for the Speed for fourteen seasons. If he never worked another day in his life, he would be fine. But he loved the game—and our team in particular—too much to walk away. Hence, why he took the post as our head coach a year ago, but it was a double-edged sword. There were times when being so close was too painful a reminder that he couldn't play.

I winked at my best friend. "But you love me anyway."

A knock sounded at my front door, and I wheeled my carry-on through the house. "There's the car now. I'll be up there before you know it."

"Fine." The man pouted like a toddler, and I couldn't help but laugh as he hung up.

Tucking my phone into my front pocket, I snatched my wallet from the entryway table. It was set to be a quick weekend trip as we were mere weeks away from training camp, but I was excited to get away. The off-season was lonely, with all my teammates retreating to their summer homes while I remained in Indy.

I could've gone home to Boston to visit my family, but I'd learned my lesson during my first summer post-divorce. All I received were pitying stares and sad sighs, and I didn't need more of that in my life. I was tortured enough already, knowing I wasn't enough to make my wife stay.

I didn't stop to realize that the driver of a car ordered on a rideshare app wouldn't come to the door before I opened it.

Standing on my front porch was a woman I'd place in her mid-thirties, dressed in a pantsuit. Her dark hair was pulled into a low bun at the nape of her neck, glasses rested on her face, and a satchel was slung over one shoulder.

I eyed her warily.

When you were a public sports figure, there were always reporters looking to get a scoop, and I was the highest-ranking member of the Speed as their captain. But it was a gross violation of privacy for one of them to show up at my home.

I crossed my arms over my chest, and my voice dripped with disdain. "Can I help you?"

Pushing the glasses up the bridge of her nose with one finger, the woman asked, "Is this the residence of Jenner and Evangeline Knight?"

Hearing my ex-wife's name on the lips of a stranger had me stumbling back a step.

"Evie?" My voice broke as fresh pain washed over me at the loss of the only woman I'd ever truly loved. "Um. Evie doesn't—"

"I'm so sorry I'm late!"

My eyes whipped up to find none other than Evie herself rushing across the lawn, and you could have knocked me over with a feather. It was as if I were watching in slow motion as the wife I hadn't seen in four years approached where I stood on the porch opposite the stranger in a suit.

She looked as stunning as ever, even more so, if possible. Dressed in a floral sundress, it was clear she'd kept to her word during our last conversation and lost some weight. Not enough to lose her curves, and maybe not enough for it to be noticeable by anyone else, but I knew every inch of that body and could tell. Her blonde hair was shorter now, barely brushing her shoulders the way it was curled around her rounded face. But it was those sparkling violet eyes that stole my breath away. Unlike the last time I'd seen her, they were so full of life.

I shouldn't be bitter that she was happy because I only wanted the best for her, but seeing that she seemed better off without me was a punch to the gut.

For a moment, I thought this might all have been a dream, and I was set to wake up at any second. That was, until she looped her arm around my waist, rose on her tiptoes to press a kiss to my jaw, and chirped brightly, "Sorry, honey. I lost track of time."

Okay, the count was still out on whether this interaction was a figment of my subconscious because this woman right here wasn't acting like my ex-wife, who'd snuck out while I was at practice four long years ago. The same one who'd avoided my calls for months before serving me with divorce papers. And the one who couldn't stand the sight of me to the point where our divorce was handled by a proxy on her end as she refused to take a single penny of our shared marital assets.

No. There was no way. Because this woman was acting as if the past four years had never happened. Like we were still a very happily married couple.

And my mind was racing, trying to figure out why.

The brunette in the suit extended her hand. "I'm Stella Randall. Nice to meet you both."

Evie took it first while I stood there, stunned. A gentle nudge to my side had me remembering my manners and shaking the woman's hand.

Then Stella said the words that rocked my world. "I'm the social worker in charge of determining if your home is a suitable environment for a child."

"Excuse me?" I gawked at the woman.

Evie's musical laughter floated through the air, but she gripped my forearm tight enough to leave nail marks. "Oh, Jenner. For the adoption, remember?"

"Adoption?" I choked out, turning my head to stare at my ex-wife.

She ignored me, turning to Stella with a knowing grin. "Men. I swear, their selective hearing is the worst, am I right?"

Stella's smile slipped as she assessed me critically. "Is this a bad time? Perhaps we should reschedule. However, I must warn you; I'm booked solid for several months, and postponing will only delay the process of getting you listed in our catalog for birth mothers to choose from."

Maybe I was having a stroke. That had to be it. God was getting me back for making fun of Maddox being the old one.

Ha ha. Very funny. If you're listening up there, I've seen the error of my ways. You can make it stop now.

"Of course not," Evie rushed to say, dragging me away from the door to allow Stella entry. "Please, come in."

Whatever was going on, Evie was clearly in the know, and for the time being, it was best to keep my mouth shut and try to gather as much information as possible until I could piece together the entire picture of why my wife was suddenly back.

Stella crossed the threshold, and Evie latched the door behind her, offering, "Can I get you something to drink?"

"A water, if you don't mind. We can review your paperwork before I walk you through the process," Stella replied.

"Perfect. Jenner, could you show Stella to the living room?"

I nodded in a daze as Evie waltzed off like she owned the place. I mean, technically, she did. Her name was on the deed to the house, and I'd never had it removed, regardless of her wanting nothing in the divorce. It just didn't feel right.

Clearing my throat, I gestured toward the couches visible from the entryway. "This way."

Waiting until Stella chose to take a seat on the armchair, I lowered onto the loveseat, praying for Evie's quick return.

Stella gave me a small smile. "It's okay to be nervous. A lot of dads are like you. They're stuck in this limbo, wanting to be excited but also terrified out of their minds. Adoption is a daunting process, and I can't imagine it's comfortable having strangers dig into your life, determining whether you're worthy to become a parent. Especially when most couples going this route have been through enough heartbreak."

"Yeah." I tugged on the back of my neck.

"I promise to make this as painless as possible so that you and your wife can move on to the next step of starting your family."

I swallowed hard at her words. The hope of Evie and me creating a family had flown out the window years ago. She'd taken that with her when she left.

"Okay, here you are." Evie returned with a glass of water, which Stella gratefully accepted, taking a small sip before placing it on the coffee table.

"Shall we begin?" Stella asked.

Evie dropped down beside me on the couch, patting my knee. "Let's. I can't tell you how excited we are about the prospect of getting final approval to move onto the next step." She gazed at me, remarking, "It's been a long time coming."

Something in the way she said that gave me pause. There was more to this story, and the minute we were alone, I would get to the bottom of it.

Stella reached into her satchel, pulling out several documents. One of them was easily recognizable, as my name stood out in big, bold letters on a marriage certificate next to Evie's—the same certificate that had been nullified by our divorce. Then, there was a copy of Evie's passport, still bearing the name Knight instead of her maiden name of Grant.

I wasn't proud that I'd done enough late-night drunken digging to know that she'd changed her name back in recent years. It was kinda pathetic, but I still wasn't over her, probably because I'd never been afforded the opportunity of closure.

"The only piece I'm missing is identification from Mr. Knight."

"Oh, silly me." Evie slapped her bare knee. "How did I miss including that?"

"So, if I could get that now, it would be great," Stella said.

Evie turned to me. "Jenner? Your driver's license?"

The look I shot to her said, *Are you out of your fucking mind?* but my body obeyed her words, standing and pulling my wallet from my back pocket and handing over my ID.

Stella took a quick scan of it using an app on her phone and then gave back the laminated plastic card.

"Perfect. Now, I won't sit here and pretend that this is a quick and easy process. There's no timeline for when a birth mother might choose your file, and even then, they have the option to interview as many prospective families as they wish. There is a very real possibility that, more than once, you'll be passed over in favor of another couple. And there is always a risk that a birth mother may change her mind and choose to keep her child. Even after they sign away their parental rights, they have thirty days to revoke that paperwork. While there may be frustration and heartbreak along the way, I find it helps to have faith that when the timing is right, you'll be paired with the baby you were always meant to bring home."

Evie clasped my hand. "I think I can speak for both of us when I say we are cautiously optimistic. Having been through years of failed fertility treatments, we are used to heartbreak and disappointment, so we have been forced to develop a thicker skin."

At her mention of our past attempts to start a family, I squeezed her hand, the memory of our shared pain still so fresh in my mind. She gripped me tighter in response, and I knew instantly that whatever was going on here, I was going to help her. I'd never been able to deny her, and I could tell Evie was banking on that now.

Stella flipped through some paperwork. "It says here, Mrs. Knight, that you're a homemaker?"

Nodding, Evie replied, "Yes, ma'am." A tiny thrill went through me as her southern twang resurfaced. She'd fought to cover the vocal proof of her roots over the years, but I guess going back home to Oklahoma was enough to revive her accent. "With Jenner's work schedule, it's important that our child has the stability of one parent home at all times."

"Mr. Knight is a professional athlete. Is that correct?"

My ex-wife peeked at me, and pride shone in her violet eyes. "One of the best players on the Indy Speed hockey team, but I might be biased."

Stella's swooning sigh reached my ears, but I only had eyes for Evie. Had she kept tabs on me like I had on her all these years? She'd always been the biggest supporter of my career, and it wasn't the same taking the ice knowing she wasn't in the stands.

It was time to add my voice to this interview—if that's what this was.

Tearing my gaze away from Evie's, I addressed the social worker who had come to our home to judge whether we were fit to become parents. "I was one of the lucky ones who met the love of their life before they hit it big. Evie has been with me every step of the way, going back to when I was a sophomore in college and she was a freshman. She never missed a game and put her education on hold when Indy signed me to my first contract, following me wherever my career took us. We've been more fortunate than most, Ms. Randall, but it would seem the thing we wanted most eluded us—the biological ability to create a family of our own."

Evie gasped beside me, her hand shaking in my hold.

Nothing I'd said was untrue. She was the one who had left me, not the other way around. And I'd never moved on. How could you when you knew you'd already met your soulmate? There wasn't another woman alive I wanted to touch, to kiss, to love, other than the one sitting by my side at this very moment—the one I thought I'd never see again.

Stella blinked rapidly, briefly dropping her eyes and dabbing at the corners. Clearing her throat, she busied herself, shifting through the papers from the coffee table. "It's clear there's a lot of love in this household. I'm sure any child would be lucky to be placed with such a charming couple."

"Really?" The hope in Evie's voice had my heart twisting. There was no denying how badly she wanted to become a mother. The one thing I'd failed to give her.

"Well, there is one more question I have about your paperwork, and then if you could take me on a brief tour of your home, I should be able to file everything when I get back to the office."

"Of course. Whatever you need. I can't tell you how relieved we are to finally take this step."

Stella picked up a form. "It says here you don't have any family in the area. Obviously, you have the means to care for a child, but it's important that you have support with a newborn. It can be a trying time for any couple, and it helps to have people you can rely on, not to mention how it benefits a child to have a larger group of people who care for them. It's certainly not a dealbreaker; we would never discriminate against couples who, for whatever reason, don't have an extended family, but it is something that might deter birth mothers from choosing your file over others."

Evie tensed beside me, so I decided to answer. "While our extended family is spread across the country, with mine in Boston and Evie's in Oklahoma, we are fortunate that the hockey community is like a large family. I have twenty brothers on the ice, and that doesn't even count my best friend who has recently become the team's head coach. Their significant others are in constant communication, attending games as a group, coordinating team events, keeping each other company while the team travels, and raising their children together. We might not be blood, but sometimes, I feel like what we have is stronger. We choose each other, have each other's backs without question, and spend more time together than any regular family would."

"I think it would be beneficial to have each of you write a cover letter—something for a birth mother to read that really speaks to your unique situation. The agency would place them at the front of your file, and it could help set you apart."

"We can do that. Right, Evie?"

When she didn't reply, I gave her a gentle nudge with my shoulder.

She jolted, exclaiming, "Oh, yes! I can have mine typed up tonight and emailed over."

Stella smiled. "Wonderful. How about that tour?"

Evie jumped up, gesturing an arm to lead Stella out of the living room. "Right this way."

I hung back as they stepped into the kitchen, trying to wrap my head around the events of the past half hour.

Evie was back.

And apparently, the two of us were adopting a baby.

I was still fuzzy on the details of how all of this was going to work and what exactly my role was expected to be, but I couldn't help but see this as an opportunity—a chance to regain what we'd lost.

I wasn't naïve enough to believe we could erase the past four years, even if it felt like this could've been an alternative reality if we'd made different choices back then—choosing to explore adoption and stay together instead of Evie bolting, adamant that she carry our baby herself. However, it was clear that Evie needed my help with this charade, so it was up to me to find a way to leverage this to my advantage.

But first, Evie had some explaining to do.

Chapter 3
Evie

Jenner shut the door after Stella's departure, and I prepared for the backlash of showing up here unannounced and dropping a bomb on him.

When I got the call from the agency in Indiana, I hadn't thought twice about hopping in my car and driving straight to Indy. This was the first one not to reject me outright, and I was so desperate for this to work out that I decided not to give Jenner a heads-up. I figured, without warning, he couldn't say no.

It was a risk, but one that had worked out so far. Jenner had played along in front of the social worker after his initial confusion at being blindsided. And from what Stella had said, it sounded like I would be added to their catalog once the paperwork was properly filed with the agency.

This was everything I'd ever wanted.

But there was still the matter of my ex-husband, who'd found himself tangled up in my web of lies.

He spun around, and for a moment, I was awestruck. I had been so focused on the interview that I'd put on my blinders and hadn't taken a good look at him until now.

Jenner and I had started dating when we were teenagers, meeting at the college we'd both attended in Arizona. He'd grown from a boy into a man before my very eyes, the transition gradual over the years. I knew every inch of muscle that remained hidden from view beneath his clothing.

Maybe it was the four years apart and not seeing him every day, but the level of handsomeness of the man standing before me had my heart racing. Had he always looked this incredible? Or perhaps it was the bachelor life that agreed with him.

Oh my God. I hadn't once stopped to consider if he'd moved on. What if there was some woman due home any minute?

Before I had any more time to freak out that some jealous girlfriend—or worse, new wife—was going to suddenly appear, Jenner sighed and ran a hand over his auburn beard.

"Evie, what the hell?"

"Look, I know you're mad—"

"*Mad?*" he huffed out. "I don't even know how to begin unpacking what just happened."

Dropping my gaze, I picked at my cuticles. "I didn't know what else to do." The admission was barely audible as my lower lip trembled, and I desperately blinked back the tears that threatened to fall.

"Evie."

My name fell from his lips like a prayer, and I peeked at him through my lashes. His tortured gaze reflected my own pain.

Jenner shook his head. "I honestly don't know whether to strangle you or hug you. What kind of mess have you landed yourself in?"

"Can we sit?" I gestured to the living room.

He checked his watch. "Might as well. I'm not going to make my flight."

I groaned. "Oh my God. I'm so sorry. I should go."

Jenner folded both arms over his broad chest. "You're not going anywhere until you explain why a social worker showed up today, and why she thinks we're still married and planning to adopt a baby."

Stepping past me, he took a seat on the same loveseat we'd shared during the interview. Taking a deep breath, I followed his path into the living room and settled onto the armchair, needing space as I laid myself bare. I wasn't blind to the irony that Jenner had been the one person I'd always felt comfortable being vulnerable with, and now I was terrified of him judging me.

For a few minutes, we simply stared at each other as an awkward silence stretched between us.

"Why don't you start at the beginning," Jenner prompted when he realized I wasn't in any hurry to speak.

Nodding, I sighed. "I'm in a tight spot, and I need help."

"I'm assuming you mean with the adoption?" He leaned forward, placing his elbows on his spread knees. "What I don't understand is why you shut me down about the subject years ago. What changed?"

Shrugging, I replied, "I was grieving back then—grieving the life I thought we would have, how it would happen. I couldn't see past it at the time. Not until I got away. The space allowed my mind to clear once the weight of expectation was no longer crushing me."

Looking skyward, he breathed out, "That's why I let you leave that day. You were so upset. I thought taking a breather would do you good, and then we could talk about our next step together. I never imagined . . ."

I had many regrets, and leaving Jenner the way I did would always sit at the top of the list.

I could admit I'd been a coward, running away and shutting down. So many nights, I'd laid awake in my childhood bedroom, wondering if I should have stayed and fought for us. But as time went on, I convinced myself that he probably hated me, and I made peace with my new reality, determined to take control of my own destiny.

"I know it's probably four years too late, but I am sorry, Jenner. I was hurting, and I didn't handle it well."

His chocolate-brown gaze settled on me. "The minute I found out where you were, I should have hopped on a plane. But I didn't want to strong-arm you into staying in a relationship you were so obviously done with."

"Well." I swallowed thickly. "After a few years, I was able to save enough money to cover the costs of an adoption and decided to pursue that option."

There was an audible rumble from deep within his chest. "If you weren't so damn stubborn, you could've had all the money you needed."

"I didn't want your money, Jenner," I shot back. "You earned it, not me."

"You were my wife!" he roared. "I took vows to take care of you!"

"Look. I didn't come here to argue."

"No," he huffed. "You came here to lie to an adoption agency, apparently."

I flinched at his accurate assessment of my deception. My desperation was driving the train now, and it was going too fast for me to stop it.

Softly, I confessed, "Six agencies turned me down."

His brows shot up. "What? Why?"

I held up my ringless left hand. "Because I'm not married."

"That's ridiculous!"

My lips curved into a wry smile. "It's their playground. They get to make the rules and decide who gets to play. No single moms allowed, it would seem."

"So, you thought it would be a good idea to put my name on the application with yours?"

Shame burned through me, knowing I'd put his reputation on the line if it were ever uncovered what I'd done.

"I need help, Jenner." My voice wavered.

He ran a hand through his auburn hair. "This seems like an involved process, Evie. How is this going to work?"

"I know it's asking a lot—"

"Stop. Let me rephrase that. What happens if someone chooses us? There's an innocent life who will be caught up in all of this. Or have you not thought that far?"

"Truthfully?" He nodded, so I continued, "I thought it was a long shot. Figured, at some point in the vetting process, they'd discover we were divorced and I'd be black-listed on every adoption list in the country. But I wasn't getting anywhere on my own, so I had to try. I got a call two days ago that they wanted to do a home visit, which was further than I'd ever made it before, so I got in the car and drove right here."

"You drove?" Jenner's eyes widened, and his eyebrows shot up.

"Well, I figured if it went well, I'd be here a while."

Reclining on the couch, he tucked both hands behind his head, blowing out a breath. "How long do you think?"

I twisted my fingers. "Not sure. Months at minimum, maybe a year? It depends on how long it takes a mom to choose my file."

"*Our* file," Jenner corrected.

"Right." I nodded. "Our file."

"That's where I'm stuck, Evie. If some mom picks us, I would assume that means more home visits, correct?"

"Yes."

"Are you back in Indy for good then? Popping in and out with a kid at will whenever the social worker calls? Correct me if I'm wrong, but won't there be unannounced visits? Am I expected to stall until you show up? And won't they expect there to be baby gear all over this place? How in the world do you expect to pull this off?"

"I don't know!" I shouted, throwing my hands in the air.

"Well, you better figure it out if you want me to go along with this."

Hope stirred in my chest. "You're going to help me?"

He scrubbed a hand over his jaw. "I don't know yet. I need to think about it, and you really need to iron out the details because, right now, it's a half-baked idea at best."

"Okay." I nodded, willing to do whatever it took to make this work. Standing, I said, "I'll let you go. I really am sorry I made you miss your flight."

"It's fine." He waved me off. "Where are you staying?"

"Don't know. I literally drove straight here. I'll grab a hotel or something tonight and figure the rest out."

"Stay here."

"What?" I wasn't sure I'd heard him correctly.

"I'll be back on Sunday evening. You can stay here until I get back, and we can talk more about this."

"Are you sure?" I asked skeptically.

"Yeah. Make yourself at home. Shouldn't be too hard," he muttered dryly.

I ducked my head. "Thank you."

He rose to stand and walked to the front door, grabbing the handle of a suitcase I hadn't noticed earlier. "It's fine. I'll see you on Sunday, Evie." Jenner opened the door and was gone before I could say another word.

Even though he hadn't agreed to help me yet, I knew I was making progress. I had forty-eight hours to put together the proposal of a lifetime to get Jenner to say yes. My entire future relied on it.

Alone in the house that had once been my home, I ventured upstairs. Jenner had left the first floor exactly the same as when I'd left four years ago, and I wondered if that also held true for the upper level.

During the home tour with Stella, I'd claimed stomach issues and excused myself while allowing Jenner to take the lead. I hadn't been ready to revisit the memories held in these rooms, not when I wasn't sure what my emotional reaction would be.

We'd bought this house right after Jenner had signed his first big contract, three years after he began playing for the Speed. To that point, we had been living in an apartment, never sure when he would get sent to Cincinnati to their minor league affiliate. But he'd paid his dues, grown into a stronger, smarter player, and was rewarded with a four-year, twelve-million-dollar contract to stay in Indy permanently.

I was twenty-three and Jenner twenty-four the day he signed that contract, and it had seemed surreal. That amount of money was life-changing, and while I didn't know how to wrap my mind around it, Jenner knew exactly what our first purchase would be—a house. We'd been married for two years, and he had declared we were no longer broke newlyweds, so it was time to act like grownups.

This was the first house we toured. I could only imagine what the realtor had thought of me with how I'd bounced around, excited over every little detail—the chef's kitchen, in-ground pool, a living room *and* a family room, and five bedrooms. That was before I'd gotten a firm handle on tamping down my accent, so that probably hadn't helped dispel the idea that the handsome, rich hockey player had pulled a girl out of a trailer park. I bet she wondered if I was pregnant, and that's why he'd married me.

Ha, I wish.

It was crazy to think back to those early days when we were so in love and couldn't keep our hands off each other. There had been so many times when we'd gotten carried away and forgotten to use protection, only to spend days or weeks stressed out that it would result in a pregnancy we weren't ready for.

It had been drilled into our heads—especially mine—that it only took once.

But we knew better now. Using contraception all those years had been pointless.

The ultimate irony was that an unplanned pregnancy early in our marriage might've been the thing to save it. Years of heartbreak could have been avoided by the arrival of an unexpected bundle of joy—one that was half Jenner, half me.

But none of that mattered now. We couldn't change the past, and we certainly couldn't change the fact that my body had failed me.

Reaching the top of the staircase, I turned left toward the master suite. The door was closed, and I pressed a palm to the wood surface, letting my fingertips trail over it slowly.

I didn't dare turn the knob and peek inside. And it had nothing to do with the fact that this was now Jenner's bedroom alone, and it would be an invasion of privacy to go snooping through it.

This was the room where our marriage had died. But if I was being honest, it most likely died in the countless doctors' offices and hospitals during those final years. Our relationship had grown so fragile over that time that a strong gust of wind would have been enough to shatter it.

My chest tightened, thinking back to that time, and I stepped away from the door.

To the right was another closed door, one that promised to be even more painful if I dared to open it and step inside. But my curiosity got the better of me, and with a steadying breath, I closed my eyes, forcing myself to turn the doorknob.

Counting to three silently in my head, I opened my eyes, and a soft gasp flew past my lips as my knees threatened to buckle. The room was exactly as I'd left it, painted a pale yellow. And instantly, I was transported to the past.

"Oh God, Jenner, I'm going to come!" I screamed as Jenner's forceful thrusts threatened to throw me over the edge.

His chest glistened, covered in sweat, each muscle defined as he kept up his punishing pace between my thighs.

"Hold it, baby," Jenner gritted out. "Wait for me."

"I can't," I whined, my back bowing off the bed as my body grew taught, each muscle tensed in preparation for an earth-shattering release.

"You can. Just a little bit longer." He slammed into me harder, making it damn near impossible to stop the freight train of my climax rushing toward me.

"Jenner!" I cried, unable to hold back, stars bursting behind my eyes as pleasure crashed over me in waves.

"Fuck," he grunted, feeling my pussy tighten around him.

A few more thrusts and he followed with a groan, his cock pulsing inside me as he came.

Collapsing by my side, he pulled me to his damp chest, stroking my hair gently.

When our breathing evened out, his hand slid down my back, gripping a fistful of my ass. "Goddamn, you're perfect. I love how fucking soft you are."

I hummed with my lips pressed against his chest in response.

You didn't often see professional athletes who made a living by treating their bodies like peak performance machines with women of my size. I'd never felt bad about being a big girl, topping out at a size twenty-eight, and Jenner had never taken an issue with it either. He always went out of his way to tell me how much he loved my body, especially how soft and curvy it was. And clearly, it had no problems turning him on. Our sex life was off the charts.

He released his grip on my backside and rolled over, slipping out of bed. My limbs still felt weighted down, so I lounged on the mattress, pulling the sheet up to cover myself while he took care of things in the bathroom.

The sound of the toilet flushing reached my ears, and I forced my heavy eyelids open in time to catch the sight of the Adonis I married walking naked toward me.

I'd grown up in the country, where men's lean muscular forms were born from years of manual labor, but Jenner's was well-defined from over a decade of playing hockey, working to hone the muscles that served him on the ice. He might be in love with my large, fluffy ass, but you could bounce a dime off his tight glutes, and his thick thighs had mine shifting restlessly, knowing the power they wielded, both on the ice and in the bedroom.

A smirk tipped up on Jenner's lips as he crawled back into bed. He leaned in for a lazy kiss, murmuring, "Is my needy girl ready for round two already?"

I bit my lip, running a hand over his bicep. "Maybe."

He chuckled, lowering his head to skim a line of kisses over my collarbone as his hand traced circles over my hip.

"I'm sick of using condoms. I want to feel you skin to skin." To emphasize his point, he dipped his hand between my thighs, teasing two fingers deep inside me.

I moaned, eyes sliding closed as my hips bucked involuntarily while he worked me over slowly.

Mind hazy, my words were breathless. "We've been over this. We have to use something, and I don't like how the pill makes me feel."

"Why do we have to use something?" *His thumb brushed my clit, and I gasped.*

"Be-because," *I stammered.* "When you don't, there's a chance of making a tiny human."

"So?"

I froze, and my eyes snapped open. "Excuse me?"

Jenner flashed me with a charming grin, the same one that had gotten me to fall in love with him years ago. "So what if we make a tiny human? Probably would be pretty cute."

"Um." *I sat up, shimmying far enough away that he was no longer touching me. This was not a conversation to be taken lightly, and I wasn't sure our rational minds would thank us in the morning if our fuzzy sex ones made life-altering decisions.*

"Problem?" *he teased.*

I leveled him with a glare. "Are you being serious?"

Jenner heaved out a sigh. "I don't know. We decided to wait until things were settled, and now that I've signed my first major contract and we've bought this big, beautiful house, it's got me thinking."

"About the B-word?"

He smiled. "Are you afraid that if you say it out loud, it will invoke the stork, and they'll drop one right into your lap?"

I shoved at his shoulder, rolling my eyes. "No. But it's one of those things where if we have this conversation, it becomes real."

"Evie." *He took my hand.* "I want to try for a"—*he lowered his voice to a whisper*—"baby."

"Really?" My heart was beating so loud I could hear it in my ears. "You think we're ready?"

Jenner shrugged. "Is anyone ever really ready?"

"Someone has to be, right?" I joked, nervous laughter falling from my lips.

My handsome husband softened, pulling me close. "You're allowed to say no. You're the one who has to sacrifice your body to make all this happen. If you want to wait some more, I'm okay with that, too."

"I just—" I sighed. "I never let my mind wander there. We were both so focused on your career getting off the ground, and I didn't want anything to distract from that."

"I think it's safe to say my career is set for a while. So, what do you say? You wanna try the family thing with me?"

He was so damn adorable that even if I wanted to say no, I wasn't sure I would be able to.

"Okay, I'll agree to do this on one condition," I said.

Jenner's eyes lit up. If he was this enthusiastic about starting a family, I had no doubts he would be an incredible dad. He was a competitor; he never gave anything less than his all.

"Name it."

"We keep this light and fun. Scheduling sex and using only optimal positions sounds like a nightmare."

His smile grew wider. "Works for me. It'll happen when it's meant to happen."

God, we'd been so optimistic back then, having no clue the storm we were sailing into.

The very next day, it had sunk in for me that we might've already made a baby, and I began to get excited. Jenner came home from practice to find me in the bedroom next to the master suite, painting it a pale yellow—that way, it didn't matter if we had a boy or a girl; it would work for either.

Little did we know this room would remain empty for years.

And I didn't realize how badly I wanted a baby until it became the one thing the universe wouldn't let me have.

There was still hope, still a chance, if I could convince Jenner to go along with my plan.

No, there was no *if*. I had to get him on board. There was no other option.

Chapter 4
Jenner

Jenner: *Hey man, I'm gonna need to take a raincheck on that drink tonight. I missed my flight. Caught a lucky break snagging a standby spot for the last one out.*

Maddox: *How the hell did you miss your flight? When I last talked to you, you were literally headed out the door.*

Jenner: *Long story. I'll fill you in when I see you tomorrow.*

I put my phone on airplane mode as I walked down the long aisle of the jet, heading for my seat.

Maddox knew better than anyone about my history with Evie, but explaining her reappearance was too complicated to do over the phone, especially via text.

Hell, it was almost too complicated for me to wrap my mind around, and I was in the middle of it all.

Did she seriously think whatever plan she concocted was going to work? There had to be checks and balances with these agencies, right? They didn't just hand babies over without doing their due diligence.

The hope shining in her violet eyes was the only reason I agreed to even consider helping her. Because I knew what the alternative looked like. I'd had a front-row seat to that show for years before she walked out.

When this all blew up in her face, she would be shattered. And I wasn't sure there was enough glue in this world to piece her back together when her last chance at becoming a mother vanished.

As I trekked further and further down the aisle, I was hit with regret that I'd been too careful with my money and refused to ever splurge on chartering a private jet. It wouldn't have put a dent in my bank account to do so, but it had always seemed frivolous. First class was fine. But now, as my gaze honed in on the middle seat in coach—my only option of making it to Minneapolis tonight—I was rethinking that logic.

Shoving my carry-on into the overhead compartment, I thanked the young woman who stood to allow me to slide into my seat. I reminded myself that it was a short flight—less than two hours—and I would survive.

As much as I would have loved to turn off my brain and veg out for those couple of hours, I couldn't stop thinking about Evie.

Despite all the years spent apart, she was still the only woman I'd ever loved. I'd never allowed myself to move on. It was as if my heart knew something my brain didn't—that someday she'd be back. And that the door would be cracked open the tiniest bit so that maybe I could figure out a way to keep her from leaving again.

She'd found a way to captivate me from the first time I laid eyes on her, and I knew even then I was a goner.

I was being a total creeper.

My boys would be laying into me so hard if they could see me now, hiding behind the trunk of a palm tree, staring at the big, beautiful blonde chatting with a few other girls in the middle of the quad. They'd be spouting off about how girls were expected to come to us because of our status as kings of the ice, being players on the hockey team at Glendale State University. Most, if not all of us, were already drafted by teams around the professional league and were biding our time in college, putting on weight and sharpening our skills, until our future team called, telling us they were ready for us to play.

That was the dream, anyway.

There were no guarantees that being drafted meant you would ever hit it big. Some guys spent years in the minor league on a two-way contract, working their asses off until they could skate onto the biggest stage in professional hockey. Others never even made it that far. Only a select few had a long-term future playing hockey waiting for them.

I wanted to believe I would be fortunate enough to make a career out of playing the sport I loved, but I was smart enough to know that even if I gave it my all on the ice, there were factors outside of my control.

So, I'd never been keen to flaunt my athletic status on campus, and certainly not when picking up girls.

My teammates might be happy to bang their way through the puck bunnies on campus, but that had never appealed to me. I wanted something deeper, more meaningful, when I was with a girl. I wanted to forget about the game and just be myself. Truth be told, most of the girls were stick thin, nothing like the blonde I couldn't keep my eyes off of as she laughed freely out in the open.

God, the idea of hefting her into my arms and getting a glimpse of her surprised face had me half hard in my hiding spot. Sure, I worked hard in the gym to keep my body performing on the ice, but with that came an added benefit of being able to throw around a bigger girl with ease. What I wouldn't give to bury my face in her pillowy breasts, maybe even fuck them. The idea of those thick thighs acting as earmuffs as I took up residence between them had my cock shifting from half-mast to full salute.

Fuck it. If I didn't approach her now, there was no telling if I would ever run into her again. Training was getting more rigorous as the season approached, and I'd have less free time to troll campus, hoping to cross paths with the blonde goddess.

Adjusting myself in my pants so I didn't embarrass myself, I left my hiding spot and strolled toward the group of ladies.

I didn't want to sneak up on them, so I stopped a few feet away before saying, "Morning, ladies. Are you new to campus?"

The four girls spun around, and I locked eyes with the blonde I'd admired from afar.

Up close, she was even more stunning, with big apple cheeks that were slightly pink from the desert sun. And her eyes. Fuck me. They were the most unique shade of purple, almost a light violet. I'd never seen anything like them.

I was still lost in those captivating eyes when one of her companions gushed, "Oh my God. You're Jenner Knight, aren't you?"

Tearing my gaze away from the blonde, I gave her brunette friend a fake smile. "Yes, I am."

The poor girl nearly swooned on the spot, grabbing onto the blonde to remain upright. "Oh, wow. You're amazing." She placed a hand to her chest. "I'm Natasha."

"Pleased to meet you, Natasha." I gave her a polite nod before returning my attention to the blonde. Extending my hand, I said, "I'm Jenner."

She quirked a brow. "Pretty sure we've already established that."

My heart skipped a beat, hearing her speak for the first time. She had a country twang I couldn't quite place, but it was endearing as hell.

I dropped my hand, which was now sweating, and brushed it against the side of my pants. Clearing my throat to make sure it didn't come out too high, I plastered on my most charming smile. "Forgive me. That was my way of trying to get your name."

She sized me up before cocking a hip. "Evangeline."

It suited her, especially the way she said it with her accent.

"That's a hell of a name."

A corner of her lips tipped up. "Well, I'm a hell of a woman."

Before I could say another word, she added, "My friends call me Evie." Turning on her heel, her friends fell in line beside her as she threw over her shoulder, "If you play your cards right, maybe I'll grant you that honor."

I was floored. There was no other way to say it. She oozed confidence, and it was sexy as hell. But nothing beat the sight of watching her rounded ass sway as she sauntered away.

That was the moment I made it a personal mission to make her mine.

It killed me that her confidence had taken a hit during the years we'd struggled to get pregnant. We had both lost ourselves during those years, our focus narrowing on a single goal that we never managed to achieve.

She seemed better now—at least from what I could gather in the hour we'd spent together—but she still wasn't back to the girl she'd been before. Maybe she would finally be whole again once she found that missing piece.

My mind was made up. Whatever Evie needed, I would give it to her. I'd never been able to refuse her, and that wasn't about to change now.

"Where the hell have you been?" Maddox's voice rose over the band playing near the dance floor.

I shrugged where I was seated, at one of the many bars placed around the lawn overlooking the lake behind Jaxon Slate's—captain of the Connecticut Comets—summer home in Minnesota. He was not only the face of the league but a stand-up guy, as evidenced by his graciousness in hosting his younger brother's wedding.

The wedding had been beautiful, set in front of the lake, but now that the sun had gone down, the party was in full swing. Since Maddox was a member of the wedding party, he had been busy most of the day, but I knew that, eventually, he would find me, demanding an explanation as to why I'd been held up in Indy.

Signaling the bartender for another round, I dropped a one-hundred-dollar bill into his tip jar when he returned with a drink for both Maddox and me. Lifting the whiskey to my lips, I savored the burn as Maddox eyed me impatiently.

When it became clear I wasn't ready to speak yet, he dropped onto the barstool beside me and sipped his own drink.

Leaning both arms onto the bar top, I bit the bullet. "Evie showed up yesterday."

There was a spray of whiskey as Maddox coughed loudly. I couldn't blame him for the over-the-top reaction to my news. I was still struggling to believe it myself. Hell, I'd checked my doorbell camera ten times to confirm her car was still out front and I hadn't imagined the whole damn thing.

"*Your* Evie?" Maddox croaked as the bartender wiped away his mess.

"I have legal paperwork stating she's no longer mine," I muttered dryly.

He cleared his throat again. "You know what I mean."

"How many Evies do you think I know?" I shot him a sideways glance.

Maddox shrugged. "Hell, if I know. Your ex-wife is the last person with that name I'd expect to show up on your doorstep."

"Yeah, well. Caught me completely by surprise, too." I threw back the rest of my drink, raising my empty glass for another.

"She's been gone for four years. She vanished without a trace and refused to face you during the divorce proceedings. So why in the world would she just come back without warning?"

I blew out a heavy breath. "She's trying to adopt a kid."

A heavy silence stretched between us even though the party raged on.

"But didn't she—"

"Yeah, I know. She wouldn't even consider it when we were together. That irony is not lost on me."

Finally daring to face my best friend, I found him assessing me with a critical gaze. His forehead wrinkled as his brows drew down. "I still don't get it. What does any of this have to do with you?"

I knew he was going to be all over my shit about this, but he was the only person I could trust. I couldn't keep this to myself, and he'd always been my sounding board.

"She needs my help."

His cat-like green eyes narrowed. "Help how?"

"What I failed to mention was that before Evie showed up, a social worker did."

Maddox tilted his head, trying to piece together the information I was giving him out of order. "I don't understand."

"I guess she's been trying to adopt for a while and has been turned down a bunch of times because she's single."

"That's bullshit!" he yelled. Then it hit him. "Oh God, Jenner, what did she do?" When I didn't respond right away, he pressed, "Please tell me she didn't do what I think she did."

I busied myself, swirling the ice cubes in my glass. "She applied using both our names, attaching our marriage certificate like we're still married."

He gripped my shoulder, turning me to face him. "Jenner, I need you to listen to me. You can't do this. I know you love her and you miss her, but this is wrong. And I'm sure, on some level, it's illegal. You're not only lying to an agency; you would be lying to some woman out there who is choosing to hand over her baby to a couple she believes is together. She's trusting a piece of herself to your care. And it's all based on lies. I need you to tell me you're not going to go along with this."

I shrugged him off as my anger rose. He might be proposing later tonight, but he couldn't begin to understand the depth of my devotion to my wife, even if our marriage was over.

"Not even six months ago, I told you if I had to do it all over again, I wouldn't have let her go. So, what am I supposed to say? Sorry, you're on your own? Watch on as her dreams are crushed once again at my hand? I couldn't give her a baby the first time, so this is my chance to make things right."

Maddox ran a hand through his dark, styled hair. "Look, I get it. But I don't think you've thought this through. Think of the innocent lives that will be impacted, not just Evie. You have to take a step back and look at the bigger picture here. This has disaster written all over it."

I slammed my glass down on the bar. "Do you have any idea what it feels like to have your heart stop beating? Because I do."

"Jenner." Maddox sighed.

"No! The minute I saw her yesterday, it was like I was shocked back to life. And I'll be damned if I go back to the way I was living before."

Before he could respond, a tiny, manicured hand slipped over his shoulder before his girlfriend, Bristol—who also served as a reporter for the Speed—came into view. The tension left Maddox's body instantly, and his face lit up with a smile at the sight of the woman he loved—the woman he was set to propose to within the hour.

She tucked herself into his side, and he dropped a kiss against her red hair.

Maddox was completely gone for her, and I couldn't deny they fit perfectly together, even if I hadn't been the biggest fan of their relationship at the start. I had been worried about my best friend's career if he was caught screwing around with one of the few female reporters traveling with the team. He was new to his position, so it would have been easy for the press to turn it into some kind of sexual harassment buzz piece.

He asked Bristol, "Having fun?"

Her pale skin was flushed, coated in a sheen of sweat from the humid summer air. At least someone was having fun tonight.

She batted her big, blue eyes at Maddox. "I wanna dance. What kind of sexual favors do I have to promise to make that happen?"

"Love." I scoffed, turning back to my drink. Then, thoughts of Evie and how we used to be as happy as my best friend and his girl hit me, and I let out a sound that could rival that of a wounded animal.

Maddox's chuckle reached my ears, but it was Bristol who spoke next. "What's his deal?"

I wasn't in any mood to rehash my life's messy turn of events.

Apparently, Maddox had no qualms about airing my dirty laundry. "Oh, nothing much. His wife showed up on his doorstep yesterday."

Bristol's gasp proved that Maddox had never divulged the details of my private life with his girlfriend. That was only a small comfort, knowing that over the next few months, everyone would be asking questions. Evie's reappearance wouldn't go unnoticed, especially if we were expected to act as if we were still a happily married couple.

Her voice was high-pitched in her disbelief. "You're *married?* Where has she been all this time?"

"Oklahoma," I grunted, tossing back the rest of my whiskey before holding up my empty glass for the second time in less than half an hour.

"Does she work there?" I should have known giving a reporter the bare minimum would have her digging for more information. It was in her nature.

"Hell if I know," I grumbled. "Haven't spoken to her in the four years since she walked out."

The bartender returned with my refill, and I gratefully accepted as he mouthed, *Last one.*

I took a sip of the amber liquid, letting it scorch a path down my throat.

Having been frozen in time since Evie left, my senses were suddenly in overdrive now that she was back. Smells, tastes, hell, even the lavender color of Bristol's bridesmaid dress seemed more vivid. It was borderline overwhelming, and the incessant questions were giving me a headache.

The lovebirds whispered to each other for a minute before Maddox said loud enough to be heard, "Jenner's got a bleeding heart. And Evie knows that, or she wouldn't have come back, begging for his help. Even though I think it's a really *bad* idea."

The reality of what I was about to do hit me at his words.

This, pretending to be married to adopt a baby, could all blow up in Evie's face. And I'd have the worst seat in the house, front and center, as her hopes were dashed once again. Maddox was right; this might be wrong, but I couldn't stand idly by when the woman I loved was so desperate that she'd swallowed her pride and begged for my help after all this time.

I was doing this, with or without his blessing.

Bristol asked, "What kind of help?"

Now wasn't the time. Tonight was not only a big night for Braxton and Dakota, who had gotten married. It would be a lifetime memory for Maddox and Bristol once he popped the question. My drama could wait until after I got a few things straight with Evie.

"Take your girl for a dance. Enjoy being in love, and let me be. You're not going to change my mind." It was a clear dismissal, and my best friend was smart enough to realize it, grunting as he stood, ushering his girl toward the dance floor.

I savored my final drink of the night, mind firmly focused on the possibility of winning Evie back.

The thing that tore us apart might very well be the same one that brought us back together.

Chapter 5

Jenner

I touched down in Indianapolis with a plan—a plan to win my wife back and give her what she wanted more than anything.

Agreeing to help her with the adoption process was only step one. But I had a few tricks up my sleeve that would tip the scales in my favor.

We had a history. We'd once had incredible chemistry. And I was banking on the fact that maybe, somewhere deep down, she still loved me as much as I loved her.

Our marriage hadn't ended because we'd fallen out of love with each other. Our bond had been severed by a circumstance neither one of us could control.

I had so many regrets about how I'd handled our divorce. I'd let her go because I didn't want to cause her any more pain. I had done enough of that for a lifetime in not being able to give her a baby. I should have fought for us.

This was a do-over, our second chance.

And I had no intention of letting Evie walk out of my life ever again.

The driver dropped me off at my house, and I unlocked the front door and let myself in.

Evie's car was still out front, so I knew she was somewhere inside, but I couldn't see her from where I stood in the entryway, latching the door behind me. It was still light outside, even though it was well into the evening, and I wondered if she'd eaten yet. If we were going to hash out the details of this very risky farce, I couldn't do so on an empty stomach.

Leaving my suitcase in the foyer, I searched the first floor before heading upstairs. The first thing I noticed was that the door to what had once been planned as the nursery was ajar.

Beyond Evie painting the room a light yellow, we hadn't done much with the space, electing to wait until it was needed before outfitting it further. The longer it remained vacant, the more it hurt Evie to step inside, and eventually, the door was left permanently closed. To see it cracked open now was like a pull I couldn't explain; my feet moved of their own volition until I reached it and pushed it wide open.

My heart threatened to burst out of my chest at what I found inside.

No longer an empty room, it contained a white crib, dresser, and changing table. Gray artwork featuring moons, stars, and clouds hung on the walls in contrast to the yellow paint and white furniture. Curtains even hung on the window along the far wall, with a padded rocking chair sitting before it.

It was like getting a peek into a past that never came to fruition—the one we should have had if things had been different.

This was Evie's dream, contained in a single room. All that was missing was a child to love.

A door unlatching sounded across the hallway, accompanied by a soft, feminine gasp.

I spun around to find Evie, dressed down in cotton shorts and a tank top. Her shorter blonde hair was pulled into a messy bun at the top of her head.

Swallowing around the lump forming in my throat, I said, "You finished the nursery."

Her violet gaze dropped to the floor. "Yeah."

"It's beautiful," I whispered.

Eyes snapping up, they searched mine. "Really?"

God, I would have given anything to reach out and touch her. I wanted to hold her close and tell her I would make everything all right for her again, that we would fill that room with a baby, and she would become a mother like she always dreamed.

I was more determined than ever to make that a reality for her—for us.

"Really," I confirmed.

"I—" Evie paused, chewing her lip. "I thought it would be helpful to have Stella add pictures to our file." Immediately, she backtracked, "But if I've overstepped, I can—"

"No," I cut her off. "It was a good idea." Peeking behind me, I asked, "You did all this yourself?"

Even without looking, I could sense her moving closer.

Her voice was quiet in her reply. "I've made my peace with doing it all alone."

Fuck, is she trying to rip my heart out?

Four years ago, I'd offered to go down this path with her, but she'd turned me down flat.

I could accept that she had been hurting in that moment—the pain overwhelming at the realization that we'd failed again after putting her body through hell in our countless attempts—but was it really better the way she was pursuing it now? Without a partner's support, fighting an uphill battle with small-minded agencies who were unwilling to give her a chance on her own?

Sighing, I turned to face her. "But you can't."

Evie shook her head. "I guess not. Lord knows, I've tried."

"Have you eaten?"

My sudden change in subject had her blinking in surprise. "Um, no. Wasn't sure when you'd be home."

I cocked an eyebrow. "You were waiting for me?"

Her round cheeks pinkened. "You're letting me stay here until I get things sorted. Figured the least I could do was make you a meal."

Evie was an exceptional cook, something that fell by the wayside in our final years of marriage when she struggled with depression over our situation. I was glad to see she'd found pieces of herself again, even if she wasn't all the way back to the sassy girl I'd once known.

"Maybe tomorrow?" I hedged, praying she wouldn't bolt when I laid out my terms. "Tonight, I was thinking we could order takeout and talk."

She ducked her head. "Sure. Sounds good."

Cartons of Chinese food littered the kitchen island, where we sat on stools, using chopsticks to eat directly out of them. This had always been our thing, going back to college when we didn't have flatware in our dorm rooms. And we'd kept doing it once we had a place of our own and no shortage of forks. We viewed it as nostalgic, a reminder of how far we'd come, keeping us grounded when the number in our bank account grew so large it was difficult to wrap our minds around.

Taking a sip from her glass of water, Evie swallowed before asking, "So, where were you this weekend?"

This was good. We could ease into the heavy stuff after we caught up for a bit.

"Minnesota. A young teammate of mine, Braxton, got married."

A knowing smile touched her lips. "Ah. I forgot the off-season for hockey is wedding season for the players."

She wasn't wrong. None of us had time to get married during the grind of the season, and with playoffs, you never knew if your team would be done in April or June, so most players got married in either July or August. There were the occasional early September nuptials, but it was a rarity since you weren't afforded much time for a honeymoon with training camps kicking off mid-month.

"It turned into a double celebration, actually. Maddox proposed to his girlfriend, who happens to be the bride's best friend."

Violet eyes grew large as Evie's mouth dropped open. "Maddox is getting married?"

"Would seem so."

"Wow," she breathed out. "And you said he's the coach now?"

I nodded. "He got hurt a few years back. It was bad enough that he couldn't play anymore. So, management offered him the coaching job last summer. He's half decent at it." Huffing out a laugh, I added, "When he doesn't let his temper get in the way."

"That sounds about right. Maddox always was a hothead. Glad to see that hasn't changed when it feels like everything else has."

"Why don't you tell me what you're up to these days?"

Evie blew out a heavy breath. "Well, before this whole thing"—she waved a hand around—"I was just biding time, I guess. My life hasn't been too exciting these past few years. I've been living with my parents—who, don't get me wrong, are amazing, but I'm a thirty-one-year-old woman—working odd shifts at the bank, and being the subject of town gossip."

My fist clenched around my chopstick, and I heard the faintest crack from the thin bamboo. As if hearing how she'd been living since leaving wasn't enough, learning that the community she called home saw fit to talk about her behind her back sent me over the edge. It was too much.

Before I could make a remark about small-town folk having small minds—knowing how well *that* would be received by the woman who was very proud of where she came from—Evie added, "Probably didn't help that Tucker came back home too."

That piece of information piqued my curiosity.

I liked Evie's brother—he was a good guy—but I couldn't say the same for his wife, and my imagination couldn't conjure a scenario where she'd be willing to move to Rust Canyon, Oklahoma, permanently.

"Tucker's back? How does Brooke feel about that?"

An unladylike snort flew from Evie's nose. "Hell, if any of us care. They've been divorced for years."

I stared at her in shock—not over the news of Tucker's divorce but that he'd finally seen Brooke for who she was. The moment I'd laid eyes on her, I knew she was no better than a puck bunny sinking her claws into a guy with tons of promise. I'd never said anything because Evie's brother seemed happy enough, and it wasn't my place to put my nose into someone else's marriage. But I could only imagine that the woman took him to the cleaners when they called it quits.

Evie took my silence as a sign to continue. "I'm sure you can imagine the talk around town. 'The Grant siblings left for the big city and came home disgraced, their marriages in shambles.' And the murmuring about how it could've all been avoided if we'd married someone from inside the community."

The idea of never having met or married Evie settled like a rock in my gut. Our relationship might have ended in heartbreak, but my life would have been missing something without her even if I never knew she existed—I was sure of it.

"Is he still practicing?"

She took another bite of lo mein, humming with a full mouth to indicate the affirmative. After chewing and swallowing, she explained, "He's got his own family medicine practice in town."

"Good for him." I couldn't hide how impressed I was. Most would see giving up a high-paying medical career in a big city as taking a step down, but Tucker had a kind heart. He loved helping people. I had a feeling running his own practice was more fulfilling than the hustle and bustle of a busy hospital.

Evie twisted her hands. "Look, Jenner, as much as I enjoy catching up, I don't exactly have time to spare."

Right. She came here for a reason. The finished nursery upstairs was proof of that.

Pushing my food away, I leaned my elbows onto the marble island. "All right, Evie. Tell me how you see this working out."

Her chest expanded with the force of her deep breath. "Okay. I've had some time to think while you were gone, and I've come to the conclusion that it's going to be a touch trickier than I initially imagined."

"Yeah, no kidding."

"You were right about the social worker making more visits. That's why I furnished the nursery. She'll want to see that we have a place set up for a baby should a birth mom choose us."

I raised an eyebrow. "So, the room's just for show?"

Evie twisted her lips. "I suppose. I'll look into getting a place in town. At least until the adoption clears, then I'll go back to Oklahoma."

"To live with your parents," I supplied, the knife twisting in my heart at the thought of her leaving again.

"Right." She nodded. "I'll have help, and the baby will grow up loved by its uncle and grandparents, surrounded by the support of the community that helped raise me."

I tapped my fingertips against the countertop in thought. "How long does the process usually take?"

Evie's head tilted back and forth. "Depends. Bringing a baby home isn't the end of it. Finalization of an adoption can take anywhere from six months to a year. But that doesn't take into account the time it takes for a mom to choose me—"

"Choose *us*," I corrected. She needed to remember that she'd hitched my star to her wagon about to drive off the cliff and into the canyon below.

"Right. Who knows how long it'll take to be chosen, and that's only the initial step. She would have the opportunity to interview us along with other couples, and as Stella mentioned, there's always the possibility she could back out. There is no guarantee this will pan out the first time we try it."

I mulled it over, rolling it around in my mind a few times. "So, we are looking at a couple of years?"

Evie deflated before my eyes. She was finally realizing how insane this plan sounded and how much she was asking of me.

"Since my name is on all the paperwork, I'm assuming that once the adoption is finalized, I will be listed on the birth certificate as the child's father?"

"I—uh." Evie was at a loss for words. I guess putting together baby furniture had occupied her mind this weekend instead of examining the intricacies of this situation.

Closing my eyes, I let out a heavy breath. "Okay, here's how this is going to work."

"Jenner, I'm sorry. This is asking too much. I shouldn't have come. This was a mistake."

The sound of the stool scraping against the ceramic tile had my eyes snapping open and my hand snaking out to snag her wrist before she could escape.

Whipping around, halfway to standing, she stared at me in shock.

"Sit down, Evie. We're not done talking about this."

That fire sparkled in the depths of her pale purple eyes, and sass filtered into her voice. "Oh, I know you're not fixin' to tell me what to do."

There she is.

I couldn't stop my lips from twitching, but I tamped down my joy at seeing her personality shine through after so long. I could celebrate my girl coming back to me, slowly but surely—both physically and emotionally—once we got this mess sorted.

"Will you *please* sit down, Evie? I want to help you."

Her jaw dropped. "You do?"

"Yes, but I have some stipulations."

Evie eased her plump ass back onto the stool. "Okay . . ."

Buckle up because it's about to get real.

"For starters, you'll stay here. There's no point in spending extra money renting out a place here in Indy. I have plenty of space for you and a baby when that time comes."

She stared at me in disbelief. "Really? That would be amazing! I can't thank you enou—"

Her words died when I held up my hand. "I wasn't done yet. Let me lay it all out before you agree to what I'm asking in return for my help."

Big eyes blinked up at me, but she nodded.

"If my name is on the birth certificate, I intend to be involved."

"What does that mean?"

"It means that if we present as a couple to some woman willing to hand over her baby, then we will both be that child's parents."

Evie's eyebrows drew down, and a wrinkle formed between them. "How do you expect that to work?"

"Come on, Evie. Do you really think I'll just hang out while you spend months caring for a baby all alone under my roof? Back away with my hands up and say, 'Not my problem?' If so, you don't know me at all. What I'm saying is that should we bring a baby home with the intent to legally adopt it with my name listed as the child's father, then I will *be* that child's father. In every way that matters."

"Jenner." She huffed out a sigh. "That doesn't work. I'm going to leave as soon as the legalities are settled."

Time to go for broke.

"That brings me to my last condition."

"Can't wait to hear this," Evie grumbled.

"I refuse to lie to an adoption agency or a birth mother. If they believe us to be married, then we *will* be married."

"I don't understand."

Reaching into my pocket, I pulled out our rings—she'd sent hers back by certified mail once our divorce was finalized—and laid them onto the island between us. Evie's eyes grew comically large at the sight of them.

"Accepting my help means you agree to get re-married."

That was all it took for Evie to jump off the stool and back away. She paced the length of the kitchen, and I could literally see the gears turning in her mind.

Finally, she paused her restless motion and yelled, "Are you out of your damn mind, Jenner Knight?"

Probably, but let's not pull at that thread.

I shrugged, plucking her engagement ring from the island and holding it up. "Those are my terms, Evie. Take 'em or leave 'em." Flashing her with my most charming grin, I asked, "So, what do you say? Will you marry me? Again?"

Both hands flew up to cover her face, and a muffled "Oh my God" sounded from behind them.

It didn't exactly sound like a yes, but we both knew she was shit out of luck if she didn't take my offer. And I wasn't naïve enough to believe there was anything to keep her from filing for divorce again after she got what she wanted out of the bargain. It would be up to me to make it too difficult for her to leave again.

From the sounds of it, I had plenty of time to convince her to stay. The gloves would come off once she got a peek at Daddy Jenner. I was gonna rock the hell out of fatherhood after walking through fire to get there. She wouldn't be able to resist me.

"It's still your plan, Evie. Only with a twist," I offered when she remained silent, hiding behind her hands.

A frustrated scream sounded, and for a moment, I thought I'd blown it. She was going to say, "Fuck off," and leave.

But instead, she lowered her hands and said, "You have a deal."

"Excuse me?" I knew her back was against a wall, but there had been a moment of doubt.

Hands on her hips, Evie narrowed her eyes. "Don't make me repeat myself. Not when you've got me bent over a barrel."

I bit back a smirk. She may have shown up and knocked my world off kilter, but I was going to come out of this on the other side as a winner.

Evie would, too, even if she didn't realize it yet.

Chapter 6
Evie

Desperation made people do crazy things. Like finding themselves standing outside a courthouse in an ivory dress, with the intention of marrying their ex-husband for a second time.

All because I was so close to achieving my dream of motherhood that I could taste it.

If legally tying myself to Jenner was how I reached the finish line after years of disappointment and heartbreak, then so be it. He'd been a good husband to me in the past—the best, actually.

Why is this a hardship again?

Oh, right. Because we'd drifted apart—correction: I'd run away—and we had both moved on.

Or had we?

I could admit I'd been stuck in a holding pattern for years since leaving Indy. The only thing I accomplished in all that time was dropping fifty pounds. And it wasn't like I'd done so by actively choosing to eat healthy and exercise. No, I'd feasted on a steady diet of tears and regret for months after arriving back in Rust Canyon when the realization hit that I had thrown away the best thing in my life.

Yeah, I could admit that Jenner still held my heart, which was why this whole idea of getting married was dangerous.

What if we went through all of this, had a mom pick us, and then he decided fatherhood wasn't for him after all? It wasn't the same as having a baby the "normal" way with your partner. There was no biological tie, nothing to bind them together. There would be nothing to keep him from washing his hands of the whole mess. He'd never asked for this.

Yes, he did. He offered adoption as an option years ago.

I shook off that thought. Neither of us were the same people we'd been back then.

Hell, I had no clue what he'd been up to all these years. Had he dated? Ever thought of settling back down? I wasn't sure I wanted to know the answer to those questions. Honestly, it didn't matter. We were minutes away from tying the knot. He would be mine again, even if in name only.

After accepting his deal—agreeing to move in, get married, and let him act as a father to a child we would hopefully adopt—I laid out a condition of my own. I wanted to ensure our profile was added to the agency's catalog before we doubled down on our legitimacy as a couple.

That bought me a few weeks—weeks during which I thought Jenner would come to his senses and call the whole thing off, sending me packing back to Oklahoma.

While I sat in limbo, waiting for something to go wrong—for the agency to uncover that I'd stretched the truth and deceived them about my relationship status—Jenner dove headfirst into training camp.

Which was why I was meeting him at the courthouse on a Friday afternoon instead of us arriving together.

Last night, we received a call that our profile had gone live, and a birth mom might request to meet us at any time. We were given an access code to the back office of the agency's website, which granted us the ability to see our page. We could double-check the information or request to attach any additional items—photos, testimonials from friends and family, or anything else we wanted to share.

With the Speed heading out on Sunday evening for a pre-season game in Chicago, Jenner pointed out that if we didn't get married immediately, it would be almost a week before we had another opportunity. And in Indiana, there was no waiting period when applying for a marriage license, so we could obtain the license and get married at the same time.

Speed Arena—where training camp was being held—was only a few blocks from the courthouse in downtown Indianapolis, so we'd agreed to meet after he was done with practice and meetings for the day.

Closing my eyes, I took a cleansing breath before releasing it and making my way up the steps of the imposing building that could easily pass for a skyscraper—at least by Midwest standards.

Pushing through the revolving glass doors, I found myself at a security checkpoint. Placing my purse on the conveyor belt for the X-ray machine, I stepped through the metal detector. I didn't know why, but I held my breath every time I passed through one. I knew I had nothing on me to set it off, but I still got nervous about hearing the alarm.

Once I gathered up my belongings, the security guard on the other side of the checkpoint asked my destination, and I explained I was there to obtain a marriage license. He took one look at the off-white color of my dress and smiled, offering his congratulations. Heat rose up my cheeks, and I ducked my head, thanking him before taking off in the direction of the elevator.

Thankfully, no one else was waiting when the brushed nickel doors slid open, and I stepped inside the lift. Pressing the button for the 12th floor, I leaned against the wall, clutching the handrail near my hips.

I can't believe I'm doing this.

A soft ding sounded, signaling I'd reached my destination, and when the doors opened, I stopped breathing. Standing there, in a suit, with a bouquet of magnolias—my favorite—clutched in his hand, was Jenner.

My hand flew to my mouth as my lower lip trembled and tears burned behind my eyes.

Jenner stepped forward, placing his hand against the elevator's sliding doors to keep them from closing while I remained frozen, unable to move.

His smile was soft, expression tender, as he said, "God, Evie. You look stunning. I'm the luckiest man in the world."

Christ Almighty, this man is going to be my undoing.

He extended his free hand toward me, and for a moment, I stared at it. If I laced my fingers with his, there would be no turning back. Within the hour, we would be married, bound together as partners in life, perhaps someday in parenthood. Coming back to Indy had been a gamble, but I hadn't realized I would be risking my heart.

Uncertainty filtered into Jenner's coffee-brown eyes. "Evie," he breathed out. "If this isn't what you want, we can turn around and go home."

Home.

That word had me jolting back to reality. If we didn't do this, I would be headed back to Oklahoma alone and childless. That wasn't an option—not when I was this close.

Steeling my resolve, I slipped my hand into his, holding on for dear life. "I'm fine. Let's get married."

For a second, we stood there as his eyes searched mine. "Are you sure?"

"Yes." I nodded, even as my knees knocked together. "I got all dolled up, might as well make it worth it."

"Okay. Good. I had the clerk draw up the paperwork for the license but couldn't finalize it until you showed up with your ID." A mischievous smile crept onto his lips. "I think, for a while there, she thought I was being stood up. And she didn't seem too torn up about it."

I brushed my hand over his lapel. "Can't say that I blame her. You clean up real good."

That roguish grin lit up his face, the same one I fell in love with when we were teenagers. "Shall we?" Jenner tilted his head in the direction of the clerk's office. Realizing his hands were full, he startled, "Oh!" He offered me the bouquet of magnolias. "These are for you."

"Thank you." I accepted them gratefully, bringing them to my nose as we walked down the hall and into the tiny office where our new marriage license awaited.

Jenner held open the door for me, and I stepped through, only to come to a halt when I saw two people waiting for us inside—one I would have recognized anywhere and another I'd never seen before in my life.

A cute redhead in a pencil skirt and blouse caught sight of us, and her big blue eyes widened as she bounced on her heels. "Oh, Jenner. Is this her?"

She had that tone of youthful optimism that betrayed her to be younger than I'd initially thought. If I had to guess, I'd place her as fresh out of college.

The tall man, standing by her side, eyed me cautiously.

"Evie." The disapproval in his voice was a stark contrast to the excitement of the woman beside him.

"It's been a long time, Maddox."

He grunted in response, and the redhead elbowed him in the side. "Don't be rude," she hissed.

Jenner squeezed my hand. "Evie, let me introduce you to Maddox's fiancée, Bristol Cooper."

Bristol squealed, running faster than a woman had any right to in heels and barreling into me, wrapping her arms around me for a hug. Jenner stepped aside to let her have her moment. She was warmth, whereas Maddox was ice. I couldn't tell if that was their typical dynamic or if Maddox still held a grudge over how I'd left his best friend. My guess was the latter.

My gaze locked with Maddox's, who was standing across the room watching us. I mouthed, *She's young*, to which he merely rolled his eyes. He was several years older than Jenner's thirty-two, so there was easily a ten-year age gap between him and the girl squeezing me tighter than a boa constrictor.

Jenner teased from beside us. "Do we need to change the names on the license? I have to warn you, Bristol, Evie does have a thing for redheads."

Watery laughter sounded from Bristol as she released me, blue eyes sparkling with unshed tears.

Who was this girl, and why was she emotional over a marriage that might be legal but certainly wasn't real in any of the ways that mattered?

"Sorry." She dabbed at the corner of her eye. "I'm just so happy for you two. Jenner's one of the good ones, you know?" *Oh, I sure do. If he weren't, he wouldn't be helping me.* "And to see the two of you reconnecting? Really speaks to true love conquering all."

I turned to Jenner with a raised eyebrow.

Even if I'd never stopped loving him, I wasn't sure he could ever forgive me for what I'd put him through. I wasn't the same girl he met all those years ago. Circumstances outside of my control had changed me and made me jaded about love and life. It wasn't all sunshine and rainbows. Sometimes, you were forced to weather storms so strong they knocked you off your feet, and you weren't sure if you would survive.

I couldn't blame Bristol, though. She was in those early days of a relationship with Maddox if they were freshly engaged. If I tried hard enough, I could remember what that was like when rose-colored glasses tinted everything you saw. The world was full of possibilities, and you wanted everyone to be as happy as you were, surrounded by the glow of newfound love.

Bristol walked back over to Maddox and tucked herself into his side. He gazed down at her adoringly, tightening his hold around her waist. When he peeked back at me, his green eyes narrowed, and the temperature in the room dropped by ten degrees.

Yep, he's still pissed at me.

"Ready?" Jenner asked by my side.

"Yeah, let's get hitched," I said with more conviction than I felt.

He chuckled. "There's my country girl."

I let him lead me to the clerk sitting behind a desk. Handing him the flowers, I dug inside my purse for my driver's license and handed it over. The middle-aged woman peeked at the photo on the laminated card before raising her gaze to scan my face, ensuring I was the person I claimed to be. Her lips pursed as she surveyed us as a couple, her eyes shifting to Jenner's with an expression almost as if to say, *Seriously, this girl?*

I was used to the pair of us being a mismatch in terms of size, but it had never bothered me—I was comfortable with who I was and how I looked. Jenner had always been the first to defend me any time someone made a snarky comment about the "fat" girl being married to the ripped athlete. He'd gone on record more than once, stating that he loved my body and that people should worry more about their own lives instead of concerning themselves with ours.

When she hummed in disapproval, Jenner's hand tightened on mine. I squeezed back, a silent gesture telling him to let it go—it wasn't worth it.

The clerk finalized the paperwork on our marriage license and instructed us to the courtroom two doors down the hall on the right. We thanked her—well, I did; Jenner's jaw was clenched too tight to get words past it—and left the small office.

Bristol's heels clicked in a quick tempo over the polished marble floors of the hallway. Stepping up beside me, she whispered, "What a bitch, am I right?" That got a small laugh out of me, and Bristol bumped me with her shoulder. "She's just jealous."

I wasn't about to point out to this young woman that there wasn't much to be jealous of. In my thirty-one years, I hadn't accomplished much. People only saw what they wanted to see. My crowning achievement could be seen as marrying a handsome hockey player, but they had no idea what happened behind closed doors, the struggles we'd faced, both individually and as a couple. Money and love weren't always enough to guarantee a picture-perfect life.

Maddox stepped past Bristol, holding open the door to the courtroom so the rest of us could enter. Jenner handed over the license to the attendant, and we took our seats on a long bench as there were a few couples in line before us.

"You okay?" Jenner whispered in my ear.

I swallowed. "I'm fine."

"I'm sorry about that back there."

Shrugging, I kept my eyes on the couple currently saying their vows as I replied, "I'm used to it."

Jenner sighed. "You shouldn't have to be 'used to it'."

"Can't change the world, Jenner. I don't fit in their perfect little boxes. It's nothing new."

His thumb stroked over my knuckles where our hands were still clasped, resting on his thigh. "You've always been beautiful to me, Evie, both inside and out."

I couldn't manage more than a nod, or I was going to start sobbing. Why was he being so nice to me after all I put him through? It didn't make any sense.

"Knight party?" the judge called out, and we stood on command, making our way down to the front of the courtroom.

Bristol stood by my side while Maddox stood by Jenner's. They were there to act as witnesses, but it was clear they fell into the traditional roles of best man and maid of honor. I suppose it was life coming full circle, as Maddox had been the best man at our first wedding ten years ago.

The judge began reciting the words of the ceremony from memory, likely having performed it dozens of times a day. His monotone voice had me zoning out, and my mind wandered to the last time Jenner and I had said "I do."

"Oh my gosh, Evie, you look so pretty!" Bex Crawford gushed when I stepped out from behind the partition in the back room of the barn that served as a bridal suite.

Mama had just done up the buttons at the back of my wedding dress, and this was my big reveal to my bridesmaids. Since I was living in Indy with Jenner and had purchased the dress in a boutique up there, this was their first time seeing me in it.

Pictures on a model didn't do it justice.

The ivory, off-shoulder, A-line dress featured a sweetheart neckline. There was a sheer lace overlay along the fitted bodice with visible boning before it flared out into flowy chiffon from my hips to my feet, which were sporting a pair of brand new, brown leather, embroidered cowgirl boots.

You couldn't get married in the country, on a farm, without paying homage to your roots. I might live in the city now, but would always be a country girl at heart.

Bex let out a wistful sigh. "Jenner is gonna keel over when he sees you."

At only sixteen, she was the youngest of my bridesmaids. When we'd needed a partner for my younger brother, Tucker, it only made sense to invite his high school sweetheart to fill that role. He was headed off to college in the fall, and they would be attempting the long-distance relationship thing, but I had a feeling it would work out. Tucker adored her. Hell, he'd even considered staying closer to home for school so he didn't have to be a thousand miles away on the East Coast. But it spoke to how much Bex cared about him that she insisted he go, that if he wanted to become a doctor, he couldn't throw away an opportunity to attend one of the best programs in the country.

I would lay good odds that their wedding wouldn't be too far off. If I knew my brother, he was only biding his time until she turned eighteen.

Folks around these parts thought nothing of a teenage bride. It was rarer to see our young people leave town to attend college.

"I would have to agree," a male voice spoke from behind. "Jenner's likely to pass out before you reach him at the altar. Good thing I'll be there to hold him up. I am older and stronger. In case anyone was keeping count."

Spinning around, I found a mischievous grin on Maddox Sterling's face. He was Jenner's best friend on the Indianapolis Speed and also served as their captain. Today, he would stand beside him as his best man.

"Oh no, I'm feeling faint myself," my best friend from college, Natasha, said in a breathy voice.

Maddox stepped forward with a predatory smirk, gripping her elbow and making a show of keeping her upright.

Yeah, if that girl had it her way, she'd be horizontal before the night was over.

Natasha was there the day I met Jenner and had been vocal for years about what a lucky bitch I was that he'd singled me out of the thousands of girls on campus. But one look at Maddox last night during the rehearsal dinner, and she set her sights on his tall, muscular form.

"Don't worry, Tash. I'll take care of you tonight." Maddox's voice was husky, and there was no mistaking the double meaning in his words. They were totally gonna fuck tonight.

Her eyes met mine, and she pretended to fan herself, mouthing, Oh my God. He's so hot.

Maddox was a gorgeous specimen, I could hand him that, but he was pretty much a man whore, sleeping his way across the country, living up to the stereotype that athletes were players both on and off the ice.

I mean, he was the perfect guy to give Natasha the night of her life, but he wasn't the type to settle down.

Unable to keep a smile from my face, I asked, "Is there a reason for the cock in the henhouse, Maddox?"

Mama tsked at the vulgar phrase but knew to leave well enough alone.

Releasing his grasp on Natasha, Maddox reached into the breast pocket of his tan suit, pulling out a large velvet box. "Actually, I was tasked with making sure this was delivered to the bride."

He stepped closer, offering me the box. There was only one thing that came in a box like that, and I knew before opening it that Jenner had gone overboard.

We'd decided that while he was on his entry-level contract, we wouldn't get carried away, electing to live modestly. He was making good money, even if it was the league minimum, but we knew his career wasn't guaranteed, so we were saving as much as we could, just in case. We were optimistic but also aware that every guy on the ice was only one bad injury away from being done playing forever.

Maddox placed the box in my hands, bent down to kiss my cheek, and whispered, "You make him really happy."

Blinking rapidly to fight back tears that were sure to ruin my makeup, I nodded, hoping he knew that I felt the same way.

"I'll leave you ladies to it. See you at the end of the aisle."

The door latched shut, and I ran my fingertips over the soft velvet. My index finger caught on the corner of something sharp on the underside, and that's when I realized there was a note.

Pulling it from the box, I slipped a piece of cardstock from inside the envelope.

Evie, my love,

You light up my life, so it's only fitting that you wear something on our wedding day that shines as brightly as you do. I can't wait to spend the rest of my life with you.

Yours, Jenner

I unlatched the box with shaking hands to reveal a stunning diamond necklace. It was nearly blinding with the way it reflected the overhead lights of the room.

My bridesmaids rushed forward, all of them swooning over Jenner's words and the beautiful piece of jewelry.

"Damn, that Jenner," Natasha teased. "Making all the other men look bad."

Swallowing thickly, I asked her, "Help me put it on?"

She squeezed my shoulder before plucking the necklace from its resting place inside the box. Natasha nudged me to step before a standing mirror, mindful of the photographer in the room and making sure this moment was captured. Reaching across my throat, she threaded the chain, clasping it behind my neck.

My fingers grazed the sparkling gems where they rested right above my full breasts, pushed higher by the corset top of my dress.

"Wow," I breathed out.

"I've been instructed to fetch the bride," my dad's voice boomed in the small space.

When I turned to face him, his blue eyes grew glassy as he took me in. Placing a hand over his heart, he said thickly, "My little girl's all grown up. You look beautiful, darlin'."

"Thanks, Daddy." I crossed the room to hug him tight.

He cleared his throat a few times, likely trying to keep his emotions in check. When he pulled back, he asked, "You ready? Your forever is waiting for you."

My heart raced, but I managed a nod, looping my arm through his offered elbow. Mama and the girls all filtered out ahead of us.

Taking a deep breath, I let my father lead me from the bridal suite toward the double doors to the barn. The interior was set up for the reception after the ceremony, but outside, there were chairs set up on opposite sides of the aisle, where at the end rested a wood arbor covered in magnolias.

Jenner stood with his hands clasped at his waist, looking as handsome as ever in his tan suit, even as he fidgeted, awaiting my arrival. His auburn hair was styled, swept away from his face, the golden hour casting the strands in a fiery glow. I had the perfect view of his sharp, clean-shaven jawline.

The moment was surreal. I was about to marry this gorgeous man who treated me like a queen. Any second, I expected to wake up from this beautiful dream.

The string quartet struck up a beautiful melody, signaling the bride's arrival. The guests stood, turning to get a peek as I began my journey down the aisle.

They might all be looking at me, but I only had eyes for Jenner. As I drew closer to where he stood, the world faded away, narrowing down to just the two of us.

Tears flowed freely down his face, and he didn't move to wipe them away. He was comfortable wearing his heart on his sleeve.

When I got close enough, he stepped forward, pulling me into his arms and dipping me back for a kiss. There were hoots and hollers from our guests as he claimed my mouth, unwilling to wait for that part of the ceremony.

My dad chuckled from where he stood beside us, joking, "Save something for the honeymoon."

That got another cheer from the crowd.

Jenner pulled away, his thumb brushing against the curve of my jaw. "Sorry, I couldn't wait. You are my dream come true, Evie."

I bit down on my kiss-swollen lower lip, knowing I would burst into tears myself if I spoke.

Straightening, Jenner kept one arm around my waist, offering his free hand to shake my father's. "Thank you, sir, for raising an incredible daughter and for granting me the honor of taking over in caring for her for the rest of her life."

Daddy shook hands with Jenner, smiling at the two of us warmly. "Take care of each other. That's the secret to a lasting marriage."

"Evie?" A familiar voice pulled me from the memory of a time when I'd been so happy and in love I could've burst.

"Huh?" I shook my head slightly to regain my bearings.

"It's your turn to take your vows. We're waiting on you."

"Oh!" My eyes widened as I scanned those gathered, all staring at me expectantly.

The judge eyed me with concern. "Is everything all right, Ms. Grant? Are you here of your own free will?"

Nodding, I rushed out, "Of course. My apologies."

Jenner squeezed my hand. My daddy had been right all those years ago, and I wished I would have listened.

During our struggles to conceive, I'd shut down, and Jenner was left in a one-sided marriage, always caring for me and getting nothing in return—unless you counted me walking out on him when I couldn't see past my pain to view the bigger picture.

The judge sighed, clearly sensing something was off. It probably didn't help that a hulking, scowling best man stood beside the groom.

"Do you, Evangeline Grant, take this man to be your lawfully wedded husband, to live together in matrimony, to love him, comfort him, honor and keep him, in sickness and in health, in sorrow and in joy, to have and to hold, from this day forward, as long as you both shall live?"

"I do," I replied.

I couldn't help but think God would strike me down for agreeing to these same vows, knowing I hadn't upheld them the first time. I was a gigantic hypocrite.

We were instructed to exchange rings—the same rings we'd exchanged during our first wedding; I still couldn't believe he'd kept them—and then the judge said, "By the authority vested in me by the State of Indiana, I now pronounce you husband and wife. You may now kiss the bride."

Since I'd already made the judge suspicious by zoning out mid-ceremony, I wasn't about to give him any additional reason to question my consent in marrying Jenner. Handing my flowers to Bristol beside me, I threaded my fingers through my husband's short hair and pulled his mouth down to mine.

For a moment, Jenner stood there frozen, our lips pressed together, but then the softest rumble echoed from his chest. His mouth opened, his tongue teasing the seam of my lips, and I let him inside. God help me, my knees threatened to buckle as he kissed me as if no time had passed, like we hadn't spent years apart—like I'd never stopped being his.

The sound of a throat clearing had us breaking apart. Flushed, I peeked around Jenner to find Maddox staring me down with a scowl.

I knew what he was thinking—that I was going to hurt his best friend again. But what he didn't realize was that coming back here and tying my life to Jenner's again had the potential to shatter me completely.

I wouldn't survive if, at some point, he did wise up and cast me aside.

CHAPTER 7
Evie

We might be married, but Jenner and I were living as roommates in the house we'd purchased together as a couple many years ago. I was sleeping in a guest room, and Jenner kept the master. There hadn't been much discussion about it since I'd moved my stuff in when he was in Minnesota for his teammate's wedding.

He kept busy with training camp and pre-season, gearing up for the official start of the regular season, so most days, I was alone.

Honestly, I welcomed the solitude.

After spending years living in my parents' house, I'd rarely had a moment to myself unless I hid in my bedroom. When Jenner was gone, I had free reign. I could almost pretend it was if I'd never left.

But that illusion came crashing down the minute I heard the automatic garage door opening each day.

Our relationship had been awkward since my return. I didn't know how to act.

Part of me wanted to show my appreciation for his assistance in obtaining an adoption that had eluded me for years by doing simple things, like cooking him meals or cleaning the house. But the other part cautioned that those actions might be seen as overstepping, and I didn't want to push it. I was already disrupting his life enough.

And, of course, Jenner being Jenner, he was ten steps ahead of me, having prepared meals delivered and hiring a housekeeper to keep on top of the household tasks.

There was nothing for me to do, and I was going stir-crazy.

I couldn't very well go out and grab a part-time job when we'd told the agency I was a homemaker. We'd already deceived them enough, and the guilt gnawed at me. With each passing day that we didn't receive a call about a prospective birth mom meeting, I believed it to be the universe's punishment for lying.

Since we were under a microscope and Jenner was a public figure, I knew I'd have to bite the bullet and attend his games, the same as when we'd been a true married couple. If the agency—or a prospective mom—looked into his activities with the team, they would expect to find me in some of the pictures.

Cameras were always on the lookout for spouses and family members in the stands when a player scored. The fans loved that tiny peek into the players' private lives and seeing their support on display. I'd found clips of myself on social media more times than I could count during my first marriage to Jenner. And all too quickly, I'd learned to turn a blind eye to the comments. People were very brave when granted anonymity behind a computer screen, and I didn't need anyone to make me feel bad about myself.

Jenner and I discussed that I would attend as many home games as I was able in order to be seen. We'd never made a public announcement about our divorce, so fans didn't know the reason for my years-long absence, but it was well-known within the tight-knit hockey community. In my mind, that was the only wild card remaining as I pushed forward in my quest to adopt. One leak from inside, and this house of cards we'd built could come tumbling down. I was banking on the fact that hockey was a brotherhood—a sisterhood for the significant others—and they would protect us as one of their own.

Tonight was the Speed's home opener, and it would be my first time returning to Speed Arena since the divorce.

Making sure my access passes were uploaded to my phone with a unique code tied to his player profile at the rink, Jenner had left hours before puck drop to warm up for the game with his teammates.

I was itching to peek into the master suite closet, curious to discover whether he'd kept any of my clothing. Everything else in the house was exactly as I'd left it four years ago, but I had my doubts that Jenner would want to come face-to-face with my personal effects day after day. Surely, he had donated everything, or at the very least, boxed them up and placed them in storage.

As much as I wanted to, I still couldn't find it within me to cross that threshold into his private space—what had once been *our* private space.

Not that much of the clothing left behind would fit me anymore—having trimmed down from a size twenty-eight to a size twenty-two—but the red and black Speed jersey brandishing his last name and number would still work. People elected to wear them oversized all the time.

It was just as well. Most significant others didn't wear jerseys to the games. I wouldn't look out of place throwing on a pair of faux leather leggings and a shimmery red tank top paired with a jacket.

Hopping into my mid-size SUV, I drove the path I knew by heart. For the four years we'd lived in the suburbs before I left, I'd made the trip into downtown Indianapolis to Speed Arena multiple times a week. It was practically our second home.

Nerves blossomed in the pit of my stomach as I drew closer to my destination. Traffic was already thick, a combination of rush-hour and fans headed into the city to cheer on the team they loved. People clad in Speed-branded merchandise milled the sidewalks, excitement shining on their faces.

Turning down a side street, I pulled up to the familiar security checkpoint at the entrance to the parking structure attached to the arena. Grabbing my phone, I swiped across the screen to pull up the code that would grant me access to park there.

There was a security guard manning the gate, and he did a double-take when he saw me pull up. "Mrs. Knight? Is that you?"

Jerry had worked at Speed Arena for decades and knew everyone who worked within its walls and their significant others. He was a testament to the entire organization being a giant family from top to bottom.

Giving him a warm smile, I chided playfully, "Jerry, how many times do I have to tell you? It's just Evie."

He chuckled. "Well, I'll be! We've missed you greatly around these parts."

"It's good to be back," I replied. And I meant it. There were as many good memories as bad ones in this place. It had just been difficult to realize that during my darkest days.

He pressed the button inside the booth to lift the gate, giving me a salute. "Enjoy the game. And don't be a stranger, you hear?"

"Yes, sir." I pulled through the gate and found a parking spot on the floor with direct access to the club level, where the family box was.

I'd decided it was best to go in blind. I didn't want to look up the current roster and worry about which WAGs—short for wives and girlfriends—I would run into and have to explain why I was back. It was going to be challenging enough, and the extra anxiety wasn't worth it.

Those women had been my friends, but because Jenner and I had kept our struggles private, they didn't have the complete picture of why our marriage fell apart. Jenner was well-liked amongst his teammates, and I was sure my sudden disappearance and subsequent divorce filing probably made me look like a cold-hearted bitch. If Maddox's attitude at the courthouse weeks ago were any indication, I wasn't in for a warm reception.

Scanning my phone at the door leading into the arena, I pushed inside when it automatically unlocked. The family box was a few doors down on the right, and I steeled my nerves, forcing myself to turn the handle.

In the hockey world, a lot could change in four years. Guys retired, some were traded, and others decided to move on after their contracts expired—whether for more money or a better fit with another team. Because of this, I was only mildly surprised when I didn't immediately recognize anyone inside the suite.

My heart squeezed, seeing a few little ones running around, most clad in Speed jerseys featuring a nameplate that read: Daddy.

That was one of the hardest parts when Jenner and I had tried and failed to create a family of our own—coming to the rink and seeing the players share special moments and memories with their children. Then there were the countless baby showers we threw as a team for each new arrival. You wouldn't think there would be a lot with a little over twenty rostered players, some of them young and unattached, but with roster adjustments each year, it added up to more little Speed babies than I could bear.

Each time, I grew lonelier, being on the outside looking in.

A toddler crashed into my legs, knocking himself off balance and onto his bum on the floor. Instead of crying, he held his tiny arms up to me, a silent gesture asking for me to pick him up. I didn't know who he belonged to, but my heart wouldn't allow me to leave him hanging.

Scooping up the boy, who couldn't have been more than two, I cuddled his warm body to my chest. "Let's see if we can find your mama, little man."

My new friend placed his cheek against my shoulder, sticking a thumb into his mouth. He was the sweetest thing, trusting me completely, and I had to fight back the wave of emotions that threatened to overwhelm me. I couldn't wait to have these moments with a child of my own.

"Oh, Ollie, there you are!" a feminine voice called from near the spread of food set up.

Turning, I found a brunette with another baby strapped to her chest in a carrier.

She rushed forward, a smile on her face. "Sorry about that. It's so hard to keep up with him now that there are two of them."

"It's not trouble at all. He's super friendly."

The woman chuckled. "That he is. Especially these days, now that my attention is split."

How is it fair she's got two beautiful babies, and I can't even get one?

I tilted my head to peek at the tiny cherub-faced infant tucked against her chest. "Absolutely precious. How old?"

She rocked on her feet, a hand absentmindedly running along the baby's back. "She's almost six weeks. Go figure, born right before training camp, so Asher is gone all the time. If I'd been given a choice, we would have aimed for early summer, but this one wasn't planned."

"Asher Lawson?" The sting at hearing how other women fell pregnant so easily without trying was outweighed by my surprise. "I didn't realize he'd gotten married, let alone had kids."

"Yeah, you know him?" I nodded, and she replied, "We've been married for three years this past summer. Ollie turns two in a few weeks, and this here is Bailey." Pausing for a moment, she laughed and shook her head.

"And I'm Tessa. Gosh, I'm losing my mind with the two littles. Didn't realize I hadn't introduced myself."

I waved her off. "No worries, you've certainly got your hands full. I'm Evie Knight."

Tessa's blue eyes bulged. "Knight. As in Jenner?"

Nodding, I couldn't help but wonder what she'd heard about me. "Yeah, I'm his wife."

She breathed out, "Wow," before recovering quickly. "Sorry. Caught me off guard to hear he's married when I've never seen him with a woman in all my time with Asher."

Smiling politely, I explained, "It's a long story."

Tessa caught on quickly that it wasn't something I wanted to share, so instead of pressing further, she elected to speak to Ollie. "Hey, bud. I was just getting you some chicken nuggets. Are you hungry?"

The tiny boy perked up at the mention of food, yelling, "Yeah! Nuggies!"

"Need any help getting him settled?" I offered.

She let out a grateful sigh and replied, "That would be great. Thank you."

There was a child-size table set up in a corner for the smaller kids, and I set Ollie down while Tessa placed a full plate before him. He didn't waste any time tearing into his meal; our brief encounter had already been forgotten.

"If you ever need someone to keep an eye on him or need a break when the team is on the road, feel free to reach out. I'm home during the day and wouldn't mind a playdate with my new friend." I stared longingly at the little boy at knee level.

For the first time, I noticed the exhaustion etched on Tessa's face as she sagged against the wall. "That would be amazing. We don't have any family close by, and I'm learning quickly how difficult managing the two of them alone will be this season."

Tessa appeared younger than I was now—maybe mid-twenties—but I could still remember those early years when I'd struggled with moving to a new place and didn't know anyone, while Jenner had an instant camaraderie with his teammates. There were many days when I questioned whether I'd made the right choice in following him to Indy.

"Even if you need to get out of the house for coffee, to have someone to talk to while Ollie plays at a park. I know how maddening it can be to be inside your head all day long."

"Wow. I'm so glad you had a run-in with Ollie. Can I have Asher get your number from Jenner?"

"Of course." The countdown clock on the TV feed inside the suite told me the game would be starting soon, so I wrapped up our conversation. "Call or text anytime. It was nice to meet you, Tessa. I'm gonna grab something to eat and then take a seat, but we'll talk soon."

"Thanks, Evie."

She turned her attention back to her son, and I felt mildly better, having made a new friend within the team, especially one with young children. If everything went according to plan, my potential future child could be their playmate. That was, if Jenner continued to insist on raising this child with me.

I couldn't stop a sigh from slipping past my lips. I didn't know how any of this was going to work out. Setting the legalities of our second marriage aside, we were in a platonic relationship, even if there was a familiarity between us. How long would he be willing to co-parent under the same roof with me before he grew tired of it—grew tired of pretending with me?

My past and present colliding became too much to reconcile, and I couldn't breathe. A dark cloud was hanging over my head, waiting for the perfect moment to unleash a storm and drown me. I knew one thing for sure: I needed to get out of here before I had a total meltdown.

Halfway to the door to the suite, a nasally voice I'd come to hate sneered, "Well, look what the cat dragged in."

Lord have mercy. I do not have the energy for this today.

Knowing that escape was impossible now that I'd been recognized, I spun around to find Juliana, Saint Booker's girl, staring at me with a malicious gleam in her eyes. Of all the people to still be hanging around all these years later, of course, it would have to be her.

Juliana had always been a troublemaker—a queen bee wannabe. She craved being the one the other ladies sucked up to, but my presence stood in the way of her achieving that goal. With Maddox being single as the Speed's captain, I'd helped organize a lot of the WAG events since Jenner was an alternate captain. And as a result, I became the enemy in Juliana's eyes.

I couldn't have cared less about planning parties and organizing gifts for the girls getting married or having babies, but I knew if I handed over that responsibility to her, she would have gone on a power trip and torn our peaceful group apart.

As she stalked closer, it felt as if Juliana was sizing me up, searching for a weakness to exploit. Eventually, an evil smirk curved on her lips, plumped up with too much filler. "I'm honestly surprised it took you this long to come crawling back." She made a disgusted noise at the back of her throat. "If I were you, I would've stayed gone. Jenner's better off without you."

I'd dealt with my fair share of mean girls over the years—what chubby girl hadn't?—but the one thing I was proud of was that I'd never let them take me down. And that wasn't about to change today.

Since news of unexpected wives seemed to be the theme of my time in the suite so far, I decided to see if I could use it to fuel my counterstrike.

I wasn't at all surprised to find her left hand bare. Saint was as vicious as Juliana, but it would seem he had enough sense not to tie himself to a viper.

Plastering a smile on my face, I made sure my voice took on a sugary sweet quality as I said, "Bless your heart for sticking by Saint all these years. Remind me. How long have the two of you been married?"

Understanding dawned that I was making a dig at her martial status—or lack thereof—and she turned bright red. "At least I'm not a fat bit—"

"If you don't want to become the villain in my next novel, I'd suggest you show some respect to our captain's wife." A young woman with dark curly hair stepped between us.

Juliana narrowed her eyes, but I was still reeling from the information bomb this new woman had unknowingly dropped on me.

Jenner was the Speed's captain? Since when? And why hadn't he told me?

Probably because you've been self-absorbed since your return.

The dark-haired woman linked her arm with mine. "If you'll excuse us, the game is about to start. Some of us are actually here to support our men instead of stuffing our faces with the free food."

Dayum. Mic drop for the new girl.

As soon as we were out of earshot, I leaned in to say, "Whoever you are, you might just be my new best friend."

Light laughter flew past her lips as she led me to the high-top counter overlooking the ice, which was being cleaned by an ice resurfacer before puck drop.

As we climbed onto side-by-side barstools, she finally introduced herself. "I'm Dakota Slate, Braxton's wife."

That name tickled something at the back of my brain. "Slate. That sounds awfully familiar."

Nodding, Dakota flashed me with a brilliant smile. "You're probably thinking of Jaxon, my brother-in-law. He's the captain of the Comets."

"Oh, that's right. He's been in the league for about as long as Jenner has."

"And he's showing no signs of slowing down. Most guys his age are starting to think about retirement, but not Jaxon. And why would he when he's still playing at such a high level? It's almost a race to see which Slate brother will be the next one to bring the championship trophy back home to Minnesota."

The realization of how long Jenner had been playing professionally hit me, and I spun around to view the other women gathered in the suite. Besides Juliana, I didn't recognize a single one of them, but they had one thing in common—they were all younger than me.

"Jeez. When did I become the oldest woman in the room?"

Dakota eyed me, likely trying to gauge my age. "Oh, come on, you're not that old."

"I didn't use to think so," I breathed out. "But I remember there being more veteran ladies the last time I was here."

"Yeah. The Speed have moved in a younger direction these past few years. From what I hear, it's what they hope will give them an edge over some of the teams with aging cores. They came really close a few years ago, the year Maddox went down. Lost in six games in the Finals."

I gawked at her. "Seriously?"

Her lips twisted as she nodded. "Was a total heartbreaker to come so close but not be able to seal the deal."

God, I'd missed so much in four years away.

"And Jenner is the captain now?" I still couldn't believe I'd heard her correctly earlier.

"Yup. It was quite the shift. Maddox to coach and Jenner to captain. And they're still as close as ever."

I muttered dryly, "Yeah, I kinda gathered that."

"Oh!" Dakota exclaimed so suddenly that I jumped in my seat, placing a hand over my racing heart. "I forgot to congratulate you on the wedding."

My head whipped around to see if anyone else was listening in, but the other ladies seemed busy with their own interactions. Turning back to Dakota, I lowered my voice, "Um, thanks. It was kinda quiet. Sorry if anyone's feelings are hurt about not being invited."

"Don't worry." She nudged my shoulder with her own. "I got the play-by-play later that night from Bristol. For a girl who accused me of being love drunk a year ago, she sure was swooning over you and Jenner reconnecting."

Okay, so that answered the question as to whether some of Jenner's teammates knew about our history.

Dakota continued, "She mentioned you might show up tonight, so I was on the lookout. Sorry I didn't get to you before Juliana did. She's such a pain."

"Glad to see not everything has changed," I teased. "But what was that bit about a villain in a book?"

Her cheeks pinkened. "Oh, that. Um . . ." There was a moment where she bit her lip, eyes shifting around the suite. "I'm an author."

I kept my voice low, asking, "Is it like a secret or something?"

"Not exactly. Just a little delicate."

"Delicate how?"

She tossed back whatever mixed drink sat before her on the counter and cleared her throat. "I write romance. Honestly, I'm surprised Bristol didn't mention it. She's my number one fan."

Now that she'd mentioned her, I realized my visual scan of the suite had come up empty for the perky redhead. "Where is Bristol? I figured she might be up here tonight, seeing as she's engaged to Maddox."

Dakota smirked. "Oh, she's in the press box."

"The press box?" Jeez, I couldn't keep up with this girl.

A snicker flew past her lips. "She reports on the team."

My jaw dropped. "Maddox is marrying a *reporter*?" That man hated the press.

"Yup." She popped the P. "And boy, what a doozy that story is."

"Guess I've missed a lot since I've been gone."

"Eh." Dakota shrugged. "You're back now, so there's plenty of time to catch up."

Yeah, but for how long?

The lights in the arena dimmed, and the pre-game hype video played on the big screen over center ice.

It was surreal to be back. Some things remained the same, while so many others had changed.

I might be seemingly slipping back into the role I'd held before, but I wasn't sure where I fit anymore—not just in my own life but in Jenner's.

Chapter 8
Evie

The lights came back on after the anthems—both American and Canadian—and the Speed, along with their opponent for the evening, the Quebec Cardinals, lined up for the opening face-off. The referee at center ice spoke to both centers briefly before they lined up their sticks opposite each other, and he dropped the puck.

I'd steered clear of hockey since the divorce. It was too painful to think about the life I'd left behind—the life I wished had been so very different. It hadn't been hard to do, considering Oklahoma wasn't exactly a hockey hotbed.

But seeing the game again after all this time had memories rushing back—hyping Jenner up before a big game, consoling him after a tough loss, or even watching other teams play each other during our nights in at home, calculating which ones we needed to win to help boost the Speed in the standings before playoffs.

Those all blurred together over time, but the one that stood out was when he'd convinced me to come watch him play for the very first time.

Coffee was life. There wasn't a soul alive who could convince me otherwise.

That's why I was currently standing ten people deep at my favorite campus coffee shop, impatiently tapping my foot and checking the time on my phone as the line moved at a snail's pace. I was going to be late for class, without a doubt.

Could I have bailed when I saw the line was out the door upon arrival? Sure, but then I'd have ended up face down on my desk while Professor Neilson droned on about calculus formulas. It seemed like such a pointless pre-requisite class. I was never going to use any of what was learned in real life.

Could I have hit up the coffee shop closer to the building where my class was? Definitely not. This was the only one on campus willing to make my favorite off-menu drink—a grasshopper frappuccino.

By the time I reached the counter and placed my order, I was twenty minutes late for an hour-long lecture. Deciding to borrow notes from a classmate, I grabbed my chilled coffee and sat down at a table near the window. Might as well enjoy this beautiful fall Arizona day.

I was still pinching myself that I'd not only gotten into the program of my dreams for international finance but that my parents had allowed me to accept and move almost a thousand miles from home. I couldn't deny the location's weather held a certain appeal when applying. The mid-seventy-degree weather in November was something I could get used to.

Accepting the change in my morning's schedule, I reached into my backpack for my laptop when a male voice spoke behind me, "Looks like we meet again, Evie."

Spinning around to find the owner of the slightly familiar voice, I discovered it to be the boy who'd so brazenly walked up to our group in the quad a month or so ago just to speak to me.

Jenner Knight.

He stood out in a crowd with his auburn hair—currently hidden beneath a backward-facing ball cap—and I'd assumed I would have seen him around after that day, but we'd never crossed paths again.

Until now.

Not wanting to appear too eager, I arched an eyebrow. "Did I miss the part where we became friends?"

I'd teased him the day we met, giving him my full name instead of the nickname everyone used. It was a test to see if he would pursue me. And for the past month, when I hadn't seen him again, I figured he'd moved on, perhaps forgotten about our brief encounter. It gave me a small thrill to know I'd been wrong.

Grabbing the empty chair at my table, Jenner spun it around to sit on it backward. Folding his arms over the back of it, his coffee-colored eyes sparkled in the sunlight streaming in through the window.

"You're right. We aren't friends yet. But I'd like to remedy that situation."

God, he was so sure of himself. I could use a man who matched me in that department.

Biting back a smirk, I eyed the Glendale State logo stitched on his track jacket. It was also visible on the T-shirt he wore beneath, and if I were a betting woman, I'd lay odds that if his hat were flipped the other way, I would find it there as well.

"Did you leave any merch behind at the campus bookstore for any of your fellow students?"

His hearty laughter filled the small coffee shop, and almost every head turned in our direction at the sound.

When he calmed down, he looked me dead in the eye. "You know, I thought you were beautiful from across the quad, but it was that bit of sass you hit me with that day that made you damn near irresistible."

Those dark brown eyes scanned me from across the table, causing my blood to heat and my thighs to clench.

I decided to make him work for it. "If I'm so irresistible, how has it taken you a month to approach me again?"

A corner of his lips tipped up. "It's a big campus. And if I recall, you barely wanted to offer me your name, let alone your phone number."

He had a point there.

"If I'm being totally honest, I've been training. There wasn't much free time to be trolling campus for the blonde who stole my breath away."

"Training, huh? What major does that fall under?"

Jenner chuckled. "Not exactly a major, but it is the reason I'm at Glendale State. It also serves as an explanation for the university-branded apparel from head to toe. I play for the hockey team."

I already knew this information, mainly because Natasha had rambled on about him for the rest of the day following our initial run-in.

Tilting my head, I questioned, "You decided to come to the desert to play a sport that requires ice?"

He flashed me with a brilliant smile. "Sand or snow, doesn't matter to me, so long as I get to play."

Thanks to Natasha, I was more equipped for this conversation than I should've been, given that I knew very little about hockey.

"Drafted or still chasing the dream?"

Jenner lifted his chin. He seemed almost offended that I would even ask. "Drafted."

Leaning back in my chair, I crossed my arms, pushing my breasts up. I was pleased when his gaze dipped to stare at my cleavage. I had big tits. Sure, sometimes they made finding clothes difficult, and going braless was damn near impossible, but in situations such as this, they were a hell of an asset.

"So, you'd say you've mastered your stick-handling skills, then?"

Eyes snapping up, his mouth dropped open on a stunned exhale. Rubbing a hand over his jaw, he muttered, "Fuck me. You're gonna take me on a hell of a ride, aren't you?"

"Only if you're lucky, hotshot," I replied.

"Am I allowed to call you Evie now?"

I shrugged. "I suppose so."

He flashed me a victorious grin. "So, tell me, Evie." *Okay, I had to admit my name sounded really good falling from his lips.* "Where do you hail from? I couldn't help but notice you have a bit of an accent."

"Little town you've probably never heard of. Rust Canyon, Oklahoma. How 'bout you?"

"We moved to Boston for my dad's work when I was a teenager, but I spent most of my childhood in Toronto."

My eyebrows shot high on my forehead. "You're Canadian?"

Jenner scoffed playfully. "You say that like it's a bad thing. Technically, yes, since I was born on Canadian soil, but my parents are both American, so I have dual citizenship."

I was intrigued. Coming to college was my first ever move. My parents had brought me home from the hospital to the same house I'd lived in my entire life. My decision to pursue international finance was motivated by my desire to see the world.

"But if all goes to plan, I'll spend most of my adulthood in Indianapolis."

Unable to contain my surprise, I said, "That's a strange choice."

He lifted a shoulder. "Not really mine. The professional team that drafted me is located there."

"Ah. I see." *I pretended like I understood, but I didn't really. I knew next to nothing about the lives of professional athletes or how the draft worked.*

"Listen, since we're friends now, Evie." His smile was infectious, and I found myself returning it. "If I got you a ticket to come to our game on Thursday night, do you think you might want to come see me play?"

I chewed on my lower lip. He was cute, and he was interested in me. There wasn't any reason to say no, other than I knew nothing about the sport he had seemingly staked his future on.

"Make it two tickets, and I think I can free up my schedule."

Pulling on the back of his neck, Jenner sounded unsure for the first time since I'd met him. "Is the second ticket for a date?"

He was even more adorable when he was nervous. Normally, I'd make him sweat, but I'd already put him through his paces enough for one day.

"I was thinking of asking my friend, Natasha. Not sure if you remember her?"

The tension in his shoulders eased, and he breathed out, "Oh, yes. Of course. Two tickets it is."

"Aren't you forgetting something?"

His handsome face took on a confused expression. "Am I?"

"Pretty sure this is the part where you ask for my phone number."

Jenner dragged a hand down his face. "Right. Sorry. A pretty girl says she's coming to my game, and my brain shuts down."

I bit back a smile. This was going to be fun for however long it lasted.

"Fucking right, baby!"

A scream from beside me jarred me back to reality. Dakota was practically standing on her chair, cheering. When I peeked down at the ice, five guys in Indy Speed red and black were hugging against the glass. That could only mean one thing: the Speed had scored a goal.

The crowd inside Speed Arena was on their feet, screaming for the home team as they took the lead.

Dakota sat down, placing a hand to her chest. "Sorry, I get so excited when Braxton scores. He works so damn hard, you know? It's not easy being Jaxon's little brother."

I gave her a genuine smile. "I totally get it. I think it's great you're so invested." Tilting my head over my shoulder at the handful of ladies milling around the suite, paying no attention to the game, I added quietly so as not to be overheard, "Not all partners care as much."

Chewing her lip, she eyed me shyly. "Can I tell you a secret?"

Oh God, if she tells me she's pregnant, I might just scream.

Bracing myself, I swallowed, nodding. "Sure."

Leaning in close, Dakota dropped her voice to a whisper. "I used to know *nothing* about hockey."

Sheer relief coursed through my veins as laughter bubbled up from my chest.

Dakota laughed with me. "Crazy, right?"

I used a finger to cross my heart. "Your secret's safe with me, darlin'. You'd never be able to tell the way you were hootin' and hollerin'."

Her blue eyes lit up. "Oh! I just *love* how you talk! Where are you from?"

"Oklahoma."

"Ooooh. Hearing you has me itching to write a small-town country series. If I did, would you help me with research? I'm a city girl, through and through."

Shrugging, I replied, "Why not? Could be fun to see my hometown portrayed in fiction."

She clapped her hands. "Awesome! I've gotta tie up my current work in progress while the guys are on the road, but maybe when they get back, you, me, and Bristol can catch up over lunch, and I can pick your brain and see if anything sparks inspiration."

"Sounds like a plan."

"And you're coming to Pipes tonight, right?"

"Um . . ." I struggled with how to respond. I'd come to the game to be seen, but I didn't want to impose on Jenner's life any more than I already had. Going out to the Speed's post-game hangout—a popular karaoke bar in Indy—with the team seemed like a step too far for our fragile arrangement.

Dakota didn't seem to notice my hesitation as she continued to chatter away. "If we play our cards right and sneak a few extra drinks to Bristol without Maddox noticing, you may get to experience the rare treat of her getting up on stage."

Intrigued, I asked, "How many drinks does it take for that to happen?"

A wicked smirk curved on her lips. "Depends on the kind of drink. We get her a double whiskey or two, and it won't take long."

"And her getting up on stage is a good thing?"

Dakota snorted, not bothering to hide her amusement. "Oh, it's fucking terrible. But entertaining as hell."

"Well, how can I say no to that?"

"You can't. Trust me when I tell you it's a show you don't want to miss."

Our conversation died off as we focused on the game being played. I grew mesmerized by the effortless skating and ease with which the players passed the puck perfectly onto their teammates' sticks. I knew how hard they'd worked to hone their skills, all with the hopes of making it to this professional stage and having the world view them as the very best.

Even if I wasn't the same wife I'd been to Jenner years ago, I was always so very proud of all he'd accomplished.

Pipes was exactly as I remembered, with its honky-tonk vibes.

The neon lights cast a glow over the dimly lit establishment as music blared from strategically placed speakers. On home game nights, the place was usually packed with fans hoping to catch a glimpse of the players or perhaps celebrate a victory with them, and tonight was no exception. Thankfully, Larry, the owner, always set up a reserved section of seating for the team.

There had been a brief flicker of surprise on Jenner's face when I mentioned that Dakota had invited me to Pipes, but he covered it quickly, declaring that he would drive us there and we could retrieve my car from the garage when he had practice tomorrow.

The bar was only a couple of blocks from the arena, but I couldn't help but notice how Jenner's hand twitched where it rested on the center console of his SUV on the ride over.

Was he upset that I'd inadvertently inserted myself into his friend group? I could only imagine his life had been peaceful in my absence, and now I'd thrown it into chaos. That was why I didn't understand why he'd been so adamant about getting remarried and playing an active role in my—our—potential child's life.

I couldn't get a good read on the man whom I'd once known better than myself.

But if Jenner's inner thoughts were difficult to interpret, Maddox made no effort to hide his. When Bristol stood on a chair, waving us over to their table the minute we walked in, Maddox's green eyes narrowed as his lips thinned.

His cool glance had a shiver rolling down my spine, but I held my ground by Jenner's side.

Folding his arms over his chest, he challenged, "Are we all just pretending like the last four years didn't happen? That it didn't destroy Jenner when you left without a word?"

Never let it be said that Maddox tiptoed around a subject. He'd played nice on our "wedding day," but it would appear that my stay of execution had been revoked. It was time to answer for my sins.

Bristol's bright blue eyes widened, and her jaw dropped open before she shrieked, "Maddox, what is wrong with you?"

I held up a hand. "It's okay, Bristol."

"No, it's not." My head whipped to the side at Jenner's dangerous tone. He was openly glaring at his best friend, jaw clenched tight. "You don't fucking speak to my wife like that. *Ever*. Do you understand?"

My eyes volleyed between the two men, the air thick with tension. I'd never seen them square off like this before.

And it was because of me.

My selfishness was ruining Jenner's life.

"Maybe we should go." I tugged on Jenner's arm, but he wouldn't budge.

"Maybe Maddox should leave. You have more of a right to be here than he does. He's not a player anymore."

Bristol's hand flew to her mouth on a gasp, and she peered up at her fiancé. The cracking of Maddox's knuckles as he tightened them into fists was audible even over the loud music in the bar.

I might not have been around these past few years, but it didn't take a genius to figure out that when Maddox went after Jenner's sore spot, Jenner had no problem returning the favor.

Green eyes glittering with rage, Maddox asked, "You want me to leave?"

"You're my best friend, but so help me God, if you disrespect my wife ever again, we're gonna have a problem."

Maddox grunted, turning away and taking a seat.

Bristol shifted on her feet. "I'm really sorry. I don't know what's gotten into him."

Jenner sighed. "I do, but he's going to have to get over it."

I nudged him gently. "Go buy him a drink."

"A drink isn't going to fix this."

"It can't hurt."

Bristol looped her arm around my elbow before speaking to Jenner. "Yeah, go hang out with Grumpy Gus, and I'm gonna steal your wife for a bit. Okay?"

He gave us a smile that didn't reach his eyes. "Have fun."

Bristol led me to the bar, where she ordered herself a whiskey neat. When the bartender turned to me, I waved him off. "Just water is fine."

The young woman by my side groaned. "Don't let Maddox ruin your night. In fact, the best way to get back at him is to order the most expensive drink on the menu." She whipped out a black credit card stamped with his name before relinquishing it to the man behind the bar. "Open a tab, please."

A lowball glass of amber liquid was placed on the bartop, and Bristol threw it back in a single gulp, twirling her finger to signal another. Pressing that finger to her lips, she said to me, "Our little secret, yeah?"

"Of course."

Maddox was a broody asshole sometimes, but I never saw him as controlling. Why were Dakota and Bristol trying to hide how many drinks she consumed in front of him?

Once her glass was refilled and a bottle of water was handed to me, we made our way back to the table. Dakota was waiting for us, and the three guys were at the opposite end, leaving some space between the two groups.

Bristol dropped onto a chair with a dramatic sigh before tossing her second drink—or at least what I'd seen as her second drink—down her throat.

"Seriously, Evie, I've never seen the two of them like that before." She paused, her forehead wrinkling. "No, wait. Once before. They were arguing at Dakota's wedding." Bristol pointed a finger at her dark-haired friend.

That must have been the wedding he'd been headed to when I showed up on his doorstep unannounced.

Dakota leaned her elbows on the table. "What did I miss?"

Bristol rolled her eyes. "Maddox was a dick to Evie, and then Jenner threatened to revoke his invite to hang with the players post-game."

"What? Why would he be mean to Evie? That makes no sense."

I sighed sadly. "Unfortunately, I know."

"Care to share with the class, Mrs. Knight?" Bristol teased.

"He's trying to protect Jenner. I get it. The way I left . . ." I blew out a heavy breath. "I've come to accept that it wasn't right, but it was one of those things where, in the moment, I was hurting and needed to get away."

Sympathy shone in Bristol's blue eyes. "I know a thing or two about running away. I'm not sure if Dakota mentioned it, but we're both from Connecticut. She followed Braxton out here after the Speed traded with the Comets to bring him here, and when things went south in my love life, I followed them both. I got out of a bad situation, and I won't apologize for it."

Nodding, I muttered, "Yeah, me too."

Dakota gripped my arm, eyes darting to the guys. "Do you need help?"

"Help?" I blinked at her.

She made a gesture toward Jenner. "Do you feel unsafe?"

Realization sank in that she thought my bad situation meant my husband was abusing me. A hand flew to my chest. "Oh God, no. Sorry if I made it seem like something else. Jenner has always treated me well." *Probably better than I deserve.* "I promise."

Relief passed over her features. "Thank God. Would have shaken me to the core to hear that Jenner was one of those guys really good at hiding his ugly side."

Bristol leaned across the table. "She took a deep dive into dark romance a little while back. Now everyone is morally gray or worse in her mind."

Morally gray. Seemed more of a fitting description for me than Jenner, especially these days.

"She's right." Dakota nodded. "My imagination runs away with me sometimes."

I gave her a smile. "Probably a good thing for an author, I bet."

She laughed. "It does come in handy sometimes, I'll admit."

A waitress stopped by the table, and Dakota and Bristol ordered another round of drinks. At their insistence, I joined them, ordering a Long Island iced tea. I figured if I was playing catch-up, I needed something strong.

There was a rowdy cheer from the crowd, and I noticed a tall man with long, blond hair almost down to his chin taking the stage. He was easily in his mid-twenties but had a boyish grin on his face as he winked at his fans. Defined muscles were visible through his tight T-shirt, and one arm was covered in tattoos down to the wrist.

The music kicked on, the heavy electric guitar indicating it was a rock-and-roll classic. Immediately, the man began jumping around on stage, his hair flying around his face as he sang like he didn't have a care in the world.

Dakota wolf-whisted, and Bristol's head dropped back in laughter.

"Do we know him?" I asked the two ladies.

"That's Goose," Bristol explained. "He's our goalie."

"How much has he had to drink?"

"Goose doesn't drink," Dakota answered.

"Seriously?" That seemed doubtful. He was way too uninhibited for me to believe that.

"Nope." She shook her head. "Sober by choice."

"Is he always that hyper?"

It was closing in on midnight, and the man had played an entire hockey game. I knew the guys had adrenaline to burn off after a win, but this guy took it to a new level.

Bristol peeled her eyes away from the display he was putting on. "Yup. He's a total golden retriever."

"A what?"

Dakota smirked. "It's a book thing. Sorry if it sounds like we are talking in code. We're used to it being the two of us. It means a guy who is peppy and happy and energetic all the time. Like a golden retriever. Get it?"

Huh. Now that she said it, I could kinda see it.

Sighing, Bristol remarked, "Can you imagine how that kind of energy translates to the bedroom? Phew." She pretended to fan herself as our server returned with a tray carrying our drinks.

"Yeah, well, you can't be all swoony over the young guy and his never-ending supply of stamina when you decided to settle down with an older man," Dakota teased.

Bristol scoffed at her friend. "Trust me, that is *not* an issue with Maddox. And even if he did lack in endurance, he certainly makes up for it in girth and length."

My eyes about damn near bulged out of my head.

Dakota noticed my distress, covering for her friend. "Don't mind her. She goes out of her way to make sure *everyone* knows she's got the guy with the biggest dick on the team. Or, I guess not 'on' the team since he doesn't play anymore, but it doesn't matter; he'd still win."

Bristol let out a pornographic moan. "What can I say? Maddox puts the 'big dick' in big dick energy, and I am so here for it."

Trying not to make it too obvious, I slid my gaze to the opposite end of the table. When I locked eyes with Maddox himself, glaring at me openly, I quickly turned back to the girls.

Even though it had been years since we'd last slept together, I hadn't forgotten that Jenner wasn't exactly lacking in that department. So, to hear that Maddox was *bigger*? Bristol was a tiny little thing; it was a miracle he didn't split her apart if that were true.

The redhead must have read my mind as she continued to overshare. "Most days, it's a struggle not only to walk but sit down." She winked. "If you know what I mean."

Dakota groaned. "We all know what you mean."

"Just saying. You need more spanking in your stories, babe."

Rolling her eyes, Dakota muttered, "I'll keep that in mind." When she noticed me sitting there, gawking at the two of them, her cheeks darkened visibly, even in the dimmed room. "If we're speaking too freely and you're uncomfortable, please stop us. When you write sex for a living and your bestie is your sounding board, there's really nothing off-limits."

I offered them a smile. "You're totally fine. No need to censor yourselves for me."

They were both so young, happy, and in love. While initially shocking, I couldn't deny that it was a breath of fresh air that they seemed to have a judgment-free relationship.

It made me miss Natasha.

When life got tough, I'd closed in on myself, shutting out everyone close to me—including my best friend. We hadn't spoken in years by the time I left Jenner, and at that point, I could have used someone to talk to. But I'd figured too much time had passed, and she wouldn't pick up the phone.

I hated how much infertility had stolen from me.

Taking a big sip from my drink, I winced at how strong they'd made it. At least I'd sleep good tonight.

Hmm. Maybe if I indulge a little too much, Jenner will carry me to bed.

Shit. Had the alcohol hit me that fast? Or maybe it was seeing him play again and hanging out post-game at Pipes with the team that made me forget all the pain of the past.

I wasn't naïve enough to believe he could ever forgive me for the mistakes I'd made, for how poorly I'd handled my grief, and for refusing to talk to him when I ran away from my problems like a coward.

"Okay. I think I'm ready," Bristol announced, standing suddenly and drawing me from my mental pity party.

"Ready?" I asked.

Dakota leaned over to bump her shoulder against mine. "Now, it's time to sit back and enjoy the show."

Bristol was still professionally dressed from the game in a blouse and pencil skirt, but as she approached the steps to the stage, she untucked her blouse, undoing the bottom buttons so she could tie the ends, baring her midriff. Next, her hands tangled in her long copper hair, twisting it into a bun at the top of her head. She kicked off her heels and sauntered boldly to the microphone.

Jenner's groan was so loud I turned my head to peek at him. He dragged a hand down his face as he muttered to Maddox, "Not again."

Maddox punched him in the arm. "If I don't get to say a negative word about your wife, the same goes for mine."

Jenner must have felt the weight of my stare because he shifted his gaze to meet mine, mouthing, *So bad*.

The music changed to whatever song Bristol chose, and she shimmied her hips, swaying to the beat. Her eyes slid closed as her head tipped back. She was definitely feeling good. I wondered how many drinks she'd had tonight because Dakota made it sound like the threshold was pretty high for her to get on stage to sing.

When she opened her mouth, I winced instantly. Jenner was right. She was terrible. But she didn't seem to care. I guess enough alcohol would do that to a girl.

A quick peek at Maddox showed him leaning forward in his chair, his eyes never leaving his fiancée. He didn't seem to mind her singing. In fact, she held his attention like she was putting on an award-winning vocal performance.

I felt a slight ache in my chest, having known that kind of love—where you accepted a person for all their strengths and flaws—and then losing it.

I would never have that again.

The song ended, much to the crowd's relief. When Bristol stepped toward the touchpad to choose another song, Maddox stood, reaching out to her, coaxing. "Baby, one was enough. Come on down."

Bristol spun on her bare heel before launching herself into Maddox's arms. He caught her easily, and her limbs wrapped around him before her mouth descended on his. I couldn't tear my eyes away as they made out like teenagers in public. Maddox dropped into a chair as Bristol shamelessly writhed on his lap.

A voice spoke in my ear. "And *that* is why Maddox isn't a fan of her getting drunk enough to sing. He might be the only person alive who doesn't mind that she's tone-deaf, but now he's going to have his hands full tonight."

Maybe it had been too long since I'd had a man's hands on me, but I was getting a little overheated watching the two of them paw at each other like there wasn't another soul in the room.

"Doesn't seem all that bad," I breathed out.

Dakota's voice carried a trace of amusement. "It's not, but he hates his players seeing her like this. But she's too far gone now, and he wouldn't be able to stop it if he tried."

Her husband, Braxton, whom I'd been introduced to earlier in the evening, approached where we sat. "Babe, it's time to go. You know I love Bristol, but the only woman I want to watch come tonight is you."

Dakota pulled me into a hug. "Well, I'm off. Enjoy your post-win sex. I know I will."

The only post-win sex I'd be having would involve a partner made of silicone.

Lucky me.

Chapter 9
Jenner

Evie was quiet on our ride back to the house. I couldn't be sure if it was because Bristol's singing had damaged her hearing or if she had something else on her mind.

She was sitting right beside me, but she'd never felt further away.

Parking in the garage, she bolted from the car before I had a chance to open her door. Seeing her flee from me triggered something deep within my soul, so I quickened my steps to chase after her.

I couldn't lose her again—not when I'd just gotten her back.

"Evie?" I called out when I saw her take a detour into the kitchen.

Rounding the corner, I found her hidden behind the door of the stainless steel fridge. She closed it, bringing a glass of water to her lips and drinking greedily.

I couldn't deny that watching her throat muscles work on the swallow had all my blood rushing south. I knew exactly what that throat was capable of.

My voice was gravelly when I spoke again. "Are you okay?"

Setting the now empty glass on the island, she folded her arms over her chest. "Why didn't you tell me you were the captain?"

That's what she's upset about?

"It happened while you were gone. I didn't think you'd care."

Hurt flickered over her features, and it gutted me. Every cell in my body screamed for me to close the distance between us and pull her into my arms to tell her how much I still loved her, but I held myself in check, not wanting to scare her away.

"Of course I care," she said, her voice whisper-soft. "It's a big deal, Jenner. You've worked hard and earned it."

I shrugged. "It's bittersweet knowing my best friend had to be knocked out of the game due to injury for me to 'earn' it."

Evie sighed, nodding. "I suppose. But I bet he sure loves bossing you around."

That had a chuckle breaking free from my chest. "Boy, does he ever."

"A little warning would've been nice, you know. I walked into that suite tonight, having no clue I was expected to be their leader."

I scanned her face, searching for any hints as to whether she *wanted* to take on that role.

"It's fine. Dakota handles most things with Braxton being the alternate captain." Which was what Evie had done when Maddox was our unmarried captain. "She's got lots of support since her sister-in-law is the wife of the Comets' captain. Bristol helps out when she's in town too, but can only do so much as she travels with the team. There's not a veteran wife up there if you haven't noticed."

Evie cocked her hip, and I bit back a smile as I braced for her signature sass.

"Oh, I noticed. But what you fail to realize, Jenner, is that *I* am the veteran wife."

I almost couldn't believe my ears, and I needed to hear her confirm what I thought she was saying.

"You want to take on those duties? To get more involved with the team and their families?"

"Isn't that what everyone would expect from me? Plus, it'll give me something to do. I can't just sit around here all the time."

Nodding, I replied, "If it makes you happy, I don't think Dakota will have any problem handing over the reins to you. She might even thank you for it, seeing as it'll give her more free time to write."

A tiny smirk curved on her lips, betraying that Dakota's status as a best-selling romance author had come up at some point during the evening.

"Make sure you get her my number, will you? I'm off to bed."

She stepped toward me, but as she walked past where I stood, I snagged her wrist, and she halted, turning her head to look at me in question.

"Thanks for coming tonight. It means a lot."

Evie ducked her head. "I did what I had to do."

And just like that, any hope that we were making progress died. She'd made it crystal clear that every action was aimed at bringing her closer to her ultimate goal.

I was simply a means to an end.

A clap of thunder boomed, shaking the house, but that wasn't what woke me from a dead sleep. No, it was the near-silent unlatching of my bedroom door.

Only one other person was in the house, and I knew exactly why she would venture into my room tonight, of all nights.

Evie was terrified of thunderstorms.

And she had good reason to be afraid. She'd grown up in Tornado Alley. Every year, there were devastating tornados that had the ability to tear entire towns apart.

Indiana, being flat, was not without the same risks, though the frequency was far less. I could count on one hand the number of times I'd heard a warning siren in my eleven years living here.

Her quiet footsteps were barely audible over the torrential downpour outside hammering on the glass windows surrounding the room. They paused when she neared the side of my king-size bed.

I held my breath, waiting for her next move.

When she simply stood there, I decided to go for broke and flipped back the covers in invitation. I would never turn her away. She had to know that by now.

The mattress dipped beneath her weight as she laid down beside me. I could feel the vibrations of her trembling, so I trusted my gut and looped my arm around her waist, pulling her closer until her back was flush with my chest.

I didn't even care that her hair was in my face as I breathed in her scent. Having her in my arms again was a dream I never thought would come true. We fit so perfectly together. I only wished she could see that, too.

"Storm?" I asked, voice roughened by sleep.

"Mmhmm."

Bold under the cover of night, I kissed the back of her head, promising, "You're safe, Evie. I've got you."

The tremors racking her body slowly eased, and her form grew lax against mine. Her soft breathing was music to my ears, lulling me to sleep.

And for just a moment, I could pretend that in the morning, she wouldn't push me away again.

My wife was an angel, and no one could convince me otherwise.

Golden hair fanned out on the pillow like a halo around her head. Rosebud lips were parted as air rushed past them with each deep breath. Facial features were relaxed in sleep, devoid of any pain or worry that had marred her beautiful face over the years.

Evie hadn't stirred when my alarm went off, or when I'd crawled out of bed. Who knows how long she'd laid awake before gathering the courage to sneak into my room for comfort. It killed me to think of her scared and suffering alone during the years she'd been gone.

I wanted to protect her from everything, but I had learned the hard way that that was an impossible task. At the very least, I'd been able to be there for her last night when she needed me.

Wanting to give her as much time to rest as possible, I showered and dressed before sitting on the side of the bed and nudging her shoulder.

"Mmph." With that, she turned over, burying her face in the pillow.

"Evie, you gotta get up, honey."

"So tired," came her muffled reply.

"I know." I dared to stroke her hair. "Tell me where your keys are, and I'll get a ride to the rink and drive your car home."

She rolled over, and I watched as the realization of where she was—in my mind, where she belonged—dawned on her face. In my bed.

Both hands flew up to cover her face, and she groaned. "Sorry."

"Nothing to be sorry about."

Evie scoffed. "I'm a thirty-one-year-old woman afraid of storms."

"Your fears are justified, given where you grew up. Everyone has something they're afraid of."

"I'm not a child anymore, Jenner."

"I wasn't aware the impact of past trauma had an age limit." A thought struck me, and I offered, "Would you believe me if I told you Bristol is deathly afraid of flying?"

Her eyebrows rose. "But doesn't she travel with the team?"

"Yep." I nodded. "First time she flew with us, she had a severe panic attack. It was so bad that she inflicted harm on herself. Damn near scared Maddox half to death, and they weren't even officially together yet. I guess she grew up near an airport, and there was a fatal crash near her house when she was a child. She's learned to cope, but it's still not easy for her."

Evie's eyes were as large as saucers. "Wow."

"As much as I'd love to stay and chat more, I do need to head to the rink. Just point me in the direction of your keys."

She began to slide out of bed. "I'll get up and take you."

I held up my hand. "Stay. It's no trouble."

Leveling me with a glare, she shot back, "Either way, I'm invading your private space. I'll head back to my room, if that's all right with you."

Standing, I nodded. "As you wish. But since you're already in here, please help yourself to anything in the closet. You'll find that it's exactly as you left it."

Her eyes darted to the closed door of what had formerly been our shared walk-in closet. I wondered if she was thinking the same thing I was—that it had been the last place we'd spoken to each other before she left.

"I suppose I should go through it and bag everything up to be donated. Nothing in there likely fits me anymore."

Before I could stop myself, I said, "I've noticed."

Head snapping up, she assessed me for a moment. Couldn't she see how much I loved her in any way, shape, or form? She was my soulmate, my perfect match. Fuck that cruel twist of fate that had ripped us apart.

Dropping a chaste kiss on her forehead, I headed for the door. "I'll be back later to pack."

Slipping into the backseat of the rideshare I ordered, I couldn't tell if we were making progress or if I was fucking it all up.

Only time would tell.

Asher Lawson, the left wing to my right wing on the starting forward line, plopped down beside where I sat at my stall in the locker room, lacing up my skates before practice.

"Dude. Evie's back?"

Asher was one of the few guys on the current team who had been around when I was married to Evie, so I wasn't surprised that her reappearance came as a shock to him.

Pulling the laces as tight as they would go, I began tying the knot. "Yeah."

He let out a heavy breath. "I almost didn't believe Tessa last night when she couldn't stop raving about a woman in the suite who was an absolute godsend while trying to deal with both kids alone at a game for the first time. I'd thought the sleep deprivation had finally gotten to her, but she was adamant it was your wife. When I asked what her new BFF looked like, she described Evie perfectly. Not too many blondes with purple eyes walking around the family box at the arena."

It didn't surprise me that Evie would gravitate to Asher's young family. I could only imagine her picturing herself in Tessa's shoes, wrangling two little ones.

Asher whipped out his phone. "I'm supposed to get Evie's number for her. She said something about going on park dates or something with the kids? Lord knows Tessa could use the company. She's struggling with being home so much since Bailey was born."

I took the offered phone and typed in Evie's cell number before handing it back. "How are you guys adjusting to two under two?"

"Not gonna lie. It's been rough. Timing wasn't great."

"You getting enough sleep?" I couldn't help but notice the dark circles under his eyes, though I hadn't noticed any dip in his performance during the game last night.

He shrugged. "Enough. I know some guys leave it all to their wives during the night, especially during the season, but she did all the heavy lifting with the pregnancy and birth. It doesn't feel right not to help out."

I clapped my teammate on the back. "You're a good man, Asher." I stopped just short of saying that I hoped I would have the chance to be as supportive of a parenting partner if that day ever came.

Braxton walked in, dropping onto the seat on my other side to remove his street shoes before gearing up.

"Hey." I nudged him. "Can you have Dakota add Evie to the WAG text chain if I send you her number?"

"Sure." He stood to strip down to his base layer. "I'm surprised Dakota didn't ask for it herself. The way she was talking this morning, Evie is the newest member of the Indy Speed chapter of the girl gang."

My brows drew down. "What the hell is a girl gang?"

Braxton rolled his eyes, but the smile never left his face. "It was something they had in Connecticut. My sister-in-law's girlfriends and the core

Comets' significant others. Since the move, Dakota and Bristol are honorary members, but I think they're trying to recreate it here in Indy."

Asher practically leaned his entire upper body over my lap. "Hey, can Tessa get in on that?"

"Don't see why not." Braxton shrugged.

Maddox stepped into the locker room, dressed in his Speed-branded tracksuit, already wearing his skates. He took one look at us, only partially geared up, and barked, "Social hour is over, boys. You have ten minutes to hit the ice, or you're skating suicides."

Nothing could light a fire under a hockey player's ass faster than that threat, and we all zipped our lips and rushed to finish getting ready for practice.

By the time I walked in the door, I had less than ninety minutes to pack and turn it around before I needed to leave for the airport. Thankfully, our first road trip was short—two games over three days—and I was an expert at grabbing only what was necessary.

Every year, we had fun razzing the rookies who showed up with a giant suitcase like they were packing for a week-long tropical vacation. It didn't matter that we'd all been in their shoes once; we had earned the right to bust the balls of the new guys.

I found Evie perched on a stool at the kitchen island with a book in her hands. She placed it face down on the countertop and raised an eyebrow at me.

A chill rolled down my spine, and I held my hands up in surrender. "Whatever I did wrong, I just want to say I'm sorry."

A smile tugged at her lips before she tapped a finger on the book. "Hockey smut? Really, Jenner?" Before I could respond, she continued, "I mean, I get it. You guys are like unwrapping a Christmas gift. The prize is hidden beneath all that bulky gear."

When she stopped, I waited a moment to make sure she was done before replying, "While I don't disagree with you, I'd be mindful of using the S-word in front of Dakota."

"What? Sex?"

I shook my head. "Smut."

A look of confusion filled her face. "Why?"

Directing a pointed look at the paperback, I explained, "That's one of hers."

Evie picked up the book, scanning the cover before turning it to face me. "No, it's not. See? It's written by someone named D.D. Morgan."

"She writes under a pen name."

Eyes widening, she gripped the book tighter. "Hush your mouth, Jenner Knight, and stop messing with me right this minute."

"Swear to God." I made a crossing gesture over my heart.

"Well, damn." A breath flew past her lips, and she opened the book again, flipping through the pages. "Now I have questions."

That had me rearing back. "What kind of questions?"

"Whether she's writing from real-life experience or not. Because, good Lord, sex in the penalty box? I'm walking a fine line of jealousy over here."

That book had been Dakota's big break, and that particular scene had threatened to break the internet. Neither one would confirm or deny that it was written about the two of them, but the smirk on Braxton's face when it was mentioned said it all. They'd most definitely christened the sin bin at Comets Arena.

When I simply shrugged, Evie shook her head, a wistful smile on her face. "Oh, to be young again."

She might be lamenting the loss of how wild and reckless we'd been in our younger years, but I was itching to discover what a mature relationship with my wife might look like.

Chapter 10
Evie

"I'm so glad we're doing this," Tessa said from beside me on a park bench while Ollie played in a nearby sandbox.

"To new friends." I held up my disposable coffee cup and tapped it to hers.

She took a sip, and I mirrored the action. It was a beautiful fall day in Indianapolis. The leaves on the trees had turned brilliant shades of red, orange, and yellow. The weather was chilly, but with the sun shining, it felt warmer than it was.

"VeeVee!" Ollie cried, running over.

My heart threatened to burst at hearing him try to say my name. He was seriously the sweetest little guy, and I wanted to eat him up.

"What's up, buddy?" I leaned forward when he got closer to put us at eye level.

He made an excited sound, pointing to the swingset on the far side of the playground.

"You want me to push you on the swings?"

His dark hair flopped in his eyes with how enthusiastically he nodded. "Peease." He clasped his chubby little hands and brought them to his chest.

I snuck a peek at Tessa. "Well, so long as it's all right with your mama."

Tessa stood, placing her coffee in the cupholder of the double stroller where Bailey was sleeping soundly. "Sounds like fun. Let's go!"

Ollie shot off to the other side of the park as fast as his tiny legs would carry him, and I laughed. "He's seriously adorable. You're so very blessed."

She sighed, smiling at her son. "It's exhausting and amazing at the same time. Does that make any sense?"

Nodding, I lifted Ollie into my arms, placing his legs strategically through the holes of the toddler swing. "Sounds about right."

"Like I would jump in front of a car for them, but I also want one minute where someone isn't touching me."

I chuckled. Sure, I'd glamorized motherhood in my mind, but I was well aware it came with its challenges, too. "My younger brother and I are three years apart, so a little more of a gap than between your littles, but my mama always used to tell us that there were days she prayed for bedtime to come quicker, but when it did, she would spend hours staring at us in our sleep instead of doing something for herself to unwind."

I gave my little friend a hearty push and relished the sound of his delighted squeals.

Tessa rocked the stroller back and forth gently. "It's funny. I have a background in education, but it wasn't enough to prepare me for becoming a mom. But I suppose having twenty-four mostly self-sufficient ten-year-olds to guide seven hours a day isn't quite the same as babies and toddlers you care for 24/7."

Mindlessly, I pushed Ollie on the swing. "You were a teacher?"

She took a long pull from her coffee cup and hummed in the affirmative. "Well, sort of. I was finishing up my degree in childhood education, where the final semester was spent student teaching in a local school when I met Asher."

The night we met, Tessa had mentioned being married to Asher for three years. I'd been gone for four, and he hadn't been attached when I left, so their courtship must have been a whirlwind romance.

"How did you two meet?" I asked, curious.

"Believe it or not, we met at the school where I was student teaching. He was the featured speaker at an assembly about kids staying active. We bumped into each other in the office when he first came in. And I mean that literally. I ran right into that solid brick wall of muscle and nearly landed on my ass. But his reflexes were lightning-quick, and he grabbed me before I could fall. I was so embarrassed when I realized he was a professional athlete. I felt like a clumsy girl and rushed off, my face on fire. During that assembly, I stood against the auditorium wall near where my class was seated, and even as he spoke to the room, his eyes kept finding mine. Three hours later, I walked out of the building and found him waiting for me. Seven months later, we were married. I was so young, and it seemed so quick, but when you meet the love of your life, you don't want to waste any more time."

Smiling, I mused, "I was pretty young when I got married, too. But unlike you, I didn't get the chance to finish my degree before following Jenner to Indy."

Tessa's eyebrows shot up. "Wait. I thought you guys just got married."

Shit. I forgot that Asher knew our history, but his young wife didn't.

I twisted the rings on my left hand. I was tired of lying, so I decided to tell the truth.

Taking a deep breath, I confessed, "Jenner and I recently got remarried. We were married once before, and things kinda fell apart."

"Oh." Her mouth formed a perfect circle. "That's why Asher was so surprised when I told him about you."

"Yeah. It was a mess, honestly. Maddox is still mad at me."

"Eh. The only people who need to be involved in your relationship are you and Jenner. If you're happy being back together, then forget everyone else."

She might be young, but she had a point. "Thanks, Tessa."

"And it's not like Maddox has any room to talk. His fiancé is *much* younger than him."

I laughed. "Yeah, and you should've seen her at Pipes the other night. Her singing. Woof."

We burst into a fit of giggles.

Tessa bent over and gripped her side. When she finally could take a deep breath, she said, "She's such a sweet girl, but—sidenote: I will kill you if you share this with anyone—last year when I was pregnant and she got on stage, Bailey went so nuts in my belly I thought she was gonna claw her way out of me just to get away from the sound."

A snort flew from my nose, and I clamped a hand over it. "Oh my God. That's hilarious."

"All teasing aside, Bristol is good for him. He was in a really dark place after the injury. At least, according to what I heard from Asher, since Maddox kinda drew in on himself."

I knew a thing or two about dark places, so maybe Maddox and I could find some common ground and move past our issues.

"I heard it was bad."

Tessa nodded. "And during the championship run, no less. I think he's got some unfinished business." She sighed. "They all do."

I wish I'd been there.

"But anyway, he took on the coaching job, and Bristol showed up. It was nice to see him come back to life."

Huffing out a disbelieving laugh, I said, "I still can't believe he's getting married."

"Love will make you do crazy things."

I raised my coffee. "I'll drink to that."

"Okay, now it's your turn to fill me in. You and Jenner were married, then divorced, and now you're married again?"

God, it had been so long since I'd had a girlfriend to talk to, and even then, I'd kept her in the dark about our private struggles. My online support groups were great because they were filled with women going through the same thing. They understood me, but it wasn't like they could reach through the computer and give me a hug.

They didn't know me the way Natasha did.

I think my reluctance to confide in her boiled down to several factors.

First, I was ashamed. My body had failed me, and then science failed me.

Second, she'd gotten pregnant twice, both times by accident.

The first time was while we were in college. She had been nowhere near ready to be a mom, so she'd terminated the pregnancy. I'd supported her—even though I could never make that choice for myself—because it was what she'd felt was best for her. The second time had been with a guy she'd been dating for about a year, and together, they decided to keep the baby.

She had what I wanted so desperately, and it came so easily that I began to resent her. But it was never Natasha's fault. The issue was with me, and I was the one to blame for our friendship slowly dying.

Regret over losing my best friend was why I decided to open up to Tessa now.

A wry laugh fell from my lips. "How much time do you have? It's a long story."

Tessa peeked at Bailey, still asleep in the stroller, before shamelessly pressing on the outside of her breasts. "It's not an exact science, but I'd say you've got at least twenty minutes before she needs to eat. Hit me with the short version, and you can flesh out the details the next time we meet up."

I nodded. "All right. Let's see. I caught his eye one day on campus, and that confident man waltzed right up to my group of girlfriends to introduce himself. He got my name but not my number. We ran into each other again about a month later, and he hit me hard with the charm. He invited me to his game, and even though I knew nothing about hockey, growing up in Oklahoma, he was cute and interested, and I figured, why not?"

She nudged me with her elbow. "You loved it, didn't you?"

"How could I not? It's unreal. I had no idea what I was missing. And that was just college hockey. I nearly died the first time I saw him play in a professional game. Well, after I fought the urge to throw up because I was so nervous for him."

"I think it's really cool you two were together when he was getting his start. That had to be special to experience. Asher was already well-established when we met."

My head tilted from side to side. "Yeah, but there was uncertainty associated with those early days. That first contract saw him move up and down between the Speed and their minor league affiliate in Cincinnati, the Crawlers. It was rough, both mentally and physically. Jenner would get in his head every time he was sent down, and we'd have to pick up our lives on a moment's notice and head to Cincy. He worked hard to prove himself, and it paid off."

"I'd say so. He's the captain now."

Looking skyward, I blew out a breath. "I still can't believe it." Lowering my head, I muttered, "And I hate that I wasn't here for it. I was selfish, and I shouldn't have left the way I did."

Tessa placed a hand on my arm. "You don't have to tell me if it's too painful."

I shrugged. "I'm used to the pain by now."

When she stared at me with sympathy in her eyes, I continued. "We got married young the first time. I was twenty-one, and Jenner was twenty-two. He'd gotten signed by the Speed at the end of his junior—my sophomore—year. I was on the fence about going with him. We'd only been together for a little over eighteen months. But I loved him, and when he got down on one knee, I was a goner."

"Been there," Tessa supplied.

"We looked into transferring my credits, but enrolling in classes with the constant shuffle between Indy and Cincinnati was too difficult, so my education fell by the wayside. I became the dutiful hockey wife, but I didn't feel like I was missing anything by not having a college degree. I was happy with my life, happy with my husband and supporting his career."

"But something changed, didn't it?"

I toed the ground. "Yeah. We decided to try for a baby."

A rush of air flew past Tessa's lips. "Oh." She understood without me having to say much more, which I appreciated.

"Yeah. It was really hard." I blinked back the tears, the emotions rushing back to the surface of how agonizing that process had been, only to yield no results. "Technically, there's nothing wrong with either one of us. We just could never make it happen. And Lord knows we tried every option. Nothing worked."

"I'm sorry." Though her voice was soft, it was full of compassion.

"Me, too. Because for as difficult as it was for me, trying in vain to conceive, it was devastating for Jenner to watch me suffer." I sniffled, remembering that morning. "I think I would have kept trying forever. But after what turned out to be our final round of IVF failed, Jenner broke. He said he couldn't do it anymore, and I wasn't ready to accept it. He offered other options to become parents, but I took it personally. It felt like he was giving up on me. So, I packed a bag and ran away."

"Where did you go?"

"Home. Back to Oklahoma. He tried reaching out." I swallowed past the lump in my throat. "So many times. But I never answered. I knew if I heard his voice begging me to come back, telling me that he loved me, I would run back into his arms. I was so deep in my depression that I knew I would drag him right down with me. So, instead of talking to my husband, I filed for divorce." I scoffed. "It took years to come back to myself and realize my mistake."

"You still love him, don't you?"

It was such a simple question, but it had my head snapping up. Tessa's lips were curved in a sad smile, but there wasn't a trace of pity on her face. She might be young, but she got it—got me.

"I never stopped," I admitted.

"So you came back."

"Yeah."

Emotionally drained, I didn't have it in me to tell her that my reason for coming back wasn't so much about my love for Jenner as it was my desperation to become a mother. Maybe someday, if my dream ever came true.

"Up, VeeVee! Up!" Ollie's sweet voice saved me from any further explanation.

He held his arms high, gesturing to be lifted, and I was happy to oblige. I might not have my own child, but this little guy helped soothe the ache in my soul, even if he wasn't mine.

Resting him on my hip, I asked, "Where would you like to play next?"

A chubby finger pointed toward the playscape. "Wheeee!"

One look at the bumpy slide visible, and I knew exactly what he wanted.

Tessa spoke from behind me as a tiny whimper reached my ears. "I'm gonna sit down and feed her. You good with him?"

I bounced Ollie. "Of course. Let's go for a ride on the slide while Mama takes care of Baby Sister."

Setting him down once we reached the steps leading up to the slide, I let him grip my finger from the side as he climbed onto the platform.

"Okay, buddy. Sit on your bum." Ollie followed my instructions while I repositioned myself at the bottom of the slide. "Now, go!"

He shoved off, flying over the bump and squealing. When he reached the bottom, I scooped him into my arms and spun him around to the sound of his delighted giggles.

"More! More!" he cried, so I set him on his feet, and we repeated the process again.

My heart had never been so full, and this wasn't even my child. I could only imagine what it would feel like someday when a little one looked up at me with unconditional love in their eyes simply because I was their mama.

Ollie was on his fifth trip up the steps when my phone buzzed in my back pocket. When it buzzed again in quick succession, I realized it wasn't an incoming text but a call. Probably my mother, wondering how things were going.

Pulling it out as I kept an eye on the toddler under my supervision, I was gearing up to fire off a text to tell her I'd call her back later when I saw a number I didn't recognize. But the Indy exchange had me curious, and I slid my index finger across the screen to answer.

"Hello?"

"Hi. I'm hoping to reach Evangeline Knight?" the female voice on the other end replied.

"You've found her. How can I help you?" I bent down just in time to catch Ollie with one hand.

"This is Miranda Williams. I'm the director of the Circle City Adoption Agency."

My heart rate kicked up, and a wave of dizziness rushed over me.

Oh God, not again.

"I'm calling with good news. We've got a prospective birth mom who has chosen your file for a preliminary interview."

"What?" I couldn't believe my ears.

"It's a first step but a big one in your adoption journey. I wanted to call you personally before sending an email so we can settle on a date for the interview that works for you and your husband."

My vision swam as tears filled my eyes. This was it. It was really happening.

"Th-thank you." I barely got the words to form.

"I'll be in touch. Enjoy the rest of your day."

A strangled noise was all I could manage before the phone dropped from my hand, and I collapsed into a sobbing heap in the middle of a public park.

I was vaguely aware of a concerned Ollie tugging at my hand or Tessa's voice calling from a distance.

There was only one thing I could focus on: I was going to be a mom.

Chapter 11
Jenner

I was itching to get back home to Evie. Mainly because every time I left the house, I worried she wouldn't be there upon my return. Her leaving the way she did had fucked with my head, and I wasn't sure there would ever come a time when that fear wasn't ever-present at the back of my mind.

But the Speed had business to attend to first, in the form of the Tennessee Rockers.

We were tied at two goals apiece, entering the third period. After winning the home opener against the Cardinals, the guys got overconfident, and we lost on the road to the Houston Heroes. It was a game on paper we should have won easily, but analytics didn't matter if you didn't show up to play.

Maddox made sure to remind us of that fact the following morning when he'd made us skate so hard that half the team was puking during practice. Lazy play wasn't going to fly under his command.

So, tonight we were busting our asses but still hadn't managed to gain the lead. Instead, we were chasing it, keeping pace with the Rockers.

I knew if we popped that net, it would be the momentum swing we needed, and the boys would blow this thing wide open.

We skated a few laps after coming out of the locker room to warm up our legs before the majority of the team settled onto the bench. I grabbed Braxton and Asher, skating with them to center ice. "Let's fucking get one and make this barn go silent, yeah?"

Braxton gave me a cheeky grin and a mock salute. "Aye, aye, captain!"

Asher stared at me with intense focus. "Where do you want me?"

I bumped his shoulder. "Time to get dirty in the crease. Take away the tendy's eyes."

Translation: park your ass in front of the goalie and block his vision so he won't see a shot coming.

Even though grim determination was etched on his face, a corner of his lips turned up. "You got it, boss."

Winking, I tossed back, "Don't let Coach hear you talking like that. He's already got his panties in a bunch."

"Then maybe he should stop wearing Bristol's thongs." His smirk grew into a full-blown smile.

"I fucking hate you guys," Braxton groaned. "That girl is like a younger sister to me. It's bad enough Maddox is sleeping with her, but you guys talking about her underwear? Come on."

"Yeah, well," I huffed. "He shouldn't have come after my wife."

My young teammate rolled his eyes. "How about we focus on the game, then get home to our girls?"

I could get on board with that.

Braxton lined up at center ice with me on his right and Asher on his left. The ref dropped the puck, and Braxton was quicker than the Rockers' center, passing it right over to me. I dug my skates into the ice and pushed toward the blue line, designating our offensive zone for this period. The winger covering me cut off my path, so I dumped the puck in deep around him.

Asher made a beeline for the blue paint in front of the net—AKA the crease—and Braxton gave chase, pushing hard to beat the defender for Tennessee, who was hot on his heels.

"Boards!" I screamed, giving directions to Braxton.

We'd played on the same line for a couple of seasons now and had built a level of trust. He didn't think twice about slamming the puck hard around the curved boards as soon as his stick touched it, narrowly avoiding a check from behind. It slid right onto the tape of Logan Ford, our defenseman manning the blue line.

Logan pulled back, his stick arching well above the level of his head, and when he brought it back down to ice level, the puck went hurtling through the air toward the net. Asher had a man tied up in front, and Souza, the Rockers' goalie, was moving his head around the mass of bodies, trying to get a clear view of how the play was developing.

Skating hard toward the net, I tracked the trajectory of the puck.

Hold it. Hold it. Now!

Timing it perfectly, I brought my stick off the ice, gripping it tightly as I put it in the path of the flying rubber disc. The impact of what was undoubtedly a hundred-mile-per-hour slapshot vibrated through the fiberglass and into my forearms, but I held steady. The puck changed direction faster than the goalie could track it, and the back of the net popped.

Asher's arms flew in the air, and he rushed me. Braxton hugged me from behind, and our defensemen joined the celebratory huddle.

"Beauty of a deflection!" Asher screamed, even though he didn't need to. The home crowd had quieted when we scored, taking the lead. "Souza never stood a chance!"

We skated in a line to fist-bump our teammates, standing on the bench before taking a seat and letting the next shift take the ice.

Maddox grumbled from behind me, "Showoff."

I didn't bother turning around, sure that if I did, I'd say something befitting Maddox, my friend, instead of Maddox, my head coach. Even though we had our issues, that was personal. It had nothing to do with hockey or our professional relationship, and I would never dare to disrespect my coach in front of the team.

But at some point, the two of us needed to have a serious conversation. He didn't have to agree with the choices I made in my life, but he needed to back off and play nice, or we would have to take a step back from our friendship outside the rink.

I didn't want that to happen, but Evie would always come first.

It was just shy of midnight when I pulled up to the house after the short flight from Nashville. A rush of relief hit me when the garage door opened and Evie's car was parked inside.

No lights were visible from the windows, so I assumed she'd already gone to bed, and I quietly stepped through the house so as not to wake her. She was more of an earlier riser than a night owl, though that had shifted during our first marriage, as she'd never missed one of my games and often waited up for me when she knew I was returning from the road.

So many things I'd taken for granted back then.

I stopped in the kitchen, dropping my suit jacket over a chair before snagging a glass of water. While swallowing, I heard a noise so soft I thought I must've imagined it.

Pausing, I trained my ears to see if it sounded again. When I was met with silence, I chalked it up to being tired. It had been a long four days, and I was ready to sleep in my own bed and eat food that wasn't takeout.

Placing my glass into the sink, I walked through the living room toward the stairs when I heard it again.

What the fuck is that?

Stopping dead in my tracks, I waited, listening. I'd stand here all night just to prove I wasn't going insane.

Come on. Come on.

There.

Whatever it was, it was definitely located in this room, so I moved to the light switch and flicked it on.

My eyes were still adjusting to the sudden brightness when a head popped up from behind the couch.

I let out a deep exhale. It was only Evie, probably having fallen asleep before she found her way up to bed.

"Hey. Didn't mean to wake you," I apologized, but when she turned to face me, any additional words died on my tongue.

There were dried tear tracks down her cheeks, and the red tip of her nose matched the puffiness around her eyes. My feet were moving before I could formulate a conscious thought.

I dropped onto the couch beside her, and my hands flew up to cradle her face. Fuck, I'd almost forgotten how soft her cheeks were as my thumbs stroked them gently. Searching her eyes, I couldn't read whatever emotion was swimming in their violet depths, and it scared the hell out of me.

Pressing my forehead to hers, I whispered, "Talk to me, Evie. Please." I wasn't above begging. Not with her.

That noise presented itself again, and that's when I realized it was the sound of her sniffling. A hiccup followed, and she took a shaky breath.

"I-I went with Tessa to the park with the kids," she began, and dread settled in my gut.

Almost too afraid to ask, I forced myself to say the words. "Are the kids okay?"

She nodded, but my relief was short-lived when she spoke again. "I got a c-call. From the a-agency." A sob bubbled up from her chest, and my heart clenched.

Fuck. They'd found out about our deception. That explained why she was a mess, curled up on the couch in the dark.

"It's gonna be okay, baby. I promise. We can look into surrogacy. This isn't the end."

Pulling back, her eyes were glassy, and she shook her head. "No, it's not that. There's a mom who wants to meet us."

The breath seized in my lungs, and I stared at my wife for a solid minute before I found my voice. "Really?"

Evie bit her lower lip so hard the edges turned white. "Mmhmm."

"Then why are you crying?" I tucked a strand of her blonde hair behind her ear. "This is what you wanted, right?"

Her teeth released that pillowy soft lip, but it trembled before she replied, "I think I'm in shock that this is actually happening."

"Come here." I gathered her against my chest. "*You* made this happen. You decided nothing was going to stand in your way, and you went after what you wanted."

When she pushed against my chest, I released her. Evie blinked a few times before whispering, "Thank you for helping me."

"Hey. Don't forget we're in this together. This is just the start, Evie. And it's gonna be amazing. *You're* going to be amazing. I know it."

"They sent an email asking for availability for an interview with the birth mom who picked up our file. I checked the dates against your travel schedule, and it looks like we can sit down together on Monday. Is that okay?"

Nodding, I swallowed. "Of course that's okay. We're gonna make this happen, Evie." Standing, I offered her my hand. "You've had a long day. Let's get you up to bed, yeah?"

It was no small miracle that she placed her soft palm against mine, especially when, until a couple of months ago, I never thought I'd see her again.

Everything was falling into place. My wife was not only back in my life but tucked against my side, and we were making progress toward starting a family.

If I didn't know any better, I would say it was all a dream.

Chapter 12
Jenner

"Evie," I knocked on her bedroom door for at least the fifth time in the last half hour. "We're going to be late if we don't leave soon."

A muffled scream sounded through the wood, but the doorknob turned, and Evie came into view.

She took one look at me and shook her head, muttering, "Nope," before turning on her heel and returning to where she had clothing scattered across the queen-sized bed inside the guest room she'd been occupying since her return.

Cautiously, I stepped across the threshold. "What's wrong?"

Evie spun around, a mix of frustration and annoyance on her face. "I can't decide what to wear." She gestured a hand toward me, accusing, "And you're in a freaking suit!"

It took everything in my power to bite back a smile, but I couldn't keep it from filtering into my voice when I replied, "Ninety percent of my wardrobe consists of suits and sweats, babe. Pretty sure sweats were not the appropriate choice today."

Her eyes narrowed, and both hands flew to her wide hips. "Don't try to be cute. This is serious."

I scanned her appearance. She looked classy in a wine-colored top with lace sleeves down to the elbow and wide-leg black trousers. "I think you look great, Evie."

She huffed, gesturing to herself. "It's not dressy enough. First impressions are everything, Jenner. We can't mess this up."

Daring to step closer, I reached for her hand. Instead of pulling away, Evie met me halfway, squeezing so tightly that I was sure I'd have an imprint of her rings on my palm later.

Keeping my tone soothing, I said, "She's not going to decide she doesn't like us based on our clothing. She chose us based on what was in our file."

Evie's lip trembled, and her eyes grew glassy. Fuck. I wasn't trying to make her cry. She'd shed enough tears over trying to become a mother to last the both of us a lifetime.

If I had anything to say about it, today would mark the end of all the heartbreak. How could any woman not see that Evie was the perfect choice to raise their child?

Her free hand rose to swipe at her nose as she sniffled. "That file is the highlight reel. What if we don't live up to the expectation in real life?"

I cupped her cheek. "You're overthinking this."

Vulnerability swam in her eyes as she stared at me. "I want it so bad."

"I know." I nodded. "And it's going to happen. Even if this mom isn't the one, I know there's one out there who will be the perfect match for us."

"Okay." Evie's lips twisted to the side. "Can you at least take off the tie? Go a little more casual?"

I chuckled. My hands flew to my throat, instantly loosening the knot holding the tie in place. "You know I'll give you anything you ever ask for, Evie."

Hanging heavy between us was the fact that I'd been unable to give her the only thing she'd wanted more than anything in this world—a baby.

But that was about to change.

"Mr. and Mrs. Knight, it's a pleasure to finally meet you in person." A silver-haired woman in a black wrap dress and flats reached out to shake our hands in the small reception area of the adoption agency's offices. "Stella couldn't tell me enough good things about you from her visit."

"We're excited to be here." I extended my hand and clasped hers, giving it a firm shake before dropping my palm to the small of Evie's back as she took her turn greeting the agency's director, Miranda.

"Shall we step into my office, and I can give you an overview of what to expect today?"

"Of course." I nodded, guiding Evie down the narrow hallway as we followed Miranda.

Letting Evie settle into a chair opposite where the director sat behind her desk, I took the one beside her. My wife's knee bounced, and she twisted her hands in her lap. I wanted to reach out and soothe her, but I knew nothing would settle her nerves. Not when the future she'd always dreamed of was on the line but so many factors surrounding it were out of her control.

Miranda opened a file on her desk. My eyes saw that Knight was typed along the tab of the manila folder. Evie had handled the application process before my involvement, so I wasn't quite sure what lay inside, but it must've been enough to catch the eye of the birth mom we would be meeting today.

"I must say," Miranda began, "you've done an excellent job expressing yourselves and your journey. It's no surprise that you were selected for an interview so quickly. You can almost feel the love you would give a child."

With a sideways glance at Evie, I asked the director, "Two months is considered quick for this step?"

She nodded. "The average is six to twelve months. We boast quite the catalog, so it says something that you were able to stand out. Even if this mom isn't the right match for you, it gives me confidence that you'll catch the eye of another."

Evie sucked in a sharp breath beside me, and it took me right back to our days of IVF.

As far as I was concerned, failure wasn't an option. This first mom had to be the one. I wasn't sure Evie could handle another tenuous, drawn-out process that yielded no results. And we'd already proven that I wouldn't be able to watch her suffer.

Miranda must not have noticed Evie's distress because she continued, "The birth mom will be waiting for us in a special meeting room. I'll sit in to mediate should either party have any questions or concerns. Keep in mind that even should you be chosen, she can change her mind at any time, even after signing away her rights once the baby is born, for up to thirty days."

"We understand." I remembered Stella, the social worker, mentioning something similar. I could only imagine if they were hammering it home, it happened more often than we cared to think.

"And I would caution you to temper your expectations that you'll leave this building today with a definitive answer as to whether the birth mom wants to continue the process with you. Many of them need time to think it over after the interview, or they may have other couples to visit with. We know time is paramount, so the minute we have information for you, we will be in touch."

From the corner of my eye, I could see Evie trembling. I was growing concerned that she wouldn't be able to hold it together during the interview.

Closing our file, Miranda stood, gesturing to the door. "If you don't have any further questions, we can head out to the meeting room."

Rising from my seat, I offered a hand to Evie. She clutched it like a lifeline, her nervous energy transferring through our clasped palms.

Leaning down, I whispered in her ear, "You've got this."

Her eyes flashed to mine, and some of the fear in them melted away. She gave me a tight nod, and together, we walked hand-in-hand behind Miranda before coming to a stop at a closed door.

This was it. On the other side of that door sat the woman who was considering giving a piece of herself over to us to raise. I couldn't imagine the strength it took to make such a monumental life decision—one that would change both her future and ours.

"Are you ready?" Miranda asked.

Evie couldn't find her voice, so I answered for both of us. "Yes."

The door was pulled open, and Miranda stepped across the threshold first to announce our presence. "Good afternoon, Paige. I'd like to introduce you to the Knights."

That was our cue, and I tugged Evie along beside me as we entered the room. But as soon as we stepped inside, I stopped short and did a double take.

I'd been expecting a woman, but instead, a girl was seated on the couch with a tiny swell of a belly visible beneath her tight-fitting shirt. She barely looked older than Braxton's sixteen-year-old niece, with her strawberry blonde hair pulled into a high ponytail and zero makeup on her face as she chewed on her nails.

"Would you care to sit?" Miranda prompted, and I realized I'd been staring.

Swallowing, I barely made it the three steps to reach the couch opposite the young, redheaded girl before I collapsed onto it.

Evie was more graceful as she settled beside me, but she gripped my hand as tightly as ever.

Pressing a palm over my racing heart, I cleared my throat before managing to say, "I'm Jenner." Turning my eyes to my wife, I added, "And this is Evie."

The girl dipped her chin. "Yeah, I know. Honestly, I feel like I know everything about you from your file."

"Paige, would you like to share with the Knights why you've selected them for this interview?" Miranda guided the young woman.

"Sure." Paige's blue eyes rose to meet our gaze. "I think what drew me in was reading Mrs. Knight's—I mean, Evie's—personal statement. It broke my heart reading about the years you two tried to start a family of your own. Not just the physical toll it took on Evie with the different attempts at treatment but the emotional ride you went through as a couple. Evie couldn't say enough about Mr. Knight's—Jenner's—constant support, explaining how he never wavered in caring for her, even when she was struggling and not herself."

I peeked at Evie in surprise that she'd shared those vulnerable moments, only to find tears streaking down her face. The sound of a cleared throat caught my attention, and a box of tissues entered my field of vision. I accepted it gratefully, pulling one out and offering it to Evie.

"Sorry," I apologized for the love of my life falling apart beside me. "It's been a really difficult journey."

Paige gave me a sad smile, her eyes shifting to my wife. "I've shed more than a few tears reading all that the two of you have been through. I can't imagine how painful it was to experience it firsthand."

Stunned, I stared at the young woman. She seemed so mature, especially in her capacity for empathy.

"But as moving as that testimony was, when I saw your wedding portrait, that sealed the deal for me." When my eyebrows rose and Paige sensed my confusion, she explained, "Seeing Jenner's red hair. It seemed like a sign." She tangled a hand in her own red tresses. "There's a good chance this baby comes out a redhead, and it just felt like they would look like they belonged with you, you know?"

Evie let out a sob, and I turned enough that she could bury her face in my chest, her tears soaking through my shirt. Her words were muffled, but I knew exactly what she was saying. "Little redheaded babies."

That's what she'd always wanted. A house full of little ones who looked like me.

Paige handled Evie's breakdown like a champ. "And that nursery? I could just picture her sleeping safely inside it."

Evie pulled back suddenly, and her head whipped to stare at Paige. "A g-girl?"

"Yeah." Paige dropped her eyes to her belly before running a hand over it.

Out of the corner of my eye, I caught Evie's fingers twitching, and I knew what she was thinking—she would never know what it felt like to grow life inside her.

As much as I hated being the voice of reason, it was required if we hoped to move forward.

"Paige, giving up a child is a monumental decision, so I have to ask: Are you sure?"

A flash of defiance entered her blue eyes, and she lifted her chin. "I'm eighteen. I'm old enough to know what I want. And while I'd like to have kids someday, I'm not ready now. I'd like to think by giving her up, I'm giving us both a chance at a better life. She'll get the chance to grow up with a couple who are well-established, in love, and ready to welcome a baby into their lives."

I had to hand the girl credit; she'd clearly given this a lot of thought, but there was one more question weighing on my mind.

"And the father? Does he feel the same way?" The last thing we needed was some guy coming out of the woodwork later and challenging our parental rights.

Paige let out a heavy sigh. "He doesn't feel any kind of way."

Alarm bells sounded in my head. "Does he know about the baby?"

She shook her head. "No." Scoffing, she added, "God, I feel so stupid. I went on a senior trip to the beach with my friends. It was our last hurrah before we all split up to different colleges around the country. Some guys were renting a house a few doors down, and we spent a lot of time with them that week. One of them was really charming, and we hooked up. It wasn't until I got home that I realized the number he'd given me was fake. When I couldn't find him on social media or listed anywhere in the town he said their group was from, it sank in that he'd been playing me all along. And then, when I found out he'd gotten me pregnant, I felt like the biggest fool. I was valedictorian of my graduating class; I was supposed to be smart. But somehow, I'd wound up pregnant at eighteen by a guy whose real name I didn't even know."

A rush of air flew past Evie's lips, and I could tell she wanted to cross the room to pull the girl into a hug but was mindful of boundaries. I was pretty sure if given the option, she would want to adopt the pair of them—mother and baby.

"What about your parents?" I asked.

"My parents had me later in life, so they're in their early sixties. They're ready to retire. It would be unfair to ask them to start all over again and help raise my baby while I went to college. And I'd prefer not to drop out. I worked really hard to get several merit-based scholarships, and those aren't easy to come by."

"So, they support your decision?"

"Yeah." Paige nodded. "I thought they were going to be so mad at me for being reckless, but they surprised me. I put a lot of pressure on myself as an only child to be perfect, and I think, more than anything, I was disappointed in myself for being duped. I don't want this baby to pay for my mistakes."

We fell into silence, so Miranda asked, "Is there anything you'd like to ask the Knights, Paige?"

Her eyes locked with mine before shifting to meet Evie's. "I only have one. Will you love her like she's your own?"

Before I could open my mouth, Evie's voice rang out strong and clear. "Yes. With all my heart."

Looping my arm around her shoulder, I pulled her into my side, saying to Paige, "She beat me to it. Same goes for me."

Tears filled the eyes of the young girl seated opposite us. "That's all I need to know."

Miranda's voice cut through the emotionally charged moment. "Thank you, Jenner and Evie, for coming in today to meet with Paige. We'll be in touch once a decision has been made."

I was halfway to standing when Paige said, "I've made my decision."

Freezing, I felt Evie tense beside me, a tiny whimper slipping past her lips. "You—you have?"

Paige gave a firm nod. "I want you to be her parents. If you want her."

A trembling hand came up to cover Evie's mouth, and I clutched her closer.

Giving the girl a smile, I replied for the both of us. "We would be honored to be that little girl's parents."

Shyly, Paige asked, "Is it too much to ask for a hug?"

Evie was across the room in a flash, pulling the teenager tightly into her arms. Her soft sniffles were loud enough to be heard from where I stood.

Locking eyes with Paige, I wondered if she had any idea how she'd changed our lives today. Given the gift she was about to bestow upon us, it didn't feel like quite enough, but I mouthed, *Thank you*.

She clutched Evie closer, and her eyes squeezed shut as tears leaked down her cheeks.

I hadn't been able to make my wife's dream a reality, but this selfless girl had. And I would never be able to repay her.

I drove us home in a daze.

After everything we'd gone through—the years of unsuccessful fertility treatments and Evie walking out on me—my brain had closed the door on the possibility of becoming a father years ago.

Now, if everything went according to plan, we would be bringing our daughter home in a little over four months.

God, that sounded strange. *Our daughter.*

But that's what she would be. Regardless of her genetics, there was no doubt that she would be ours. Evie and I would be the ones who got to love her through the countless sleepless nights, the skinned knees, and temper tantrums.

I couldn't wait.

Pulling into the garage, Evie got out of the car and went into the house, but I remained in my seat. I needed a minute to myself to process how quickly my life had changed course.

A few months ago, I'd thought Evie was gone forever, but now she was back, and the family we were always supposed to have was within reach.

It seemed almost too good to be true, but I wasn't about to question my good fortune.

Taking a deep breath, I exited the vehicle, pushing into the mudroom. Reaching the kitchen, I found Evie standing there, gripping the marble counter of the island, her head hanging low.

Panic hit me with the force of a tidal wave. "Are you okay?"

When she raised her eyes to meet mine, I stumbled back, seeing the haunted look in their purple depths. Today, we'd taken a huge step toward obtaining everything she'd ever wanted, but looking at her now, you would never know it.

"Evie," I said her name softly. "What's wrong?"

Her eyelashes fluttered down to kiss her cheeks, and the anguish in her voice when she spoke shattered my heart. "I know this isn't what you wanted."

"What?" I needed more clarification.

Throat bobbing on a swallow, she opened her eyes. "I know you wished I'd stayed gone."

Disbelief rushed over me, and I yelled, "Are you fucking kidding me?"

Evie flinched, and I felt like the biggest asshole, but she'd caught me off guard.

Did she honestly believe that? After how hard I'd tried to contact her when she'd left? After how I didn't hesitate to deceive an adoption agency so she could get the baby she so desperately wanted? After we'd gotten remarried and I expressed my desire to raise a child together?

"How could you think that?" I rasped. "You're the one who walked away, Evie."

"Because you gave up on us!" she cried.

My eyebrows shot up high on my forehead. That wasn't the story I remembered. Not by a long shot.

"I never gave up. I cared more about you than anything in my life. I still do. You have to know that."

Evie dropped her eyes to the floor. The truth of my words was likely too much for such an emotionally demanding day, but she needed to hear them.

"I'm broken. You deserve better," she whispered.

I finally snapped, done tiptoeing around how I felt about her and done allowing her to believe that this situation—our marriage—was temporary.

It was time to clear the air.

Crossing the room in three giant strides, I barely heard her gasp as I turned her around, caging her against the island with my arms. She peered up at me, and I brought my face so close to hers that our noses were practically touching.

My chest heaved, and I tried in vain to rein it in now that our bodies were pressed flush. I hadn't been this close to her in years, yet it was like no time had passed. My physical response was immediate—heart racing, cock hardening.

"It's time to make one thing very clear, Evie," I gritted out. "You are my goddamn wife. I should have never let you walk away the first time, and I'll be damned if I let you get away ever again. If you so much as try to leave me, I will hunt you down and drag you back by any means necessary."

Her eyes widened, and her lips parted on an exhale.

Then, Evie did the absolute last thing I would have ever expected. Arching her hips, she rubbed shamelessly against my raging hard-on, and I couldn't bite back a groan. Heat flared in her eyes, and that was as good as a green light in my book.

My mouth crashed down on hers without warning, and she opened for me instantly, her tongue battling with mine. Her hands slid into my hair, maneuvering my head to where she wanted it and moaning when I tugged her lower lip between my teeth.

She tried to pull me closer, but I stepped back, wiping my mouth with the back of my hand. Our ragged breathing mixed in the air, our chests rising and falling rapidly, trying to recover.

Evie couldn't hide the pain of rejection that flashed across her face.

Well, we can't have that, can we?

I was nowhere near done with her. I never would be.

Shucking my suit jacket, I tossed it behind me, not caring where it landed. Rolling up my shirt sleeves, I never took my eyes off hers.

"Drop to your knees and show me how much you've missed your husband." The command was firm, leaving no room for argument.

The pale skin of Evie's cheeks pinkened, but she didn't hesitate, stepping forward and sinking down until she was kneeling on the ceramic tile. Her mouth was so close to the erection tenting my pants that I could feel the warmth of her shallow breaths through the fabric.

"Don't be shy. Take it out, baby."

Her tongue darted out to lick her lips, and my cock wept in anticipation.

Even though I hadn't been with anyone since she'd left, it had been far longer than that since I'd enjoyed sex.

Physical intimacy was the first thing to take a hit when we realized our path to parenthood wouldn't be an easy one. Evie had become hyperfocused on achieving her goal, and that meant temping, charting, and sex on a schedule in optimal positions only.

I'd always loved her with all my heart, but somewhere along the way, we'd drifted apart under the weight of expectation.

This was our chance to reconnect, to regain what we'd lost.

And I wasn't about to waste it.

Hands tugging on my belt brought me back to the present. As soon as the buckle was undone, Evie pushed the button through the loop and dragged down the zipper. My cock was eager, jutting through the opening as soon as it was given freedom.

Peeking up at me, Evie slipped her fingers beneath the waistband of my boxers and tugged, shoving both them and my pants down my thighs. Cool air met my fevered skin, but still, heat simmered beneath the surface, threatening to boil over.

Her fingers wrapped around my shaft, and my head dropped back as a throaty groan rumbled up from my chest. "Fuck, yes."

Emboldened by my response, she stroked up and down my length with the perfect pressure. If I wasn't careful, I could lose myself in her touch before enjoying the pleasure of her lips wrapped around me.

Almost as if she could read my thoughts, her tongue darted out, licking the underside before sucking the head into her hot little mouth.

I forced my eyes open. This was too stunning a sight to miss.

Staring up at me, Evie took me deeper before pulling back and using her tongue to tease my sensitive flesh. Even with her mouth full, she still managed a tiny smirk before bobbing up and down my length, increasing her speed and pressure like a pro.

"Fuck, baby. Your mouth was made for sucking my cock."

I tangled my hands in her hair, toes curling inside my dress shoes as I tried to stave off my release. I never wanted this to end.

When she hummed, it settled deep within my balls, and I knew time was running out. The tipping point was when a slight gag sounded, making my cock swell. I couldn't hold back any longer.

Gripping her hair tighter, I forced her head back. Tear tracks ran down her face as I shoved myself impossibly further down her throat.

"Swallow every fucking drop, baby, like the dirty girl you are."

Chapter 13
Evie

Mouth stuffed full of my husband's cock as he held an iron grip on my hair, there was no other choice but to obey his filthy command.

I might be the one down on my knees, but I held all the power in this position. He was unraveling before my very eyes. I did this to him—made him lose all control. And I fucking loved it.

Moaning from a combination of his words and the insistent throbbing between my thighs, I felt his dick swell a split second before the first spurt of hot cum slid down my throat. He was shoved so deep that I couldn't taste it, but I was entirely focused on making sure I swallowed every drop as he demanded.

When he began to soften, I kept sucking, and he released me suddenly, stepping back enough that his cock slipped from my mouth.

"Jesus, Evie," Jenner panted. "What are you trying to do? Kill me?"

Feeling more myself than I had in ages, I taunted, "What? More than you can handle, hotshot?"

He barked out a laugh. "Fuck, I've missed you."

Rising to my feet on shaky legs, I cocked a hip. "Are we going tit for tat on proving that? Or am I going to be getting off alone in my room?" I flashed him a sexy smirk. "Just like every other night I've spent under this roof since I've been back."

That was enough to spur Jenner into action. Even with his pants down around his ankles, he was lightning-quick, closing the gap between us and gripping two fistfuls of my ass before lifting me onto the island.

"What did you just say?" His tone bordered on deadly, but I knew he'd never hurt me. My teddy bear of a man was still there, buried deep under a haze of lust.

I simply shrugged. I knew I was pushing his buttons.

A growl vibrated through his chest. "Are you telling me that you've been across the hall, touching yourself this whole time?"

"'Course not." When Jenner narrowed his eyes at what he deemed a lie, I clarified, "Toys are much more effective at getting the job done."

I gasped when his fingers dug into my flesh so hard I knew he'd leave bruises.

"You always were a smartass." His voice was husky and low. "Let me rephrase my question. Who were you thinking of when you came, baby?"

There was no use in lying, so I told him the truth. "You. It's only ever been you, Jenner."

An eyebrow arched on his handsome face, a question in his eyes.

I gave a subtle nod in reply.

We'd always had this canny ability to speak without words, and it was a comfort to know that hadn't changed.

Jenner knew I came to college as a virgin and that he was the first man I'd ever had sex with. Our silent exchange told him that he remained the only man I had ever been with, even with all our time spent apart.

His Adam's apple bobbed on a swallow. "There's been no one else for me either, Evie. I couldn't move on. Not when I still loved you."

My heart threatened to explode. Never in my wildest dreams could I have imagined us finding our way back together. Not after how I'd left.

Since my return, I'd been so worried that he'd grow tired of the drama I brought into his life, dreading the day he would ask me to leave. That fear had been sufficiently laid to rest.

He was going to fight for me, for us, for our new family.

Everything was finally right in the world again.

With trembling hands, I reached up to undo the buttons of his dress shirt, skimming my hands over his muscles as I worked lower. Pushing the sides wide, baring his stunning form, I didn't hide my appreciation for his hard work in the gym. I hadn't thought it possible, but he was even more ripped than the last time I'd seen him naked.

"Had a lot of free time on my hands," Jenner murmured, nuzzling my neck.

I tipped my head back on a sigh, loving the feel of his lips on my skin.

My fingers trailed over the rounded muscles of his shoulders, taking my time relearning every hard plane of his body. "Looks like it was time well spent."

"No." He pulled back, gripping my chin and forcing me to look into his eyes. "I would have rather had you."

A sudden wave of sadness crashed over me. I'd caused us so much unnecessary pain.

"Hey," he said softly. "You're here now. Nothing else matters. Okay?"

Squeezing my eyes shut as I nodded, I desperately tried to keep the tears at bay. I was so sick of crying over everything.

I dared to peek at him, and so much love shone back at me that my breath caught in my lungs. I threw my arms around his neck, holding on for dear life as an overwhelming rush of emotions threatened to drag me under.

My throat was tight, but I managed to confess, "I love you, Jenner."

His arms banded around my waist, pulling me tighter against his chest. "I love you, too, baby. So fucking much."

"Will you show me?"

Jenner pulled back and searched my eyes. "Promise you're never going to leave me again?"

Swallowing around the lump lodged in my throat, I nodded. "Promise."

Hands moving to cup my cheeks, he poured all the love he felt into a tender kiss. My position on the counter put me at the perfect height to feel the brush of his renewed erection nudging against my inner thigh.

Smiling against his lips, I reached down and grabbed it, relishing the sound of his groan as he tore his mouth away.

"Don't even think about it," he warned.

I gave him an exaggerated fake pout. "But I just got it back."

With a playful roll of his eyes, he gripped the back of my thighs and pulled, making me squeal as my back met with the cool marble of the kitchen island.

"We have all the time in the world for you to use my cock for your pleasure, babe. But right now, if I don't get to taste you, I might die."

Sighing dramatically, I waved a hand. "Very well. If you must."

The sound of his pants being kicked away reached my ears as Jenner's hands skimmed along the waistband of my trousers. He pushed my shirt up enough that I could pull it over my head. Brown eyes like melted chocolate roved over my bared skin, and he sucked in a sharp breath.

Fingers trailing lightly over my waist and over my belly, he said reverently, "You were always so beautifully soft. Fucking perfect."

My teeth descended on my lower lip. No one had ever appreciated my body in its natural form the way Jenner had. He saw every flaw as an asset and worshipped them all.

"Lose the bra, baby. I want to see every stunning inch of you," he commanded. "It's been too long."

Arching my back, I reached a hand between my body and the marble to flick the clasp before slipping the garment down my arms and tossing it aside. Jenner went to work undoing the fly of my pants and sliding them down my legs.

"Goddamn. My wife is looking fucking delicious spread out on my kitchen counter," Jenner rasped.

Hearing him call me his wife gave me a small thrill. Even when we were divorced, a part of me had always known I belonged to him. I hadn't realized he felt the same.

With his warm hand on my bare ankle, he moved his touch higher, lightly grazing over the dimpled skin and faded stretch marks along my inner thighs until he reached the edge of my panties. Both of his thumbs stroked the sensitive skin there without dipping inside.

My hips bucked, trying to make contact where I was throbbing for him.

His responding chuckle washed over me like warm honey. "Tell me how much you need me, Evie."

A whimper flew past my lips. "Please, Jenner."

"Hmm." His hands moved back down to my knee to tease the inside of the joint, and I let out a whine. "That didn't seem like quite the right answer."

Desperate for relief, I had zero patience for his games. Sitting up on my elbows, I lowered one hand to shift my panties over my ass, wiggling out of them and kicking them off.

"If you're seeing fit to tease me, then I'll handle it myself," I taunted, putting one hand between my legs and rubbing a firm circle over my clit.

Keeping eye contact with Jenner standing between my open thighs, I silently dared him to take action.

Raising an eyebrow, he held my gaze until my soft moan split the air, and then he dropped it to stare at my pussy. Oh God, his intense attention there had the first sparks of an orgasm firing off, and I rubbed faster, chasing my pleasure.

Back bowing, my muscles locked in preparation. And just when I was about to tip over the edge, an iron grip locked around my wrist and wrenched my hand away. I let out a desperate sob as my release was stolen from me.

Leaning down, Jenner pressed his tight torso to my chest as he held my arms immobile beside my head. I tried rocking my hips, seeking friction any way I could get it, but he had me pinned tightly to the countertop.

His lips were a breath away from mine; his voice was husky but held a trace of amusement. "I'd almost forgotten what a feisty girl you are."

"Let me come, Jenner," I begged.

"Don't worry, sweetheart," he crooned. "You're going to come plenty."

"You're talkin' an awful big game for someone who has failed to take action," I shot back, breathless.

"You want action?" Jenner practically snarled.

"Maybe too many years out of practice, and you've forgotten how to please a woman." I let a little sass leak into my tone.

His chest vibrated as a growl worked its way up his throat. "You're going to pay for that."

"And yet, you're still talkin'."

That final remark seemed to spur him into action.

The warmth of his body was gone so suddenly that I shivered at the loss. It took a minute for my mind to figure out exactly where he'd gone, but when I felt his hot breath fanning against the slick flesh between my thighs, I caught up right quick.

My eyes rolled back into my head on a deep moan at the first pass of his tongue. "Oh God."

He pulled back, eyes peeking over my pussy. "Is this what you wanted, baby?"

"Yes," I hissed as he swirled the tip around my clit.

When he speared his tongue inside me, I nearly levitated off the counter. One of his thick forearms banded over my waist, holding me down as he feasted on me without mercy. His mouth didn't need words to express that he never thought he'd have the chance to taste me again—it showed in the way he ate at me greedily.

"Jenner," I breathed out.

The hum he let out had me jolting against his face.

"Did you miss this, Evie?" His words were muffled against me, but I heard him clear as day.

Panting, I confessed, "Every minute of every day."

That must've been the correct answer because Jenner latched onto my clit, tugging gently with his teeth as he thrust two fingers inside me, curling them just right so I saw stars. A ragged gasp split the air, and I found myself barreling toward a hard-earned release. No one else would ever own my body like my husband, and I'd been a fool for thinking I could live without him.

Pressure built at my core, coiling tighter and tighter. Even with the warning, I wasn't prepared for the intensity of the climax Jenner coaxed from me. A surprised scream flew past my lips as tears leaked from my tightly shut eyes, and violent tremors left me trembling uncontrollably.

I was vaguely aware of Jenner moving from his perch between my thighs as I lay limp across the island. This would have to be my bed tonight because there was no way I had the energy to move.

"Fucking hell, baby. You taste as sweet as I remember." The words were said as Jenner kissed a trail up my belly before sucking a nipple into his mouth.

Moaning, I willed my heavy arms to move to push him away. I couldn't take any more.

A weak hand pushed at his face, and he merely smiled against my flesh.

"Oh, honey. You didn't think we were done, did you?"

"I can't," I protested, my voice hoarse from screaming.

His teeth toyed with the hardened nipple in his mouth while his fingers plucked its twin. "I think we both know you can, Evie." He chuckled. "Maybe you're the one who's out of practice."

Damn him for throwing my own words back at me. And I hated that he was probably right. A self-manufactured orgasm had nothing on anything Jenner could provide.

I sighed in relief when he abandoned my breasts, but it was short-lived as he tugged me into a sitting position. Slumping against his chest, I threw my arms around his neck. Holding tightly to the man I'd always loved, I could hear his heart beating strongly—a heart I knew had never stopped beating for me.

That knowledge warmed me down to the tips of my toes.

"Think you can walk?" Jenner murmured against my hair.

A scoff sounded from my throat. "No way."

Pressing a soft kiss at my temple, his hands moved from my upper back to my ass, gripping two fistfuls. "Not a problem. I've got you."

In an instant, I was held tightly in his strong arms, and we were moving through the house.

One of the most intoxicating things about being with Jenner was his ability to throw me around with ease. When he lifted me, there was never a grunt, a huff, or any signs of strain. He made me feel weightless.

Setting me down on unstable legs, he continued to support me as he spun me around and bent me over the arm of the couch. His hand on my back pushed my chest further into the cushions so that my toes barely touched the ground.

"Jenner." I wiggled my ass, wondering if he was going to fuck me or spank me. Honestly, I could probably handle a spanking better than another orgasm.

His calloused palm slid over the wide globes of my backside, squeezing roughly as he spread me open for him.

Guess that answers that question. A hard fucking from behind it is. God help me.

"Do you know how many nights I dreamt of this pussy?" His deep voice sent a shiver down my spine.

My head thrashed on the couch cushions. "Tell me."

"Every fucking night, Evie. It didn't matter that you were gone. I only wanted you."

I whimpered as he notched himself at my entrance. "I'm yours, Jenner."

"Damn right, you are."

He thrust inside me so forcefully that I cried out, clawing at the couch, trying to get away. I was too sensitive, and it felt like I might actually split apart at the seams. I hadn't been kidding when I told him I couldn't handle another.

"Fuck." He sucked in a sharp breath. "Being inside you feels like home."

Jenner's hand tangled in my hair as he set a punishing pace. My hips were slammed against the arm of the couch so hard that I knew I'd have a line of bruises across my lower abdomen.

I was mindless with pleasure as an endless stream of sobs slipped from my parted lips. A second orgasm slammed into me before a third came right on its heels.

Grunting behind me, Jenner forced out through what I could only assume were clenched teeth, "That's right, baby. Take my cock like you were born to do. Let that pussy milk me dry."

His words didn't just tip me over the edge; they threw me over with such force that I blacked out from the intensity of the pleasure crashing over my body.

I was just coming to when I felt Jenner's cock slip from inside me, accompanied by a rush of warmth.

His ragged breathing mixed with mine, and I felt him hovering behind me.

"Damn, if that isn't the most breathtaking thing I've ever seen. You bent over the couch in *our* home, with my cum dripping out of your pussy."

Almost if on command, the pussy in question clenched, and Jenner groaned as cum audibly leaked onto the floor beneath me.

A soothing hand grazed over my sweaty back, and in a flash, the kind, caring man I married was back. "You did so well, baby. Let's get you cleaned up."

Gently, as if I were the most precious thing on Earth, he pulled me into his arms and carried me up the stairs, where he ran a warm bath in the master suite. Climbing in behind me, he held me tight, whispering words of love and promises of our future together.

Falling asleep against his chest in the king-sized bed inside the master bedroom was as natural as breathing.

I was exactly where I belonged.

Chapter 14

Jenner

Evie was still asleep when I slipped from the warmth of our bed. That's precisely what it was—our bed. After last night, there would be no argument about her moving back into the master suite with me.

We were starting a family. After all we'd been through, it almost didn't seem real, but it was happening. And we were doing it together.

But there was still one thing weighing on my mind, and that had me rising early to get to the rink well ahead of practice.

Stepping into the walk-in closet, I dressed quickly, throwing on a pair of joggers and a Speed-branded hoodie. I was tying my shoes, perched on the edge of the window seat, when Evie stirred, stretching her arms over her head, back arching like a cat's.

Her soft hum had my dick stirring with memories of her making the same sound while her lips had been wrapped around it.

Last night might have marked our reconnection, but it was only one chapter in the long story of our love. It had been rocky at times, but somehow, we'd found our way back together and were facing the future we always pictured.

Standing, I walked to the side of the bed as her lashes fluttered open slowly. A smile crept onto my face as I peeked down at the beautiful woman I was lucky enough to call mine laid out before me.

My voice was roughened by sleep as I mused, "Damn, aren't you a sight, looking freshly fucked in our bed."

She reached out a hand to me, and I met her halfway, loving the feel of her smooth palm against my rough one.

"Am I dreaming?" Evie asked. "Yesterday seems too good to be true."

She wasn't wrong. Everything about yesterday had been perfect.

We were months away from becoming parents and were back in each other's arms.

Kneeling onto the bed, I lowered my head to press a kiss against her lips, whispering, "If it is, I never want to wake up."

Eyes growing glassy, her voice was thick as she whispered, "We're getting a baby girl."

Both my hands cupped her face, and I pressed my forehead to hers. "Yeah, we are. And she's so lucky she gets you for a mom."

Evie squeezed her eyes shut, and twin tears leaked down her face, but I kissed them away quickly.

"No more tears, baby. All our dreams are about to come true."

Letting out a shaky breath, she nodded.

When I pulled away slightly, her eyes roved over my appearance. "You headed to the rink? What time is it?"

"Too early for you to be getting out of bed. In fact, you should be waiting right here, naked, when I get back."

That had her flashing her teeth in a sexy smile. "So bossy, Mr. Knight."

"Don't you forget it, Mrs. Knight." I nipped at her lower lip. Shoving off the bed, I stood, explaining, "I have something I have to handle before practice, but I'll be back this afternoon at the usual time."

"Anything special you'd like to eat for dinner?" she offered.

I wasn't sure if she was setting me up or not, but there was only one answer to that question. "You."

Heat flared in her uniquely violet eyes, and I stifled a groan, watching her thighs press together beneath the thin sheets.

"I have to go, but I'll see you later, babe." I leaned in for one more kiss, moaning into her mouth when she slipped me a bit of tongue.

"Fine," she huffed playfully. "Can't be lounging around as a housewife if my husband doesn't go to work."

"I love you, Evie."

Eyes sparkling, she replied, "I love you, too."

I could stare at my wife all day, but I had business to handle. Or rather, a best friend.

So much for a relaxing morning.

Taking the elevator inside Speed Arena to the executive floor, I made my way to the door of Maddox's office. We needed to clear the air.

Knocking, I pushed inside when his voice called out, "It's open!"

His brows drew down when he saw it was me and not another member of the coaching or management staff. "Hey, man. You're in early. Practice isn't for a couple of hours."

Latching the door behind me, I leaned against it, electing not to take a seat opposite his desk.

"Right now, I need to talk to my best friend and not my coach."

Maddox sat back in his chair, folding both arms over his chest. "Okay . . ."

"I need you to sort out whatever feelings you have about Evie's return, and I need you to do it fast. You know I love you like a brother, but she's the most important person in my life. Don't make me choose between the two of you because I can promise she will win every fucking time."

His green eyes narrowed at the mention of my wife's name. "Jenner, listen—"

"No. You listen," I cut him off. "I won't allow your surly attitude toward my wife to be a dark cloud hanging over our heads—not when we're about to become parents."

Whatever rebuttal he had planned died on his lips when I dropped that bombshell. "What? It's really happening?"

I gave a slight nod in confirmation. "Just yesterday, we met with a teenager who wants to give us her baby girl."

Maddox rubbed both hands over his face, groaning. "Jesus Christ, Jenner. What the hell is wrong with you? Don't you feel even the least bit guilty about lying to a teenager to get a baby for your ex-wife? Don't you see how wrong this is?"

Gritting my teeth, I snarled, "Evie is my *wife*. Legally and in every way that matters. We aren't lying to anyone."

"Excuse me?" His dark eyebrows rose high on his forehead. "What does that mean?"

Shrugging, I explained, "I made my position very clear last night, and she feels the same way."

"Oh my God." Maddox stared at me in disbelief. "You've got to be fucking kidding me. Are you seriously saying you're fine snapping your fingers and forgetting all she's put you through? I was there, man. It wasn't pretty picking your ass up off the floor when she left you in pieces."

"She's back. That's all I care about now."

"But for how long?" he challenged. "What's it going to take to spook her into running again? This time, after you've fallen in love with a kid."

My temper flared, mostly because he was poking at old bruises and insecurities that still nagged at the back of my brain.

Clenching my fist, I yelled, "Enough!" Maddox's lips clamped shut, drawing into a thin line, making his displeasure clear. "Don't you get it? My sun rises and sets with her. That's it. End of story. She's what makes my life worth living, and don't you dare try to tell me that you wouldn't take Bristol back in a heartbeat if something beyond your control ripped the two of you apart. So, you either get on board and treat my wife with respect, or we can have a relationship where you're just my head coach and I'm your player."

A few beats of silence followed my outburst. Finally, Maddox sighed. "You really think she's back for good? That you're going to pick up where you left off?"

Dropping onto one of the chairs in his office, I ran a hand through my hair. "She promised."

He caught himself as he was about to roll his eyes at me. "She promised to love and cherish you for the rest of your lives. I was a witness." A scoff sounded. "Both times, actually."

Maddox was the only one I had shared our private struggle with, so I didn't think twice about revealing a piece of my conversation with Evie the night before. Judging from Bristol's surprise over my having a long-lost wife at Braxton's wedding, I knew I could trust him to keep anything I said between us.

"I don't think you can ever truly understand what it's like to watch the woman you love suffer like I have. It wasn't just the physical pain of treatments, but the crushing blows to her mental state every time we failed. I should have waited to have the conversation about exploring other options. I was hurting in a different way, and my timing was shit. Evie had already had a meltdown that morning, and I couldn't stop my knee-jerk reaction when she mentioned trying again. If emotions hadn't been so high, maybe we could've talked about my feelings rationally instead of her getting instantly defensive." Raking a hand across my jaw, I explained, "She thinks I gave up on her."

Across the desk, Maddox gawked at me. "What? How could she ever think that?"

"She was upset and blamed herself for not being able to get pregnant. So, when I said I couldn't do another round of IVF, she felt personally attacked. You should have heard her last night, saying she's broken."

"Fuck," he said on an exhale. "I had no idea."

"That's just it, Maddox. You can't judge her for doing what she did because she was out of her mind with grief. She was watching this beautiful dream she had for our future slipping away, powerless to stop it, and then I came in out of left field after being the most supportive husband on the planet and told her I was done. We lost four long years, and I refuse to lose another second with the woman I love."

Maddox's eyes closed briefly. "I'm sorry, man."

"I'm not the one you need to apologize to."

He nodded. "You're right. I'll talk to Evie."

"Good."

The tiniest hint of a smile touched his lips. "You're seriously getting a kid?"

I huffed out a disbelieving laugh. "Almost doesn't seem real. But yeah."

"Wanna place odds on whether or not she ends up carving it up on the ice like Slate's daughter?"

Braxton's older brother, Jaxon, had five kids. Only the youngest two were biologically his, as he'd married a single mom. His daughter, Charlie, was six, and Braxton often shared videos of her playing hockey because he was extremely close with his niece. That little girl was fearless, going after boys nearly twice her size. And she always had the biggest grin when she was out there. You could see it from the stands.

Shrugging, I said, "I don't care if she loves hockey or hates it, so long as she's mine."

"You're gonna make a good dad, Jenner."

"I'm just glad to have the chance."

We settled back into our easy rapport for the first time in months.

A weight had been lifted from my chest, having hashed it out with my best friend and knowing that, moving forward, he had my back.

I only prayed everything would be smooth sailing from here on out. Evie and I were due.

Chapter 15
Evie

Jenner and I got lost in each other for a few weeks, settling back into a real relationship.

He went to the rink on the days the team was home, and I kept busy preparing for our upcoming arrival. At night, we either ate dinner together—reconnecting on a deeper level—or I was in the family box cheering him and the Speed on as they competed on the ice.

A couple of weeks before Christmas, I got a text message from Paige, letting me know she was going to the doctor for an ultrasound before she went home for the winter break. She asked if Jenner and I would like to join her, and I jumped at the opportunity. After letting her know that Jenner would be out of town with the team, I offered to pick her up at her dorm and even suggested taking her out to lunch afterward.

When she accepted, I did a little happy dance before calling Jenner with the news. The Speed were out in California, and I'd thankfully caught him before his pre-game nap. He shared in my excitement while also lamenting that he wouldn't be there to see our little one for the first time.

I kept to myself that Paige would probably be more comfortable if he weren't there. He'd seen just about everything in a gynecological capacity short of witnessing birth through all my treatments over the years, but she was a teenage girl, and he was technically a stranger. Truthfully, I hoped to bond with her a little, to make her feel even more confident in her decision to choose us as her baby's permanent parents.

Pulling up to the address she'd sent, I eyed the building on the campus of Indianapolis Tech, where Paige said she lived. It appeared to be an older dorm-style structure, and I worried it might not have an elevator. Then, my gaze shifted to the sidewalk, covered in a thin layer of snow that hadn't been salted yet. Images of her slipping and falling on concrete filtered through my mind, and my anxiety shot through the roof.

I held my breath as Paige appeared at the entrance, and she crossed the distance to hop into the passenger seat of Jenner's SUV. I'd taken it today because it had all-wheel drive, and I wasn't taking any chances with my precious cargo.

Paige gave me a bright smile as she buckled her seatbelt. "I'm going to enjoy a month at home in the Florida sun. Growing up, I always wanted to see snow. Now that I have, I'm curious: can I get my T-shirt to say I conquered a northern winter, and I never have to do it again?"

I burst out laughing as I pulled away from the curb, driving toward her doctor's office. Even though life had thrown her a curveball in the form of an unexpected pregnancy at eighteen, she still had a sense of humor. I admired that about her.

"Florida sounds nice," I mused. "I will say, I miss Arizonian winters myself."

Her blue eyes brightened in my peripheral vision. "Ooh! I've never been, but all the pictures I've seen of the desert landscapes are stunning. And I'm willing to bet they don't capture its true beauty."

I nodded, keeping my eyes on the road. "There's nothing quite like a desert sunset."

"Did you used to live there?" Paige asked eagerly, and her friendliness set me at ease.

"Actually, that's where I met Jenner."

"Really?"

"You bet. I was just about your age, a freshman in college. Jenner was a year ahead of me, playing hockey on scholarship."

Her snap sounded loudly inside the cabin of the car. "That's right. I remember reading that you two met in college. But I must've skipped over the part where you mentioned where you attended." Paige let out a dreamy sigh. "Was he as handsome back then as he is now?"

I bit back a giggle at the teenage girl crushing on my husband. Couldn't say I blamed her. He was so freaking hot that, most days, I couldn't believe he was mine.

"Maybe not so much handsome as adorable," I replied. "He's definitely matured a lot since then, but you've seen our wedding portrait, and that's not too far off from what he looked like at nineteen since we married young."

"No beard, though," she noted.

"No. That's new," I remarked.

The beard was something he'd grown during my time away. It added to the sex appeal that man had going on, and I'd be lying if I said I hated the red marks it left behind on my skin.

When we arrived at the medical clinic where Paige's OB had an office, I dropped her off at the front, grateful to see they'd taken the care to salt. Parking, I met her inside the waiting area, sitting beside her and chatting until they called her back for her appointment.

We were ushered inside a room with a large flat-screen TV mounted on the wall opposite the gurney, where Paige took a seat, reclining as she pulled up her T-shirt in preparation.

It had been over a month since our initial meeting at the adoption agency, and I hadn't noticed how large her belly had grown, hidden by her bulky coat in the car. I couldn't stop staring at the round swell; skin pulled taught over where the baby—my baby— was growing.

Even though all my dreams of motherhood were about to come true, there was still that tiny pang of longing in my heart that I'd never get to experience carrying a baby of my own. It had taken years to come to terms with that truth, but the ache never fully went away.

Paige must have noticed that I was staring because she said softly, "You want to feel?"

I jolted in my seat at her bedside, eyes going wide. "Oh, it's okay. I'm sorry if I made you uncomfortable. It's just . . . I always imagined."

Her warm hand gripped mine and placed it on the bare skin of her belly.

"Let's see." Paige moved my hand around, pressing firmly until—

My gasp rang out loud and clear in the tiny room at the press of something against my palm. "Oh my God," I breathed. "Was that—?"

Her wide smile reached the corners of her eyes as she nodded. "That was an elbow or a knee, I'm sure of it. Kicks are a little sharper."

"Wow." I stared at her belly in amazement.

"Pretty cool, huh?"

"Absolutely incredible. Is she active often?"

Paige tilted her head from side to side. "Active enough that I've never worried there was something wrong. She gets a little feistier after I've eaten something sweet. And she loves to party all night and sleep during the day."

"Ah, so we've got a troublemaker on our hands," I teased.

"Most redheads are."

Her reply made me laugh. " It's a good thing I've got experience handling them." I winked at Paige.

The baby tucked safely inside her belly gave another roll, and I asked, "Is it strange? Feeling her move around in there?"

Paige's gaze dipped to the rounded swell beneath our hands, and a corner of her lips turned up. "A little. Seems surreal to think there's a tiny person in there."

"Yeah," I breathed out in wonder.

For a while, we sat in silence. I wasn't sure what Paige was reflecting on, but I couldn't stop marveling at the movement beneath my palm.

There was a knock at the door, and a woman in scrubs entered. She introduced herself as the ultrasound technician and sat on the stool in front of the piece of equipment that would allow us to take a peek at my baby.

I still couldn't believe this was really happening. After all this time and countless failures, my dream was months away from becoming a reality.

The tech smiled at Paige. "Did you bring your mom with you today?"

"Um." I blinked at the woman in shock. With only a thirteen-year age gap between us, it would be a stretch for me to be old enough to be Paige's mother.

Paige rubbed a hand over her exposed bump. "No, she's *her* mother."

The woman's eyes widened, bouncing between the two of us. "Oh." She covered her surprise quickly, exclaiming, "Well, isn't that wonderful! Let's take a peek at the little one and see how she's doing."

Squirting some gel on Paige's skin, the tech moved the wand attached to the bedside machine over her protruding stomach. The wall-mounted TV came to life, and a moving black-and-white image appeared on the screen.

My breath caught in my throat. Squirming around in high-definition was a baby. Visible was their perfectly shaped head, the tiny flicker of their heart beating, and long limbs moving about.

In an instant, I fell in love.

"There she is," the technician remarked. "And as far as I can tell, still a girl."

Paige laughed, but I sat there stunned, unable to take my eyes off the beautiful baby I would soon meet and call my own.

Fingers gripped my hand and squeezed. "You okay?"

I barely managed a nod as my vision blurred. "Sorry." I frantically wiped away the tears streaking down my face.

"Don't be," Paige said softly. "It sets my mind at ease knowing she's going to have a mom who loves her this much before she's even born."

Blowing out a shaky breath, I asked, "Are you sure this is what you want? She's so perfect."

Paige didn't falter. "I can't take care of her the way that you can. She belongs with you and Jenner."

I couldn't imagine the strength it took to come to the decision to give away a baby at such a young age. I wasn't sure I would have been able to do it.

Paige had my utmost respect because she was mature enough to see that she was giving them both a fighting chance at a bright future. In doing so, she was making me whole, giving me a second chance with my husband, and gifting us with a family we never thought we would have.

The tech was professional and kept quiet while Paige and I had a private moment. When we grew silent and our attention returned to the screen, she remarked, "Everything looks right on track. It's exactly what we'd want to see for twenty-six weeks."

She handed Paige a towel to clean up as the machine spit out a strip of pictures.

Uncertain, she glanced between us, the black and white prints held in her hand. "Who wants these?"

"Give them to Evie." Paige pulled her shirt down, covering her belly.

My fingers traced over the image of the baby in black and white. "You don't want even one?"

She shook her head and replied, "She's not my baby."

Nodding, I swallowed around the lump in my throat. "Okay. You hungry?"

A bright smile lit up the teenager's face. "Starved."

I offered my hand to help her sit up, and she took it. "Wherever you want. I'm buying."

Paige's blue eyes sparkled with mischief. "Ooh. That's a dangerous offer. I could have some fun with this."

There wasn't any amount of money I could spend that would repay this girl for how she was about to change my life. Hell, I'd give her every last cent we had, and it wouldn't feel like enough.

Paige dipped a french fry into her chocolate milkshake before tossing the whole thing in her mouth and moaning in pleasure.

Even though she'd teased about going somewhere expensive for lunch, we'd found ourselves in a quiet diner on the edge of campus.

I picked at my food. I couldn't stop thinking about that damn unsalted walkway outside her dorm, and my brain went down a dark path picturing doomsday scenarios.

Finally, I worked up the courage to ask, "Do you have a way to get around campus for the spring semester? I know you're not used to snow, and people drive like idiots when the weather gets bad."

Paige shrugged. "I usually take the bus."

"We could lend you a car—one that's all-wheel drive and top-rated for safety."

Her lips twisted in thought. "That's a nice offer, but I don't think it's necessary."

"Are you sure?" I pressed. "It really wouldn't be a problem."

"Just seems kinda pointless. I'll be taking my courses online next semester."

"Oh?" My eyebrows rose.

"Yeah. I figured with the baby due in March, it would be easier. I won't have to worry about running around, trying to get to class when I'm about to pop, and I can keep up with assignments and video lectures while I recover from the birth."

Damn. Paige continued to blow me away. She was handling this situation like an adult—which I suppose she was, but a very new one. I could only imagine the mess I would have been had I discovered I was pregnant at her age.

"Are you scared about that part?"

Paige drew a path through the ketchup on her plate with a fry. "I know it's gonna hurt, but it's what my body was made for, right?"

I fought the urge to flinch at her statement. *My* body apparently wasn't made to carry and deliver a baby.

She continued, "I've heard that if you get the drugs, it hurts a lot less."

"Part of our contract with the agency has us covering all your medical bills, so if you want an epidural, a doula, whatever, you can have it."

Her forehead wrinkled. "I'm not sure what a doula is, but thanks?"

"It's a professional trained to support you during labor," I explained.

"Oh." Paige chewed on her lower lip. "I was kind of hoping you might want to be there."

My heart hammered against my ribcage, and I placed a hand over my chest. "Me?"

"Yeah, I thought maybe you'd like to be in the room when your daughter is born. Not sure I'd feel comfortable with Jenner being there, though."

A wry laugh fell from my lips. "Yeah, I think you two might be on the same page with that one. That poor man has seen enough to last a lifetime."

She peeked at me shyly from beneath her lashes. "So, you'll be there?"

I reached for her hand across the table. "Of course. But are you sure you don't want your mom?"

Shaking her head, she replied, "It doesn't make any sense for her to fly out here and hang around when we don't know exactly when the baby will be born. Since I'm in the dorms, she'd have to camp out in a hotel, which would be really expensive."

"Paige. Jenner and I will gladly pay to fly your mom out here and put her up somewhere nice if that's what you want."

"It's not just that." She sighed. "I kinda figured I'd save her being there for when I do this for real someday, you know?"

God, she'd thought this through end to end.

"That makes sense," I agreed.

Today had been heavy, and I wanted to lighten the mood. Signaling for the waitress to bring the check, I asked Paige, "Do you have any more classes today? Or is your afternoon open?"

The girl across the table perked up. "Free as a bird. Why?"

Flashing her with a conspiratorial grin, I teased, "Oh, I don't know. Was thinking of doing a little shopping. Wondered if you might want to join me?"

Crossing her arms on the edge of the table, she leaned forward. "What kind of shopping?"

For a second, I feared that I was about to upend the balance we'd struck, but I shook it off. Paige had already proven she was stronger than any of us could have ever imagined.

"What would you say to some new clothes? I couldn't help but notice your poor jeans were hanging on for dear life with a hair tie holding them closed at the button. I'd love to buy you something more comfortable."

She waved me off. "Oh, that's okay. If I'm going to be hanging around in my dorm, I can just lounge in my pajamas. They're oversized enough."

Other than taking her out to lunch, she'd declined every offer I'd made this afternoon, and I wanted—no, I *needed*—to do something for her. She was giving me the ultimate gift, and that deserved my gratitude.

Jenner and I were more fortunate than most and made sure to give back to the community because we'd been so blessed. I knew firsthand how money could change a life, and since we had plenty of it, I was determined to use it for good.

Today, I wanted to spoil the selfless teenager sitting opposite me.

But today's lunch location showed she was actively trying not to take advantage of the situation. Most likely, she didn't want us to think that she'd only chosen us because we were well-off and only did so because there was something to be gained from that selection.

If Paige had done her research into adoption—which, as a smart girl, I would lay odds that she had—I could imagine she'd read the stories about people "buying" babies. As someone whose focus had narrowed to nothing outside starting a family, I could see how that highly illegal market came into existence. When you hit so many dead ends, the desperation gnawed at you incessantly. Hell, it's how I'd ended up back in Indianapolis. If a couple had the means, they would be willing to pay any price to obtain a child. Young girls in trouble would make an easy target for vultures facilitating these deals—they needed someone to take their baby, and the money offered would be too attractive to pass up.

The whole idea was disgusting to me. I might have done some shady things to get to this point, but I would never exploit the situation of a scared, pregnant teen for my benefit.

There were two innocent lives involved, and anyone with a conscience would condemn such a practice.

"Paige," I said softly. "I want to do something nice for you. It would make me happy to take you shopping."

She stared at me silently, chewing her lower lip, but finally, she replied, "If you really want to."

Making sure to leave cash on the table to cover our bill, I extended my hand to help her stand from the booth.

Bumping shoulders with her, I said, "Shopping, then nails. How does that sound?"

A tiny smile crept onto her pretty, young face. "Amazing. Let's do it."

Bonding with my baby's birth mother would be good for both of us. I could gain more insight into the girl who would share DNA with my daughter, and she could get a feel for the type of nurturing mom I would be to the baby she was giving away.

I still couldn't believe I was going to be a mom.

Chapter 16
Jenner

"Knight, move your ass!" Maddox screamed from the bench.

He had every right to yell at me. I was dragging tonight.

We all had those days when you were a little off-kilter, but I hated letting the team down, especially since I was their leader. I was expected to set the tone, and like lemmings jumping off a cliff, those men were following my example on the ice, even when they shouldn't.

The San Diego Surf were one of the worst teams in the league, and we were playing down to their level. So much so that they were kicking our asses and making us look like we were a youth hockey team playing against professionals.

We were being outskated, outhit, and outscored.

Sweat ran into my eyes as I hustled to the bench for a line change.

Plopping onto my seat, sandwiched between my linemates, I about damn near jumped out of my skin when Maddox's voice spoke directly into my ear. "What's going on with you tonight?"

"Fuck!" I screamed, levitating a foot off the bench. "Give a guy some warning next time!"

"Seriously, man. Everything okay at home? Because this isn't like you."

I shook my head, eyes tracking the movement of the players on the ice. "Just having an off night. Not sure why."

"Need a minute to reset?" he offered.

"Nah. Maybe I need to stir some shit up, get the blood pumping. You know what I mean?"

There was silence from my coach/best friend behind me, and I turned to find him smirking with an evil gleam in his striking green eyes. "Do it."

"Yeah?" I arched an eyebrow.

He lifted one shoulder before letting it drop. "Got nothing to lose. They're kicking our asses, so might as well see if we can jump-start the boys. But don't do anything stupid, like getting yourself injured."

"You got it, boss." I gave him a mock salute and a wink before hopping over the boards and onto the ice.

Digging my skates in, I pushed myself harder than I had the entire game. Stick down hard on the ice, I kept up with Asher after he picked off the puck on a failed D-to-D pass by the Surf. The defenseman, who had been meant to accept the pass, hustled back, pushing Asher to the outside. But my left winger didn't care, firing a shot at the goalie, which he promptly gloved, having been given enough time and distance to track it.

Seeing my opportunity to rile up our opponents, I didn't stop skating when the ref blew the whistle to signal a stoppage in play. Instead, I turned both my skate blades perpendicular to my torso and came to a hard hockey stop, spraying the goalie with a thin sheen of what we liked to call snow.

It was an intentional maneuver—definitely unsportsmanlike—meant to piss off the Surf. The number one rule in hockey was that no one messed with your goaltender and got away with it.

As expected, someone jumped on my back as the goalie shoved at me with his blocker from the front. A mass of bodies formed before the net, both teams fired up and swinging.

I used my elbow to shuck off the man from behind, just enough to spin around and get in a punch of my own. My gloves flew off as I rained down hell upon the man I was squared up against, satisfied when his helmet flew off.

"You're a fucking asshole, Knight!" he screamed as he got in a quick jab to my jaw.

"Yeah, yeah," I grunted back. "Go cry to your mama. Better yet, send her down here. I bet she hits harder than you."

Fire flashed in his eyes, and he roared as he lunged for me. I dropped my shoulder when he tried to pull me into a headlock and flipped him over onto his back. The sound of the wind being knocked from his lungs was an added bonus to knowing I'd won the fight.

Glancing around, I saw the rest of my line still duking it out as refs tried frantically to break them up. Braxton dropped his guy, then Asher followed suit, settling once and for all that the Speed were tougher than the Surf.

We might not win the game tonight, but we'd made them our bitch.

The biggest downside to a West Coast road trip was taking the red-eye flight back home. With closer opponents, we were home around midnight, maybe a little later, and could sleep in our own beds that night. Though our team plane had larger seats than a commercial flight, sleeping sitting up wasn't good for stiff joints and muscles.

Because of that, Maddox had declared that he was issuing a maintenance day upon landing. This provided an opportunity for guys on the team to get treatment—whether it be physical therapy, massages, or dunking our bodies in an ice bath. The hockey season was a grind; our bodies got beat to hell, so we had to take good care of them.

A day off had never sounded better—not when I knew Evie was waiting for me at home. Maybe I'd surprise her by booking a couple's massage. She never said no to being pampered, and she deserved it with how stressed she'd been leading up to Paige choosing us.

Winter nights were long, so it was still before dawn when I arrived home at 6:30 AM. I didn't even bother grabbing my bags from the trunk, too excited at the prospect of sliding into bed with a still-sleeping Evie.

The first thing I noticed was the shopping bags lining the hallway from the mudroom to the kitchen. A curious peek inside revealed tons of baby clothes, along with other items like bottles, burp cloths, and pacifiers. I smiled to myself, thinking of Evie carefully picking out each item as she pictured putting them to use with our daughter.

Stepping into the kitchen, a black-and-white photograph pinned to the stainless steel fridge caught my eye. Venturing closer, my heart skipped a beat.

Pictured, clear as day, was the tiny profile of a baby.

My finger traced along the tiny outline of a button nose in wonder. She was beautiful. And she was going to be ours.

Quietly climbing the stairs, I pushed into our master bedroom, surprised to find Evie sitting up in bed, a book obscuring her face from my view.

"Hey," I said softly so as not to startle her.

The book fell to her lap, and she smiled at me. "You're home."

Immediately, I began shedding my clothes, piece by piece, until I was left only in my boxers. Pulling back the covers, I crawled into bed beside her, sighing when our skin touched. Ten days on the road was far too long to be away from her. Sure, we'd spent four years apart, but now that I had her back, even a few hours felt like torture.

Tapping at the book cover, I joked, "Weren't you just teasing me about reading hockey smut?"

Evie rolled her eyes but turned sideways so she was tucked securely against my chest. I would never again take holding her in my arms for granted.

"Dakota's extremely talented, and it's important to support someone writing about the sport who actually knows what they're talking about. I had lunch with her while you were gone, and she told me about how hockey romance has blown up, but many of the books in the subgenre are written by authors jumping on an emerging trend and don't include much gameplay on page. I guess it was Bristol's idea for her to jump on the hype train, but did you know that's how she met Braxton? He helped teach her the game so she could write it accurately and give her readers the best experience."

I kissed the top of her head, breathing in the scent of her shampoo. "Yeah, I did know that."

"Anyway, that was her big break, and now she's this kickass best-selling author, and people are rabid for her books. But instead of writing faster to please her growing fanbase, she's working toward opening an indie bookstore here in Indianapolis to help other authors. I guess it's difficult to get your books into stores when you publish independently, and that's her dream. So, she's making it happen while supporting others like her. Isn't that great?"

Chuckling, I held her tighter. "Dakota's a pretty great girl. I'm glad you two hit it off."

"And boy, can that girl write the spice. I kept expecting God to strike me down with how racy some of the scenes were."

My cock stirred, thinking of Evie getting turned on reading romance, but exhaustion pulled at me. Sleepily, I murmured, "Saw you did some shopping while I was gone."

She buried her face in my chest. "Yeah. Paige helped."

That caught me off guard. "Oh, yeah?"

"I took her to lunch after her appointment, and the poor thing's clothes hardly fit. So I begged her to let me buy her some. Of course, most of the stores that carry maternity clothing also have baby items, so we browsed for a bit, and I bought anything she smiled at. I kinda like knowing Paige will still leave her mark on our daughter. Even if it's through something simple, like selecting the baby pajamas she wears."

Smiling, I nuzzled my cheek against her hair. "That does sound nice. Was the appointment good? I saw the picture on the fridge."

That had Evie pulling from my arms, turning around, and bouncing on her knees in excitement, eyes bright. "Oh my God, did you see her? Isn't she perfect?"

This moment was what I had always wanted for her. And I thanked God it was finally happening.

"Stole my breath away," I confessed. "She's healthy?"

Evie nodded. "They said everything looked great. Right on track for her March 20th due date. Can you believe it? In three months or less, we will have her in our arms!"

"Unreal." That single word was said on an exhale.

"Oh!" she exclaimed. "And I didn't tell you the best part!"

Her joy was infectious, and I found myself smiling. "What's that, babe?"

"Paige asked me to be with her when she has the baby. I'm actually going to be in the room when our daughter is born!"

My heart swelled, and I cupped her cheek. "I'm so happy for you, Evie."

Her violet eyes scanned my face. "You're okay with her only wanting me?"

"Of course. It's a very private and vulnerable moment. I'm glad she wants to share it with you, but I'm just fine hanging in the waiting room."

Evie launched herself at me, her arms circling my neck. "This is really happening, Jenner."

"It's gonna be so great."

I couldn't stifle a loud yawn, and she pulled back to peek at me. "Didn't sleep well on the plane?"

"Not especially. Hated being away from you."

"Mmm," she purred, curling into my side, allowing us to sink onto the pillows. "What time do I need to wake you for practice?"

"Maintenance day," I mumbled as sleep threatened to drag me under. "Lay with me until I fall asleep, and then we can go to the spa for massages later."

"Sounds like the perfect day." Evie sighed happily.

With my eyes closed, moments away from unconsciousness, all I could think was that every day with Evie in my arms was perfect. And we had an unlimited string of them up ahead.

With Christmas only days away, my teammates and I walked down the hall of the children's hospital in Indy. Every year, we visited with the kids and their families who would be stuck in the hospital for the holidays.

It was always tough facing the reality that some of our youngest fans were fighting life-threatening illnesses. But this year, it struck home for me, knowing I would soon become a father.

Our baby girl was healthy for now, but I was sure most of these families had brought their bundles of joy home after birth, never expecting that they would find themselves here, in some cases, watching their children fight for their lives.

I'd already watched my wife suffer for years, and it had nearly broken me. If something ever happened to our daughter, I wasn't sure I would survive.

We split off into pairs—a high-profile player with a lesser-known one—and let the hospital administrator in charge of today's event direct us toward the rooms we were assigned. My partner was Griff Thompson, a rookie who served as our fourth-line center.

The poor kid looked nervous as we approached the door to the first room we were expected to visit.

I gave him a reassuring pat on the back, "You okay?"

Swallowing, Griff nodded. "Yeah, just don't like hospitals. My dad was sick when I was growing up."

"I'm sorry to hear that. Must've been tough."

"Yeah." His voice grew thick.

"If this event is dredging up too much for you, there's no shame in sitting it out. I would never want to put you in a situation that causes mental distress."

"Really?" Relief stole over his young face. "You sure Coach won't be mad?"

"You let me handle Coach. He might seem like a pissed-off grizzly bear most of the time, but he's not heartless."

Griff let out a heavy exhale. "Thanks, Jenner."

Tilting my head, I prompted, "Go ahead. Get out of here before anyone notices. I've got you covered."

I waited until he'd pushed through a stairwell door and was out of sight before I stepped inside the hospital room. There was a little boy, who couldn't have been more than eight or so, sitting up in bed with tons of wires leading into the neck hole of the gown he wore and a clear oxygen tube across his face under his nose.

The boy's parents stood from their chairs as I approached with a smile plastered on my face and my hand extended. "Hi there. I'm Jenner."

The dad shook my hand. "Jeff, and this is my wife, Maria."

"Nice to meet you both." I turned to the boy in the bed. "And who do we have here?"

Jeff stepped up to his son's bedside. "This is Finn."

I approached the bed, crouching down a bit so I was on his level. "Hey, Finn. Nice to meet you, buddy."

Finn gave me a weak smile, but the only response I got was a faint wheezing sound, and I peeked at his father in question.

Jeff explained, "Finn has severe heart failure. He has trouble breathing and is too weak to talk most days. He's on the transplant list."

Jesus. I couldn't begin to imagine what this family was going through. To know that another child had to die for yours to live? I fought hard against the shudder that threatened to roll through my body at the thought.

Taking the boy's hand, I squeezed gently. "Well, that's okay, bud. We don't have to talk. How about I read you a story?"

His head moved enough to indicate a nod, and I pulled up a chair. Tears were in his mom's eyes as she handed me a well-loved copy of a popular children's book.

I sat with Finn for the next hour, reading to him until he drifted off to sleep. His parents thanked me profusely for visiting, and I wished them all the best. That's all I could do.

I knew better than most that there were some things money couldn't fix, no matter how much of it you had. I would have given up every penny I'd ever earned for Evie, just like I could bet Jeff and Maria would pay any price to ensure their son's survival.

My takeaway from the day was that I needed to enjoy every moment with my family. You never knew what curveball life was going to throw your way.

Chapter 17
Evie

Holiday music filtered through the kitchen speakers as I helped prepare a meal for our closest friends.

The Speed were only afforded four days off this year, and the first game after Christmas was on the road, cutting it down to three. So, we decided to host a little get-together to celebrate since most of us wouldn't be seeing our families.

I didn't mind cooking for a large group. I'd grown up helping my mama in the kitchen as far back as I could remember, and our extended family could rival that of any other back in Rust Canyon. I guess that's what happened when you were related to the original settlers a century and a half back.

What I *did* mind was Maddox in my kitchen.

Thankfully, Dakota was working alongside us, providing a buffer between me and my husband's best friend, who wasn't exactly good at concealing his displeasure over my return to Indy.

I wanted nothing more than to finish up so I could spend time with Ollie and Bailey before Goose arrived, dressed as Santa, to surprise them and give them gifts. That man was the biggest goofball and leapt at the chance to play jolly old Saint Nick for the kids. It certainly didn't hurt that it grated on Maddox that Goose—whose real name I'd learned was Sasha—was always unflappable and peppy.

If we were going with Dakota's dog analogies to describe the men, Maddox was the German shepherd to Goose's golden retriever.

Dakota excused herself to use the restroom, and I itched to flee the room myself. The last thing I wanted was to be alone with Maddox.

"Um." I searched my brain for a reason to be anywhere else. "I think I'll go see if anyone needs their drinks refreshed."

I was halfway to the living room when Maddox called out, "Evie, can we talk for a minute?"

My back was to him, but I cringed. It was Christmas, a time of happiness and joy. I didn't want to have it ruined by a man who could barely stand to be in my presence.

"Maddox, I need to check on my guests."

His heavy sigh reached my ears. "Please? I'd like to clear the air between us."

Fuck my life.

Spinning around, I braced both hands on the kitchen island. "What do you want, Maddox?"

The large man standing opposite me tossed a dishtowel over his shoulder before folding both arms over his massive chest. "I haven't been fair to you lately. Frankly, I've been a total asshole."

I snorted over his astute self-assessment.

"I owe you an apology for how I've acted, Evie, but I need you to understand where I was coming from." Maddox ran a hand down his face. "You don't know what it was like for him when you left and then went radio silent on him. You were—no, *are*—his entire world. It broke him when you served him with those papers. For a while after you left, he thought you might come back, but that made it crystal clear you were done, that he wasn't enough for you. Without you, he was barely a shell of a man.

"So, yeah, I was a little angry when you showed up with your hidden agenda. I thought you were using my best friend, knowing he wouldn't turn you away."

I hung my head in shame because that's exactly what I'd done.

Maddox kept speaking, his words flaying my heart wide open. "You leaving Jenner shook me to the core. I was there when you said your first vows and watched him bawl like a baby when you walked down that aisle. You two made me believe in true love. And then you shattered his heart and, along with it, my faith that a couple so deeply in love could conquer any obstacle."

My chest tightened, making it hard to breathe. But as much as it hurt to hear what Jenner had been through in my absence, I needed Maddox to know our time apart hadn't been easy on me either.

Rubbing my fingers over the ache in my heart, I spoke. "Those years without Jenner were hands down the worst years of my life. I sunk into a depression so deep I could hardly get out of bed most days. I had this perfect man who adored me, but I couldn't give him a family."

Tears threatened behind my eyes, but I blinked them away. "You've seen him in there with Ollie and Bailey. That man was meant to be a father. And I thought I was stealing that from him. So, when he suggested we stop trying, I saw our future slipping through my fingers. I reacted in a way that was driven by deep internal pain. I've had enough time to reflect on my actions to realize that I was wrong. But by the time I figured it out, it was too late. So, I dug my heels in rather than change course, convinced that I'd made my bed and would be forced to lie in it. Never in a million years could I have pictured myself back here, getting a second chance with Jenner. So,

I can assure you, Maddox, the only one at risk of getting their heart broken this go around is me because the only way I'm leaving again is if he kicks me out."

"Then I guess you're back for good because Jenner would've done anything to have you come home. I wouldn't put it past him to have been wishing on shooting stars and tossing coins into fountains, hoping for a miracle."

"I'm glad you were there for him, Maddox. He's lucky to have a friend like you who cares so much about him."

He shrugged. "He's not my biggest fan right now. But he was right to be upset, and he called me on my bullshit. Jenner's a better man than me. I'm not one to use my words when someone comes at the woman I love." Maddox's fists clenched along with his jaw, eyes taking on a faraway look like he was lost in a not-so-pleasant memory.

"You're his best friend. You two will figure it out."

"What about us?" he asked. "Can we be friends again?"

My lips tipped up in a smile. "That depends," I teased.

"On what?" One of Maddox's dark eyebrows rose.

"If you're willing to finish up in here so I can play with the kids."

He chuckled. "Yeah, I think I can manage that to help out a *friend*."

"Friends, it is," I agreed.

Dakota breezed into the kitchen, eyes darting between the two of us standing on opposite sides of the island. "Y'all sorted?"

I shook my head in amusement. "Listen to you. You'd fit right in if I took you down to Rust Canyon tomorrow."

"Really?" Her blue eyes sparkled.

"Maybe you can convince that husband of yours to come down for a visit this summer. For research." I threw her a wink.

She bounced on the balls of her feet. "Oh! That would be amazing!"

I held my hand out to her. "Maddox said he's got the kitchen handled. Let's go kick our feet up while we wait for him to wait on us."

Dakota threw me an impressed look before shooting a sideways glance at Maddox. "Well, shit. That must have been one hell of a talk."

"Oh, you should have seen him. Got down on his knees and begged me to forgive him." I shot a smirk at Maddox, whose head tilted toward the ceiling as he shook his head.

"Run along before I change my mind," he grumbled, but there was a hint of amusement in his tone.

We giggled as we hustled out of the kitchen to join the rest of the crew gathered in the living room.

Jenner had moved the coffee table earlier so the kids would have room to play on the floor. I'd gone a little overboard with my holiday shopping, excited to buy toys for children I adored, and the second they arrived, I allowed them to open their mountain of gifts. Asher simply shook his head, mentioning that they had more toys than they knew what to do with, but Tessa understood my need to spoil them, and we shared a secret smile.

The adults were on the couch while Ollie pushed a giant firetruck across the floor. Bailey was asleep, tucked against Asher's chest. I couldn't help staring at the gentle way he stroked her tiny back; his cheek pressed against the top of her head as if it were the most natural thing in the world.

Jenner's fingers brushed mine, and I peered down to where he was seated on the couch. His brown eyes shone with love as he smiled up at me. "Wanna come sit?"

I nodded, but instead of taking a seat beside him, I dropped to the floor at his feet. Ollie's head snapped up, and he ran over to me, launching his tiny body into my chest.

"Hey, little man." I squeezed him in a tight hug. "You like your new firetruck?"

"Hee whooo! Hee whooo!" Ollie screamed, mimicking the sound of the siren.

Laughter bubbled up from my chest. "I'll take that as a yes."

The little boy snuggled closer into my chest, patting the cleavage visible from the neckline of my top. "Soft VeeVee," he murmured, and I wondered if he was about to join his baby sister in dreamland before Santa arrived.

Jenner's amused voice said from behind us, "Watch it, buddy. Those are mine."

Ollie reared back to glare at my husband over my shoulder. "No! My VeeVee!"

Chuckles sounded around the room at the toddler's claiming statement.

Peeking behind me, I saw Asher nudge Jenner with his shoulder. "Better watch out, man. I think you've got some real competition there. The kid's a charmer, and it looks like he's gunning for your girl."

Jenner's smile brightened, his eyes never leaving mine as he replied to his teammate. "Can't say I blame him. She's the most beautiful woman I've ever laid eyes on."

Heat rose to my cheeks.

Yes, we were married. Yes, we'd been intimate for nearly a decade combined over our two marriages. But it would never get old, knowing he found me attractive. He'd never expected me to transform myself to meet society's standards of "beauty." Jenner had always loved me just as I was—even when I hadn't loved myself.

A knock at the front door pulled us from our private moment in the middle of a gathering of our closest friends.

Bouncing Ollie on my lap, I brightened my voice. "Who could that be?"

"I'll get it," Jenner announced, rising from the couch.

I shifted to sit on my knees with Ollie standing before me. I couldn't wait to see his reaction to Goose dressed as Santa. He was a smart little guy, but

I prayed he wouldn't recognize the man behind the beard. It would ruin what I hoped to be a magical moment for my little friend.

Jenner glanced over his shoulder at me with his hand on the doorknob, and I nodded, letting him know we were ready.

The door was barely cracked open before it was flung wide, and there was a booming "Ho, ho, ho!" as Goose, dressed in a red velvet suit with white cuffs, came into view.

The terrified screech that assaulted my ears had me wincing. Ollie turned tail and ran to hide behind the Christmas tree.

Poor Goose's face fell. "He doesn't like me?"

Jenner shut the door and clapped him on the shoulder. "Maybe he just needs a minute to warm up to you."

Goose stepped closer to where we sat, but Ollie screamed, "No! No!"

Glancing at Tessa to see if she wanted to take the lead since he was her son, she gave me a subtle nod, letting me know it was okay for me to comfort the little boy.

Crouching down near his hiding spot, I offered him my hand. "It's okay. Santa came to bring you presents."

Glassy eyes met mine as one tear rolled down his chubby red cheek. "No, VeeVee. Peease no." His sad little voice broke my heart.

I opened my arms to him, and he burrowed his face against my chest, his tears soaking the fabric. Stroking his soft hair, I asked, "Is it okay for Santa to leave the presents?"

He nodded, and I locked eyes with Goose. "It was a good idea in theory but not so much in practice. Time to pull the plug."

The grown man who was always happy-go-lucky pouted. "Aw, man."

Jenner tugged him away. "Come on, big guy. I'll show you where you can change."

A few minutes later, the men returned with Goose dressed in street clothes.

Instantly, Ollie perked up. "Goose!" He ran from his spot on my lap and wrapped his arms around the goalie's calves.

Goose shook his head, but his near-permanent smile was back on his face. "Oh, *now* he likes me."

Asher chuckled. "Better luck next year."

Bending down, Goose gripped Ollie around the waist before flipping him upside down and blowing raspberries on his belly. The sound of the toddler's squeals filled the air. "Yeah, sure. As soon as he warms up to me, Bailey will be afraid. You're not gonna fool me twice on this one."

"We doing presents or what?" Maddox stepped into the room, holding a flat box covered in holiday-themed wrapping paper.

Our small pod had decided to focus on the kids since the adults had everything we could ever need, and they'd already opened everything—minus the ones held in Santa's sack.

"I know we said no gifts," he explained, coming closer to where I stood, "but I was hoping you might allow an exception."

He held the box out to me. Even though we'd hashed out our differences in the kitchen, I couldn't help being apprehensive.

Maddox shook it. "Come on. Consider it a peace offering."

Warily, I accepted the package. My eyes shifted to Jenner, who shrugged, making it clear he knew nothing about this.

Dropping onto the couch, I ran my hands along the seam where tape held the edges together, slipping my fingers beneath it and removing the paper. I uncovered what looked like a white clothing box.

My brows furrowed. What in the world could Maddox have bought me that fit inside a box so small?

Pulling the top off, I gasped. Nestled inside the white tissue paper was the tiniest Speed jersey I'd ever seen. My fingers traced over the racecar logo stitched on the front.

"What is it?" Tessa asked from across the room.

Swallowing, I lifted the garment. I'd known it was Jenner's jersey from the C stitched on the breast, but seeing the back was what had tears leaking from my eyes. Above the number seventy-five, the nameplate read: DADDY.

"Maddox," I whispered, locking eyes with the man. "I don't know what to say."

A smirk curved on his lips. "Thank you is always a good place to start."

Before I could utter the words, Dakota blurted, "Oh my God, are you pregnant?" She turned to her redheaded best friend, accusing, "And you knew and didn't tell me?"

Bristol held both hands up. "I didn't know anything about this."

I was at a loss for words, but Jenner always had my back. "No, we're adopting."

Tessa was at the park the day I got the call from the agency, so she had some idea of what we were going through, but I hadn't spoken a word about Paige choosing us to anyone.

My new friend gushed, "Oh, you guys. That's amazing! I'm so happy for you!"

Asher chimed in. "Yeah, congrats. That's great news."

Braxton, Dakota, and Goose all offered words of excitement and congratulations, but Bristol narrowed her eyes at her fiancé, huffing, "You sure kept this one close to the vest, didn't you?"

Leaning down, he brushed a kiss over her lips. "Sorry, love. Can't overrule best friend confidentiality."

"Hmm. I suppose I'll have to allow it." Turning to face me, a smile lit up her face. "Tell me all about it! I love babies." She slid a glance at her bestie. "Unlike Dakota here."

"Hey!" Dakota protested. "I like babies. I just don't have much experience with them, is all."

"Don't worry, we'll fix that." Braxton dusted her cheeks with a kiss.

"Look what you've done," Dakota teased me. "He's gonna be back on the baby train again."

That comment surprised me. Did she not want kids? It wasn't for me to judge, but for someone who wanted them so badly, it was difficult to understand why some couples chose to remain child-free. I guess to each their own.

"Yeah, yeah. It's no secret Braxton wants all the babies." Bristol waved a dismissive hand. "But I want to hear about Evie and Jenner's baby."

My trembling hands lowered the infant-sized jersey back into the gift box.

"Well, we haven't quite been blessed enough to create a family the traditional way," I began. There were sympathetic expressions from everyone in the room, including Goose, the only single person in attendance. "So, we decided to explore other options. And last month, a teenage girl going to college in Indy picked up our file and decided that we were the ones who should raise her baby girl as our own."

"Aw." Bristol clasped her hands together over her chest. "A girl? So precious."

Tessa wiped a tear from her eye. "Our girls are gonna grow up together."

A watery laugh fell from my lips. "I can't wait."

Goose clapped Jenner on the back. "Dude, you're gonna be a dad. That's wild."

"Been a long time coming." Jenner's eyes never left mine.

"I'd like to raise a toast," Maddox's deep voice called out. Everyone grabbed their drinks. "To Jenner and Evie as they embark on this new phase of life. I know the journey has been difficult, but I couldn't be happier for the two of you."

Everyone murmured their agreement, and we drank.

This was our chosen family. They were the ones who would share in all the important milestones that lay ahead. I couldn't have picked a better group of people to have supporting us as we embarked on this new adventure.

Chapter 18
Jenner

"Good Christmas, baby?" I nuzzled Evie's neck from behind as she stood at the sink, rinsing dishes after our guests had left.

She hummed, the vibrations tickling my chest with how closely I held her. "Yeah. It was so special watching Ollie's expressions while he opened his presents."

"Just think of how magical it will be next year when it's our baby girl."

Wiping her hands on a towel, she turned and looped both arms around my neck. "I can't wait."

With a house full of guests all night, we hadn't had a moment alone, and I'd been itching to get my hands on her since the moment she walked down the stairs earlier this afternoon. She looked stunning in a blue sweater that made her eyes pop over winter white skinny jeans. Her shiny blonde hair was pinned behind one ear with a jeweled clip as it curled over the opposite shoulder.

"Have I told you how beautiful you are tonight?"

A soft smile curved on her lips as they silently taunted me to claim them. "Maybe. But I'll never tire of hearing it, so if you feel compelled . . ."

Dipping my head, I brushed my lips over the corner of hers, and she sighed. Moving along her jaw, I murmured, "You're even more beautiful than the first time I laid eyes on you. And I can't believe you're mine. I'm so fucking lucky you chose me, Evie."

"Pretty sure I didn't have much of a choice once you set your sights on me," she breathed out.

Trailing a path of kisses down her neck, I sucked on the sensitive spot where it met her shoulder. Her moan had my cock hardening, and I knew I wouldn't be able to tease her for long. I needed to be inside her and soon.

"I mean this time, baby. You came back to me all on your own."

Evie sighed, threading her fingers into my hair and tugging until I lifted my head to meet her eye.

Tongue darting out to moisten her lips, she swallowed. "Didn't feel like a choice then, either. It's a wonder I didn't come running home sooner."

Fuck. That's all I needed to hear. Evie had never stopped loving me. We were two halves of the same whole, always meant to find each other.

My mouth crashed down on hers in a punishing kiss. She was mine, and I was going to make sure she knew nothing could change how I felt about her.

Evie moaned, her hips shifting enough to rub against my straining cock. Patience waning, I ripped my lips away, panting, "Upstairs. Now."

When she didn't move, I growled, "I'm going to give you to the count of three, and if your luscious ass isn't halfway up the stairs by the time I get there, I'm gonna turn it red. Understand?"

Her plush lips parted, and her eyes grew wide, but she still didn't leave the warmth of my arms.

"One," I barked, my tone harsh.

That jolted her into action, and she ran through the kitchen, disappearing from sight.

I palmed my cock over the fly of my jeans. Soon. So fucking soon, I would be buried so deep inside her that we would be one.

"Two!" The sound of her scrambling up the staircase reached my ears.

"Three!" The word was barely out of my mouth before I marched through the house, intent on making Evie come so many times she forgot her own damn name.

My footfalls were heavy on the steps leading to the second floor. I wanted her to be a dripping, whimpering mess before I even reached her. Anticipation was a powerful tool; tonight, I would use it to my advantage.

Pushing through our bedroom door, I arched an eyebrow when I found her still fully dressed, standing by the side of the bed.

"Was I not clear?"

Wide violet eyes stared at me as she stammered, "I b-beat you."

Clicking my tongue, I scolded, "You should know better by now, Evie, baby. I expected you to be naked and waiting for me."

Those eyes narrowed as she countered, "You're changing the rules."

"I can do whatever the fuck I want!" I roared, closing the distance between us.

Evie remained rooted to the spot as I gripped two fistfuls of her sweater and tugged. Threads popping filled the silence before I tossed the ruined garment aside.

"You've gotta be fucking kiddin' me." Fire flashed in those violet depths that had captivated me for my entire adult life. "That was brand new."

"You think I care?" I challenged, my voice gruff as my breathing grew ragged. "Next time, you'll think twice, now, won't you?"

Her hands came to rest on my pecs, and she shoved with all her might, but she didn't manage to move me an inch. When she pulled back to try again, my hands snaked out to circle her wrists, twisting her around and bending her over the side of the bed. Arms pinned behind her back, she struggled against my hold.

Leaning over her, my lips kissed the shell of her ear as I spoke. "You ready to behave now, sweetheart?"

"Fuck you," she spat.

I couldn't hold back a dark chuckle. "Oh, baby, you know it only turns me on more when you get fired up like this." I ground my erection against her ass to prove my point.

A tiny whimper sounded from deep within her throat.

There it is.

"If you promise to be a good girl, I'll give you back your hands."

Her head turned to the side, and she nodded. "Please."

Holding both her wrists in one hand, I rose to standing. She looked so fucking hot like this, with her ass front and center, that I couldn't help myself. My free hand pulled back before cracking across one cheek. Her resulting yelp was muffled by the bedsheets.

"That's for not being naked when I arrived," I explained, releasing my grip and stepping back.

Evie flipped over and immediately unbuttoned her jeans, sliding the tight fabric down her legs until she could kick it away. Her panties and bra went next, leaving her gloriously naked, spread out on our bed.

"Fuck, babe," I groaned, dragging a hand over my jaw. "I can see how wet you are from here." I inhaled deeply, and the scent of her arousal infiltrated my senses.

Fucking Evie was a full sensory experience—the sight, the smell, the taste. All of it combined was enough to bring any man to his knees. Yet I was the only one able to call this incredible woman my wife.

Restlessly, she shifted as I took my time drinking her in. "Please, Jenner," she begged, plucking at her nipples.

Unbuttoning my shirt, I commanded, "Tell me what you want, Evie."

"You," she moaned, hooded eyes meeting mine.

"Aw, come on." I tsked, kicking off my jeans. "You can do better than that. Do you want my fingers? Or maybe my mouth? Not sure you can handle my cock, or can you, baby?"

"Yesssssss." The word was drawn out like a hiss.

"You're so goddamn greedy for me, aren't you?"

Her head bobbed as her fingers slid between her thighs. Stroking my cock, I watched as she rubbed tight circles over her clit, pleasuring herself.

Evie was stunning like this—skin flushed, legs parted wide as her hips bucked, chasing her orgasm.

"Go ahead. Make yourself come, and then I'll lick you clean."

"Jenner," she moaned, body growing taut as she teetered right on the edge.

"You're fucking breathtaking. Make that pussy cry for me."

Back bowing, Evie gasped as I watched her shatter at her own hand. That was my signal, and I dropped to my knees before she could recover, lapping at her with my tongue, relishing the sound of her squeals. I knew she was sensitive, but I didn't care. If I had it my way, she'd pass out from pleasure before the night was through.

Her heels dug into the mattress, and she tried to shift away, but I locked my arms around her thick thighs, holding her in place. Grazing the little bud with my teeth, I flicked against it until her legs shook uncontrollably, and a rush of moisture ran down my throat.

When I pulled back, I found Evie lying limp with her eyes closed. I wiped the back of my hand over my mouth. "Delicious."

"You're a bad man, Jenner Knight," she panted.

Crawling over her sated form, I teased, "And we've only just begun, my love."

A whine flew past her lips. "I can't."

"You can and you will. We're not done until I say we are."

Evie draped an arm over her eyes. "Then good luck to you doing all the work because my muscles feel like jelly."

"It's adorable you think that's gonna stop me."

"I can feel my heartbeat in my pussy. Have some mercy. It's Christmas."

"Exactly," I teased, tugging a nipple between my teeth. "It's the season of giving. And I intend to give you so many orgasms that you have no other choice but to remain in bed and watch holiday movies with me all day tomorrow."

She let out a deep groan. "Please don't make me watch the one where they hold everyone hostage at the holiday party, and then the off-duty cop goes vigilante. It's not a Christmas movie."

"The hell it's not!" I argued.

"It's an action movie," Evie huffed.

"Yeah. At Christmas. Therefore, it's a Christmas movie."

"Whatever. Do me a favor and put me into a sex coma so I don't have to suffer through it."

"That was the plan all along, but I'm glad you're finally on board, babe."

Skimming my lips down her body, I pressed a soft kiss to her pussy before crossing to my side of the bed, my eyes never leaving her prone form.

A tiny wrinkle formed between her eyebrows. "Where are you going?"

I flashed her with a wicked grin. "I've got a little gift for you."

"If it's a butt plug, you can forget it right now. We've been over this too many times to count. Exit only, mister."

"Noted." I opened the top drawer and pulled out the item I'd stashed, waiting for the perfect opportunity to use it.

"What in the hell is that?" Evie flipped onto her belly, crawling closer to get a better look as I slid the silicone ring over my shaft.

Pressing the button on the attachment, it came to life, the vibrations settling in my balls and making me groan.

"Vibrating cock ring."

"Is the vibrating part meant for you or for me?"

"Both." I gripped my throbbing length, tugging against the sensation.

"Well, are you gonna stand over there playin' with yourself all night, or are you gonna share your new toy?"

I cocked my head, continuing to stroke myself as she licked her lips. "What happened to *I can't?*"

Sitting up, she shot back, "You know what? You're right. I can't. I'll just grab my pajamas and a book, and be out of your hair. Holler for me when you're done."

Evie scooched toward the edge of the bed opposite where I stood, but I was faster. Lightning-quick, I pounced, wrapping my arms around her torso from behind and rolling her beneath me as she squealed.

Notching my hips between her thighs, I forced her legs wide open. The vibrating attachment pressed against her clit, and Evie moaned, rocking against it.

"You done being a brat?" I rasped, sinking my teeth into the soft flesh of her neck.

"Never." Her head thrashed from side to side.

"Wrong answer, baby." My lips brushed against her skin as I spoke. "Now I've got to punish you."

"Please," she begged.

My cock was drenched from rubbing against her dripping pussy. Centering myself, I drove home in a single thrust, satisfied when Evie cried out in response.

"Is that what you wanted?" I pulled back before snapping my hips forward again.

"Yes!" Her breathless voice was almost my undoing.

"But this isn't about what you want, is it? It's about what I want."

Instead of setting a pace that would drive her wild, I kept my cock buried deep inside her, grinding my hips so the vibrator on the cock ring was pressed flush against her clit. She couldn't escape the sensations the way I had her pinned, spread beneath me.

Evie's eyes flew wide when she realized what I was doing. Resting my weight on my elbows beside her head, I cupped her cheek, rubbing my thumb over the soft curve.

Her neck arched, eyes squeezing shut as tears leaked out, and I knew she was close.

"That's it, baby. Come for me. You're so damn stunning when you fall apart."

Lips parting, a whimper escaped as her pussy clamped down on my dick, and tremors racked her body as she found her release.

Grunting, I rose onto my knees, ready to take my pleasure now that I was satisfied with hers. Well, mostly satisfied; I planned to take her over the edge one more time with me.

Fingers digging into her generous hips, I held her immobile, driving my cock into her heat faster and faster, the vibrations teasing her with each slam before I took them away again.

As she sobbed beneath me, Evie's body became mine to command.

"You're mine, you know that?" I gritted out, so close to losing myself that I could barely think straight. Evie was too far gone to reply, so I kept going, "This pussy was made for me, no one else."

This woman might be the only one on Earth who could unleash this side of me. When we were together, I became this demanding, possessive man—a sharp departure from the playful, caring one I was on a daily basis.

But I loved that she knew me like no one else. These moments were for us, and she craved this dynamic as much as I did.

Lust darkened my vision, but I wanted one more from my wife.

Reaching a hand up, I circled her throat, pressing my fingers into the pulse points beneath her jaw. Evie gasped, instantly reacting to the reduced flow of oxygen to her brain. I'd only ever done this to her a few times, but each one was still vividly imprinted in my memory—she never came harder than when I choked her.

Her inner walls fluttered around me, and my balls drew tight as I pounded into her harder than I ever had before.

Pupils blown wide, Evie's mouth opened and closed as she attempted to draw in air. Releasing my grasp on her throat acted like a detonator. She exploded beneath me, her climax so strong that she let out a hoarse scream as her pussy tightened in a vise grip.

"Fuck!" I shouted; my orgasm ripped from me with such force that I stopped breathing.

Rocking my hips, I emptied myself inside her as she continued to squeeze me, sucking in every last drop like the greedy girl she was.

Spent, I pulled out and collapsed beside her.

Evie's chest rose and fell as her harsh breathing sounded loudly in the air. It was music to my ears, knowing I was the one who'd pushed her past what she thought her body was capable of.

When I traced a hand down her sternum to her navel, she swatted me away. "No more."

Chuckling, I ran my nose along her shoulder. "Okay, baby." Removing the silicone ring from around my softening cock, I offered, "Let me clean you up?"

Evie placed a hand over what was no doubt her racing heart. "I'm not moving from this spot."

"Mission accomplished," I teased. "Gonna be a great Christmas."

Sliding off the bed, I moved to the bathroom, wetting a washcloth with warm water to wipe the mess from between her thighs.

Returning to her side and cleaning her gently, it struck me.

From here on out, every Christmas would be better than the one before because we'd finally be a family. Our daughter was the only missing piece.

Chapter 19
Evie

"Do you think she'd like brunch at the Winchester?" I asked.

Dakota smirked, holding up her champagne flute containing a mimosa. "She's not picky. So long as there's booze. Hell, we could probably do it at Pipes, and she'd love it."

"Yeah, that's a hard pass." I couldn't stop the full-body shudder at the memory of Bristol's singing.

Tessa and Dakota laughed out loud, both having been witness to Bristol's unique vocal stylings.

The team was out of town, which meant Bristol had gone with them as part of the traveling press pack. That gave us the perfect opportunity to plan her bridal shower thrown by the Speed WAGs.

"But seriously"—Dakota sat back in the booth we occupied in a quaint little breakfast spot in an up-and-coming Indy suburb—"it sounds girly, with just a touch of class, and I think it's perfect for her. Great idea, Evie."

"I'll call them this afternoon to see if they can fit us in before the playoffs. Dakota, you've got her registry info, right?"

"Yep. I'll send that over as soon as I'm back at my computer."

"Thanks. As soon as I have that and we confirm a date with the hotel, I can get the details to the rest of the ladies, and we should be good to go."

Tessa nudged me gently with an elbow. "You're so good at all this."

I shrugged. "It's like riding a bike. I used to handle all this back when Maddox was the captain." Letting out a wry laugh, I joked, "Never would have thought I'd be planning a shower for the girl who finally got the team's resident bachelor to settle down."

Dakota leaned her arms on the table, a smile creeping onto her face. "It's crazy how well they work together, even with the age gap."

Nodding, I agreed, "Wouldn't have believed it if I hadn't seen it with my own eyes."

"Well, well. What have we here?" A voice akin to nails on a chalkboard had me wincing.

We all turned to peer up at the woman who had interrupted our peaceful gathering.

"What do you want, Juliana?" Dakota narrowed her eyes.

"I should think it would be obvious." Juliana folded her arms beneath her fake breasts, putting her cleavage on display through the top of her sports bra. She looked like she'd recently come from the gym—bleach blonde hair set in a high ponytail, wearing skintight workout pants that matched the bra, with only a light zip-up overtop. I could only imagine she was worried that Saint would drop her ass like a bad habit if she so much as gained a pound, considering how she'd always gone out of her way to remark on my size.

"Spit it out." I rolled my eyes, not in the mood for her antics.

"I came to join the party planning committee." Juliana plastered a saccharine smile on her face.

"Sorry, darlin'"—I made sure to match her fake sweetness—"planning is done by ladies attached to leadership. Last I checked, Saint doesn't have a letter on his jersey."

That struck a nerve because her dark eyes narrowed into thin slits. But she must have remembered her objective and quickly schooled her features. It didn't have quite the desired effect because her attempt at a smile looked more like a grimace.

"I was hoping you might make an exception, seeing as I'm the most senior WAG."

Tessa was quick to correct her. "No, I believe that would be Evie. Which is fitting, seeing as she's the *captain's* wife."

Juliana wasn't ready to go down without a fight and countered, "If you remove the four years she was gone, I've got her beat."

"Sorry, it doesn't work that way," I shut her down.

Her temper finally got the better of her, and she snapped, venom dripping from every word. "You all can't just waltz in here and take charge. Not when I've been here the whole time. And don't get me started on the reporter."

"That reporter has a name." Dakota's icy tone had me shivering.

Juliana scoffed. "Yeah, well, rumor has it that Maddox didn't even know it the first time he fucked her."

My jaw dropped open, but Dakota shoved to her feet, getting up in Juliana's personal space. "And you wonder why no one likes you." She pointed to the door. "Why don't you get out of here before you dig the hole any deeper."

A flush of red crept up Juliana's neck, and she spun on her heels and stormed off.

Dakota dropped back into her seat with a heavy exhale. "She's such a witch."

"I feel sorry for her," Tessa said softly, and our eyes shifted to her.

"You shouldn't. She's a miserable human being and tries to drag everyone down with her," I huffed.

Tessa's lips twisted. "That's kinda my point. She must be hurting inside to lash out like that."

Dakota cut in. "Maybe, but that doesn't give her the right to badmouth other people."

"That's true," Tessa conceded. "All I'm saying is, you never know what someone is struggling with."

"Ugh," I groaned. "Leave it to the mom of the group to have perspective."

"It's those darn kiddie cartoons. They're always hiding life lessons in those things."

We all burst out laughing. She wasn't wrong.

When we calmed down, Dakota directed her next question at Tessa. "So, are you guys planning to get away during the All-Pro Break?"

Tessa sipped her mimosa, nodding. "Yeah, we're gonna take the kids down to Florida. I'd prefer the Caribbean, but we've been so busy juggling two kids that we haven't gotten around to applying for a passport for Bailey."

"Send me pics, especially if you make it to the beach," I begged.

"Of course. Ollie's my little water baby."

My heart swelled, thinking of the sweet little boy I'd made such a connection with.

"And who knows, maybe someday, the fans will like your husband a little less, and you guys can come with us," she teased.

I winked. "Maybe I can convince him to fake an injury next year."

"Oh yeah, Maddox will just *love* you for that," Dakota snickered.

"And with my luck, they'll send Asher in his place," Tessa added.

"Hmm." I tapped my chin. "Didn't think this one through."

"How about this? We plan a summer trip instead?"

"Yes!" Dakota cried. "You guys could come up to our new lake house in Minnesota. We've got tons of space."

I held my glass up, and the other two ladies touched theirs to mine. "A lakeside summer retreat it is."

Tipsy, I stepped out of the backseat of the car, sighing when the warm desert air wrapped around me like a blanket.

Jenner held his hand out for me, but I ignored it, instead snuggling right into his chest. It vibrated with his chuckle, tickling my face, and I giggled loudly.

"Okay. Guess we're gonna need help with the bags because you are two handfuls this morning, wife."

"Mmm. Handfuls," I purred. "You know I love when you squeeze my ass."

"Heads up, Jenner," Braxton called out, and the next thing I heard was a sharp crack near my ear, making me jump.

"What in the world?" I shrieked.

"Water, baby. You gotta hydrate." He pressed a bottle of water to my lips, and I sucked down the cool liquid greedily. Maybe he had a point. I'd lost count of the refills my champagne flute had seen on the flight to Vegas.

Dakota's voice spoke next. "Let her know we'll be by the pool most of the afternoon. When she's feeling up to it, she should join us."

I perked up. "Ooh. The pool? Let's go now!"

Jenner banded his arms around me as I tried to flee his hold. "Maybe a nap and more water first, babe. Don't need you drowning on me."

My lower lip pushed out in a pout. "You're no fun."

His lips brushed over my temple. "I will gladly hold the title of party pooper if it means keeping you alive long enough to meet our little girl."

I gave an exaggerated sigh. "Fine. You win."

Over my head, he told our travel partners, "We'll catch you later. I'm gonna get her upstairs."

My vision swam slightly as Jenner urged me through the casino floor toward the elevator bank. His grip around my waist was tight enough that I leaned into him, knowing he would support me as I swayed.

Twin sliding doors pulled back to reveal an empty elevator, and I got an idea. The second we were enclosed inside and the carriage began its ascent toward our floor, I spun around, using two hands to shove at Jenner's chest.

Usually, my muscular husband was immovable, but the element of surprise worked in my favor, and he stumbled back, slamming against the mirrored wall. Taking advantage of his shocked state, I pounced, gripping two fistfuls of his auburn tresses and pulling his lips down to mine.

Jenner groaned, his lips parting enough that I could slip my tongue inside. Fuck, he tasted like whiskey, and a bolt of lust shot straight between my thighs.

Speaking of thighs . . .

I edged my knee between Jenner's, so I could grind my core against his toned thigh, seeking relief. I was throbbing, desperate and needy for him. There was no doubt he'd blame my sudden horniness on my intoxicated state, but I knew better. I was hot for him all the time but was better at hiding it in public when I was sober.

"Evie." Jenner tore his mouth away, panting. "We can't do this here."

My hand skimmed down his chest, cupping his erection through his jeans, making him hiss. "Don't tell me you don't want this."

"Fuck." His forehead pressed to mine. "Cameras, babe. They have video feeds inside the elevators. No one gets to see you but me."

Ugh. I hated it when he was the voice of reason. But I had to admit that I wasn't looking to have a low-budget sex tape of us circulating on the internet.

The elevator came to a stop, the doors opening.

"This is our floor," Jenner remarked, steering me down the hallway.

An app on his phone acted as the key when he tapped it against the sensor above the doorknob. A digital unlocking sounded, and he pushed the door open to our suite.

I pulled from his grasp when the view from the massive window caught my eye. The Las Vegas Strip was laid out before us, the flat desert landscape making it easy to see for miles beyond the city to the mountains in the distance.

"Just think of how beautiful this will look at night," I breathed.

Arms encircled my waist as lips pressed against my neck. "Not more beautiful than you, baby."

I turned around to face him, smirking. "Then maybe you'll just have to fuck me up against it tonight so I can enjoy the view while you make me scream."

"I could be persuaded," he murmured, dusting kisses along my jaw until he reached a sensitive spot behind my ear. "But first, you need to rest. Sleep off some of that champagne."

Pulling away, I yanked off my tank top.

Jenner's head dropped back on a groan. "Evie."

"What?" I teased. "I need to shower off the plane before I get into bed."

He stepped back, eyeing me. "Oh yeah?"

"Mmhmm." Biting my lip, I shimmied out of my leggings, leaving me only in a bra and panties. "Join me."

Fire lit up in his coffee-colored eyes, and he dragged a hand over his mouth. "You're gonna be the death of me, woman."

Sauntering toward the ensuite bathroom with an exaggerated sway of my hips, I shot back over my shoulder, "But what a way to go."

"Fuck it." His words came out rough, and a shiver rolled down my spine.

Jenner ripped off his T-shirt, stalking after me in only his jeans, looking like something out of a sexy photoshoot. I was so turned on by the sight that I was probably going to explode the minute he touched me.

Dangerously close to overheating from a combination of lust and alcohol, I elected to keep the water cool when turning on the shower. The last thing I needed was to pass out and ruin the sexy fun we were about to have.

Stepping out of my panties, I unclipped my bra, letting it slide to the ground. My breasts ached when they spilled free, so I gripped them, plucking the nipples as a moan flew past my lips.

"Starting without me?" Jenner teased from behind.

I spun around in time to see his jeans fall away, revealing his cock, standing thick and proud. Saliva filled my mouth, and even though I was desperate for a taste, I had another idea.

Stepping under the spray of water, I sighed in relief as it cooled my heated skin. It only granted me a temporary reprieve as a burning hot wall of muscle pressed against my back.

My head lolled onto Jenner's shoulder on a moan, my ass rubbing against his stiff cock.

"How do you want me, baby?"

God, I loved it when he let me take charge.

A wicked grin curved on my lips as I pumped some of the hotel-provided body wash into my hands, rubbing them together to work up a lather.

Spinning around, I dropped to my knees, working the slippery soap over my breasts and into the valley between.

When I pushed my boobs together, it became clear what I wanted, and Jenner's eyebrows rose. "Yeah?"

My head bobbed, and I licked my lips. "Fuck my tits, baby."

A deep groan echoed off the shower walls, and Jenner gripped his cock, stroking it a few times before feeding it into the tight space between my breasts.

Towering above me, he braced one hand on the shower wall as he gave the first shallow thrust of his hips. His free hand fisted in my hair and tugged, forcing me to meet his burning gaze.

"You look so goddamn hot on your knees for me, Evie." The ache between my thighs intensified at his words, and I shifted restlessly as he increased his pace.

Breathless, I tried to push him over the edge. "Mark me, Jenner. Come all over my face."

His balls slapped against my stomach as he slammed his cock between my breasts harder and harder.

"Stick out your tongue," he commanded, releasing his grasp on my hair.

Obeying, I opened wide, anxiously awaiting the moment he unraveled.

"I can't hold back anymore, baby." Those were Jenner's only words of warning as thick ropes of cum shot wildly onto my neck, my tongue, and my cheeks before sliding down my wet flesh and onto my cleavage.

Jenner's eyes were closed, and his chest heaved. "Jesus. You're fucking incredible, you know that?"

His praise warmed me from head to toe, and I beamed up at him. Releasing my hold on my breasts, I rose to standing.

Cupping his face, I peppered kisses along his jaw. "You're not so bad yourself."

Hands anchored on my hips, and he rasped, "Your turn. Then naptime."

"So bossy," I teased.

Jenner barked out a laugh. "You fucking love it when I tell you what to do."

I bit back a smirk. He wasn't wrong.

I'd gladly let him boss me around for the rest of our lives.

"Evie! Over here!" Dakota's voice shouted the minute I stepped into the pool area of the resort we were staying in for All-Pro weekend.

Feeling refreshed after an orgasm and a nap, my sunglass-covered eyes scanned until I found her lounging beneath a shaded cabana with a blonde woman.

My flip-flops slapped on the concrete as I made my way over to the pair.

Dakota gave me a knowing grin. "That nap must have been amazing. You're glowing."

Heat rushed to my cheeks, and I nodded. "It was good."

"Mine, too." She winked. Gesturing to the woman beside her, Dakota said, "I know some of the guys know each other already, but have you met my sister-in-law, Natalie?"

"No." I smiled. "This is my first time at one of these things. It's nice to meet you, Natalie."

"Join us." Natalie patted the massive bed beneath the canopy. "Jaxon gets selected for the All-Pro game a lot but seems to have bad timing with injuries and hasn't made it to one in years, so this is a first for me, too."

Dropping my bag, I took a seat, reclining back onto my elbows. "Thank God they sent us somewhere warm. I might've cried if we were spending the weekend in Salt Lake City."

"I'll drink to that," Dakota chirped, signaling to a nearby member of the staff that we wanted to place an order.

I knew I shouldn't imbibe after how sloppy I'd gotten on complimentary champagne during the flight, but invisible peer pressure got to me. I didn't want to be the wet blanket not drinking when my companions were, so I agreed to a round of margaritas.

One round turned into two, and the three of us were feeling relaxed, lounging beneath the cabana. That was, until a young voice cried out, "Mommy!"

Natalie groaned, sitting up. "It was nice while it lasted."

Wet footsteps on concrete reached my ears, and I pushed onto my elbows in time to see a raven-haired toddler throw himself into Natalie's open arms.

"Sorry, Mom." My eyes shifted to a teenager with black hair twisted into a messy bun at the edge of the pool. "I kept him busy for as long as I could."

"It's all right, Amelia. It was only a matter of time." The teenager turned away and glided through the pool until she reached a group of children of varying ages.

"Max, my main man!" Dakota's chipper voice spoke from my other side as she reached an arm over my torso to offer the toddler a fist bump. Instead of returning the gesture, the little boy buried his wet face in his mother's chest.

Natalie let out a weary sigh. "I took for granted how much the older ones clung to their dad. I hardly get a moment of peace with this one. He only wants me. All. The. Time."

I couldn't help but smile, knowing that if our little girl wanted to cling to me 24/7, that would be just fine with me. After how long we'd waited to become parents, I was intent on showering her with all the love I had to give.

"How old is he?" Before she could answer, I mused, "Doesn't look much older than Ollie."

Head tilting to the side, Natalie asked, "Who's Ollie?"

"Asher Lawson's little guy," Dakota explained.

"Ah, I see." Natalie ran her hand through her son's black hair. "Max, here, turned three in October, but he's small for his age." Her lips twisted in thought. "Or maybe he's not. It's hard to tell sometimes. My nephew was born the same day, and he's a tank, almost as big as Charlie, my six-year-old daughter."

"Mommy! I wanna swim!" Max cried.

"Guess we're getting wet today, ladies. How about another round to take the edge off?" she suggested.

Dakota agreed before I could decline. I guess one more wouldn't hurt, right?

Scooping the little boy into her arms, Natalie made her way to the stairs at the shallow end of the pool. Dakota and I followed suit, accepting our third margaritas in plastic cups from a poolside server as we stood in waist-high water.

"He's precious," I said to Natalie, sipping my drink.

Max was wrapped around her chest like a koala, and I could tell she was exhausted, but she smiled down at the little boy. "Thank you. He was the last piece of our family we didn't know we were missing."

Dakota laughed, saying to me, "The first day I met Natalie was when Max was born. She was all hopped up on pain meds and about damn near jumped out of bed to strangle Jaxon when he suggested they have more."

Natalie huffed, "Five is plenty. Thank you very much."

Once upon a time, I'd pictured Jenner and me with a large family. We'd been so young when we began trying and were blessed with the means to support a gaggle of children, but it wasn't in the cards. The adoption process had been so emotionally draining that I wasn't sure I would want to go through it again. I would be perfectly content with one child. It was more than I thought we would ever have.

"How about you, Evie? Have you and Jenner ever considered starting a family?"

It was a perfectly innocuous question, coming from someone who'd had no trouble getting pregnant on their own multiple times. Most people didn't think twice when asking a couple about their private family planning. They couldn't understand how painful it was to dig at that open wound if they'd never struggled. I couldn't count the number of times I'd had to offer a tight smile when someone noted how long Jenner and I had been married and asked when we would start having babies.

But for the first time in nearly a decade, the question didn't make my heart hurt.

"Actually, Jenner and Evie are adopting," Dakota answered before I could.

Natalie's brown eyes widened as she realized her unintentional misstep. "Oh. I didn't realize." A brilliant smile grew on her face. "I think it's wonderful you're exploring a non-traditional route to parenthood. There are so many children out there who need a loving home."

I returned her smile. "We're really excited about it."

Without warning, something slammed into the back of my head, and I yelped as pain radiated through my skull. My drink fell into the water, and my hand flew up to cradle where the injury had occurred.

"Beau Alexander Slate!" Natalie yelled, making me wince.

A remorseful voice came in reply. "I'm really sorry, Mom. But Jameson kept throwing it over my head, saying I couldn't get it past him."

"You come over here right now and apologize to Mrs. Knight," she demanded.

Tenderly touching the spot where apparently I'd been beaned with a football, I expected to have a bump there later, but thankfully, it would be well hidden under my hair.

"Knight, like Jenner Knight?" A boy who was maybe ten or eleven, with the same dark hair as his siblings, entered my field of vision.

"Beau . . ." Natalie's voice carried a hint of warning. "I have half a mind to not let you out on the ice tomorrow night after what you just did."

His dark brown eyes grew wide, and his lower lip trembled. The poor thing looked like he was about to cry. "I'm real sorry, ma'am."

Blowing out a heavy breath, Natalie added, "I'm sorry, too, Evie. Their sibling rivalry has been off the charts lately. Jameson thinks he's too cool for his little brother, being in high school while Beau's still in elementary school. A five-year gap doesn't seem huge when they're little, but it's starting to hurt now."

I gave the boy a kind smile. "No harm done. I know a thing or two about getting in a tussle with your brother. But I can promise you, when you're both grown-ups, you'll find that you forget about all the fights and become friends."

Beau gave me a doubtful look, but with age came wisdom, and I had no doubt that he and his brother would form a closer bond when they were both older.

"Are you really Jenner's Knight's wife?" he asked me shyly.

Nodding in confirmation, I replied, "Sure am."

"He's pretty good, but my dad's better."

I bit back a laugh at his loyalty to his father because his mom was not amused.

"Beau! Where are your manners?" Natalie cried. "You're dangerously close to strike three. And the more you push it, the more I consider counting the first strike as two; it was that bad."

Dakota threw her arm over the boy's shoulders. "Don't worry, bud. I bet if you agreed to wear a Slate Speed jersey, Uncle Braxton could get you an ice pass for the skills competition."

"Nothing like being undermined in front of your kids," Natalie grumbled.

"Aw, come on, Nat. It's part of the perks of being the fun aunt—letting them do all the things their parents tell them they can't."

"Pretty sure you're supposed to do it behind my back."

"Kinda hard to do that when it's going to be on national television." Dakota smirked.

Beau beamed up at me. "Just wait until my best friend, Knox, sees me out there. He's going to be sooooooo jealous his dad didn't get picked for the All-Pro Game. But someday, we'll both be out there for real. We're both gonna go pro like our dads and play for the same team."

I raised an impressed eyebrow. "Well, with confidence like that, I bet you will."

He swam away, and I opened my mouth to tell Natalie how adorable he was when a wave of dizziness crashed over me suddenly. I reached a steadying hand toward the pool's edge, shaking my head, hoping it would pass.

"Evie, are you okay?" Dakota's concerned voice broke through my fuzzy brain.

Closing my eyes, I nodded, but then a rush of heat stole over me as my stomach lurched, and I bolted from the pool. On unsteady feet, in urgent need of a restroom, I scanned the area for a sign indicating its direction. The nausea grew too insistent, and I knew I was out of time, so I went for the next closest thing: the trash can.

Stumbling forward, I gripped the sides as everything I'd eaten that day made a sudden reappearance. Heaving uncontrollably, I heard Natalie and Dakota talking about calling Jenner. With my head in a trash can, I begged them not to, knowing he would be headed out soon to the fan meet-and-greet to kick off All-Pro weekend.

I'd just had too much to drink. I would survive. Even if it didn't exactly feel like it at the moment.

Chapter 20

Jenner

Frowning at my phone as it lit up with a familiar name on an incoming call, I swiped my finger across the screen. "Dakota?"

"Hey, Jenner." I immediately disliked how nervous she sounded. "We kind of have a situation down here at the pool."

My heart rate kicked up, and panic trickled down my spine. "What happened?"

"Evie's, um—"

"Dakota, I need you to talk to me." I was half dressed—suit pants on, shirt still unbuttoned—but immediately went to work putting on shoes because whatever was going on didn't sound good.

"She's passed out."

I blew out a heavy breath. "How much has she had to drink?"

There was a pause on the other side of the line before she answered, "Not that much, Jenner. But there is the head injury to consider."

"What the fuck?"

My feet were moving, and I was halfway to the elevator when she explained, "Beau kind of hit her with a football."

Eyes darting between the elevator and the stairwell, I shifted restlessly. I knew the elevator would be faster, being thirty floors up, but I hated waiting for it to arrive.

"I need you to tell me the exact sequence of events, Dakota."

"Okay, so we had a few drinks." I would have rolled my eyes if I weren't so concerned about my wife's well-being. "And then we got into the pool with the kids. Beau and Jameson got into some kind of pissing contest, and the football they were playing with was thrown right into the back of her head. She was fine for a while after that, but then she swayed a bit, going pale before she jumped from the pool and started puking in a trash can."

"How long after that did she pass out? And how long has it been since she took the hit to the head?" I stepped into the elevator, and tapped my foot impatiently during its descent. The floor numbers crept down at a snail's pace on the way to the lobby level.

"She's been out for only a few minutes. The ball hit her maybe fifteen or twenty minutes ago?"

The doors slid open, and I ran around the casino floor in the direction of the pool. "I'm almost there."

Hanging up on Dakota, I burst onto the pool deck, and it didn't take long to find them. Jaxon Slate's middle son was crying quietly where he sat on the concrete near where his mom and aunt were standing, gazing down at my unconscious wife.

Red-rimmed brown eyes peered up at me as I approached, and the young boy whispered hoarsely, "I'm really sorry."

I didn't have time to console him, so I offered him a quick squeeze on the shoulder as I focused on Evie.

Crouching beside her prone form, I ran a hand over her blonde hair, feeling the lump forming at the back of her head. Taking a deep breath, I kept my voice calm as I said, "Baby, can you hear me?"

Evie groaned, turning her face into the cabana bed beneath her. "Noooooo. I told them not to call you."

The fact that she was instantly roused by my voice was a good sign.

"They did the right thing. We need to get you checked out."

Eyes still closed, she shook her head. "I'm fine. Just a combination of too much heat and too much booze."

"You left out the head injury."

A hand lifted weakly. "That was nothing."

"Evie, we don't know that for sure. Not until a doctor examines you."

Violet eyes snapped open suddenly, and she screamed, "No!" so forcefully I stumbled back.

I understood where she was coming from. We'd spent far too much of our marriage inside doctor's offices, where Evie had taken the brunt of the poking and prodding during different procedures. But I would never forgive myself if something happened to her because she refused medical treatment for an injury of this nature.

Frustrated, I dragged a hand over my face. "How about this? We have a few team doctors on hand this weekend. They're experienced at diagnosing concussions. Let's get you upstairs, and one of them can take a look at you."

She chewed on her lower lip as her eyes focused on me. Her fingers trailed over the bare skin of my chest, visible from where my collared shirt had been left open. "You have an event tonight."

"I'll call the whole damn weekend off right now, Evie, if you refuse to let someone check you out. Nothing matters more than you. Nothing."

That seemed to get through to her because she nodded. "Okay."

I smoothed the tangled hair away from her forehead. "That's my girl. Let's get you upstairs."

Evie shook her head. "I don't want to move. I want to sleep."

"I know, baby, but we can't leave you here." Standing, I entered the passcode on my phone and handed it to Dakota. "Can you walk up with us to handle the elevator and unlock the door to our room so I can carry her?"

Dakota's concerned blue eyes darted to Evie. "You think she's gonna be all right?"

"Most likely." I nodded. "Doubt a ten-year-old's got a strong enough arm to do permanent damage."

"Don't let him hear you say that." She cast a look at her nephew. "His older brother goading him over that exact thing is how she took the hit."

Ah, boys.

Returning to the cabana, I eased one arm under Evie's knees, the other beneath her armpits. "Think you can help me out and hold onto my neck, baby?"

Evie let out a soft whimper but looped her arms around my neck so I was able to hoist her into my arms. Her swimsuit was still wet from being in the pool, and dampness seeped into my clothes, but I didn't care. I wasn't going out tonight; I already knew that.

The only thing that mattered was making sure my wife was all right.

Thankfully, with Jaxon's help, I was able to get in contact with the Comets' team doc, who had made the trip to Vegas for the league event this weekend. I'd helped Evie change into her pajamas and she was tucked in bed by the time he arrived.

My girl whined during his examination, complaining that she wanted to go back to sleep. Standing at the foot of the bed with my arms crossed, I watched on, my body vibrating with tension.

Dr. Weston peeked over at me, declaring, "She doesn't show any signs of a concussion."

Relief washed over me so forcefully that my hands dropped to the mattress, and I had to breathe through the darkness creeping in from the sides of my vision.

"Thank God," I breathed.

A hand clasped my shoulder. "You sure you don't need to be checked out, too?" There was humor in the doctor's voice, but I wasn't in the mood for jokes.

Pushing off the bed, I took a deep breath. "Nah. I just needed her to be okay." Running a hand through my hair, I asked, "Any guesses as to what caused the episode? The girls said it happened suddenly."

He eyed my wife, who now lay unconscious on the bed. "You said she'd been drinking before the incident?" I nodded. "It's entirely possible the bump to the noggin was an unfortunately timed coincidence."

"Yeah. But she's usually better at holding her liquor," I mused.

Shrugging, Dr. Weston replied, "You never know which bartender is going to have a heavy pour. And if they're good at what they do, you don't even notice you've had too much until it's too late. Keep an eye on her tonight. If she's not better tomorrow, you've got my number."

"Thanks. I appreciate you coming up." I walked him to the door.

Once he was gone, I slid into bed next to my wife, prepared to keep a watchful eye on her until she woke.

"There's the little troublemaker!" I skated toward Beau Slate, who was dressed in full gear to accompany his dad on the ice for the All-Pro Skills Tournament.

Behind the cage on his helmet, his brown eyes widened when he saw me. "Is Miss Evie okay?" he asked timidly.

"Right as rain," I confirmed.

"I didn't mean to hit her, I swear."

"I know, bud." I placed a gloved hand on his helmet and gave his head a little shake. "All is forgiven."

Beau chewed on his lower lip. "My mom was real mad."

Jaxon skated over, having overheard our conversation. "He's not kidding." The face of the league shuddered. "Nat's not a yeller, but last night, I was worried someone was going to call security on our room. Took hours to convince her to let him out on the ice tonight."

"Evie wouldn't have wanted to see him punished so harshly, or at all, for that matter. It was an accident. We all know that." I dropped to a knee before the boy. "You said your best friend is watching tonight?" Beau nodded. "How about we give him a show?"

"Yes!" Beau screamed excitedly. "Knox is a year older and gets to do all kinds of things before me."

"I happen to have a spot in the goalie shootout. Wanna take my place?"

"Oh boy," Jaxon muttered. "You have no idea the grenade you're about to throw into that friendship. Those two are as competitive as it comes."

"Remind me, who is Knox's dad?" I asked Beau.

"Benji Mason," he replied.

"Hmm. Can Knox shoot as good as his dad?" Benji was a sniper. He had a quick release and could place a puck into the net with precision.

"Yeah." The little boy sighed.

A wicked grin curved on my lips. "He ever score on a pro goalie, though?"

Beau caught my drift, and his brown eyes sparkled with mischief. He knew that he'd have bragging rights on his buddy for years to come. "No, sir."

"Then this is your shot." I winked playfully. "Don't blow it."

"Wait till I tell Charlie!" He skated over to where his younger sister was hanging out with Braxton. From what I'd gathered over the years, my young teammate had a tight bond with his niece.

When I stood, Jaxon simply shook his head. "You didn't have to do that."

"I know. But I felt bad for the little guy. Broke my heart to see him crying poolside yesterday."

"Natalie mentioned you guys are planning to adopt?"

I chuckled, having forgotten how fast news traveled within the hockey community. "Yeah. A little girl due next month."

"That's great, man. You excited, scared shitless, or both?" Jaxon teased.

"Scared out of my mind, but probably not in the same way as most expectant fathers."

"Oh yeah?" He raised an eyebrow in question.

I spun my stick in my hands. "We walked through fire to get here, and I almost want it more for Evie than I want it for myself. But—" I let out a heavy sigh. "There are no guarantees, even though a mom chose us. A lot can still go wrong."

Jaxon nodded in understanding. "I hate to break it to you, Jenner, but parents live in constant fear, even after the kid is born and they get to take them home. They worry about their child's health, their safety, and whether they'll make the right choices when they're out of your sight. It's fucking terrifying, but the most rewarding thing you'll ever do in your life."

"And you've got five of them. Should I be lighting a candle for you in church?" I joked.

We shared a laugh before he replied, "Couldn't hurt. Just remember, I have teenagers. Bigger kids, bigger problems." He rubbed a hand over his face. "But seriously, though, if I can give you one piece of advice as someone who has been through it a couple of times before, it would be to enjoy every day. You'll find yourself looking forward to the next milestone, so much so that you don't focus on the stage you're in. Soak in the days when all they want to do is sleep on your chest to the sound of your beating heart. You'll never get that time back."

Emotion clogged my throat, thinking about sharing those moments with our daughter and watching Evie become a mom.

Swallowing, I managed to say, "Thanks, Jaxon."

"From what I saw of you and Beau, you've already got what it takes to be a great dad."

"I hope so." The words were barely a whisper.

Maybe they were a prayer. If they were, I hoped someone was listening.

Chapter 21

Jenner

The day after we got home from Vegas, our happy little bubble burst.

We got a call from the adoption agency asking us to come in for a meeting. The director's administrative assistant said it was urgent and that they needed to see us immediately. The Speed were still on break, so we told them we'd be right over.

Evie was in full-blown panic mode on the drive to the agency's office.

"Do you think Paige changed her mind? I haven't heard from her in a few days. Should I reach out?"

I reached my hand over the center console to grasp hers. "We don't know what's going on. Let's just sit tight until we do."

"Jenner, we were so close." Her voice broke, and along with it, my heart.

I wanted to give this woman the world, but I had failed time and time again.

"It's gonna be okay, I'm sure of it." The lie slipped easily from my tongue. I wasn't sure of anything. Deep in my gut, I knew this meeting was the end of the road on our adoption journey—at least, in regards to one involving Paige.

During the rest of the drive, I mentally berated myself for getting excited, for forming an attachment to the baby Paige carried, and for already thinking of her as ours. I should've known better. All of it seemed too good to be true.

Evie clung to me as we walked the hallways of the agency and were told to wait in the director's office because she was in the middle of an interview between a birth mom and prospective parents.

Sitting side by side before an empty desk took me right back to the last time devastating news had been delivered to us.

I gripped Evie's hand while we waited in the fertility specialist's office. "I'm sure everything's fine."

She chewed nervously on her lower lip. "What if it's not?"

"We're young," I countered. "They said it's not unusual for it to take over a year to conceive. And I'm not sure we can even count it as a full year when we missed the ovulation window five times because I was on the road."

Evie shook her head. "I just know something is wrong with me."

"Maybe it's me," I offered.

Tears welled up in her pretty purple eyes. "I have a bad feeling about this, Jenner. I don't know why."

"Hey." I moved from my chair to kneel before her, wiping away a tear that slid down her cheek. "I love you, Evie. So, no matter what the results of these tests are, we will figure it out. Together. Okay?"

Squeezing her eyes shut, she nodded but couldn't stop a sob from bursting free. I tucked her against my chest, holding on for dear life, praying with everything I had that the doctors were prepared with a plan—that we could overcome this obstacle and find our way to becoming parents.

The door to the office opened, and Evie let out a whimper.

Pulling back enough to kiss her, I whispered, "I've got you."

I retook my seat as Dr. Burton dropped onto his desk chair. He gave Evie a kind smile, offering her a box of tissues. Sniffling, she pulled a few from the box before blowing her nose.

When he left the box on the edge of the desk, my heart sank.

Clearing his throat, Dr. Burton began, "Mr. and Mrs. Knight. Thank you for coming in today. I felt it was best to share the findings of your tests in person."

Evie's hand reached out blindly for me, and I gripped it with both of mine, providing the anchor she so desperately needed, even if my world was about to crumble right alongside hers.

"They were bad, weren't they?" *she asked, her voice hoarse from crying.*

Tapping the file on his desk, he replied, "No. Not bad. But they were inconclusive."

"Inconclusive?" *I questioned.* "What does that mean? More testing is required?"

The doctor opened the file—our file. "There's nothing in here to suggest that you shouldn't be able to conceive a child naturally."

"So..." *Evie paused, likely trying to work through his words in her brain.* "There's nothing wrong with either one of us?"

"Not that I can tell. Since you've been trying for over a year and have been unsuccessful in conceiving, that does mean I can diagnose you with unexplained infertility." *Evie sucked in a sharp breath, so he rushed to explain,* "Try not to panic. I know it sounds scary, but getting that diagnosis means we can explore options. And it doesn't mean that you couldn't get pregnant on your own next month."

"What kind of options?" *I asked.*

"To start, we can try some medications to increase your follicle production. I must warn you, however, that this could lead to a multiple pregnancy."

My wife squeezed my hand. "That's a risk we're willing to take."

If this weren't such a serious situation, I might've laughed. It was one thing to willingly agree to twins or triplets in a state of desperation, quite another to deal with the realities of carrying, delivering, and raising multiple babies at the same time.

"We can try that for six months or so," Dr. Burton continued, "and if that doesn't do the trick, we can move on to IUI, where we would place the sperm directly into your uterus to increase the likelihood of conception."

"And if that doesn't work?"

"The final option is IVF, which is a much more invasive and taxing process. Not to mention costly."

It was my turn to speak up. "Money is no object."

Yeah, it sounded pretentious, but it was true. And I needed Evie to know that I was willing to sacrifice everything I had for her.

"Right." Dr. Burton nodded. "If you're all set to go down this road, I can have a prescription waiting for you at the front desk, and we'll take it from there."

"Yes. That's what we want." Evie's voice grew eager.

"Perfect, let's give that six months and see if we can't make a baby."

"Thank you." Standing, I offered my hand to the doctor Evie's brother had referred us to. He was the best in the Midwest, and we'd traveled to Chicago to visit him.

He shook my hand. "Hopefully, you'll have no cause to come back this way, and you'll be sending me pictures of a chubby-cheeked little cutie before this time next year."

Leading Evie from his office, I whispered in her ear, "We've got this, babe. We just needed a little boost, is all."

And I truly believed it.

The door to the office opened, and in stepped the agency's director, Miranda Williams. Her poker face was shit, and the stern frown on her lips had dread rolling down my spine.

Sitting behind her desk, she folded both hands atop the polished wood, getting right down to business. "I'm afraid we have a problem."

Add a terrible bedside manner to the lousy poker face.

Evie whimpered by my side, but instead of comforting her, I leaned forward, challenging, "What kind of problem?"

My mind skipped right over Paige backing out to something being wrong with the baby. I wasn't sure which scenario was worse because both would kill Evie.

Miranda didn't falter at my harsh tone. "It's come to our attention that you falsified records to obtain this adoption."

And just like that, the rug was ripped out from beneath us.

A hand flew up to Evie's mouth to stifle her sob.

After all this time, we'd thought we were in the clear. If they were going to discover our deception, we figured they'd have done so long before now—not when we were mere weeks away from bringing home our daughter.

Willing myself to remain calm, I decided to play dumb, in case they didn't have the whole picture. Maybe there was some way we could work around whatever they'd found and still make this adoption happen.

"I'm not sure what records you're referring to," I countered.

Miranda held my stare. "We received an anonymous tip that you and Mrs. Knight have been estranged for quite some time, and your 'reconnection' coincided with when our agency accepted your application."

Anonymous tip? What the fuck?

Only a handful of people knew about the adoption, and each one was thrilled for us to start a family. So, who the hell ratted us out? And why?

When I didn't respond, Miranda continued to speak over Evie's quiet sobs. "Upon further investigation, we were able to pull up a divorce decree for Jenner and Evangeline Knight dated four years ago."

"Did your research also bring up that we were recently remarried?"

Evie perked up, crying, "We are married!"

Miranda sighed. "That may be, but you were not at the time of your application."

I wasn't done going to bat for our family. "Ms. Williams, I assume you've read Evie's cover letter?" She nodded in confirmation. "So, then you know the hell we went through trying to create a family the traditional way. I can't imagine it would come as a surprise to you that our years of treatments yielding no results caused a strain on our marriage. The emotional toll was extremely high."

Turning to Evie, I held my hand out to her, which she gratefully accepted. "I love my wife. That's a fact, and it's remained true through all our ups and downs. I can't change the fact that I was unable to give her a baby, but I would move heaven and earth to make her dream of motherhood come true. Are you going to sit there and tell me that shifting the date on a piece of paper up two months would really make a difference to you and your agency?"

"Mr. Knight. I'm sorry, but my hands are tied. You and your wife have misrepresented yourselves, and there's no telling what else you might've lied about. I cannot allow your adoption to proceed, as I would feel uncomfortable placing a child in your home. Today marks the end of your relationship with our agency."

The color drained from Evie's face the same way hope leaked from my chest as reality sank in.

My wife jumped up from her chair, throwing a hand over her mouth as she ran from the room, muttering, "I'm going to be sick."

I was on my feet in a flash, poised to chase after her, but I couldn't resist one final parting shot at the woman who'd just broken my wife's heart.

"Are you happy now? You've crushed her dream."

Her tone didn't hold a trace of remorse or sympathy. "I'm sorry, but you did that yourself."

And fuck, if I didn't hate that she was right.

Chapter 22
Evie

I closed myself inside a bathroom stall and hung my head into the toilet. Every time the director's words telling us the adoption was dead echoed in my brain, my stomach clenched, and I heaved.

My heart ached, not wanting to believe it was really over, but my head knew I had fucked up, and there was no coming back from what I'd done.

There was a knock on the external door leading to the hallway in the office building. It creaked open on squeaky hinges, and I heard Jenner's voice call out, "If there's anyone in there, fair warning, I'm coming in to get my wife."

When no one answered, he pushed inside.

"Evie, honey?" His steps stopped on the other side of the stall. "Can you open the door?"

Swallowing against the bile rising in my throat, I let out a groan.

"I'll lay on my belly and crawl underneath if I have to. Dirty bathroom floor or not. Nothing is going to stop me from getting to you." He sighed, and a thud sounded high on the stall door. I could picture him dropping his forehead against it. "Let me in, baby."

Baby.

A sob broke free from my chest. I wasn't sure I'd ever be able to hear him call me that again without feeling like a knife was slicing my heart wide open. Because there would be no baby for us. And it was all my fault.

"I'm so fucking sorry," Jenner whispered, barely loud enough to be heard over the sound of me openly weeping.

Weakly, I reached a hand out to flush the toilet, watching the water swirl in the bowl before disappearing, just like my dreams. I would never get to hold that baby girl in my arms, never get to tell her how much I already loved her, never get to be there for her when she thought the world was ending like mine was now.

Leaning back against the wall, I flicked the lock, and the door burst open, revealing a distraught Jenner.

He took one look at my tear-streaked face and closed his eyes, pain lacing his words. "Oh, Evie."

How could I live with myself knowing that I'd done this to him? That I was the one dragging him down? Again.

It was more than any single person should have to bear.

Turning on his heel, he moved to the sink, and the sound of running water filled the room. When it stopped, Jenner reappeared, dropping to his knees before pulling me into his arms. The rough pads of his fingertips grazed my neck as he swept my hair to the side before placing a damp paper towel over my clammy skin.

"I've got you," he whispered into my hair.

I was a mess, and he deserved someone better, someone stronger. But I'd made Jenner a promise—I wasn't leaving again. Truthfully, with a broken heart, I simply didn't have the strength, even if that's what I wanted, which I didn't.

But it didn't stop me from feeling guilty that we'd ended up right back in the same place after all these years. With me broken and him stuck taking care of me.

For days, I lay in bed, practically in a catatonic state, staring at a wall in the master suite as the minutes ticked by, forced to relive the worst moment of my life.

The only time Jenner left me was to go the rink when he needed to for practice or games. I knew he was suffering, too, but I didn't have the capacity to see beyond myself at the moment.

Life felt meaningless. I mean, what was the point?

Some might argue that I was loved by a man utterly devoted to me and condemn my selfishness. Hell, if my head weren't so fucked up, I would probably agree with them. Jenner was everything a girl could want, but I'd had my heart set on this beautiful picture of a family that would never come to be.

His face appeared before me one day, and he brushed away the tangled strands of blonde hair that had fallen into my eyes. "Hey." I didn't respond. "As much as I hate to leave you like this, the team is headed on the road. It's only a couple of days, over to Detroit and Pittsburgh. Dakota's gonna pop over and check on you while I'm gone." Jenner sighed. "And when I get back, I think we need to discuss getting you some help. I love you too much to see you like this, Evie. We'll figure this whole thing out, I promise."

I only blinked at him in response.

I didn't need help. I needed our baby girl.

Jenner tried calling while he was gone, but I declined every single attempt.

What was there to say to each other? He'd warned me from the start that this was a terrible idea—lying about our marital status—but being the good guy he was, he'd gone along with it anyway. And that's why I'd come back; I'd known he couldn't tell me no. The one time he had, I'd left him.

He'd kept his word to have Dakota stop by to check on me, but I couldn't force myself out of bed. Using the app on my phone connected to the doorbell camera, I told her I wasn't in the mood for visitors. But that didn't stop her from trying to bring me food twice a day.

I felt empty and hollow, and my heart ached.

I couldn't sleep because, every time I closed my eyes, I was forced to relive the moment when we were told it was over—that we would never be parents.

For hours a day, I simply stared at the lock screen on my phone. It featured an ultrasound picture of that beautiful baby girl we'd thought for a short time would be ours forever.

When my battery died, I didn't bother getting up to recharge it, deciding that it was time to let go. Obsessing over what would never come to be would only serve to drive me insane.

On the bright side, that meant I didn't have to feel like a selfish bitch when Jenner called and I didn't answer.

Why would he still want to be with me after all I'd done? I had thrown his life into chaos more than once, and instead of running screaming, he chose to double down, time after time.

I couldn't give him a baby, and now he'd have to deal with my mental health issues. I was some prize, that's for sure.

The doorbell rang, and I groaned. It was likely Dakota with a dinner drop attempt, but I couldn't send her away without my phone. And since that was what she'd come to expect, if I didn't answer at all, she would worry, call Jenner, and he'd send in the cavalry—which, in this case, meant my mom. That was the last thing I needed to deal with right now.

Mentally preparing to haul my ass out of bed, I took a deep breath. My nose wrinkled, catching a whiff of my been-in-bed-for-a-week-and-haven't-showered smell. Maybe that would be enough to scare Dakota away, and she wouldn't come back. I mean, a girl could hope.

Pushing up on my elbows, I swung my legs over the edge of the mattress. My vision blurred when I sat up, but a quick shake of my head cleared it.

You can do this. Get up, tell her, "Thanks, but no thanks," and then you can get back in bed.

My feet touched the cool wood floor, and I stood. I was steady for the first two steps, but then the room began to spin, and I faltered, reaching blindly for something to stabilize me. I caught nothing but air as darkness crept into the corners of my vision.

Vaguely aware that I was falling, I felt no pain as unconsciousness pulled me under.

Chapter 23

Jenner

Straight to voicemail. Again.

Frustrated, I threw my phone into the stall assigned to me inside the visiting locker room deep within Lakers Arena in Detroit.

Evie had completely drawn in on herself after the agency cut ties with us, effectively ending our pending adoption. I couldn't reach her. And I didn't just mean on the phone. She was so deep inside her grief that she wouldn't let me in—wouldn't let me help her.

God, it killed me to see the light dimmed from her eyes. She'd lost the will to fight, which scared the living daylights out of me.

In the back of my mind, I couldn't help but wonder if she'd give up on us next. Because without the possibility of getting a baby, she didn't need me anymore. Love hadn't been enough to make her stay the first time.

"You okay, Captain?" Braxton eyed me.

"Not really." I ran a hand over my beard.

"Worried about Evie?"

"Yeah. Her phone's been off all day."

Braxton and Dakota were the only ones I'd told what happened. Usually, Maddox was my go-to confidante, but in this case, I wasn't in the right headspace to hear him say, "I told you so." He'd been against deceiving the adoption agency from the start, warning that it was going to blow up in our faces.

An added benefit of opting for my younger teammate was that his girl was back in Indy and could check up on Evie while the team was on the road. Not that Dakota had gotten my wife to open the door, but at least she'd reported back that Evie had at least spoken to her, which meant she hadn't run.

Braxton gave me a sympathetic smile. "Dakota will be headed over there soon, and the good news is we'll be home tonight, and you can check on her yourself."

"Yeah," I agreed, but something in my gut warned that there was more to it than a turned-off phone.

Over the years, I'd gotten good at compartmentalizing my private life while on the ice, and tonight was no exception.

I was fucking buzzing out there. Every time my skates touched the ice, adrenaline surged in my veins, and I pushed harder, outmaneuvering the defenders for the Michigan Lakers with ease. They couldn't stop me as I got low to avoid their checks and squeezed around them, leaving them hustling to catch up as I barrelled toward their goalie.

Suddenly, it was just me and Braxton. The puck was on my stick, and my eyes slid over to track his movements. He matched me stride for stride, and

I knew he'd be ready. We'd practiced this a million times; the only wild card was Byers in the net and his reaction to our play.

My job was to get him out of position so Braxton could have the easy score. I had to make Byers believe I was the one who was going to shoot, get him to forget about my center waiting at the back door with no one to defend him.

As I got closer, Byers backed into the net, trying to predict where I was planning to place the puck so he could block it. Pulling my stick back, I gave the appearance of readying to take a shot, and he squared up, dropping into a butterfly and raising his glove.

Fuck, he made this so goddamn easy that I almost laughed.

Instead of shooting straight at him, I slid the puck over to Braxton, who held his stick hard on the ice. A tiny tap the second the rubber disc hit his blade, and it was headed straight for the wide-open net. Byers realized his mistake too late, extending his glove hand to stop it, but it had already popped the netting.

Braxton whooped, throwing both hands in the air, and I rushed over to wrap him up in a bear hug as the rest of our teammates on the ice crowded around us in celebration.

"Like taking candy from a baby!" Logan Ford, our defenseman, shouted, and that took the wind right out of my sails.

It was all the reminder I needed that I was out here playing a fucking game while my wife's whole world was falling apart.

There had to be a way to fix this. And I was going to find it.

"Jenner, can you tell us what happened out there?"

Stripped down to my skintight base layer, I wiped the sweat from my forehead before shoving my Speed ballcap on backward. The media was a necessary evil postgame, and usually, after a win, I was happy to answer their questions. But tonight, I barely managed to suffer through it, only focused on getting home to my wife.

"Care to expand on that question?" I asked the male reporter, who had his phone set to record shoved in my face.

"There was a noticeable shift in your energy level after the goal you assisted on to Braxton Slate."

I gritted my teeth. "Not sure what you're talking about." I was well aware that had been a turning point because my mind couldn't focus on the game. Before he could press further, I snapped, "I'm happy to answer questions about the *team* play tonight in our victory over the Lakers. As you pointed out, I played a key role in assisting Braxton with what turned out to be the game-winning goal. I'm not sure we need to deep dive into every shift played on the ice, do you?"

That had him zipping his lips and retracting his phone.

Good. Maybe the others would take the hint.

"If you don't want to talk about your piss-poor performance after playing the hero, why don't you share with our friends how your adoption is going?"

My head whipped to the side so fast I heard something in my neck pop. When I caught the smirk on Saint Booker's face three stalls down, I saw red. "The fuck did you just say?"

Bristol's soft voice called out from the back of the press pack in warning, "Jenner—"

I held up my hand to cut her off, eyes narrowing on Booker.

"Oops." He raised a hand to cover his mouth, pretending to play coy. "Was I not supposed to share that? Was it a secret?"

Suddenly, I was standing, the pieces clicking into place—the anonymous tip. But I still didn't understand why.

"It was you?"

Saint cocked his head to the side. "What's wrong, Cap? Trouble in paradise?"

Fists clenching in rage, I closed the gap between us, getting in his face. "You better start fucking talking."

Maniacal laughter burst from his lips. "Your wife messed with the wrong girl. Even I'm not dumb enough to get on Jules's bad side."

Jules. That was his girlfriend, Juliana. I knew she and Evie had never gotten along, but what the hell did this have to do with our adoption falling apart?

Before I could ask, Saint volunteered the information. "Guess they had a little run-in a few weeks back. Jules found Evie and her little posse planning a bridal shower for Coach's girl and offered her assistance. But instead of playing nice, they froze her out, telling her to take a hike. She hung around, out of sight, and when your wife excused herself to go to the bathroom, that's when it got real juicy."

Growling, I gripped the front of his shirt, but he remained unphased.

"While she was gone, the others started talking about throwing a surprise baby shower for your wife. That was the first Jules had heard about you two having a baby, but with Evie being a bigger girl, it became one of those questions—is she just fat, or is she pregnant?"

I swear to God, I was going to tear him apart with my bare hands.

"But it didn't quite add up when she watched them order a round of mimosas. So Jules did a little digging, only to find out that our beloved captain and his wife were in the market to adopt. But that's where it hit a snag. She uncovered that our golden boy had lied about his relationship with his estranged wife—or ex-wife, in this case—to apply. She couldn't in good conscience allow some poor, unsuspecting woman to give up her baby to such an immoral couple."

This motherfucker's girl had blown up our lives because of petty jealousy over team social status?

That knowledge tipped me over the edge, and I couldn't hold back any longer.

Releasing my grasp on his shirt, I pulled back my fist and clocked him square in the jaw. When it didn't provide any relief or satisfaction, I did it again.

Saint stumbled back, falling onto his ass on the seat of his stall. Murderous intent filled his blue eyes, and he pounced, knocking me off balance until we crashed onto the locker room floor, a tangle of limbs as we wrestled for position to beat the shit out of one another.

I was deaf to the commotion around us; my focus narrowed on making Saint pay.

"Hey! Break it up!" a voice boomed in the small space as hands pulled us apart.

My chest heaved, anger still consuming me, as I fought against whomever held me back.

"Let me go!" I screamed.

Maddox's scowling face filled my vision. "Not until you tell me why my captain is attacking his teammate."

"Me?" My eyes widened at the accusation that I was the one in the wrong. I reached around his massive frame to point my finger at Saint. "That asshole fucked with my family!"

Shocked, Maddox spun around, asking Saint, "What's he talking about?"

The cocky fucker simply shrugged, a smirk on his busted-up face.

Peeking back at me with an eye roll, Maddox said, "If he doesn't want to share his side of the story, I can't help him. Why don't you explain, then?"

There was a dull throbbing beneath my eye, and I hissed when I darted my tongue out, tasting blood where my lip was split. But nothing hurt more than my heart, knowing I'd failed Evie. I was the one who'd put her in Juliana's orbit when I insisted she attend games so we could be seen as a couple. If I hadn't . . . maybe we would still be on track, excited about impending parenthood.

Maddox must have seen the despair on my face because he gripped my bicep, ushering me from the room.

He found an unoccupied training room and sealed us inside.

Sighing, he ran a hand through his dark hair. "What's going on?"

Dropping my gaze to the floor, I whispered, "They found out."

His confusion was audible. "Who found out what?"

"The adoption agency. Called us in last week to tell us they knew our paperwork wasn't above board and killed the adoption."

Maddox sucked in a sharp breath. "Shit."

I dared to peek up at him, confessing, "Evie's a fucking mess, man. She's been in bed for days, won't talk to me, won't eat, won't sleep. I've tried calling her this whole time we've been gone, but she won't pick up. Dakota's been going over a couple of times a day to check on her, but she won't answer the door. It's like her heart has been ripped right out of her chest, and she doesn't know how to go on."

"Jenner, I'm sorry." His words were genuine, even if he'd cautioned us this would happen from the start.

"And if that wasn't bad enough, Saint fucking Booker saw fit to taunt me in front of the press. Come to find out, his girlfriend was the anonymous tip the agency received, telling them to dig deeper into our relationship. All because the girls wouldn't let her help plan Bristol's bridal shower."

My best friend's chest rumbled. "I should've let you kill him."

I blew out a heavy breath. "I'm glad you didn't. He's not worth it. The only thing I care about is getting home to her, so can we wrap this up and get on the road?"

Maddox nodded. "Yeah. You let me handle Saint. I've been sick of his shit for a while, but you don't fuck with your own teammates. I'm willing to bet I can get him to waive his non-trade clause by the end of the week."

"If I never see his face again, it'll be too soon," I muttered.

Tilting his head toward the closed door, he said, " Let's get you out of here and cleaned up. It's time to go home."

What did it say about me that I was terrified of what awaited me when I got there?

Every light was off when I arrived home. If Evie hadn't gotten out of bed, as I suspected, it wasn't much of a surprise.

There had been a moment of anxiety when I pushed the button on my garage door remote, but it vanished quickly when I saw her car parked in its usual spot. In the state I'd left her, it would have come as a hell of a shock that she had found the strength to get out of bed and drive anywhere, let alone back to Oklahoma as she'd done before. But I wasn't sure I would ever shake the fear that one day she would just vanish.

Moving through the quiet house, I made a beeline for the master suite. I didn't bother to stop to take off my suit jacket or shoes. Checking on Evie was my top priority.

Pushing into our bedroom, I froze. The covers were flat on the bed, indicating she wasn't in it.

Fear skittered down my spine, and I turned to check the bathroom. When that search came up empty, I dared to call out, "Evie?"

I was met with only silence in response.

Fuck. I should've never left her in the state she was in.

Stepping further into the bedroom, I was headed to check the walk-in closet next. The unimaginable began creeping into my brain when I saw it around the corner of the bed—Evie's limp hand lying along the hardwood floor.

My heart dropped to my stomach.

"Shit."

My feet couldn't move fast enough to get to her. When her unconscious body came into view, limbs splayed awkwardly, I dropped to my knees, cupping her face.

"Evie, baby. Wake up," I begged, desperate for her to open her eyes. "Please." That last word came out strangled.

Torn between needing to keep my hold on her and calling for help, I finally managed to reach a hand into my pocket and pull out my cell. Typing in the three numbers kids were taught at an early age to memorize, I pressed the speaker function before tossing it onto the floor.

When the call connected, a female voice spoke clearly on the other side of the line. "9-1-1, what's your emergency?"

"My wife," I rasped, emotion making it hard to speak. "She's unconscious."

"Okay, sir," the reassuring voice said in response. "Do you know how long it's been since she lost consciousness?"

I shook my head, even though I knew the dispatcher couldn't see me. "No. I just got home and found her like this."

"Can you check to see if she has a pulse?"

My blood ran cold, but I forced my hand to move from her cheek to press two fingers below her jaw. Relief washed over me at the faint pulsing I felt beneath her pale skin.

"Yes, but it's not very strong."

"I'm sending an ambulance. Can you confirm your address?"

"It's 528 Poplar Lane."

"Great. There's one in the area, and it should be arriving in less than five minutes. I'm going to stay on the line with you until they get there, okay?"

I swallowed against the lump in my throat. "Okay."

"The more information the EMTs have, the better. Can you tell me if you notice any signs of head trauma on your wife?"

My fingers grazed over Evie's soft face. "No, but she did take a hit to the head a little over a week ago. She was cleared of a concussion at the time and hasn't shown any symptoms since that would suggest the doctor who checked her over was wrong in his assessment."

"Good. How about any underlying health conditions?"

"No, nothing."

"Medications she's currently taking?"

I paused, eyes flicking to the bathroom, where I knew there were leftover pain meds from past injuries I'd incurred on the ice.

Slamming my eyes shut, I admitted to the woman on the phone, "Not that I know of, but she has a history of depression and was in the midst of a bad bout of it before I left on a work trip."

"Do you think she might've taken something?" There was no judgment in her tone. She was simply trying to gather facts.

"I don't want to think so, but in her current mental state, I can't be sure."

I was wound so tight I nearly jumped out of my skin when there was a heavy pounding on the front door.

"I think the ambulance is here," I breathed out.

Calmly, the dispatcher explained, "I know it's difficult, but you're going to have to leave her to answer the door. They can't help her if you don't."

The last thing I wanted to do was relinquish my hold on Evie, but I knew she needed the help of the EMTs.

Kissing her forehead, I whispered, "I'll be right back, baby."

Running down the steps, I flung open the door before turning on my heel and sprinting back up without a word to the two men waiting on the other side. They wouldn't have been called if it wasn't an emergency and would figure it out.

Following behind me, they stepped inside our bedroom, kneeling to check on Evie.

The first one asked, "You found her like this?"

"Yes."

The second one studied me instead of focusing his attention on my wife like his colleague. "What happened to you?"

"What?" His question didn't make any sense.

He tapped two fingers below his eye. "Your face."

Shit. Everything that had happened tonight prior to walking into this room had been forgotten the moment I found Evie lying there.

Not only did the memories come rushing back, but so did the pulsing pain beneath my eye socket, which had only been made worse in a pressurized airplane cabin. I probably looked like I'd gone a few rounds with a heavyweight champion versus an asshole who'd landed two punches.

"Got in a fight," I mumbled.

EMT Number Two's eyebrows rose. "With her?" His gaze darted to my unconscious wife.

"No!" I yelled before realizing that raising my voice wouldn't make my statement any more believable. Shaking my head, I explained, "I play hockey."

EMT Number One rolled his eyes before chastising his partner. "Jesus, Kyle. You don't recognize him? He's the freaking captain of the Indy Speed, for Christ's sake."

"Sorry," EMT Number Two—Kyle—said. "I had to ask."

I ran a hand down my face. "Yeah. I get it. How about you worry a little less about me and a little more about my wife?"

He nodded. "Stay with her. We're going back down for the stretcher, and we will be right back."

I barely noticed the two men leaving but heard the wheels of the portable bed upon their return.

It took some coaxing for me to move back enough to allow them to maneuver her onto the stretcher, hook her up to monitors, and then work together to carry the whole setup down the stairs. I trailed them helplessly, barely managing to lock the front door before climbing into the back of the ambulance with the EMT delegated to care for patients during transport to the hospital.

He locked the stretcher in place and tapped on the partition between the back and the cab to let the driver know we were ready. I flinched when the siren blared, and the vehicle lurched forward, speeding down the quiet suburban streets.

Throughout the drive, I leaned forward to stroke Evie's hair, whispering that everything would be okay, hating that I didn't know if I was feeding her lies.

We came to a stop outside the emergency room of the nearest hospital, and the back doors of the ambulance swung open. The EMTs moved the stretcher onto solid ground before rushing her into the building. I had to run to keep up as they relayed all the information they'd gathered so far to a team of waiting doctors.

They pushed through a set of doors leading to the back of the unit, and when I went to follow, a woman in scrubs stepped in my path. "Sir, you can't go back there."

I gestured a hand toward where they walked further away with Evie. "That's my wife."

She gave me a small smile, nodding. "I understand that. If you can give me her name, I'll make sure someone comes out to brief you on her status."

"I need to be with her." My voice weakened, knowing that even if I tried to plow through the woman half my size, she'd call for security, and then I would never get near Evie.

"I know it's hard," she replied. "But in order to help her, our team needs to be able to focus, and it's difficult to do that with a panicked spouse in the room."

"Evie," I said hoarsely. "Her name is Evangeline Knight. Just please help her," I begged.

"We'll do everything we can for her," she promised before turning and heading toward where they'd taken Evie.

Desperation clawed up my throat as I collapsed outside the swinging doors where the love of my life had disappeared.

I couldn't lose her. Not like this.

Chapter 24

Jenner

"Knight?" a voice called out into the waiting room.

Shoving off the chair I'd been sitting in, I practically ran to the doctor in scrubs and a white overcoat, who was holding a tablet.

Placing a hand over my chest, I breathed out, "I'm Evie's husband. Is she okay?"

He nodded. "She's stable."

I slumped against the nearest wall, almost unable to remain standing as relief at his words rushed over me. "Thank God."

"If you want to follow me, I can take you to the room we've moved her to, and we can discuss her condition."

"Yes, of course." Pushing off the wall, I followed him through the double doors and into the area I'd previously been barred from entering.

We moved through several corridors until we reached a room with a cracked-open door. From where I stood, I could tell the lights inside were dimmed.

Turning to face the doctor, I gave him an expectant look, ready for him to share what he knew about what had happened to Evie.

Instead, he huffed out a small laugh. "Sorry. I just have to say I am a huge fan."

For the love of God. Is this guy for real? Does he not realize now's not the time?

Not wanting to seem ungrateful for the care he and his team had provided my wife, I gave him a tight smile. "Thank you."

"Seriously, my whole den is decked out in Indy Speed red and black. I think this year could be our year."

My patience was barely hanging on by a thread, and it took everything in me to keep my tone level. "I appreciate the support. But right now, my wife is my sole focus, as I'm sure you can understand."

The ER doctor seemed to remember where he was and nodded. "Right. Of course." He tapped on the tablet he held. "Her toxicology report came back clean, so we can rule out any kind of self-induced overdose, which I believe was a concern?"

Nodding, I swallowed. I hated that my mind had even gone there, but she'd been in such a bad place when I left that I couldn't be sure.

"Since she was alone when she lost consciousness, we also made sure to run a CT scan to rule out any head trauma. It came back negative."

Folding my arms over my chest, I said, "All I'm hearing is what's *not* wrong with her. Have you managed to figure out why she passed out? And is she awake yet?"

The doctor shook his head. "She's still unconscious, but there's nothing to suggest that she won't come around soon. From what we can tell, your wife is extremely dehydrated. It's possible she experienced a sudden drop in blood pressure, which caused the fainting episode."

Okay, that made sense. She'd been in bed for a week and had refused most offerings of food or drink. As soon as she was discharged, I'd be forced to make some hard choices about her care. There was only so much I could do on my own, and maybe it was in her best interest to be checked into an in-patient facility—somewhere they'd have eyes on her 24/7—at least until her mental state improved enough that I didn't have to worry about leaving her alone.

"Has her morning sickness been severe?"

The question was like a bucket of ice water being dumped over my head, and I jolted. "Excuse me?"

Almost as if he hadn't heard my request for clarification, he continued, "I'm going to have OB come down and check on her, see if they want to admit her for observation. Then—"

I held a hand up, cutting him off. "You need to back it up a step. I think you have the wrong patient."

The doctor frowned, peeking down at the tablet. "No. It says right here: Evangeline Knight. Is that not correct?"

"Yes, but you're talking about morning sickness and an OB. You must have made an error because my wife can't get pregnant."

"Her HCG levels would suggest otherwise," he countered. "In fact, they're so high, I'd say she's pretty far along. Nearing her second trimester if I had to guess."

"Sec—" The words died on my tongue. After all this time? There was no way. I simply couldn't believe what he was telling me.

Clearing my throat, I found my voice again, leveling the doctor with a glare. "You better be fucking sure before I walk into that room and tell my wife that what she's struggled for years to achieve has suddenly become a reality. She won't survive a false positive."

He nodded in understanding but didn't waver. "Blood tests don't lie, Mr. Knight. And like I said, I plan to make a call to OB, and we can have them confirm."

"So she's—" I paused, taking a deep breath with my eyes closed, almost afraid to say the words. "She's really pregnant?"

"It would seem so, and I'm guessing by your reaction, this news is coming as a surprise?"

I scoffed. "Surprise is an understatement. You have no idea the hell we've been through."

He offered me a smile. "Glad to see it's a happy surprise, then. Shall we go in and see her?"

In a daze, I nodded, allowing him to push through the door ahead of me.

Light from the bright hallway behind us illuminated the room, and I caught my first sight of Evie since I'd watched them wheel her away. She looked so weak and helpless, lying there in a hospital bed, hooked up to all kinds of monitors.

When her soft moan reached my ears and her head shifted on the pillow, I rushed to her bedside, grasping her hand with both of mine and squeezing. "Hey, baby. Can you hear me?"

"Jenner?" she rasped, her voice barely audible.

"It's me. Can you open your eyes for me?"

Evie's lips turned down in a frown, but her eyelashes fluttered against her cheeks before violet eyes peered at me from beneath heavy lids.

"There she is." Tears fell freely down my face. I'd been so fucking scared when I found her, worried I'd never get the chance to tell her how much I loved her, how she was my world, and that she would always be enough for me.

She tugged her hand out of my hold, reaching up to cup my cheek. "What happened to you? You're hurt."

I shook my head. "Don't worry about me. I'm fine."

Her eyes flitted about the room. "Where am I?"

"The hospital. When I got home, you were passed out on the bedroom floor. I didn't know what had happened."

Evie placed her free palm against her head. "I remember the doorbell ringing. My phone was dead, so I got up. Then everything went dark."

The doctor cleared his throat, and her eyes snapped to him standing at the foot of her bed. "You gave your husband quite a scare, Mrs. Knight."

Flicking her gaze to me, she asked, "When can we go home? I don't want to be here."

"Soon, I promise. They, um, they want to run some more tests."

"Why?"

I turned my face into her palm, kissing it gently, trying to work up the nerve to tell her what the doctor had told me in the hallway.

"Evie, baby—" My voice broke, and I couldn't force myself to say the words. I still couldn't believe it was true, and I wouldn't survive watching her heart break again if it wasn't.

"Jenner." Her lower lip trembled. "You're scaring me. What's wrong?"

When I peeked at the doctor, he nodded, so I turned back to my wife.

"They think you're pregnant."

Her eyes went wide, and she jolted in bed. "What? No. That's—that's not possible."

"Mrs. Knight." The doctor stepped in. "When you came in, we ran standard blood tests, which came back showing a significant level of the pregnancy hormone, HCG. Judging from those numbers, you're several months pregnant."

Evie shook her head. "No, that can't be right. I've had regular periods."

"It's possible you were experiencing breakthrough bleeding, which is very common early in pregnancy."

Whisper-quiet, she said, "But I can't get pregnant. We tried." Her eyes squeezed shut, and her voice wavered as she added, "So many times."

"I won't pretend to know your exact circumstances. All I can tell you is what the results of our testing uncovered. Fertility is a tricky business, and you never know what's going to shift the odds in your favor."

Evie peeked at me before asking the doctor, "I've lost some weight since the last time we tried. Could that have helped?"

He nodded. "It's entirely possible."

"Is this real?" she asked in disbelief.

Honestly, I still couldn't wrap my mind around it either.

"I'm going to have OB pop down to do an ultrasound. That will help determine exactly how far along you are and set your minds at ease that this is really happening." The doctor tapped the foot of the bed. "But let me be the first to offer my congratulations."

I wasn't leaving Evie's side, so I nodded my thanks as the ER doctor left the room.

The minute he was gone, I broke down. Burying my face against Evie's soft waist, I wept. It was all too much, and I couldn't hold it in any longer.

What if I'd lost her tonight? What if I'd lost both of them if there truly was a baby?

Having her walk away was one thing. At least I'd known she was safe. But the thought of living in a world she wasn't in? It was too much to bear.

In a complete role reversal after the years I'd been her strength in the storm, Evie ran her fingers through my hair. "I'm okay, Jenner. I'm right here."

I clutched her closer, pressing my ear to her chest, comforted by the sound of her beating heart.

"I was so scared, baby," I admitted.

"I know, and I'm sorry I put you through that."

Peering up, I wiped beneath my nose with the back of my hand. "I'm the one who should be sorry. I should've never left you."

"You had to go."

"No. You were in no state to be left alone. If I'd been there . . ." My words trailed off.

Evie sighed. "Honey, you were there. For days. And it didn't make any difference. Because my heart stopped beating when we lost a chance to be that sweet girl's parents." Her fingertips ghosted over her lower abdomen. "And if there is a baby in here, it's not a replacement for what we lost. I'll never not think of what it could have been like to have her in our lives, to raise her as our own."

I nodded my agreement. "Me, too."

"Knock, knock!" A chipper voice sounded from the doorway, and I whipped my head around to find a woman in pink scrubs wheeling in an ultrasound machine.

This was it. The moment of truth. We were about to find out if, against all odds, we'd done what we once thought impossible—create a baby of our own.

"You must be Evie."

The woman gave my wife a bright smile. Hadn't anyone told her it was the middle of the night?

She placed a hand over her chest, introducing herself, "I'm Wendy, and if it's okay with you, I've come down here to check and see if we can get a peek at what's going on based on your blood tests."

Evie let out a heavy exhale; she was likely as nervous as I was. "Yeah, okay."

"Great." Wendy positioned the ultrasound machine on the opposite side of the bed from where I sat, before rolling over a stool from the corner of the room so she could take a seat.

She began typing on the keyboard attached to the wheeled cart.

"Let's see." Wendy hummed. "Do you know the date of your last period?"

Evie chewed her lower lip. "I had one only a couple of weeks ago. Does that mean . . ." The unspoken end of that sentence hung heavy in the air.

"That's okay. Try not to panic. Lots of women experience bleeding while pregnant that can mimic a period."

I was no expert when it came to the inner workings of the female body, but I knew that bleeding during pregnancy was cause for alarm, and dread settled like a rock in my gut.

"Since we're not certain how far along you are, we'll try to keep it minimally invasive and attempt an abdominal ultrasound first. If we can't get a clear picture, I'll switch to the transvaginal wand, as that's the best way to pick up on very early pregnancies."

Evie reached for my hand, and I threaded my fingers through hers as she responded, "Okay."

They must have changed Evie into a standard hospital gown at some point after her arrival because that's what she wore now as Wendy pulled the hem up from beneath the blankets to expose her soft belly.

Wendy noticed Evie's free hand trembling because she gave it a quick squeeze. "Deep breaths, mama. You got this."

Mama. We were only seconds away from discovering if we would become parents.

Gel was squeezed onto Evie's bare skin, and Wendy glided a wand through it, her eyes trained on the screen turned in her direction.

"There you are, little one."

Those words had the breath freezing in my lungs, and Evie let out the tiniest whimper.

"There's really a baby?" I dared to ask.

Wendy nodded. "You bet. Why don't you take a look for yourself." She grabbed the side of the screen, but just as she was about to turn it around, she paused. "Wait a minute."

"Jenner." Evie sobbed my name, but it barely broke through the haze of panic buzzing in my ears.

My head dropped to the side of the bed, and I silently prayed to whomever was up there that this wouldn't be ripped away from us. We'd been through so much already; couldn't they see we were due for a break, for fate to turn in our favor for once?

"Sneaky little bugger," Wendy said, amusement lacing her words.

Peeking up, I saw the moment she turned the screen around, showing not one but two wiggling forms in black and white.

Evie gasped. "There's two?"

Wendy's smile grew wide as she pointed to one of the babies. "This one was hiding, which is quite impressive for this gestational age. If there's more than one, I should have been able to see it right away at fifteen weeks."

My jaw dropped. "Did you say *fifteen* weeks?"

"Mmhmm," she confirmed.

Evie found her voice next. "That's almost four months! There's no way." She glanced in my direction. "That would have been . . ."

Wendy cut in. "Well, the first two weeks are technically before conception occurs, so if you're looking to do some quick math, these little ones came to be about thirteen weeks ago. That puts you at sometime around early November."

I locked eyes with my wife, and color rose to her cheeks. She was thinking the same thing that I was. The timing lined up with when we'd physically reconnected—first in the kitchen and then with her bent over the edge of the couch.

"Well, I'll be damned," I whispered, staring in awe at the two babies on the screen. Swallowing, I asked Wendy, "Are they—are they healthy?"

"As far as I can tell," she replied. "I am going to recommend you call your own OB tomorrow and schedule a follow-up once you're discharged, since a twin pregnancy is automatically designated as high-risk, and you'll need extra monitoring. If you can promise me that, I'll see what I can do about them letting you go home as soon as your IV drip finishes."

"Yes, we can do that." Evie nodded.

"I want you to take it easy for a few days. Hydrate, and if you can manage it, small frequent meals. Nothing too strenuous activity-wise until we can be certain you won't pass out again, okay?"

"I'll make sure of it," I vowed.

Wendy removed the wand and wiped the gel from Evie's belly. "Perfect. I'll print some pictures of these little buddies and then talk to the doctor handling your chart. Hopefully, we can have you home before lunchtime."

Evie shifted the fabric of the hospital gown down to cover herself, and I reached over to take the offered pictures of our babies as Wendy congratulated us and left the room.

"Jenner. There's two of them."

"Uh-huh." I couldn't stop staring at their tiny little bodies.

"Two," Evie repeated.

"Yeah." I had whiplash from the emotional roller coaster of the past few hours.

"What are we going to do with two of them?" Her voice rose in panic, and I forced myself to drag my eyes away from the images of our babies.

"Hey, hey, hey." I placed the strip of photos across her legs before settling onto the bed beside her, stroking my thumbs over her cheeks as I cradled her face. "It's going to be okay."

"How?" She held up two fingers for emphasis. "Two."

I bit back a chuckle. "Don't you see, honey? We wanted it so badly for so long that when it finally happened, we were rewarded with a two-for-one special."

"But—but—but—" Her chest heaved with each attempt to formulate her rebuttal.

"It's a lot, I know. But we can handle it. Together. Okay?" I tried to reassure her the best I could, but I knew her mind was racing.

"Are you sure?" Evie's voice trembled.

"I've never been more certain of anything in my life," I promised. Reaching down, I grabbed the pictures, bringing them into view. "Look at them. They're beautiful. And they're ours. Made with love." I let out a shaky breath. "I love you so fucking much, Evie."

Tears leaked from her eyes, and she nodded. "I love you, too."

"We'll figure everything else out. I don't want you to worry. All your focus should go into taking care of yourself so you can grow our babies." My hand automatically came to rest over her belly, where our children were hidden from the world.

"Our babies," she whispered, tracing a fingertip over the outline of first one, then the other.

"We're going to have the family we always wanted, baby. You and me, and these two little ones."

Years of heartbreak had led us to this hard-earned moment, and I had every intention of making the most of it.

Chapter 25
Jenner

I'd briefed Maddox on the situation before we left the hospital, and he had told me not to worry about anything other than taking care of my family. The Speed would survive without me for a few games, and he would handle the press.

When we got home, I found myself constantly answering the door to accept deliveries of flowers or food from various members of the team. They'd all sent their well wishes via text, offering support in any way we might need while Evie regained her strength and we wrapped our heads around our new reality.

Evie was settled on the couch, bundled up in a pile of blankets, watching sitcom reruns before a roaring fire in the living room, when the doorbell rang for at least the twentieth time that day.

"You'd think they'd coordinate and spread it out over a few days," I grumbled as I trudged to the door. "There's no way we can eat all this food before it goes bad, even if she is eating for three."

Flinging the door wide, arms ready to accept whatever item had been sent by my teammates this time, I nearly stumbled back in shock when I saw who waited on the other side.

"Paige?" I blinked to make sure I wasn't seeing things, but sure enough, a very pregnant teenage girl was standing on our doorstep.

"Um, hi." She shifted on her feet.

We stared at each other for a full minute, but when she shivered, I was jolted back to my senses. Stepping back from the doorframe, I made enough room to permit her entry. "Come in. It's freezing out there."

Timidly, Paige ducked her head, crossing the threshold.

I shut the door and turned around, leaning against it. "What are you doing here?" Then, a thought occurred to me, and I blurted, "Didn't the agency contact you?"

"They did." She nodded. "And I'm sorry if this isn't okay, but I didn't know what else to do."

"Jenner, what was it this time?" Evie's voice called from the living room.

Concern for my wife outweighed everything, and I worried that seeing Paige would send her into a tailspin. She was still mourning the loss of the baby girl Paige carried, even though we had two babies of our own on the way.

"The past week has been hard on Evie," I explained to the young girl. "If you tell me what you need, I can try to help."

Paige peeked over her shoulder toward where she'd heard my wife's voice. "I need to talk to you both. Please." Her blue eyes pleaded with me, and against my better judgment, I guided her through our home, coming to a stop once we reached Evie.

Eyes still locked on the screen above the mantle, Evie groaned. "Whatever it is, I can't eat another bite. I know they're trying to show how much they care about us, but half of what they sent over is going to go to waste."

"It's not food," I said.

"Oh Lord, they didn't take to sending stuffed animals, did they? I swear, if there's a life-sized teddy bear or other woodland creature, I won't feel the least bit bad donating it. We're going to have enough to deal with without that cluttering up the house."

"Evie. We have a guest."

"Who—" Her words halted when she turned her head and caught sight of the teen standing by my side. "Paige?" Evie sat up suddenly.

"Whoa." I placed a hand on her shoulder. "Take it easy, babe." My heart still hadn't quite recovered from last night and having her rushed to the hospital.

A sob sounded from my right, and I turned in time to watch Paige's face crumble as she broke down in tears.

"Oh, honey," Evie cooed. "Come here."

Paige ran around the edge of the couch, throwing herself into Evie's arms. My wife mothered the girl pressed against her chest so effortlessly, holding her close and whispering words of comfort. It came so naturally to her. Our kids had no idea that they had this incredible woman waiting to love them.

Feeling like I was intruding on a private moment, I stepped into the kitchen to grab both ladies a glass of water. Evie's hydration was at the forefront of my mind after her fainting episode, and I wanted to minimize any risk for Paige as well.

Returning to the living room, I found them both sniffling, their eyes red-rimmed from crying. I set my offering of water on the coffee table and sat in a nearby chair.

Evie smoothed damp strands of strawberry blonde hair away from Paige's face. Sadness crept into her voice as she said to the girl, "As happy as I am to see you, I'm not sure you should be here."

Paige's lower lip trembled, and she nodded. "They told me not to contact you, but—but it didn't feel right. I needed to see you." Her eyes slid over to where I sat. "Both of you."

"I'm not sure what they told you—"

"They said you weren't fit to adopt! That I couldn't give you this baby." Paige's hands clutched at her swollen belly.

Evie squeezed her eyes shut. "I'm afraid it's a bit more complicated than that."

"I don't care!" Paige cried. "All I know is that she belongs with you guys."

Tears trailed down my wife's cheeks as she admitted, "I messed up, Paige. I'm the reason they're blocking our adoption. I lied on our forms, and they found out. I knew better, but I did it anyway. Because I wanted a baby so badly. And it was wrong."

"Lied? Lied how?"

Evie opened her mouth several times, never uttering a sound as she struggled to explain our deception.

"We were divorced when Evie applied," I offered.

Paige turned to face me, her blue eyes burning with questions. "I don't understand."

I took a deep breath. "You've read Evie's account of our infertility struggles." The teen nodded. "Well, there was a part of a story she purposely left out. Trying and failing to have a baby on our own was stressful, and it placed a strain on our marriage. I love Evie with everything I have, but she was suffering, placing blame on herself for our inability to conceive. Eventually, it became too much, and she needed to get away. Letting her go is the biggest regret of my entire life."

She frowned. "You said you *were* divorced. Does that mean you're married now?"

"Yes," I confirmed. "Evie tried to adopt on her own during our time apart but wasn't successful in getting herself listed in any agency's catalog as a single woman. Out of options, she applied using her married name, attaching our original marriage certificate. When they accepted her—us, really—she found her way back up to Indy, and that's when I found out about the whole thing. I agreed to go along with it because I knew how much becoming a mother meant to her, but she doesn't know I had ulterior motives."

"You did?" Evie asked.

My vision honed in on the woman I'd loved since I was nineteen. "I saw your return to my life as a gift, one I wasn't going to take for granted. That's why I laid out my conditions. I wanted you so tangled up with me that it would be damn near impossible to separate us. My greatest mistake was letting you go, and I was determined to keep you for good this time."

To Paige, I said, "We were remarried about six weeks before we met you."

"And the agency found out." Evie's voice broke on that admission.

The girl looked between us, declaring, "I don't care."

"What?" I wasn't sure if I was asking for clarification or for her to say it again.

"I don't care," she repeated. "The timing, the legalities—none of it matters to me. I chose you. You are who I want to raise her. I don't want to pick another couple." Paige peeked down at her bump. "If you haven't noticed, I'm kinda running out of time, and I refuse to hand her over to the state, having no say in where she's placed. But I can't keep her. I can't. *Please.*" That last word dripped with desperation.

Evie reached out to grasp Paige's hand. "Honey, I'm sorry, but it's not up to us."

Paige gestured around the room. "You guys are rich, right? Can't you make it happen? Take the adoption private? Without the agency?"

I let out a sigh. "We could . . . but there's something else we need to tell you."

Concern filled her young face. "Okay . . ."

"Evie's pregnant."

Paige's face fell as that truth sank in. "Oh. I see." She stood, stepping away from the couch. "I'm sorry I came here and bothered you both." Her gaze flicked to Evie. "I'm so happy for you."

When she turned toward the door, a single word caught my attention. "Jenner."

Evie's pale purple eyes pleaded with me, and I knew I was a goner.

Twenty-four hours ago, our plans for the future were in shambles.

We'd spent months planning for one baby—the one tucked safely inside Paige's belly—only to have that dream ripped away. Then, we'd gotten the surprise of a lifetime, finding out that after years of trying, we were set to become biological parents to not just one but two babies that Evie was carrying.

It would be sheer insanity to double down and accept Paige's offer to adopt her baby. Doing so would mean three babies separated by, at most, four months if Evie managed to make it full-term with the twins.

But my one design flaw was that I'd never been able to say no to my wife, and I wasn't about to start now. That baby girl was already ours in her mind, and I'd been witness to the devastation it caused when she thought we'd lost her.

Rising to my feet, I called out to the retreating form of the girl carrying our daughter. "Paige, wait."

The teenager turned around slowly, fresh tear tracks staining her pretty face.

"I think we can make this work." Hope lit in her eyes at my words. "On one condition."

"Jenner . . ." Evie warned, having been on the receiving end of my "conditions" before.

I held up my hand, letting her know I had this.

"I'm listening," Paige said, stepping closer.

I knew it was a risk, but it was one I was willing to take.

"You become a part of our family." Evie's soft gasp reached my ears. "You're giving us a piece of yourself, entrusting it to our care, so I think that entitles you to a permanent place in our lives."

Paige's pale red eyebrows drew down. "But I want you to be her parents."

"And we will be," I agreed. "But I'm a firm believer that a child can never have too many people in their life who love them. We can work out the details later on how we want to handle your role, but I think I can speak for both myself and Evie when I say we don't want to say goodbye once the adoption is finalized. I can understand if this is too much for you, and if you want, we can limit your interactions to, say, maybe only her birthday and Christmas. But she should know where she comes from and know you loved her enough to give her the best possible life, even if it wasn't with you."

Chewing on her lower lip, Paige mulled over my offer.

Finally, she hedged, "If I agree, you'll take her?"

Peeking back at Evie to make sure this was what she wanted, she only offered me a tiny nod before crying out, "Yes!" and jumping up from the couch and rushing over to pull Paige into a hug.

I jolted seeing her move so quickly. These next few months were going to be stressful, making sure she stayed safe while pregnant.

When they broke apart, Paige peeked down at Evie's belly. Four months along with twins, you couldn't tell she was pregnant yet, but I had a feeling that when they wanted their presence to be known, she'd pop overnight, and I couldn't fucking wait.

"And she's going to be a big sister?" Paige touched her bump.

"She's got her work cut out for her." I chuckled.

"What do you mean?" Her forehead wrinkled.

Evie gave Paige a shy smile. "We're having twins."

The shock on her face likely mirrored ours when we'd heard the news. Wide-eyed, she breathed out, "Wow. Two?" Then it hit her. "Oh my God, you're going to have *three* babies?"

Shoving both hands into my pants pockets, I rocked back on my heels. "Would seem so."

Paige huffed out a laugh. "And here I am, not ready to take care of one." After a beat, she asked, "Are you sure you want to do this?"

Giving her a warm smile, I replied, "The only thing I've been more sure about in my life was marrying Evie. This is the family we are meant to have, just not in a way we ever saw coming."

Chapter 26
Evie

Jenner insisted on driving Paige back to campus since she'd used a rideshare app to get to our house. Before they left, he tucked me into bed, warning me not to get up until he returned.

Reluctantly, I rolled my eyes and agreed. I knew I'd given him the scare of a lifetime last night, but I was feeling a lot better after being pumped full of IV fluids at the hospital and eating a few small meals throughout the day.

Yes, I was pregnant. Yes, it was high risk. But I wasn't made of glass. Women had twins every day. His overprotective hovering was going to get old real fast; he needed to loosen up.

My fingers ghosted over my still-soft belly. If I hadn't seen their tiny bodies on screen, I wouldn't have been able to believe there were two babies nestled beneath the skin. And to discover I'd been pregnant for months without realizing it?

I shuddered, thinking that if I hadn't landed myself in the emergency room, I could've been one of those women you saw on the news who wound up giving birth on the toilet, having no clue they were expecting.

The garage door sounded, signaling Jenner's return, so I shuffled around in bed, working my way to sitting upright in anticipation of his arrival.

His handsome face appeared at the threshold of our master suite, but he didn't enter. Instead, he crossed his arms, leaning against the doorframe as he surveyed me.

Smirking, he said, "And then there were three."

"Are we crazy for doing this?" I finally voiced aloud the question plaguing my mind for the past hour.

Jenner shrugged. "Go big or go home, right?"

I huffed out a laugh as he drew closer. "Not really sure that applies in this case since we already have two on the way. We're already going to have our hands full. Are you sure this is what you want?"

"Come on, Evie. We both know it would have killed you to let Paige walk away tonight. She had her world flipped upside down, the same as us when the agency blocked the adoption. The three of us spent months preparing for you and me to be that baby girl's parents. That was the plan until suddenly it wasn't, and while it was a loss for us—one I know you were never going to recover from—Paige still had to face the reality that she had a baby due in less than six weeks who didn't have a home secured. That girl's been through so much already. I couldn't stand by and let her worry that that baby—one we already loved—would end up in the system, or worse, she'd be forced to raise it herself when she wasn't ready to do so."

He sat on the edge of the mattress, and I crawled over to loop my arms around his chest from behind, kissing the nape of his neck. "You're a good man, Jenner Knight. The best I've ever known."

His head turned enough that he could graze my cheek with his lips. "I would do anything for you, Evie. And if that means we go from zero to sixty on this parenting thing, then so be it."

"You think you can make it happen? With so little time left before Paige delivers?"

Jenner nodded. "I'll call our lawyer in the morning. A private adoption where both parties are agreeable should be pretty straightforward."

"Thank you." I squeezed my eyes shut as emotions rose to the surface.

Hearing my soft sniffles, Jenner turned us so he cradled me against his chest, stroking my hair. "I know, baby. It's been a rough week."

I could only manage a nod as all the ups and downs played on repeat in my mind.

"You should probably get some rest," he whispered against the top of my head.

The moment he said it, I was suddenly exhausted and didn't put up a fight as he helped to situate me beneath the covers. Jenner dimmed the lights before stripping down to his boxer briefs and climbing into bed with me.

Sleep was moments away from pulling me under when he said, "Our lives are about to become busier than ever, and if the thought of it is this overwhelming, I can't begin to imagine the reality. And after last night . . . the last week, really . . ." Jenner let out a heavy exhale, and my heart squeezed, knowing I'd put him through the wringer. "I think it's really important that we get you in to see someone who can be your sounding board when life seems unmanageable. We both know I'm not enough."

Tears leaked from my eyes, my voice watery when I vowed, "You're enough for me, Jenner. I love you."

His fingers danced across my cheeks, wiping away the moisture. "I love you too, Evie, but I couldn't reach you this past week. Nothing could. And it was fucking terrifying." After a shaky breath, he admitted, "When I found you last night, there was a split second where I feared that you'd done something to harm yourself. That you'd finally decided that you couldn't live with the pain anymore and ended it."

I shook my head. "I would never."

Brown eyes filled with sadness stared into my soul. "You were in such a dark place. You'd thought you had lost your future. And while I realize I might not be enough for you, you will always be enough for me. Kids or no kids, *you* are my life. That has never changed. Not when you struggled to get pregnant, not when you left me, and not when we lost the adoption. The thought of living in a world without you in it? It's unimaginable. You are irreplaceable to me, Evie.

"I'm not going to sit here and pretend that I will ever know all you've been through and all you're going to deal with as we move forward, not just with the adoption but with your pregnancy. Having someone else to talk to who can be objective while we navigate this new phase of life can't be a bad thing, right?"

Jenner's hand slid from my face, moving down my body until it came to rest over my still-fluffy belly. "I'm not asking you to do it only for me. I'm asking for all of us."

I sighed, placing my hand over his. "I know it sounds like a good idea, but when they hear about how bad off I was last week, they'll want to put me on medication. And I won't risk anything harming these babies."

A thought struck me, and I let out a loud gasp, hands flying to cover my face as I groaned, "Oh my God."

"Evie, what's wrong?" Jenner's voice took on a high-pitched quality in his panic. Even though I couldn't see him, I could feel his hands roving over me, searching for a potential source of pain. "Talk to me, Evie," he begged.

"Vegas." The word was barely audible with my mouth covered. "And Christmas. Fuck!"

Jenner's hands stilled. "What?"

Peeking through my fingers, I found my husband kneeling over me, a concerned expression etched across his face.

"Such an idiot," I muttered.

Jenner's eyes slid closed, and he took a deep breath. "I'm gonna need you to elaborate on that. Which one of us is an idiot?"

I scoffed. "Here I am, worried about the effects of pharmaceuticals on our unborn children, when a week ago, I was partying it up in Sin City, having such a good time I practically mauled you in an elevator and then got sick and blacked out poolside."

"Babe," he said on an exhale, leaning down to cup my face so I couldn't avoid looking at him. "You didn't know you were pregnant."

"It doesn't matter!" I shouted. "You think that's going to erase any kind of damage my ignorant actions caused? This is probably our only shot. What if I messed it up already?"

One of his dark red eyebrows rose. "Okay, let's slow it down for a minute. We're about to take on three infants in the next few months, and you're worried about getting *another* chance? How about we focus on the hand we've been dealt first."

I gritted my teeth. "Don't you dare be a smartass right now, Jenner Knight. You know what I mean."

"I do." He nodded. "But we just saw them this morning and were told they were perfectly healthy."

Fear had my chest tightening and my lower lip wobbling. "What—what if they were wrong? What if they're not healthy? And I'm the one who did something to hurt them?"

Lowering his head, Jenner dusted his lips over mine. "God would have to be a real sick fuck to give us this gift, only to take it away. He owes us one after the hell we walked through to get here."

"How can you still believe in someone who let us suffer for so long?" I whispered.

"How can I not? If the world went without suffering, we'd never truly appreciate the good things when they happened. Sure, we've endured more than our fair share, but it's evening out now. We're being showered with blessings and will have three beautiful children to raise, even if it's not quite the way we imagined it when we were younger and first began trying to create a family."

I eyed him skeptically. "You really think that's how it works? That the big guy in the clouds runs some kind of system of checks and balances?"

The corner of Jenner's lips quirked up. "Why not? After thinking I'd never see your beautiful face again, never get to hold you in my arms, you found your way back to me, and now everything is how it should've always been."

"So, what? You think this was all some sort of test? To see how much we could handle before we broke?"

"No. But I do think there was a guiding hand when all those small-town country adoption agencies turned you down. When you had no other options, something—or someone—led you back here."

Rolling my eyes, I muttered, "You're crazy."

A teasing smirk crept onto his face. "Maybe I'll sign us both up for therapy."

"A comedian, too." I tried and failed to bite back a smile."

Satisfied I was no longer spiraling, Jenner resumed his position, lying by my side. "Seriously, though. I'm sure everything is fine. But tomorrow, when we follow up with your doctor, we'll voice our concerns."

"Yeah," I breathed out, still uncertain I hadn't caused our babies harm.

"Hey." He gently cupped my cheek, turning me to face him. "No matter what, they're our kids, and we are going to love them. Okay?"

Jenner's confidence and unwavering love were the only things that could settle my mind enough to fall asleep. But he was right. There was nothing we could do about my past actions; the only thing we could do was tackle any ramifications head-on.

"Everything looks great." Dr. Roberts wiped the ultrasound gel from my exposed stomach.

"Really?" I was still in a daze at seeing our little miracles wiggling around for the second time in as many days.

"Really," she confirmed with a nod as I pulled my shirt down.

"And I didn't hurt them by overindulging during the holidays and while on vacation a couple of weeks ago?"

Dr. Roberts grasped my hand. "You're not the first woman to not know she was pregnant right away, Evie. From what you've told me, it's not like you're the type to have a daily glass of wine to unwind at the end of the day, but instead, you engaged in a few instances of social drinking. Like I said, they look perfect."

Jenner's hand squeezed my shoulder, and his breath fanned my ear as he whispered, "Told you."

I shot him a glare, but my relief at hearing the babies were healthy outweighed my annoyance at his self-assurance.

"Now," Dr. Roberts began, pulling away and reaching for the tablet containing my patient chart. "Let's talk about what you can expect with a multiple pregnancy."

Jenner whipped out his phone, ready to take notes. He wasn't the type to do anything by half-measures and would likely follow the doctor's instructions to a T.

"You're in a unique situation where you've skipped over the first trimester and are barreling down the track toward delivery. As I'm sure you're aware, twins are less likely to make it to full term. Even when they do, we like to induce, or plan a C-section—depending on the babies' positions and your personal preference—no later than thirty-seven weeks to limit a chance of fetal mortality."

I sucked in a sharp breath, reaching blindly for Jenner's hand to serve as an anchor against the paralyzing fear gripping me in a chokehold at the thought of losing one or both of these babies.

Thankfully, my husband was steadfast, his warm palm sliding along mine, not flinching when I gripped him tight enough to cause pain.

Dr. Roberts continued, "So you're looking at less than twenty weeks between now and delivery. From what I can tell, these little buddies are identical. They're sharing a placenta, even though they have different amniotic sacs. This poses additional risks because they share a blood supply, which requires more frequent monitoring."

"What kind of risks?" Jenner asked, concern lacing his tone.

I squeezed his hand as if to say, *Not helping, babe.*

"What we'll be watching for is to make sure that one of them doesn't begin stealing more resources from its twin." Even though she was laying out some serious information, Dr. Roberts chuckled. "Consider it a test run to see how well these two decide to share before they make it out of the womb."

"Is there anything we can do to limit the risk?" Jenner was all business.

"Unfortunately, there isn't. But with frequent monitoring, we should be able to catch any issues—if there are any—early."

"How frequent?" I dared to ask.

She gave me a bright smile. "You're going to be sick of my face by the time we're through, but on the bright side, you'll get tons of extra peeks at your little ones. We'll do a scan every two weeks until you hit thirty-two weeks, then once every week after that—if you make it that far—until delivery."

Swallowing, I mused, "That's a lot."

"It is," she agreed. "But it's the best way to head off any issues at the pass." Dr. Roberts set the tablet down on the countertop resting along the wall of the exam room. "Now, I want you to listen to me very carefully, Evie. If, at any point, something doesn't feel right, I don't want you to hesitate to call the office—or the on-call line if it's after hours—before getting yourself to the nearest emergency room to get checked out. Too many moms brush things off, thinking it's silly to get checked out over every little twinge or gut feeling. But I want you to promise me you won't second-guess yourself and get to a hospital straight away."

She must have seen the panic her stern demand caused because she softened. "I'm not going to sit here and scare you with a laundry list of extremely rare potential complications. Just know that I'd always rather we be overly cautious and send you home with it being a false alarm. Okay?"

I let out a shaky breath, gripping Jenner's hand tighter. "Okay."

"And I know this is probably the last thing you want to hear, but try to keep stress levels to a minimum." When my eyes shot to Jenner's over my shoulder, she added with humor in her voice, "I know hockey games can have your heart rate spiking, but try to remind yourself that it's just a game."

"Um." Chewing my lower lip, I confessed, "It's not that."

"Oh?" One of her dark eyebrows rose.

Jenner answered for me. "We also happen to be adopting a baby expected to be born next month."

Dr. Roberts's face transformed into one of stunned disbelief.

Yeah, welcome to the party, doc.

"As you can probably imagine, Evie's pregnancy came as an even greater shock as we'd begun to explore an alternative path to parenthood."

"Well." She huffed out a laugh. "When you two decide to do something, you make sure to go all out."

"Apparently." My free hand slid over my belly.

"I don't recommend the type of sleep deprivation that comes with a newborn during a high-risk twin pregnancy," she remarked. "So, Dad is going to have to step up for nighttime feeds. And might I suggest a night nanny for when he travels? I have several we've had patients work with in the past that I can recommend."

A night nanny? That seemed a little excessive.

I was sure I could handle getting up once or twice a night with our daughter when Jenner was on the road. Paige wasn't due for another six weeks, and there was the possibility with a first baby that she'd go past her due date. That would put us at the end of March or early April. Sure, the Speed were playoff-bound, but they didn't have any trips remaining that were very far away or for extended periods of time. The West Coast trips were out of the way, which was a blessing right about now.

"Sure. Wouldn't hurt to have a list. Just in case," I replied.

"Perfect. I'll make sure they have that ready for you when you stop up front to make your next appointment. In the meantime, I want you to stay on top of eating—even if it's smaller, more frequent meals—and drinking lots of water. Rest when you feel tired, but light exercise will do you good."

"Thank you, Dr. Roberts." Jenner stepped from my side to offer her his hand to shake.

"It's my pleasure. You two have been ready to become parents for a long time, and I'm glad it's finally happening." She gave my shoulder a squeeze on her way to the door. "See you in two weeks."

I could only manage a nod with how my mind was racing. This was a lot to take in, even before you added in the baby girl we had promised Paige we'd raise.

Just wait until my mama heard about all of this. She'd always warned me that I had a tendency to bite off more than I could chew, and one day, it was gonna land me in a heap of trouble.

But so long as I had Jenner by my side, I knew we could handle it. Or at least, that was the hope.

Chapter 27
Evie

"Cum sponges!" Bristol cried from her perch on a plush armchair at the front of the event room inside the Winchester Hotel. Her bright blue gaze locked on her best friend seated at our table, and she clutched a package to her chest. "Dakota, you know me so well."

The ladies in attendance all laughed, but I spun in my seat to face Dakota. "What in the hell is a cum sponge?" Shaking my head, I muttered, "You know what? I probably don't want to know."

My young friend giggled, downing her second—or maybe it was third—mimosa. Setting down her glass, she held up both hands. "Okay, hear me out on this one."

Another fit of giggles gripped her, and she placed her head on the table, taking a few deep breaths to settle herself. Bristol wasn't the only one who enjoyed a party before noon where alcohol was served.

"They're a cylinder-shaped sponge on a stick." She paused. "You know what? It'll be better if I show you."

My eyes widened as she darted across the room on unsteady legs, reaching into whatever bag contained the item in question before returning.

Plopping back down on her chair, she unzipped a clear plastic bag, producing a singular sponge.

Dakota took one look at the horror etched on my face and smirked. "Don't worry. I'm not going to actually show it in use. This is more of a theoretical visual demonstration." Offering me the one she held, she said, "Here, you take this one."

Cautiously, I reached out to grip the plastic stick protruding from the end of the sponge.

Clearing her throat, Dakota began, "Okay, so it's the same insertion tactic you'd use with a tampon. But instead of absorbing blood, it soaks up all the cum. And you don't leave it in there. Just spin the stick a few times and remove it. Then voilà! No leakage."

As someone who hadn't used a condom in nearly a decade, I was mildly intrigued. "Does it really work?"

Her head bobbed enthusiastically. "You bet! Bristol was hooked on them long before I lost my V-card to Braxton. And then when I did, she insisted I try them. Now, I have a brand endorsement deal because I've used them in a few too many of my books, and the company that makes them is loving how many readers have run to buy their product. So, of course, when a free box showed up on my doorstep the other day, I couldn't resist throwing a pack into Bristol's gift since she was the one who turned me on to them."

"Hmm." I eyed the sponge held in my grasp. "I'll have to check that out."

"Yeah, I'll bet you're getting all the creampies now that you're preggo." Dakota's eyes dropped to the vicinity of my belly. Even though I wasn't showing yet, the skin around our growing babies was becoming firmer to the touch.

My face flamed. I knew these girls were close, but I wasn't about to volunteer that, since learning I was pregnant, Jenner hadn't touched me once. Maybe I didn't need these cum sponges after all.

Tessa piped up beside me. "I still can't believe you're gonna have three babies all at once."

"You and me both," I breathed out.

I was still wrapping my mind around the whole thing. Yes, three babies was a lot to take on, but one of the things I was working on with my therapist was breaking it down day by day. If I looked at the situation as a whole, it would be easy to become overwhelmed. We had several months before three babies were a reality, so right now, we were focused on the one due in a matter of weeks.

"You know"—Dakota held up her champagne flute for a refill from a passing waiter—"I should be pissed at you."

"Me?" I placed a hand to my chest.

"Yeah, you." She narrowed her eyes. "You've given Braxton baby fever."

Okay, it was kinda adorable that her young husband was already itching to start a family. It reminded me so very much of Jenner at his age. I only prayed their path to parenthood would be easier than ours had been.

A blur of copper came into my field of vision, and suddenly, Bristol's arms were encircling Dakota's neck from behind. "Oh, don't you go blaming Evie. Braxton has wanted a gaggle of kids since before the two of you even hooked up."

Dakota huffed. "Yeah. What's wrong with that guy?"

I couldn't stop the smile that spread onto my face. "He loves you so much that he can't contain it," I offered in explanation. "The only choice left is to let it grow."

"Yeah, well, if it hurts half as much as when he took my virginity, I'm not in any rush."

Tessa snickered as she said, hidden beneath a fake cough, "No comment."

Pointing an accusing finger at Tessa, she screamed, "I knew it!"

Bristol waved a hand to a member of the wait staff. "Water over here for this one. She's cut off."

Dakota's brow furrowed. "Hey!"

"You'll thank me later," Bristol promised. Turning to me, she said, "You'll have to forgive my bestie. When she drinks too much, it acts like a truth serum. Apparently, childbirth is high on her list of fears. Who knew?"

"Listen, lady. You would be terrified, too, if the first time you met your sister-in-law, it was hours after she'd given birth, and in her drug-induced delirium, she made sure you knew how wide everything got stretched out." Dakota extended her hands, curving them to form a circle where her fingertips didn't quite touch. "Yowch." Her curls bounced as she shuddered.

Tessa tilted her head from side to side while wrinkling her nose. "That's eerily accurate."

I grimaced, reality sinking in that I might have to endure that twice over. I wasn't sure the surgical option and resulting recovery were any better.

Bristol clapped her hands, seemingly eager to change the subject. "So, Evie, do you have a best friend from back home in Oklahoma who's gonna swoop in and steal all your attention from us once news reaches that you're about to have an instant family?"

"No." I shook my head. "When I went off to college, I lost touch with a lot of people. Well, not so much lost touch as our interests kinda drifted apart. Not a lot of people leave Rust Canyon, and many of my friends got married young and stayed home to support their husbands. Not that I didn't do exactly that, but going to college set me apart. Then you throw in the rising star athlete I married, and we just weren't on the same life path anymore."

Bristol hummed, hugging her best friend tighter. "What about college, then? There has to be someone from your past who will be excited about your news."

Nostalgia hit me square in the chest, looking at the pair of women across the table. From what I'd gathered over the past few months since my return, they had been college roommates, and seeing them made me think of my own ride-or-die. The one I hadn't spoken to in years.

Immediately, Bristol picked on my silence. "Ooh. See, I knew there was someone! Tell us all about her before she shows up. It's a very serious business vetting girl gang members."

"Girl gang?"

The redhead waved her hand around the small table where it was me, herself, Dakota, and Tessa. "Yeah, that's us." She nodded solemnly. "It's very exclusive."

I let out a laugh. "Yeah, I can see that. Glad I made the cut."

Letting go of Dakota, she rushed over to hug me. "Of course you did, Evie. We love you."

Blinking back tears, I cursed the damn pregnancy hormones for making me weepy at the drop of a hat.

"Aw, no!" Bristol exclaimed when she pulled back. "I didn't mean to make you cry."

I waved a hand before my face, but my shaky voice wasn't very convincing. "I'm fine."

Bristol gestured for Tessa to scooch over a seat so she could sit beside me. "What's wrong?"

Squeezing my eyes shut, I whispered, "I did have a best friend in college. But we don't talk anymore."

A soft, warm hand found mine. "You don't have to tell us about it. I'm sorry if I brought up bad memories."

Sighing, I faced my new friends. "We didn't have any kind of falling out or anything like that. Jenner and I kept our infertility struggles to ourselves. I didn't want anyone to know, didn't want the constant looks of pity. My college roommate, Natasha—who also happened to be my maid of honor when we got married the first time—got pregnant by accident in the middle of all of it. Seeing her have the perfect little family was too much, so I stopped taking her calls. I know it sounds selfish. That I just let our friendship die because I couldn't get over my own issues."

Tessa said, "You were in self-preservation mode, Evie. A good friend would understand that. You should reach out. I'm sure she'd be happy to hear from you."

I shook my head. "No, it's been too long."

Dakota chimed in. "If Bristol ever stopped talking to me? It would suck for sure, but if she tried reaching out after all this time? I would jump at the chance to hear her voice and catch up on all I'd missed in her life."

My eyes slid to the redhead by my side. "Yeah . . . there's also something else I didn't mention."

"Why are you looking at me when you say that?" Bristol asked cautiously.

"I'm ninety-nine percent sure Natasha hooked up with Maddox the night of my wedding."

A wicked grin curved on her face. "Then I guess we're even. I fucked his brains out the night you remarried Jenner."

The four of us burst out laughing, the earlier undertone of sadness fading away.

The redhead wiped a tear from the corner of her eye. "Seriously, though. It's no secret that Maddox had an active sex life before we got together. I did, too. I can't be mad about some woman he slept with when I was"—Bristol counted on her fingers, trying to do the math—"thirteen."

Stunned, I couldn't believe how mature she was being about her partner's past. I didn't want to know about a single one of the women Jenner had been intimate with before we'd met. The urge to play the comparison game would be far too strong.

Dakota snorted. "Yeah, you weren't so breezy about it when it came to Hannah and Maddox having a history." She cupped a hand, stage-whispering to those of us not in the know, "Hannah Moreau, as in Coach Moreau of the Comets's daughter."

Bristol glared at her best friend, pointing a finger in her direction. "That was different, and you know it."

"Why? Because you always wanted to be her when you grew up?"

Lips twisting to the side, Bristol admitted, "Maybe . . ."

"Let's share with the group why you were ridiculous to be even a little bit jealous. One—she's freaking married. And two—you're the younger, hotter model." She threw in a wink for good measure. "Less mileage."

I clapped a hand over my mouth to try and stop the laughter bubbling up from my chest.

Bristol flicked her wrist, dismissing Dakota. "Don't listen to her; she's drunk. Any friend of yours is a friend of mine."

"Speaking of friends," Dakota began, "where is the Wicked Witch?"

A shiver rolled down my spine at the thought of Juliana and her nastiness.

"Oh, didn't you hear?" A smug satisfaction sounded in Bristol's voice.

"Hear what?" I asked.

"Maddox benched Saint indefinitely for the little stunt he pulled. After a week of trying to get his agent to coerce management into overriding the decision, he realized it was pointless. So, he waived his no-trade clause, and they shipped him off to Alberta."

My jaw dropped. "Wait, what stunt?"

"You seriously don't know?" I shook my head, so she explained, "Juliana is the one who blew the whistle on you with the adoption agency. And Saint was dumb enough to gloat to Jenner about it."

While I remained speechless that I hadn't heard about this in the weeks since the incident at the agency, Tessa remarked, "It's so cold up there her fake tits will probably freeze."

Bristol leaned both elbows on the table. "They might, if Saint hadn't dumped her ass for fucking up his career with her vindictive bullshit."

"Karma, you gotta love it." Dakota raised her freshly filled glass. "Evie ends up with everything while Jules gets kicked off the gravy train."

"I'll drink to that!" Bristol cheered, and everyone raised their glasses.

No one warned me that double the babies meant I'd be getting up twice as much in the middle of the night to pee. Rolling out of bed, I rushed to the bathroom before my bladder exploded.

Damn, Jenner and his forcing me to drink ridiculous amounts of water.

A relieved sigh rushed past my lips when I made it in time, but when I returned to bed, I noticed Jenner wasn't in it.

"Babe?" I called out, only to be met with silence.

Checking my phone quickly, I saw it was nowhere near morning, so where the hell could he be at this time of night?

Throwing a cardigan over my loose sleep shirt, I padded into the hallway. Soft music reached my ears, and there was light coming from the cracked-open door of the guest bedroom.

Curious as to what he was doing in there in the middle of the night, I stepped closer, pushing inside. Jenner stood with his back to me, dressed in paint-splattered clothes, as he used a paint roller on a stick along the wall.

"Whatcha doin'?" I asked softly so as not to startle him.

Jenner spun around, the roller stick suspended in the air. "You shouldn't be in here. The paint fumes are bad for the babies."

Folding my arms over my breasts—which I could've sworn had doubled in size in the few weeks since learning I was pregnant—I leaned against the doorframe. "I'll go back to bed if you tell me why you're painting in the middle of the night."

Sighing, my husband replied, "Couldn't sleep. I got to thinking about all the things we need to get ready, and I needed to do something to settle my mind."

"So, you decided to redecorate?"

"Yeah. The yellow nursery has been waiting for Baby Girl for months. Which worked out pretty well when we found out she was getting two little brothers." His mention of our twin boys had my hands dropping to my belly. It still didn't feel real. "I had this navy paint sitting in my trunk and figured if I was up anyway, I could at least be productive."

"I'm surprised you didn't opt for Indy Speed Red."

Jenner shrugged. "Hearing about Braxton's upbringing and the pressure placed on him to follow in his brother's footsteps, I don't want our sons to feel like they don't have options, that they can't carve their own paths, follow their own dreams. I thought a space theme would be kinda cool, you know? Boys like rocket ships, right?"

A smirk found its way onto my lips. "Is that your way of saying *you* like rocket ships, Jenner?"

"I mean . . . if they offer me a ride into space tomorrow, I'm totally taking it." A boyish grin curved on his handsome face.

"Come here." I crooked my finger

He set the paint roller down and stepped closer. Once he was within reach, I cupped his jaw, running my thumbs over the soft texture of his beard.

"Is it okay?" he asked quietly. "If you want to do something else, I can scrap it and start over."

"It's perfect." I pressed my lips to his. "They're going to love it. And not because space is 'cool,' but because their dad poured his heart into it."

Jenner peeked down to the swell of my belly between us, and I followed his gaze.

"I don't think I've ever been this happy, Evie," he whispered.

"Me, neither," I agreed. "Feels like a dream, and I never want to wake up."

If we were this thrilled at the idea of our growing family, I was certain our hearts would burst when we finally met our children.

Chapter 28

Jenner

Sweat ran into my eyes and my vision blurred as I made my way back to the bench. Dropping down between Asher and Braxton, I grabbed the towel next to my water bottle to wipe the sweat away from my brow, cleaning the clear plastic of my visor for good measure.

"Fuck," I panted, trying to catch my breath after a hard forty-five-second shift. "Can't get a breakout pass for shit tonight."

"No kidding," Asher agreed.

In an arena located in midtown Manhattan, we were playing against our divisional opponents, the New York Freedom. They were buzzing on the ice while we were simply trying to survive.

Most of the game was spent struggling to make it out of the defensive zone. It almost felt like they could see our intended plays before they materialized and were always perfectly positioned to break up our passes.

That, and they were laying the heavy hits tonight.

I rolled my shoulder, a twinge beneath the skin reminding me of a check I'd taken into the boards during the first period. I had played through worse, but I made a mental note to have one of the trainers hit me with a cortisone shot during the intermission.

"Slate line!" Maddox barked. "Back on the ice!"

Almost muscle memory at this point, the three of us jumped over the boards and onto the ice, skating hard to where the defenseman for the Freedom was holding the puck behind his own net as they also executed their own line change.

Braxton charged the lone D-man, trying to force him to throw away the puck, while I cut off the pass to his forward, situated at the blue line. I almost smiled at the predictability of it as I kept my stick hard on the ice to intercept the pass.

I could feel the forward at my back, chasing me down as I charged the net, where Braxton now stood tied up with the defenseman. Time seemed to slow down as I assessed the goalie's stance and where I wanted to place the puck for the highest chance of scoring. If I could get him to drop, I'd need to snap the puck immediately to try and get it over his shoulder before he could get his glove up to catch it. But when he squared up, trying to peek around the bodies of both his teammate and mine, blocking his view, I made a split-second decision.

Pulling to my right, I locked eyes with the netminder, Monroe, as I pulled back my stick like I was going to take a close-range slapshot. The Freedom defenseman also tracked the move, pushing Braxton in front of where he expected the shot to land so he would take the brunt of the block. Bringing my stick back down to the ice, I didn't shoot the puck with as much force as I could muster. Instead, I pulled it to the left, chipping it into the open net on my backhand before anyone could react and stop me.

My arms shot up in celebration, and Asher skated closer, screaming, "That's my fucking captain!"

I chuckled, but damn, if it didn't feel good to get one on the board when the ice had been tilted toward the Freedom most of the game. If we could play solid defense for the rest of regulation while Goose continued to stand on his head, as he so often did, then we might just squeak out of this one with a win.

In mid-March, the playoff picture was still muddy for some teams, but the Speed were sitting pretty at the top of the division. Securing that top spot would mean home-ice advantage, so losing to a divisional opponent at this time of year wasn't an option.

The five of us on the shift for the goal scored skated toward the bench, reaching our gloved hands out for a line of fist bumps from our teammates. As I skated the length of the bench, various positive sentiments were thrown out.

"Atta boy, Jenner!"

"Cap made Monroe his bitch!"

"Let's get another one and blow this wide open!"

We all knew that stats didn't matter. The team with more shots didn't automatically win. It was about making the most of quality chances and minimizing mistakes on the ice. The Freedom were clearly outplaying us, but we were the ones with a one-to-nothing lead.

As I rested on the bench while the second line took the center-ice face-off, Maddox tapped me on the head. "Nice read on that, Knight. How's the shoulder?"

"Fine," I gritted out.

Truth be told, the wind-up on the fake slapper had tweaked it, but I didn't want to be pulled from the game. Not when we had a chance to turn the tide and pull out a win.

"Good," my best friend and coach grunted. "Keep it up."

I nodded my agreement before squirting some ice-cold water down the back of my neck to help cool me off and maybe numb the pain until we made it to intermission.

The next time the guys got the puck deep inside our offensive zone, our line went out again.

The Freedom executed a seamless breakout, passing the puck from behind their net to the neutral zone before chipping it deep on the dump and chase. Thankfully, our top defenseman, Wyatt Banks, got there first, slinging the puck up the boards where I skated to gather it and either carry it out or pass to Asher or Braxton if they were already headed into the neutral zone.

My stick blade had barely touched the puck when I heard Braxton scream, "Get down!"

I had just enough time to catch a flash of motion from the corner of my eye, recognizing Freedom defenseman Ian Yates coming at me full force. Normally, that wouldn't bother me; hits were a part of the game, and I'd taken my fair share of them throughout my career. But it was the fact that his skates had already left the ice that made me take notice and follow Braxton's warning without a second thought.

Abandoning the play and the puck at my feet, I dropped like a rock, narrowly missing Yates's flying leap that had him crashing head-first into the glass wall and crumpling onto the ice beside me.

"What the fuck?" I shouted, scrambling to my feet as Yates struggled to get up.

That motherfucker had been gunning for a high hit to the head, and I was damn lucky Braxton had seen it coming in time to warn me to avoid it. With how hard Yates had hit the glass, I would have ended up with a concussion, if not worse. That idiot was lucky he hadn't snapped his own spine playing reckless.

A shudder ran the length of my spine at how close I'd come to a serious injury with a family to care for. Skating to the bench, I needed a minute to get my head straight before I could focus on the game again.

Dropping my forehead to rest against the edge of the boards once I was seated, I took a few deep breaths, trying to calm my racing heart.

I'm okay.

I ducked, and he missed.

I'm gonna make it home to Evie in one piece tonight.

Maddox's voice spoke from behind me. "Jenner, you're done for the night."

Head whipping up, I turned to face him. "Aw, come on. Don't tell me the concussion spotters called down. He didn't even touch me!"

My coach and best friend shook his head. "It's not that. You're about to become a dad."

"What?" I was on my feet instantly, but then fear gripped my heart. "No, it's too soon."

Maddox placed both hands on my shoulders, looking me in the eye. "It's Paige, not Evie."

The air left my lungs in a rush. "Thank God."

The tiniest hint of a smile curved on his lips. "Good luck, man. You're gonna need it."

My teammates moved out of the way so I could rush down the tunnel and strip out of my gear. There was a half-second of hesitation where I debated skipping a shower, but I quickly realized they probably wouldn't let me on a plane if I stunk like sweat and hockey gear.

Scrubbing the stench off me as quickly as possible, I barely took any time to towel off before throwing on my gameday suit, grabbing my phone and wallet, and running out of the arena.

Evie and I were going to become parents tonight.

Given how long it had taken me to get home from New York City, I thought we would already have a baby.

But no, I'd been sitting in this tiny maternity ward waiting room for eight hours without a single update.

I had total faith that Evie had it handled, but that didn't mean I wasn't a nervous wreck. I could respect that I wasn't needed or wanted in that room, but the unknown was killing me.

The longer this dragged on, the more I began to worry.

Was Paige okay? Was the baby?

Had a complication arisen, and no one saw fit to tell me?

How was Evie holding up? Was she making sure to eat and rest as she helped support Paige?

There were too many variables, too many things that could go wrong.

Needing to expel nervous energy, I began to pace.

Ironically, I hadn't gotten the medical attention I needed for my shoulder due to my abrupt departure from the game, and the muscles had locked up during the two-hour flight home. I hissed, trying to roll it as I carved a path through the square room—back and forth, back and forth.

"Is there a Jenner Knight in here?" My head whipped around to discover a nurse in pink scrubs at the entryway to the waiting room.

"That's me," I called out.

A rush of emotion hit me when I saw her smile brightly as I stepped forward. "There's someone who's ready to meet you."

I nearly sank to my knees as relief crashed over me. Pressing my hand to my chest, I dared to ask, "Did everything go okay?"

The nurse nodded. "Birth mom and adoptive mom and baby girl are all doing great."

"Thank God," I breathed out.

"If you want to follow me, I can take you to them now."

Nodding, I fell into step beside her. "That would be great."

We came to a stop outside a room with a pink placard affixed to the door reading: *It's a Girl!* The nurse gestured for me to enter. "They're waiting for you."

Taking a deep breath, I forced my feet to move, knowing that my life would never be the same once I crossed that threshold.

A curtain divided the space, and from the other side, I could hear a soft cooing I knew was coming from my wife. My heart exploded when I pushed the fabric aside to find Evie rocking back and forth, a tiny bundle of blankets resting in her arms. She'd never looked more beautiful, holding our daughter to her chest, the swell of her belly where our sons rested now impossible to ignore.

It was crazy to think that we hadn't known she was pregnant only six weeks ago, and now she was sporting quite the baby bump. It was like our boys had decided one day to make their presence known. And to think they'd only be a few months behind their big sister in their arrival.

"Hey," I said softly around the lump in my throat.

Brilliant but tired purple eyes peeked up, and a smile formed on Evie's face. "Hey. You wanna come meet your daughter?"

I nodded but held up a finger. "Yeah. In a second."

Instead of stepping toward my wife, I went to the bedside of the teenage girl who had given us the world. Paige had the tiniest hint of a smile on her face as I approached, but she didn't lift her head from the pillows.

We'd spent some time together in the past month as we prepared for this moment, so I didn't think twice about smoothing some stray hair pieces from her face. "How are you, sweetheart?"

Her blue eyes slid closed, and she whispered, "Tired."

I fought back a chuckle. "I'll bet."

"She did so good, Jenner," Evie remarked, still rocking our baby girl. "She was so brave."

"I'm so proud of you both." Paige's eyes opened, and I gripped her hand, resting above the blankets. "And if I forget to tell you a million times over during the next several years, Paige, thank you."

"No, thank you," Paige countered. "You're going to give her such a beautiful life."

"I hope so." I wasn't sure if I'd said the words aloud or if they were a prayer. "Rest now. We can visit later when you're stronger, okay?"

Her head bobbed lazily as her lips parted on a sigh, and she fell asleep before my eyes.

"Jenner?"

Turning, I walked toward my wife. When I reached where she stood, I held my breath, hand reaching up as I pulled the blankets away to catch the first glimpse of our daughter's tiny face.

My palm flew to my chest, where my heart threatened to burst free of my ribcage. This was better than any adrenaline rush I'd ever experienced.

"She's perfect." I dared to reach out and graze her soft pink cheek with my fingertip.

"Counted all her fingers and toes myself," Evie teased. "I know that's usually the dad's job, but you'll get your chance soon enough."

"Yeah." I huffed out a laugh at the reminder that our family was far from complete.

"You want to hold her?"

Suddenly nervous, I shifted on my feet. "Uh, yeah, sure." When Evie offered me our daughter, I halted her. "Other arm." I extended the crook of my left elbow.

Eyebrow raised, she asked, "What happened?"

I shrugged with my good shoulder. "Took a hard check into the boards. Didn't have time for treatment since I got pulled off the bench to come home. I'm sure I'll be fine once the trainers get their hands on me. Can't have anything keeping me from snuggling with this little cutie pie."

Evie eyed the injured arm. "Maybe sit down first, yeah?"

"Good idea. You come sit with me. I don't even want to know how long you've been on your feet tonight."

The sassy woman I married rolled her eyes at me. "It's morning, in case you haven't noticed."

"Oh, I noticed. I was the one watching time tick by at a snail's pace all damn night." I gestured to the bench seating along the wall of the room, making sure she was settled before taking a seat myself.

There was an awkward little exchange on the handoff, but a warm, feather-light weight settled in my arms, and my world shifted on its axis. This baby girl was completely dependent on me—on us—to care for her, to cherish and guide her for the rest of her life. The responsibility I now carried was heavy, but I welcomed it.

Years of struggle and heartbreak had brought us here. We were finally a family.

Evie beamed down at the baby in my arms. "Look at her, sleeping like an angel."

"Beautiful. Just like her mama." I moved my head enough to brush my lips over hers. Hammering the point home, I said, "You're a mom, Evie."

Eyes filling with tears, she nodded, pressing her forehead to mine. "Still can't quite believe it."

"This little one is going to know so much love. Because she was so very wanted."

Pulling back slightly, Evie's violet eyes lit up. "I forgot the best part!" Even in her excitement, she kept her voice soft, mindful of our newborn and the girl who'd given birth to her both asleep in the room.

Smirking, I teased, "If this is your *oh wait, there's more* moment, I think we already have that covered with the twins."

Evie raised a hand to shift the knit pink cap covering our daughter's head, revealing a tuft of strawberry-blonde hair.

"Paige was right. She's a little redhead," Evie declared.

Unable to stop myself, I dipped my head, placing a soft kiss atop the baby's head. "Hope."

"What?"

Locking eyes with my wife, I repeated the word. "Hope. I think that should be her name."

Stunned, Evie blinked at me. "You do?"

"Maybe there was a reason we ran through those baby name books a million times and never managed to narrow our choices down to have a shortlist. Because deep down, I already knew what her name was."

"Why Hope?"

Even though it hurt like hell, I reached my free arm across my torso to cup Evie's face, stroking over the skin of her cheek with my thumb. "Because that's what she represents. That you never gave up hope of one day becoming a mom. Even when we were apart, it remained your driving force until we reached this very moment, with our daughter held safely in my arms."

Lip trembling, Evie whispered, "Hope. Yeah. I like it."

"Welcome to the world, Hope Knight," I whispered to our daughter.

The sleeping infant had no idea that she'd changed our lives. Not only that, she'd saved our marriage, a task which I had once written off as impossible.

Hope was the ultimate symbol of our new beginning and bright future.

Chapter 29
Evie

The tiniest cries filtered through the video monitor on the nightstand, rousing me from sleep. Rolling over in bed—not an easy feat with a basketball-sized belly in the way—I extended an arm over the edge to grab it.

A hand on my shoulder stopped me. "I've got her. Go back to sleep."

Hope had been home with us for two weeks, and Jenner hadn't let me get up in the middle of the night to feed her once when he wasn't traveling. We'd caught a lucky break in the schedule, and he'd only been gone overnight twice, but I had managed on my own those couple of times just fine.

Sure, it sucked having your sleep suddenly interrupted by a newborn, having to trudge down to the kitchen to heat a bottle before changing their diaper, and trying to stay awake long enough to feed them and put them back to bed. But those moments when it was just us? Just me and Hope in the quiet of the night? They were special, even if I was exhausted out of my mind. I wanted to cherish this time when she was our sole focus before her brothers arrived and chaos ensued.

"Babe," I protested. "You had a game tonight. I can get up."

"Nope." Jenner's voice brooked no argument. "Doctor's orders, remember?"

Thankfully, it was dark, and he couldn't see my eye roll as he crawled out of bed and slipped out of the room.

My OB wanted us to be cautious, but all our monitoring had been perfect so far, and this week, I'd hit twenty-four weeks. Sure, it wouldn't be ideal if the twins decided to arrive this early, but at least we'd reached the point where the medical team would do everything they could to ensure our boys had the best chance at survival. With each passing week, the odds grew greater.

I could only pray they inherited some of my stubbornness and all of Jenner's tenacity, staying put for as long as possible and coming out fighting.

It didn't matter that I wasn't the one getting up with Hope tonight; now, I was wide awake. Shifting on the mattress, I tried to find a comfortable spot. It wasn't only my belly in the way these days, but this stupid pregnancy pillow Jenner insisted I needed. I'd protested that it was too big, taking up nearly half of our king-sized bed, but he wouldn't take no for an answer, listing out all its benefits—reduced heartburn and water retention, improved blood circulation, less stress on my spine.

Grudgingly, I could admit it did reduce some of the aches and pains associated with my rapidly expanding belly, but right now, I wanted to chuck it from the second-story window.

It also didn't help that my t-shirt grazing over my nipples was turning me on, the pulsing between my thighs growing more insistent by the minute. I was never going to fall back to sleep with that situation going on down there.

I let out a frustrated groan. Jenner and I hadn't been intimate once since discovering I was pregnant, but I was so horny most days I couldn't see straight. Not that I'd confided in him about that little tidbit. With him not making a single attempt at initiating sex in almost two months, I wasn't about to force him to help me take the edge off. Clearly, my changing body wasn't appealing to him.

Checking the time on my phone, I estimated I had at least twenty minutes before he was done feeding Hope and returned to bed. That was more than enough time to scratch the itch in private.

Deciding I needed to make this quick, I grabbed a vibrator from my nightstand. I owned a few different types, but you could never go wrong with one that had dual ends—one with a clit-sucker, the other with a G-spot stimulator. That thing could get me off in five minutes flat.

Clothing was already becoming a struggle for me, and with a newborn to care for, there hadn't been time to shop. Panties were the first thing I'd outgrown, so I was currently bare beneath the oversized shirt I wore to bed.

Finding myself already soaking wet, I had no trouble sliding part of the toy inside me before pressing the buttons that brought it to life.

A sigh slipped past my lips as the vibrations and sucking action worked in tandem. This was exactly what I needed. My hips bucked, chasing my pleasure as I coiled tighter and tighter.

Just like that.

A little more.

Almost there.

"False alarm." Jenner's words had my eyes popping open, and I couldn't stop the gasp that tore up my throat.

Concern filled his voice as I heard him step closer. "What's wrong?"

Frantically, I tried to hit the buttons to turn off the vibrator, but it wasn't quick enough.

"What's that sound?"

"N-nothing." I cursed myself for stumbling over the word that came out breathy.

My eyes had adjusted to the darkness of the room enough that I could see when Jenner crossed both arms over his chest and raised an eyebrow. "Didn't sound like nothing."

Now, I was stuck. Because my hand was still between my legs, and Jenner's eyes were scanning me critically. If I made even the tiniest move, he'd track it, and my little solo sexy playtime would be discovered.

"Don't think I won't stand here all night, Evie."

Stubborn man.

Releasing my grasp on the toy, I brought both hands out from beneath the covers, huffing, "Fine. I needed a little relief."

Jenner cocked his head. "Relief? What kind of relief?"

I widened my eyes before tilting my head to indicate where my thighs rested open, hoping he got my meaning.

Understanding dawned as he tracked my gaze, and his defensive posture loosened. "Oh!"

"Yeah." I cringed. "I thought you'd be gone longer."

"You thought..." Jenner's words trailed off. "Do you do this often?"

Annoyance simmered beneath my skin, and I snapped. "Don't you dare make me feel bad about this. Not when you've been keeping your distance."

"This is *my* fault?" He placed a hand over his chest.

"Listen, buddy. I'm hopped-up on pregnancy hormones, and they're making me horny. All. The. Time. And it's not like you've stepped up to do the job, so I've had to take care of it myself."

"All the time." Jenner repeated my words in a dazed voice. "Like, when I'm in the house?"

The man had caught me masturbating while he'd left the room to feed our daughter. Did he really need me to spell it out for him?

"Let's just say the detachable showerhead has gotten quite the workout lately," I muttered.

Jenner cleared his throat. "Um. I don't know—"

I cut him off. "I get it. You don't need to say anything."

"Oh, yeah? What is it exactly that you get, Evie?"

Shoving the blankets lower, I gestured to my belly. "It's a little hard to ignore our sex life died when I got pregnant. The only thing I can't settle on is if it's my body that repulses you, or if it's the idea of them being between us that freaks you out."

His eyebrows shot high on his forehead. "You think I'm repulsed by you?"

Tired and cranky that I didn't get the release I'd so desperately needed tonight, I let out a weary sigh. "What else am I supposed to believe?"

"Let's get one thing straight: I've never been more turned on by your body than I am right now. You're fucking gorgeous growing our babies, just like I always knew you would be. Total honesty, you aren't the only one getting off alone in the shower."

"Then what's the holdup?" I demanded. I needed to know why we weren't fucking like rabbits every chance we got.

Dragging a hand down his face, Jenner replied, "I don't want to hurt you. Hurt them." He eyed my swollen stomach.

I scoffed, finally reaching down to remove the toy and bring it into view. "Trust me, if orgasms were gonna hurt anyone, they would have done so long before now. I'm getting myself off multiple times a day at this point."

"And you've had bleeding."

"Months ago," I countered. "And it's not just the vibrator and the showerhead. I've been fucking myself with the replica dildo I got at my bachelorette party." Natasha was to blame for that one, but Jenner had been a good sport and had allowed a cast to be made of his dick when we were young and stupidly in love.

"Jesus fucking Christ, Evie."

He was right there; I just needed to throw him over the edge.

Narrowing my eyes, I threw down a challenge that I hoped would do the trick. "So, what's it gonna be? You gonna take what's yours? Or let a piece of silicone take your place?"

Chest expanding on a deep breath, he said, "Okay."

"Okay? Okay, what? You didn't pick an option."

Instead of answering, Jenner hooked both thumbs into the waistband of his boxer briefs and dragged them down his muscular thighs, revealing how turned on he was by my changing body.

All business, he asked, "How do you want to do this?" I was already scrambling to my knees on the mattress when he added, "There's only a few options. I don't want you on your back."

Scoffing without a second thought, I muttered, "Okay, Dad."

Like a switch was flipped, Jenner stepped forward suddenly, fisting a hand in my hair, forcing my head back. Nipples hardening painfully, I swallowed, silently begging for him to let me have it.

Voice gruff, he snarled, "Oh, is that what you want, Evie? You want Daddy to come in here and fuck you until you're screaming the house down?"

My mouth dropped open. We had a daughter and two unborn sons who would one day call him Daddy, so why the hell was that so hot?

Deciding to blame it on the pregnancy hormone horniness, I rasped, "Yes."

With my head held firmly in his grasp, Jenner lowered his mouth to trail a path down my neck. I arched into his touch, silently begging for more as my blood heated to the point of boiling.

Against my skin, he murmured, "That's too bad. You've been a naughty girl. And naughty girls don't get what they want."

A whine slipped from my parted lips as I shifted my hips, trying to ease the ache between my thighs.

Jenner released me so suddenly that I fell back against the pillows.

"Shirt off," he barked. When I stared at him, stunned, his voice rose. "Now!"

Gripping the hem of my T-shirt with trembling fingers, I drew it over my head, hearing the soft hiss from my husband before the fabric cleared my vision.

"Fucking breathtaking." His huge palm pressed against the taut skin of my belly. "Don't you ever think I don't want you, Evie, because I love your body in every shape and size. Right now, though?" His free hand grabbed mine and brought it to his cock, positioning my fingers around the stiff shaft. "I've never been harder in my goddamn life than at the sight of you big and pregnant with my babies."

On a whimper, I looped my arm around his neck, pulling his mouth down to meet mine. The first pass of his tongue had me moaning, my grip tightening on his cock as I began to stroke him. I was desperate and needy; my hand moved faster, trying to drive him as crazy with lust as he'd always driven me.

He tore his lips away, our combined panting filling the silence of the room. "Evie, slow down."

"I can't," I breathed out. "I need you. Right fucking now."

A rumble sounded from his chest as both hands skimmed down my sides. "As much as I love this ass"—he gripped two fistfuls for emphasis—"I want to watch your face when you come around my cock. There isn't a more beautiful sight in this world."

Breathless at his words, I could only manage a nod.

"Up."

He didn't have to tell me twice. I climbed off the bed, allowing Jenner to toss the U-shaped pregnancy pillow across the room.

His tightly toned body reclined on the mattress, and he snapped his fingers sharply. "What are you waiting for?"

Fucking hell. Bossy Jenner had always been my favorite, and with desire gripping me in a chokehold, I was close to exploding from his words alone.

Kneeling on the edge of the bed, I allowed Jenner to offer me a hand to steady myself as I climbed over his prone form to straddle his lap. The first brush of his hard length against my slick pussy had a tremor rolling down my spine.

"You're a goddess, you know that?"

His hands came up to cradle my belly before sinking lower and brushing through my slit. I sucked in a sharp breath as he teased a tight circle over my throbbing clit before venturing lower and sinking two fingers deep inside.

Before I had a chance to move against his touch, he removed his fingers, holding them up to show that they were coated in my arousal.

"Fucking drenched for me," he murmured before licking the digits clean, moaning as he did so. "Delicious." The remark was said while he smacked his lips.

Writhing over his hard length nestled between my thighs, I was losing patience.

A smug smirk crept onto Jenner's face. "Look at my wife. So desperate to ride my cock."

"Mmhmm." I bit my lip, the friction of skin against skin almost enough to tip me over.

Fingertips dug into the soft flesh of my thighs. "You're in charge, baby. Take what you need."

That was all I needed to hear. Rising on my knees allowed his shaft to point toward the ceiling, and I maneuvered over it. Stabilizing myself with both hands pressed to Jenner's abs, I shifted until the crown of his cock nudged at my entrance.

With a slowness so agonizing my quads screamed with the effort of holding back, I lowered myself onto his dick until I bottomed out, and we both groaned.

"Holy shit," I breathed out.

It didn't matter that I had a carbon copy of this man's cock in my nightstand drawer and had used it more times than I could count over the past decade; nothing would ever come close to the real thing.

Jaw clenched, Jenner gritted out, "You're killing me, Evie. I need you to move."

Rocking my hips, I tested the feeling of fullness, reveling in the faint pulsing I felt from the pronounced veins along his length buried deep inside me.

When Jenner's hands came up to cup my breasts, I threw my head back on a moan, hissing when the rough pads of his thumbs brushed my nipples. They'd become overly sensitive these past few weeks, and I circled my hips in response to his touch.

"That's it, baby. Ride my cock. Just like that." His words of encouragement had me moving faster.

He pinched my nipples, tugging the distended peaks with his fingers.

Without warning, my muscles seized, and I cried out, "Yes! Oh God, Jenner!" as I shattered, the force of my climax so strong it felt like my soul left my body.

My hips moved on their own as I chased every last ounce of pleasure from the intense orgasm that had snuck up on me.

"Jesus, babe. Where the fuck did that come from?" Jenner's voice sounded distant through my fuzzy hearing. "Your pussy has never squeezed my cock so hard."

Panting, my chest burning with the effort to fill my lungs with air, I placed my hands atop his on my breasts.

"So sensitive," I breathed out.

"Oh, yeah?" He rolled my nipples, causing me to let out a guttural groan. Chuckling at my response, he said, "Your tits are irresistible right now. So heavy and full."

"Uh-huh." If I wasn't careful, he would have me coming again just by playing with them.

Jenner shifted beneath me, and I gasped, shoving off his cock, the sensations overwhelming.

Growling, my husband sat up, snagging my wrist as I tried to escape.

"It's—it's too much," I explained.

Eyes searching mine, his voice was husky as he asked, "You want to stop?"

My gaze dropped to the hard cock jutting out from his hips.

"No." The harshly uttered word had my head snapping up. "Don't you dare worry about me right now. I'll be just fine if I don't get to finish. Tell me what you want."

Chewing on my lower lip, I took a mental inventory of my body.

My pulse could be felt between my thighs, the throbbing matched the beating of my racing heart. The lightest brush of his cock on my clit, when I'd sat atop him had been borderline painful with the extra blood flow down there since becoming pregnant. My nipples were practically orgasm detonators at this point, and though I was getting myself off multiple times a day, I wasn't sure how many I could handle back to back.

No matter what Jenner said about not caring if I left him with blue balls tonight, that had never been my style. I gave as good as I got. Always. And tonight wasn't about to become my first exception to that rule.

There had to be a position we could use that wouldn't have my belly in the way in which he didn't touch my nips and featured minimal rubbing against my clit.

My eyes widened as it struck me.

Jenner eyed me carefully. "I'm almost afraid to ask what's going on in that mind of yours." His fingers grazed my temple before pushing sweaty hair behind my ear.

"Switch with me."

His brows drew down. "I said I don't want you on your back."

I rolled my eyes. "Get up, Jenner. I've got this."

A doubtful expression flickered over his features, but he shifted positions with me. Once he was fully behind me, I dropped onto my elbows, presenting my ass to his view.

Groaning, he palmed one cheek. "Fuck, yes. I can get on board with this."

Satisfied, I shifted my hips from side to side in invitation.

"But I wanna make one adjustment first."

My head whipped around in confusion. What was he talking about?

Extending his arm, he snagged the pillows from his side of the bed, sliding them under my hips, providing a cushion for my belly.

Lips twisting to the side, I couldn't help but think that I'd married the most caring man alive. He always put me—and now our family—first, and I was so damn lucky he was back in my life.

His fingers moved up the sides of my belly, over my hips, the featherlight touch teasing goosebumps to the surface of my skin. Wanting him to grip me harder, I whined when he removed his hands.

My forehead pressed to the mattress, and my hands fisted the sheets. Jenner knew exactly what he was doing. He was asserting his control the only way he knew how since he couldn't—or wouldn't—fuck me hard in my condition. Anticipation became his method of choice.

And fuck, if it wasn't working.

Every nerve ending I possessed was on high alert as I waited for the moment he would make a move and claim me in a way only he ever had. I moaned into the bedding, hoping that would be enough to spur him on, but still, nothing.

His harsh breathing set me on edge. I wanted to scream at him to do something but knew that would only make him drag this out longer.

A flash of fire seared through the flesh of my backside, and I gasped.

"Sorry, baby," Jenner's husky voice sent a shiver down my spine. "This juicy ass was just begging to be bitten."

Holy fucking shit.

I was about to ask him to do it again when his cock nudged against my waiting pussy.

"Please," I begged, breathless.

Jenner teased just an inch inside. "Is this what you need?"

A moan slipped past my lips. "More."

Another shift, and his dick slid in further. "Better?"

My head thrashed from side to side. The man was a master of the tease, and he knew how to play my body like an instrument.

Panting, I tried desperately to have my mind relay the proper signals to my mouth. "All." I sucked in a ragged breath. "All of you."

Done with games, Jenner surged his hips forward until he was buried balls deep, and my gasp layered over his guttural groan.

"So deep," I whimpered.

Fingers digging into my hips, his voice was strained. "You okay?"

"Fuck me, Jenner."

"Yes, ma'am."

Jenner reared back, his hard length dragging against every inner nerve ending and setting them on fire. I held my breath in anticipation of him slamming home, but instead, he slid back inside slowly, grinding against me once our bodies grew flush. The move had him pressing against that secret spot inside me, and I clawed the sheets.

"You feel so fucking good," he grunted from behind me.

He repeated the action, never increasing his pace.

"I could watch my cock disappear into your perfect pussy all night. The sight is damn near mesmerizing."

Gritting my teeth, I bit back a retort that I was glad he was having fun because I was frustrated out of my mind that he wouldn't just rail me hard. Every time his cock surged deep, I felt the first teasing hint of an orgasm, but it wasn't building the way I needed it because he wasn't hitting that spot rapid-fire.

Bracing one hand on the mattress, I reached my other arm back, digging my nails into Jenner's hips in an attempt to urge him along.

"You need to come, baby?"

"God, yes."

He removed my hand from his body, placing it back onto the mattress as he caged me in from above, our sweat mixing as his chest pressed against my back. That changed the angle of our connection, and I groaned when he rubbed me just right, both inside and out.

I squealed when his fingers brushed my clit, but with how he had me pinned, I wasn't able to escape his touch, no matter how overwhelming.

"Bite the sheets, baby." A shiver rolled down my spine at his silky-smooth words.

When I didn't obey immediately, too far gone to lust to compute his meaning, Jenner's voice grew more commanding. "That wasn't a request. Bite down."

Swallowing thickly, I managed to open my mouth and clamped down on the material right before me.

"That's my girl," Jenner rasped.

Fuck, that was almost enough to throw me over.

My response was muffled by a mouthful of fabric, as were my screams, when his fingers pressed firmly, rubbing tight circles over my clit as he resumed pounding into me from behind.

Electricity shot outward from my core, lighting me up like a Christmas tree. Tears leaked from the corners of my tightly shut eyes as the pleasure crashed over me in waves so intense it felt like I might black out.

"Goddamn, I could watch you come all day."

I could barely hear Jenner over the blood rushing in my ears.

His grunts were hot in my ear as he thrust three more times before stilling, his teeth latching onto the skin of my neck as he spilled himself deep inside me.

As soon as he finished, Jenner gently eased me onto my side, our connection intact, even though his cock was softening.

He pressed a palm over my heaving chest, directly above my heart, his fingers spreading wide over my sternum. "I hate that you thought for even one second that I didn't want you."

My hand covered his. "You know how it is when I get stuck in my head."

"Evie." He kissed the sweaty skin of my bare shoulder. "I've wanted you since the first time I laid eyes on you." His soft chuckle vibrated through his chest, and it warmed my heart. "I never told you this, but I was hard for the entirety of our first meeting."

"What?" I turned my head so I could see him.

"It's true. One look at you, and I knew I needed to get my hands on you. And then you sassed me, letting your confidence shine through, and that physical attraction I felt blossomed into something more."

I huffed out a disbelieving laugh. "You're joking."

"Nope. Your body has always turned me on, even when I didn't know if I'd ever get a chance to be with you." His palm skimmed between my breasts and came to rest on my belly. "This doesn't change anything for me."

My eyes squeezed shut. "I'm sorry."

"You have nothing to be sorry for. But maybe the next time your thoughts run away with you, come talk to me. We're always stronger together, okay?"

"Yeah," I agreed with a sigh.

"And now that we've got that issue out in the open. If you need relief, and I'm around? You come to me. Understood?"

The tiniest smile crept onto my lips. "You got it, boss."

His resulting laughter lightened the heavier mood, and I relaxed enough to fall asleep, held in his strong arms.

Chapter 30

Jenner

It didn't matter that it was early afternoon. I knew better by now than to come into the house and make a ton of noise. If one or both of my girls were sleeping, I didn't want to risk disturbing their much-needed rest.

Stepping through the silent first floor, I had a suspicion that was the case today. And I wasn't mad about it. With a game tonight, I couldn't think of anything better than slipping into bed beside my wife and having her warm body pressed against mine as I took my own nap in preparation for the grind on the ice later.

But as I climbed the stairs, I heard a faint sound coming from the open door to Hope's room. Venturing closer, I took a peek inside, and what I encountered stole my breath away.

Evie was seated in the glider rocking chair near the window, her legs working to keep a rhythmic motion as she fed our daughter a bottle and sang to her softly.

It didn't matter how many years we'd pictured the moment we would become parents; nothing could compare to the reality. Warmth spread from my chest, and my heart threatened to burst watching my wife love on our little girl.

This was the role Evie had been born to play.

Everything was already perfect, having Hope in our lives, and I couldn't begin to imagine how incredible it would be once our boys joined us, turning our tiny family into a large one overnight.

"Hey," I said softly, stepping inside.

Violet eyes, filled with love, looked up, and my stunning wife smiled. Speaking to our daughter, she whispered, "Look, Daddy's home."

I extended my hands. "Want me to take her?"

Evie shook her head. "No, I'm good right here. I'll finish feeding her, and then you can burp her and put her down."

"Sounds like a deal." I knelt at her feet, content to watch on as my wife and daughter's bond grew by the day.

We'd fought hard to achieve our ideal version of domestic bliss, but now that we had it? There was nothing more beautiful in this world.

"Jenner!" My name uttered on a pained cry had me bolting upright in bed.

In the middle of the night, our bedroom was dark, and my brain was so groggy that it took a moment to process what I was seeing.

Evie was writhing on the mattress beside me, her face pinched in pain as she gasped for breath.

Fuck. I'd known we would be on high alert for the next few months, but I thought we had more time. She'd only hit twenty-seven weeks yesterday.

Tamping down my panic that it was far too soon for our sons to be born, I tried to keep my voice calm when I spoke. "Talk to me, Evie."

Teeth gritted, she hissed out, "Cramp."

Relief surged through my veins.

"Tell me where."

Fisting the pillow by her side, she sucked in a sharp breath. "Leg."

I wasn't a stranger to muscle cramps and knew how agonizing they could be when they came upon you suddenly. Kneeling beside my wife, I palpated down the leg closest to me first, then switched to the other and worked my way up. The minute I pressed into her upper calf, she screamed.

The muscle was locked tight beneath my touch, and I knew it was only going to hurt more before it felt better.

"Breathe," I coached as I dug my thumbs in, rubbing tight circles against the hard knot beneath the skin.

"Can't," Evie panted before letting out another series of screams when I hit a particularly tender spot.

I shifted my stance on the bed, straddling her uninjured leg so she didn't kick me out of reflex.

"I've got you, but try to relax, babe."

"Fuck off," she gritted out, and I had to bite back a smile. Labor was going to be a real picnic with this one.

"I know it's hard, but you have to try. Deep breaths, okay? Focus on that while I try to get your calf to loosen up."

My girl whined but forced herself to slow her erratic breathing.

"That's my good girl. You're doing great," I praised.

Wryly, she remarked, "That doesn't have quite the same impact outside of sex."

I chuckled. "There she is."

Beneath my fingertips, her muscles finally gave way under the counter-pressure, and Evie flopped back with a relieved sigh.

"That sucked," she breathed out.

"I'll bet." I shifted off the bed and headed for the bathroom. "I'm gonna rub you down with some of my muscle salve, and hopefully, you won't be too sore tomorrow."

Returning to the edge of the bed with the container in hand, I had barely unscrewed the lid when tiny cries filtered through the baby monitor.

Evie threw an arm over her eyes. "Fuck. I'm sorry."

"Don't be." I patted the side of her thigh. "Honestly, I would have been impressed as hell if she could sleep through all that."

Her nose wrinkled. "Was I that loud?"

"Let's just say we'll be lucky if the neighbors don't call the cops thinking I tried to kill you," I teased back. "You stay here. I'll bring her in and then work on your leg while you feed her."

She nodded, and I padded out of our bedroom. Hustling downstairs to the kitchen, I warmed a bottle before pushing into the nursery right off the master suite.

Our little girl was pissed at having her sleep interrupted, and I couldn't blame her. No one enjoyed being jarred from a restful slumber like the three of us had been tonight. Though, Evie had had it the worst of all of us.

"Hey, little one. Did Mama wake you up with her hollering?"

I reached into the crib before cradling Hope to my bare chest. It would never get old feeling how perfectly she fit there.

Giving her a quick change, I brought her into our room, declaring, "Someone's wide awake and ready to party."

Evie was no longer reclined. Instead, she sat up in bed with one leg tucked beneath her and the other outstretched. Sitting like that, her belly dipped low enough to brush the mattress, and I marveled at how it got bigger with each passing day.

"She's not the only one," my wife grumbled, pressing both hands to the sides of her swollen stomach. "Would seem my middle of the night screamfest woke them all up."

Coming closer, I pressed a kiss to her forehead. "Can't say I blame them. FOMO is very real, and it sounded like you were having a good old time without them in here."

She shot me a dirty look. "Not exactly the kind of screaming good time I prefer."

"Shhh," I teased, widening my eyes and placing a finger over my lips. "Not in front of the kids."

The love of my life rolled her beautiful eyes. "You're ridiculous."

"I know." I winked, handing her our daughter first and then the bottle. "But you love me."

"Only God knows why," Evie shot back, but there was humor in her voice.

Once I was sure she had Hope handled, I went to work rubbing the salve into her leg. Her soft sighs of relief went straight to my dick, but I told him to calm the hell down. Not only was our daughter in the room, but this woman had been in total agony less than half an hour ago. Now was definitely not the time.

"How much water have you been drinking?" I asked, focused on kneading her sore muscles.

When Evie didn't reply, I peeked up, only to find her chewing her lower lip guiltily.

"Evie..." I gave her a disapproving sigh.

"I get busy, okay?" Her tone grew defensive. "I'm dealing with a lot." She threw a pointed look at our daughter.

"Did you enjoy tonight?" I challenged.

"You know I didn't. Don't be a smartass."

"You're missing the point. If you want to minimize the risk of it happening again, you need to make sure to stay well-hydrated. Something you should be doing anyway."

"I know. And I'm trying. I swear."

"Okay." She'd been through enough tonight, so I let it drop with the intention of finding a way to make it easier for her to stay on top of her water intake.

Propping Hope on her shoulder, she patted her tiny back gently. A soft burp sounded, and Evie peeked over her shoulder to stare at our infant daughter.

"She's out like a light," she whispered.

"Good." I gently eased Hope into my arms. "I'll put her back down, and then it's time for all of us to get some rest."

For once, Evie didn't argue, shifting down the mattress until she could curl onto her side.

I kept telling myself the worry would lessen once the twins were here, but I knew I was fooling myself into thinking that. In reality, I would have even more people to love and protect and care for.

But I couldn't fucking wait.

Hooking my keys beside the door to the mudroom, the first thing I heard was Hope's cries echoing throughout the house.

The hairs on the back of my neck raised instantly, my feet moving up the stairs before my brain caught up. The PTSD of finding Evie unconscious was still too fresh in my mind, and knowing she could go into labor at any time had me on edge.

Finding Hope screaming in her crib did nothing to quell my panic. There was no way Evie wouldn't go to her the moment she heard our daughter crying. Even if she was napping herself, she always got up. And I knew that because I loved catching glimpses of them on the baby monitor app on my phone when I wasn't home.

"Hey, hey. It's okay, honey." I scooped up Hope, bouncing her as I strode from the room in search of my heavily pregnant wife.

"Evie!" I called out but received no response.

Fuck, she was nowhere to be seen in our bedroom. My pulse kicked up, and I found it hard to breathe.

Please, God, let her be okay.

The only place remaining that I hadn't searched was the ensuite bathroom. Approaching the open door, I hear the softest sniffles over the blood rushing in my ears.

"Baby?"

Turning the corner, I found her sitting on the floor, propped against the massive jacuzzi tub. Head in her hands, she wept quietly.

Momentarily paralyzed by fear, I froze at the threshold.

"Evie, honey?" I tried again.

She lifted her head, and her red-rimmed eyes peered at me.

Cautiously, I stepped into the room. "Didn't you hear Hope crying?"

Her gaze honed in on our daughter, who was held tight to my chest. "I—I—" she began, but burst into tears before she could finish whatever she'd planned to say.

Dropping to the floor beside her, I used my free hand to brush away the tears lining her cheeks. "What's going on?"

She reached beside her and produced a roll of toilet paper, holding it up without a word, like I was expected to know exactly why she was so upset.

"Ummmmm." I stretched the word out, hoping she would pick up on my confusion. When she didn't, I prompted, "Is there a problem?"

Switching from sadness to rage in an instant, she chucked the roll at the opposite wall. My eyes widened in shock just before she screamed, "You bought the wrong brand!"

Holy shit.

That's what this was about? Toilet paper? Seriously?

This was my first real glimpse of pregnancy mood swings, and I was struggling with how to respond. Honestly, I was mildly terrified of my wife at the moment.

Even though every cell in my body begged me to ask what was wrong with the brand I'd purchased, having taken over most of the shopping these days, I bit my tongue. We didn't need to pour gasoline on this hormone-induced fire.

"I'm sorry, Evie. I didn't know. Next time I go to the store, you can make me a detailed list including what brands you prefer for our household products."

Giving myself a mental pat on the back for my placating reply, I was shocked when she yelled, "What the hell am I going to do until then? I can't use *that*!" She pointed an accusing finger at the roll that had unraveled when she'd launched it across the room.

"Okay." I held a hand up in surrender. "I'll go out right now. I'll even take Hope with me so you can have a moment to yourself."

Sniffling, she wiped the back of her hand beneath her nose. "No, you don't have to do that. She can stay here with me." Evie held her arms out to take our daughter.

Without hesitation, I handed Hope over, knowing that her sweet baby snuggles could make any day brighter.

Evie kissed the top of Hope's head, breathing in the scent like it would cure all that ailed her.

The sight of my two girls gave me the courage to say the thing that had been plaguing my mind for weeks. "I think it's time that we bring in help."

Evie's head whipped in my direction; her lower lip trembled, her voice small as she asked, "You think I can't take care of her?" She clutched our daughter closer to her chest.

Before my wife could dissolve into an emotional puddle again, I explained, "Actually, just the opposite. You take such good care of her that you're forgetting to take care of yourself." I placed my hand on her belly. "You can't forget that you're the sole caretaker for these two right now. Taking care of yourself is taking care of them."

Her gaze dropped to where I touched our unborn sons, resting beneath the bump. "I know. It's just—" Evie sighed heavily. "It's a lot of work caring for a newborn."

"You're right, it is," I agreed. "It's a major adjustment for anyone, let alone someone dealing with a high-risk multiple pregnancy. You have to cut yourself some slack here, babe. It's okay to let others help you."

"B-but I'm her mom, Jenner."

"And that won't ever change. She's never going to love anyone as much as she loves you. Our days of this cute little trio are numbered. Before we know it, you and I are going to be outnumbered. Hiring a nanny has always been on the horizon, but I think it'll be good for all of us if we make that move now. Don't you think?"

"Yeah." Evie nodded. "You're right."

Pressing a kiss to her temple, I whispered, "I only want what's best for you, for Hope, for our boys. Always."

Her head shifted to rest on my shoulder, and we sat on the cold bathroom floor for a while, our family unit sharing a moment of peace after the sudden storm.

Chapter 31
Evie

"Babe!" Jenner shouted as he came in from the garage. "I have a present for you!"

My eyes shifted to Emmy, our new nanny, seated on the opposite couch, where she was folding Hope's laundry during naptime.

Nervous laughter left my lips. In the past, that phrase was usually a lead-in to sex. "Jenner, Emmy's here."

Confusion filtered into his tone. "Yeah, I know." Coming into view, he held up a gift bag.

"Oh." Heat rose to my cheeks.

Coming closer, Jenner smirked. Leaning over the back of the couch, he kept his voice low, saying in my ear, "Aw, baby, did you think I was gonna give you my dick?"

I could have sworn Emmy's lips twitched with the effort to hold back a smile. Guess I should get used to people thinking we were sex maniacs; we were about to have three kids less than half a year apart.

Rolling my eyes, I smacked at his chest the best I could the way I was seated. "You said you have a present?"

"Yes!" His brown eyes sparkled, and he rounded the couch to plop down beside me. Thrusting the gift bag into my hands, he bounced in his seat. "Open it."

I eyed him carefully. What could he have gotten me that had him this excited?

Pulling the tissue paper out first, I frowned when the item inside the bag was uncovered. Gripping the attached handle, I pulled out the massive insulated tumbler I saw every woman at the park with.

"Do you like it?" Jenner leaned forward. "I got the purple one to match your eyes. And the best part is, it'll help you up your water intake. Eighty ounces a day sounds like a lot, but you only need to fill this twice to hit it. Isn't that great?"

It was such a thoughtful gesture; I almost felt like a brat for not matching his level of excitement.

His face fell when I remained silent for too long. "Oh shit. Did you want a different color? I can take it back. Or I don't and get you another one anyway. It's better to have more than one. Less washing."

"No. It's not that . . ."

"Then what?"

I took a cleansing breath. "Isn't it bad enough that we were forced to buy a minivan?"

Jenner cocked his head. "What's wrong with the minivan? That thing is kickass. It has more horsepower than my SUV!"

That had me laughing. He was fully locked in on dad mode.

"I feel like I'm one Pilates class away from being a complete suburban mom stereotype with this thing." I waved around the massive tumbler.

Jenner leaned in close, lowering his voice like he was sharing a secret. "Evie, you *are* a suburban mom."

Did he think I didn't know that?

Huffing out a sigh, I said, "What if I don't feel like announcing it to every stranger on the street?"

My husband, bless his soul, had the courage to snicker. "Pretty sure the three newborns will do that for you."

Emmy giggled, and that was all it took for me to laugh, too. Okay, maybe he had a point.

Patting his knee, I pursed my lips together, letting him know I wanted a kiss, but there was no way in hell I was moving my body to lean closer with this big ole belly in the way.

Taking the hint, he shifted closer and pressed a soft kiss to my lips.

"Thank you, Jenner."

His smile was blinding in response. "Now, was that so hard?"

I chucked a pillow at his head, and his laughter boomed so loud that Hope's cries sounded from upstairs. But how could I be mad about him waking her when he was hands down the most attentive husband and father I'd ever encountered?

We were damn lucky to have him.

"I know we planned this appointment for my afternoon off, but I can't get out of this mandatory team meeting," Jenner apologized the minute he made it through the door after practice.

I stared at him in disbelief. "Seriously? It just 'came up' out of nowhere?"

He sighed. "I'm really sorry. I didn't know anything about it until I got to the rink this morning. I only had time to stop off at home and check on you before I went back."

"Why bother?" I huffed.

"Because Emmy couldn't make it in today, and I don't like you being at home alone for so long."

Even though I'd been initially resistant to bringing in help, Emmy had been an absolute godsend. She was an extra set of hands I hadn't realized I needed when Jenner wasn't around.

"I'm going to have to cancel the appointment." I gestured to my massive stomach. "I can't fit this thing behind the wheel anymore. As you well know." I narrowed my eyes, annoyance at this man and the wrench he'd thrown in my day rising by the minute.

"Actually . . ."

A knock sounded at the front door, and he walked toward it, tossing over his shoulder, "I got you a ride."

Before I could ask who he could have enlisted to drive me to my bi-weekly ultrasound and check-up, he opened the door to reveal a smiling Dakota.

She waved enthusiastically, not bothering to greet me before declaring, "We're gonna take your car, okay? It makes the most sense since it's all set up with Hope's car seat."

I raised an eyebrow at my husband.

Jenner pressed his hands together in a pleading gesture. "I know it's a last-minute change, and those can be upsetting . . ."

He was likely referencing my meltdown over toilet paper, but I couldn't be held responsible for the hormones turning me into a crazy person right now. That was my story, and I was sticking to it.

"But the second round of the playoffs starts tomorrow, and the coaching staff wants to make sure we are prepared to take on the Philadelphia Rebels. They took the second spot in the division this year, and we've seen enough of them over the season to know how tough they play."

My attempt at taking a deep breath was foiled by my limited lung capacity, with two little humans pressing on my diaphragm. Without the ability to center myself, agitation leaked into my voice. "Whatever. We can just reschedule."

Jenner and Dakota shared a look before my husband locked eyes with me. "I hate that I can't be there, babe, but I'd really like for you to go and check on our little munchkins. Please?"

Dakota chimed in, "You're actually doing me a favor. I could use this experience for research."

Outnumbered, I let out an aggravated sigh. "Fine." I hooked a thumb over my shoulder. "Van's in the garage."

Jenner helped get Hope buckled into her carrier before latching it into the base and letting the automatic door slide shut. He dropped a kiss on my cheek after he helped me into the passenger seat and said, "Text me with an update, okay? I'll have my phone on the whole time."

I nodded, keeping my lips firmly shut. I knew if I opened them, I would likely snap at him, and that wasn't fair. I had no right to be upset about him needing to go to work. If he worked a regular nine-to-five gig, I wouldn't be upset about him being unable to duck out in the middle of the day. I'd simply grown spoiled that he was free most afternoons, with the tradeoff being that some evenings he had games and other times he traveled.

Dakota smoothed her hands over the steering wheel. "Oooh. This thing is a tank, but it's kinda nice."

As she backed out of the garage, I peeked over at her and teased, "You in the market? I could be persuaded to sell."

Light laughter filled the enclosed space, and she pointed a finger at me. "Oh, no. I see what you're trying to do."

She'd made her feelings pretty clear at Bristol's bridal shower that she wasn't ready to start a family yet.

Assessing her as she drove the familiar route to the medical center, I asked, "Then what are you researching since you're not interested in a baby for yourself? Are you thinking of writing a pregnant heroine in one of your books?"

"Maybe." Dakota's head tilted from side to side as she kept her eyes on the road. "I've been toying with the idea for a while. It's something I've yet to add to my repertoire. Truth be told, I'm terrified."

I folded my lips, biting back a smile. "Because of the oh-so-lovely graphic description you got from Natalie?"

She snorted. "No, but you'd think that would be enough to scar a person for life." Dakota shot a pointed look at my belly. "People really hate a pregnancy trope. I mean, sure, I'm not ready to sacrifice my body in that pursuit yet, but I've never minded reading it. And while I can appreciate that not every book is for every reader, I just can't wrap my head around the vehement response some people have to seeing pregnancy on page. They go out of their way to attack it online while, in turn, making other readers who enjoy it feel ashamed when asking for recommendations. So, yeah, it's mildly terrifying to venture into those rough waters."

Humming, I countered, "Have you ever considered that those who can't or don't want to read such a storyline might be like me? That they've spent years struggling, so even seeing other women pregnant in fiction is a knife to the heart? When they pick up a book, they want to escape, not be reminded of the pain in their real life."

Dakota nodded slowly. "Yeah, I can see that. It's why content warnings are so very important. I'm always careful to lay out any minor thing that might be considered a trigger so readers can make the best choice for them when deciding to read my work."

"But while it might be something I steer clear of in my leisure reading, I don't know that I would go out of my way to attack it on a public forum. There's simply no need to incite a riot over a personal preference."

"I agree. There's nothing else out there that splits the reader community quite like a surprise pregnancy trope. I'm sure there's also the camp that feels like it's forcing a relationship. And I can understand that, too. Look at Jaxon and Natalie, for example. Sure, Jaxon always loved her, but if it weren't for Charlie, there's no telling if he'd have ever gotten the chance to work his way into her life. I'm not saying every couple who has been dealt an accidental pregnancy is meant to be—because not all of them are—but I'm in the business of writing fiction. It doesn't always have to be super realistic; it just has to give you the warm and fuzzies."

She made a good point, and it was interesting to hear an author's perspective. Dakota's peek behind the curtain of the romance industry made me want to scope out some of these "surprise" pregnancy stories.

After all, I was living it, even if my situation was different than most portrayed in print.

"See, it was good I tagged along," Dakota chirped as we got back into the car after my appointment. "I've never heard of pelvic rest before."

"Lucky you," I grumbled, not exactly in the best mood.

Pelvic rest meant all extracurricular activities *down there* were off-limits until after I delivered. At a touch over twenty-eight weeks, I was looking at another two months if the boys decided to stay put until my induction.

Jenner had just gotten over his fear of touching me, and now it was completely hopeless. Those orgasms were the only relief I had when pain pulled at my hips and back almost constantly. Lugging these two around daily was beginning to take a toll on my body.

"But, oh my God, was that ultrasound cool!" Dakota gushed. "Do you really get to see them like that all the time?"

I nodded. "Every other week."

"They're like, tiny people in there! And they were moving around so much!"

Her excitement was slowly pulling me from my sulking over losing sex. A smile tipped up on my lips, and when I dropped a hand to my protruding belly, I was promptly rewarded with a strong kick. "Yeah. They're little gymnasts in there."

"You mind if I stop off for coffee? I stayed up way too late last night writing and need a little kick."

"Sure." It wasn't like I had anywhere else to be. Outside of doctor's appointments, I usually didn't leave the house—the having a newborn and being pregnant combo was a killer.

Dakota turned off into a trendy little downtown area near my house. The sidewalks were bustling with stay-at-home moms pushing strollers, college kids hanging out between classes, and retirees enjoying an early dinner at outdoor patio seating. It was a beautiful spring day, and it seemed like the locals were enjoying it.

Lugging myself out of the van, I had to admit the fresh air felt good. Maybe we could open the pool soon, and I could get some pain relief by floating.

"Here, I've got her," Dakota offered before I could grab Hope's carrier from the backseat. She'd been super helpful at the appointment, handling the baby while I was otherwise occupied.

The coffee shop had a pink and brown striped canopy where a few patrons enjoyed their pastries and beverages outside. The big picture windows had been painted from the inside, showcasing stenciled outlines of various types of coffee—latte, Americano, iced.

When I pushed inside, a bell rang over the door, signaling our arrival, but before I could step even two feet inside, a chorus of voices shouted, "Surprise!"

Blinking, I stumbled back, bumping into Dakota behind me.

It took a moment, but I was finally able to piece together what was going on. Blue and white balloons filled the space, in addition to ones spelling out B-O-Y in baby block letters. And the women who had shouted were all ones I knew—the Speed WAGs.

Already highly emotional after my appointment, the idea of them throwing me a surprise baby shower was too much. But when one face in the crowd caught my eye, it threw me over the top.

Hand trembling, I brought it to my mouth as a sob escaped. "Oh my God, Tash?"

My long-lost best friend strode forward and pulled me into her arms the best she could with my belly in the way. She even smelled the same, and I breathed in deeply the scent of her, clutching her tighter, almost as if I were afraid she would disappear if I let go.

"I can't believe you're here," I managed to get out through the sniffles.

Pulling back, Natasha peeked down at my bump fondly. "Look at you."

"Yeah." I dropped my gaze.

"I only got a quick rundown about what's been going on, but I wish you'd reached out. I would have wanted to support you in any way you needed. You have to know that."

I swallowed, emotion making my voice thick. "It was too hard. The feeling of failure and the shame that accompanied it were suffocating, and I couldn't talk about it."

"Well, I'm ready to leave the past behind us because we have more pressing matters to discuss."

Curious, my head snapped up. "Oh, yeah?"

Leaning in close, she said, "Can we just talk about the hot young thing Maddox snagged?"

Surprised laughter bubbled up from my chest. "She's something."

"I am telling you, Evie, she shocked the hell out of me when she called. Didn't waste any time letting me know she knew I'd slept with her fiancé and then breezed right into the shower invite."

"Sounds about right." I peeked over Natasha's shoulder to find the redhead in question buzzing about the room.

Natasha gave a slight shake of her head. "Not sure I'd be so progressive and open with one of Frank's ex-lovers." Frank was the man who'd gotten her pregnant before we drifted apart, and it sounded like they were still together.

Damn, it felt good to slip back into our easy rapport. It was as if no time had passed when, in reality, it had been nearly seven years.

A smirk curved my lips. "Well, don't forget Maddox has probably slept with half the population of the Midwest by now."

Dreamily, she sighed. "Yeah, he was such a manwhore. But holy shit, his dick." Natasha held out her forearm. "Never seen one like it."

"So I've heard," I muttered dryly, reminded that I wouldn't be getting the D anytime soon.

Turning so we were both facing the women gathered, her gaze honed on Bristol. "He always did have good taste, though. Likes the stunningly beautiful ones with spunk."

I snickered. "You say that now, but you haven't heard her sing."

Humming, she replied, "All you've done is intrigue me. Now, it's like I *have* to hear her sing."

Shaking my head, I grimaced. "Trust me. You don't. Your ears will thank me."

Before Natasha could say anything more, a tiny, familiar voice cried, "VeeVee!"

I searched the room, and Ollie came into view, running toward me. Stopping short, his eyes widened, and his mouth dropped open. "Whoa, VeeVee. Big belly."

We hadn't had a chance to hang out in a while, so he was seeing me big and pregnant for the first time.

Not missing a beat, he gripped the hem of his shirt with both chubby hands and lifted. Pushing his soft little belly out, he declared, "Me big belly too!"

"Okay, this kid is adorable," Natasha declared. "Who does he belong to? Because I'm about to sneak him out of here in my purse."

Smiling fondly at the little boy, I ruffled his dark hair. "This is my buddy, Ollie. His dad, Asher, plays with Jenner."

"Believe it or not, I remember him. He was a rookie the last time we talked. And now he's got kids?" Tash shook her head. "Damn, time flies."

The soft whimper behind me had me turning to find Hope rousing from sleep.

Natasha tracked my gaze and gasped. "Oh, Evie. She's precious."

Fresh tears sprang to my eyes, thinking of how close we'd come to losing our chance at raising Hope. There was no question that she belonged in our life, in our home.

"Wanna help feed her?" I offered. "Her little brothers are not super fond of her using them as a resting place. They go berserk when her weight settles over them when she takes a bottle."

"Hells yes, Auntie Tash wants to bond with our sweet little ginger princess. I was born for this moment." She crouched down to speak to the baby in the carrier. "We are gonna spoil you rotten. Yes, we are!"

Seeing my best friend with my daughter warmed yet another frozen place in my heart.

The shower began winding down, and I was still in shock at the sheer generosity of the people in our lives. We wouldn't need to buy a single thing for the boys. They'd even secured us a triple stroller since Hope wasn't much older, and we'd need to cart all three around for a few years.

But the best gift of all was having the time to reconnect with Natasha. We filled each other in on our lives over the past seven years, and I'd learned that she'd finally agreed to marry Frank three years ago, and their son, Teddy, was about to turn eight. We made plans to get our families together once the dust settled on both the season and our new additions.

"Tash, holy shit! Is that you?" Jenner's voice sounded from near the door of the quaint coffee shop.

My best friend stood, striding toward my husband and pulling him in for a hug. When they broke apart, she beamed at him. "Hey, Red, looking good. Love the beard. Meshes well with the whole dad thing you've got going on."

His head tipped back in laughter, causing his Adam's apple to bob along his throat.

"Tell me, Jenner, how many of those pearly whites are fake these days?" she teased.

Jenner flashed her a dazzling grin. "Aw, come on, Tash. You know it's rude to ask a man his number."

Natasha looped an arm around his neck. "Fuck, I've missed you. Now, tell me how in the world you let my girl go, and then I need the deets on how the hell you found yourself here with a baby together and two more on the way."

"Long story," he mused. "How much time do you have?"

She pretended to check a non-existent watch. "Not much. Give it to me quick and dirty. That's just how I like it, right, Maddox?" Natasha winked at Jenner's best friend hovering near the door.

"Jesus." Maddox dragged a hand down his face. "How the fuck does this keep happening to me? Are you all hiding in a closet somewhere? The ghosts of Maddox Sterling's past conquests, ready to be paraded in front of my future wife?"

"Don't worry, big guy." She waggled her fingers at him, the diamond on her left hand catching the light. "I'm happily married. And your little firecracker called *me*, so you can take it up with her."

"Fucking unbelievable," he muttered, going in search of his spirited fiancée.

Jenner crossed the room, placing a kiss on my lips before taking a seat and snagging Hope from Dakota's arms.

"A meeting, huh?" I arched an eyebrow at him.

"Yup." The cocky bastard smirked, making sure to pop the P.

"Your sons are fine, by the way." Sarcasm seeped into my tone.

"I know." He winked. "You already texted me the update."

Even though I was giving him some attitude, I couldn't be upset by the extremely thoughtful gesture of those closest to us, wanting to shower our baby boys with love.

Cuddling our daughter, he addressed Natasha. "Let's see. Long story short, the biggest mistake of my life was not chasing after Evie when she left. We fell into this really bad place of blaming ourselves and thinking we weren't enough for the other. For the record"—he met my eye—"that was never true. So, when she blew back into my life with a crazy scheme to adopt a baby, I was a lovesick fool and couldn't turn her away. But you know Evie. She's nothing if not stubborn. She fought back at every turn, keeping me at arm's length, and for a while, I was content to let our frozen hearts face off. Until one night, she said the most ridiculous thing about me never wanting her to come back, and I decided to make it crystal clear just how much I wanted her." His giant palm came to rest on my belly. "Pretty sure that's the night these two rascals were conceived."

Natasha clicked her tongue. "No one can say the two of you have a boring story. That's for sure."

She had that right. Nothing about our lives was set to be boring ever again.

Chapter 32
Jenner

"Save the icing for cupcakes, Knight! It's not doing you any favors in getting your tired ass off the ice!" Maddox barked from the bench as I gritted against the burn in my thighs after being stuck in the defensive zone for two minutes straight.

He was right. I was stuck out here after an icing because we couldn't change—that was the rule. But the Philadelphia Rebels could, and their fresh legs would be an advantage. It would be easier for them to skate around us, setting up plays while we were sluggish, moving in slow motion as we tried to stop them from scoring.

Putting my head down, I lined up for the defensive zone face-off. If we won it, we had a chance to clear the zone and get it deep into our offensive zone so we could get to the bench and let the next shift take over. If we didn't, the Rebels would be in prime scoring position.

This was Game 3 of the second round, played in Philly. We'd won both games at home but couldn't allow them to claw their way back into this series. The sooner we closed it out, the more time we'd have to rest before hopefully playing in the Eastern Conference Finals. We'd been there once before during my tenure with the Speed and were all itching to get back. Each game won was a step closer to winning a championship.

The ref dropped the puck, and I focused on tying up my man while Braxton battled against the Rebels' center, Riggs. Unfortunately, Riggs chipped it back to his defenseman, who walked the blue line—skating laterally along it—before finding an opening and pulling back for a slap shot. The time it had taken him to shoot allowed two of his teammates to block Goose's vision, and he was unable to see the puck as it sailed over his right shoulder and into the net.

The home crowd in Philly went nuts, and their victory song blared over speakers as our opponents skated to their bench for a line of fist bumps.

"Fuck!" I screamed, slamming my stick against the ice before skating to our bench.

Maddox's jaw was clenched, but he kept his comments to himself. He didn't need to say anything; I knew I'd fucked up by icing the puck prior to that face-off. I'd had the time and space to skate it to the red line before sliding it into our offensive zone, but I was so fucking tired my brain was mush. The only thing I could focus on in that moment was getting it out of the defensive zone so I could get a break.

Oh, I was getting my break now, all right. It just came at the cost of putting my team in a hole.

After dropping Game 3 to the Rebels, Maddox went hard on us in practice the following day. The main focus was special teams, as we'd had opportunities on the power play the night before but hadn't cashed in.

Had even one of those resulted in a goal, we would have gone to overtime to determine the winner.

I was on the power play unit with three other forwards—Braxton, Asher, and Eli Clifford—while Wyatt Banks served as the sole defenseman. The objective was simple: use the man advantage to score a goal. Your opponent only had four skaters, so they couldn't guard all five of you. Passing was key, finding the open man while keeping the other team guessing and preventing them from boxing us out. But ultimately, you wanted to get quality shots on goal. Hell, at this point, with how poorly we'd executed our power play, getting pucks to the net was more vital. Even if a goalie blocked a shot, there was always the chance of scoring on a rebound.

The old adage was that championships were won in practice; you only collected them at games because you should be practicing how you expected to play.

Well, if that were true, we wouldn't be winning a championship anytime soon. Or at least, I wasn't.

Pucks were bouncing right off my stick and onto the penalty kill team's, for them to shoot it down the opposite end of the ice—icing rules didn't apply during a power play for the team down a man; it was the most effective way to kill them by wasting time.

I was struggling, plain and simple, and everyone could see it.

Asher pulled me aside during a water break because he could tell my off-kilter performance stemmed from deeper issues.

"You doing okay?" he asked before squirting a long stream of water into his mouth.

"Yeah, can't seem to get the puck to stick today."

"You sure it's got nothing to do with worrying about your girls back home?" Asher challenged. When I merely grunted in response, he continued, "I get it, man. It's hard for your head to be in the game when you're thinking about your family. And you're dealing with a double whammy. First off, you've got a newborn at home, causing you to suffer with the dad guilt of being on the road. Then throw in the pregnant wife and the uncertainty of when she's gonna pop out a litter, and your stress levels are probably high enough to give you a stroke."

Tilting my face skyward, I blew out a breath. "I've already been pulled off the bench once to rush home and head straight to the hospital. But this time is different." I swallowed. "It's Evie."

"I know." He placed a gloved hand on my shoulder.

"Maddox keeps asking how he can help—well, when he's not barking up my ass to quit fucking up—but short of making me a healthy scratch for every away game from here until the end of the season, there's nothing he can do. And even if that was an option, I've made a commitment. I'm the leader of this team, and I set the tone. The world doesn't stop because my personal life is weighing too heavily on my mind."

"Don't forget you've got allies back in Indy who are ready and willing to step in if you need anything. Tessa and Evie have grown close, and I know my girl would do anything for yours. So, even if it's someone to hang out with so she doesn't go stir-crazy, hit me up. And then, there's Dakota, who is a total night owl when we're on the road. I'm sure she wouldn't mind writing at your house if you're worried about Evie being there alone without the nanny around at night."

I groaned. "Fuck, Asher. I'm still trying to recover from finding her passed out in the middle of the night after coming home from the road."

He cringed. "Sorry. Just going off of what I'd be thinking in your shoes."

"You're right. She probably shouldn't be alone at night right now. Just in case. My mind's been racing constantly, and that one slipped through the cracks."

Asher chuckled. "Glad something good came from our little chat. But seriously, don't be afraid to ask anything you guys need."

"Thanks. Appreciate it."

I had no idea how I was going to survive until the season ended or the babies were born—whichever came first.

"Knight! McCall wants to see you when we get back to the hotel." Maddox stepped into the locker room to convey that message before turning on his heel and walking right back out.

Great. That's just what I need.

Jared McCall was the Speed's general manager. A former player and champion, he knew the game well, and it had worked in his favor when taking on the role of a team builder. He'd been smart about drafting prospects with unrealized potential in later rounds that had led to our current success and future potential as a team. We had our star power, but we also had a strong backbone; our third and fourth-line guys were solid. They could battle it out with the top lines of our opponents, and you needed every line working to secure a championship—hockey was not a game of individuals.

If he wanted to see me personally, I could only imagine it had something to do with my subpar play as of late. My team looked to me to lead by example, but I was failing spectacularly. A ship without a vigilant captain was sure to sink.

Resigned to having my ass handed to me by the man in charge, I knocked on the door to his hotel suite once the team bus brought us back after practice.

I was prepared to be a yes-man, agreeing with every point McCall made because I didn't have a valid excuse for my mind being elsewhere. Players had pregnant partners and babies at home all the time, and it didn't impact their play. They could compartmentalize and do their job—something I had been good at doing until recently.

So, it took me entirely by surprise when he opened the door with a smile, exclaiming, "Jenner, you made it!" Stepping aside, he offered, "Why don't you come in, and we can talk."

Eyeing him, confused as to why he was in such a chipper mood when I'd been playing like shit, I crossed the threshold before awaiting further instructions.

The door latched behind me, and Jared gestured toward a small seating area. "Let's sit down."

Nodding, I dropped onto one of the armchairs. Jared sat opposite me and reclined, propping one foot on the opposite knee.

"How's Evie holding up?"

The man had four children; of course, he would ask about my pregnant wife.

There was a tension that never quite left my body when we were on the road. Not lately, at least. Thoughts of her, our newborn daughter, and unborn sons were constantly on my mind, setting me on edge at the idea of something happening while I traveled.

Sighing, I replied, "Exhausted, as I'm sure you can imagine."

"Of course." He nodded. "Our middle girls are twins, so I've been in your shoes. If you think it's tough now being on the sidelines, just wait.

The chaos is coming. Our oldest son was four when the girls were born, so I can't imagine handling three babies so close in age."

"We've been extremely blessed." Even though we were in a difficult situation at the moment with me having to be away, I couldn't deny that we'd been handed the opportunity to have an instant family. Our lives would be full of love and laughter with our three children.

"That you have," Jared remarked. "Which is why I asked you to meet with me today."

My eyebrows raised, my curiosity piqued. "Yeah?"

"I want you to know that you and your family have the full support of the Speed organization. While I know it's difficult to be away with the uncertainty surrounding when Evie will deliver, we want to alleviate some of the stressors that accompany traveling with the team during this time."

"Because I've been playing like shit," I muttered, peeking at my lap.

Jared barked out a laugh, and my head snapped up. "Why don't you pull up my stats from the time before my girls were born? They aren't pretty. You don't have to explain yourself to me. And it's why I'm offering my help."

"Help how?"

"For starters, from here until the end of the Speed's run in the playoffs, whenever we travel—wherever we travel—there will be a private plane on standby to get you home as quickly as possible if the need arises. I know it's only a small comfort, but it could cut hours off your travel time compared to dealing with commercial flights last minute."

He had a point there. I hadn't been able to get a direct flight from New York to Indy when Hope was born, and that had tacked on an additional two hours. I would never forgive myself if I missed the birth of my sons and wasn't there to support Evie in that moment.

"That's very generous." I ducked my head.

"Maddox can be a bit of a hardass, but he agreed that you needed some peace of mind. He's always looked out for you."

Chuckling, I replied, "Yeah, he's okay some of the time."

"Which is why we've also arranged for a chef to prepare dinner in your home for the duration of the season. Having a newborn is challenging and time-consuming, and can often mean a momma forgets to eat. Let us take that worry off your plate. Every day, Evie will have nutritious food to eat while she cares for your daughter and continues growing your sons. How does that sound?"

I was at a loss for words. "Jared, this is too much."

He shook his head. "I wish I could do more. You've been an incredible asset to this team for years and seamlessly stepped into the role of captain when Maddox could no longer play. We owe you a debt of gratitude for your years of service and continued commitment to making our team better. Your family is our family, and we take care of our own. No exceptions."

"Thank you. I don't know what else to say because that almost doesn't feel like enough."

Jared smiled. "It's not anything more than someone once did for me a long time ago, and I never forgot it." He stood, making it clear that our meeting was over.

He walked me to the door, but before he opened it, he asked, "You've been doing the belly lift trick with her, right?"

I tilted my head. "What?"

Stepping back, Jared demonstrated with an imaginary partner before explaining, "You stand behind her and lift her belly up from below. Takes tons of pressure off her hips and lower back. Give it a try when you get home. Give your girl a little relief while she's carrying the entire load, yeah?"

Dazed, I stared at my GM. "Thanks for the tip."

Moving closer, he clapped me on the back. "Anytime. Buckle up, though, Jenner, because you're about to go on one hell of a ride."

I wouldn't argue with him there. Life was coming at us faster than we could have ever imagined, but I wouldn't change it for the world.

Home at last, I was surprised to find all the lights on inside the house upon arrival. Stepping through the rooms, it didn't take long to discover why.

Like angels, both my girls were passed out in the living room with the TV still on.

Hope was in her bouncer beside the coffee table, and Evie lay on her side on the couch.

Taking a seat on the coffee table, I leaned forward to brush some of the blonde hair off Evie's face.

"Hey," I whispered. As much as I hated to wake her when she was finally catching some rest, I knew she would be extra sore tomorrow if I left her here.

Black eyelashes fluttered against her cheeks a moment before hazy purple eyes peered at me. A smile curved on her plush lips when she focused enough to see who had woken her.

"You're home." Her twang was more pronounced when she was groggy, and it did things to me, but I told my dick to calm down. There would be no hanky-panky until our boys were delivered safe and sound.

"Mmhmm." I softly stroked the curve of her cheek with the pad of my thumb.

"Did you win? I tried to stay up, but—" Evie let out a soft sigh. "I just couldn't keep my eyes open a minute longer."

"Yeah, baby, we did. One more to go, and we're in the Conference Finals."

"That's good." Her eyes drifted closed again.

"Why don't we get you up to bed? I bet your pillow is waiting for you."

"Stupid fuckin' pillow," she grumbled.

I bit back a laugh. To this day, she still couldn't admit it helped to have the pregnancy pillow supporting her back while the other side tucked between her knees alleviated her hip pain. But she wouldn't be the stubborn woman I married—twice—if she ever said I was right. And God knows I loved her for it.

Slipping an arm beneath her shoulders, I eased her into a sitting position, even as she whined, eyes still shut. A wrinkle formed between her brows, and she shifted. "Dammit. Now I have to pee."

"Sounds about right." I tried and failed to keep the smile from my voice.

The tiniest hint of purple was visible from her thinly cracked eyelids. "Glad my misery amuses someone."

Kissing her forehead before standing and offering her a hand up, I replied, "You know I hate seeing you uncomfortable. Just thought it was a given that any time you wake up at night, you'd need to go to the bathroom, so it was kinda funny that it seemed like you were surprised by it, is all."

Evie stifled a groan as I tugged her from the couch.

"I'm gonna get Hope settled. You okay to make it to bed? Or do you want me to tuck you in first?"

Rolling her eyes, she waddled past me in the direction of the downstairs powder room. "Take care of our daughter, but if I'm not up there in ten minutes, it's because I fell asleep sitting on the toilet."

I placed a hand over my mouth, my body vibrating with the force it took to hold back laughter. I could respect she wasn't in the mood, but the mental image she painted was too much.

Once Evie was out of sight, I scooped up Hope, who only let out the tiniest whimper at being moved. Not knowing how long she'd been out, I was careful not to wake her as I transferred her to her crib and turned on the white noise machine.

For a while, I rested my forearms on the crib rail and simply stared at her. I still couldn't get over how stunningly perfect she was. And it almost felt like she'd changed in the four days I'd been away. I wanted time to slow down so that I could memorize every moment of her being this little, but I knew that's not how it worked.

How many times had my parents said when we were growing up that it was over in a flash, and they couldn't believe how fast the time had flown between when they'd brought us home from the hospital and when they'd watched us embark on our adult lives? When you were younger, you thought they were full of shit because it was crawling by for you, but I finally got it. They'd been right all along.

"You gonna stare at her all night, or you comin' to bed?" Evie's tired voice reached my ears, and I turned to find her standing at the door to the nursery.

"Coming, babe. Just missed her and wanted to soak up a few extra minutes, even if she's asleep."

"Not even two months old, and she's already got you wrapped around her little finger," she teased.

"Guilty." I rose to my full height and made my way over to where my wife stood. Cupping her face, I leaned in to whisper against her lips, "I have a soft spot for the beautiful girls in my life."

Evie let out a stuttered breath, and I took that opportunity to kiss her long and slow. My love for this woman had never dulled, even during our time apart, and if possible, it had blossomed even further since her return.

I swallowed her moan, but when she used both hands to shove against my chest, I stepped back, breaking our connection.

Fingers pressing against kiss-swollen lips, she chided, "Not fair, Jenner."

"I know." I blew out a breath. She wasn't the only one who was sexually frustrated at the moment. "Let me make it up to you."

Arching an eyebrow, she folded both arms over her chest. "And how do you expect to do that?"

Placing my hand on the small of her back, I guided her from our daughter's nursery, silently latching the door behind us. Once we entered our master suite, I pulled her into my arms and spun her around until her back was pressed to my chest.

Evie turned her head to peek back at me. "What are you doing?"

"You'll see." I pressed my lips against the skin of her neck.

Lately, she hated fabric rubbing against her belly, so at home, she usually only wore cotton shorts and a sports bra, and tonight was no exception. I skimmed my hands along the bare sides of her swollen stomach, and she jumped in my arms.

"Your hands are cold."

"I'm sorry." Immediately, I moved to pull my hands away, but she reached up to place hers atop them.

"No, I'm hot all the time, so it feels nice."

"Oh, good." Reaching lower, I cupped the underside of her belly and gently lifted.

Evie immediately melted in my arms, her muscles relaxing as she leaned into my hold. "Holy shit," she breathed out. "What kind of magic is this?"

"You like it?"

"Like it?" she huffed. "Babe, forget sleeping tonight because I'm gonna need you to do this all night. Where has this been all my life?"

All of my tension slipped away, at finally being able to give her some relief. I'd felt helpless for most of her pregnancy, so if I could do this one small thing to help ease her pain, I would happily do it for as long as she liked.

"Little trick Jared McCall told me about the other day. Said it helped his wife."

While we gently rocked from side to side, Evie moaned. "Jared is my new favorite person."

I let out a near-silent laugh. "That's not all."

"Oh, yeah?" Her voice took on a faraway quality, like she was falling into a dream state.

Nuzzling the top of her head, I explained, "He's got a jet on standby for when the team travels, in case I need to get home in a hurry."

"That's nice of him."

"On top of that, he's got a chef coming in to make dinner for you—for us—for the rest of the season."

Evie simply hummed.

Since she was so relaxed, I decided to push my luck.

"I was thinking . . . I don't love the idea of you being here alone when I'm gone. Maybe we call in one of the moms to come visit and keep you company?"

Groaning, she pulled from my hold and turned to face me. "We have Emmy."

"We do," I agreed. "But she's not here at night. And her job is to take care of Hope. I want someone here to take care of you."

Evie threw both hands on her hips, temper flaring. "I'm not a child."

"Never said you were, honey. But I worry. And I'm struggling with it to the point where it takes up all the space in my mind when I can't be here. It took ten years off my life when I found you unconscious in this very room only a few months ago. I just want to know that, should anything happen, someone is here to help you until I get home."

She must have seen the anguish on my face at that memory because she finally relented. "Okay."

"It's up to you who we fly in to help out. I know your mom is set to come in late June anyway, so we can bump up her ticket. Or we can bring in mine until the end of the season."

"You boys set to win it all this year?" my wife asked, a hint of challenge in her tone.

"That's the plan."

Nodding once, Evie declared, "Then call your mom. I'm sure she'd want to be around to watch her boy raise the trophy."

"I'll do that first thing tomorrow."

I stepped closer, helping to ease her onto the bed and position her in a way that she was most comfortable before sitting on the edge. Leaning over, I pressed a soft kiss to her lips. "Get some rest." Then I shifted until my mouth hovered directly over her belly, whispering, "You too, boys. Let your mama sleep."

Evie's hands tangled in my hair, an expression of pure love on her face when I peeked up. As long as my family was safe and sound, I would want for nothing else in this life.

Chapter 33

Jenner

After taking down the Rebels in five games and battling it out with the Miami Storm in a back-and-forth series that took six games to settle, the Indy Speed were headed for the championship round against the Chicago Crush.

The past two seasons hadn't gone our way, but through perseverance and grit, it would seem that the third one was set to be the charm. We'd finally made it back to the Finals. This time, we were determined to emerge victorious.

After our trip to Philly, I was in a much better headspace. Knowing multiple people were going out of their way to support our family had lifted a huge burden off my shoulders, and I was able to focus on the game, which was what I was paid to do.

My mom had been in town for three weeks now, and though Evie would never admit it, she liked the company.

Pam Knight was a natural caretaker, and she made sure my wife didn't lift a finger, which I wholeheartedly appreciated. She got her to appointments—going more frequently now that Evie had hit the thirty-two-week mark—and ensured that she was eating enough, drinking enough, and getting plenty of rest, which was easier said than done at this point.

Did it suck knowing my wife and daughter weren't in the stands as we took this next step? Absolutely. But I knew how taxing attending a game would be for Evie, and even watching on TV, staying up late enough to witness its conclusion was often a struggle.

While we'd been the top seed in the Eastern Conference, the Crush held that distinction in the Western Conference. Since they had more regular season points than us, they were the ones who held home-ice advantage for this series. That meant we were headed on the road for Games 1 and 2 in Chicago.

We dropped Game 1, losing by a score of four-to-two, but made the necessary adjustments as a team to beat the Crush in Game 2 two-to-one.

Back in Indy for Game 3, we were firing on all cylinders. The hometown crowd's energy lifted us up, and we were buzzing—executing perfect passes, laying the big hits to separate our opponents from the puck, and cashing in on quality scoring chances. We won big, beating the Crush five-to-nothing.

Game 4 was more of a grind. Chicago wasn't going down without a fight. They made us work for every zone entry, every shot, and challenged us in the corners. Neither team had scored a goal through fifty-five minutes of regulation. If we remained scoreless for another five minutes, that would mean a sudden-death overtime.

The extra time would wear on both teams, so to lose would not only be a mental hit but a physical one.

Thankfully, Goose did what he did best, being a brick wall and not letting a single shot past him. On one particularly skillful block with his pads, he kicked the puck out to the half wall, and I was able to scoop it up and make the stretch pass to Braxton in the neutral zone. He and Asher were off to the races, challenging the lone defenseman for the Crush.

I could see the move before it happened. Braxton flicked the puck to Asher, whose stick barely touched it before sliding it right back over to our young center. The goalie and defenseman had both locked on Asher as the shooter and were caught completely off guard when Braxton sniped from close range, scoring the game-winning goal with less than sixty seconds on the clock.

We were riding high on our return trip to Chicago for Game 5. We were up three-to-one on the Crush in the series, which meant we only needed one more win. Even when we had been in the Finals three years ago, we hadn't come this close. Each time we took the ice from this point forward, we had an opportunity to secure the championship and have our names immortalized in silver like so many greats who had come before us.

It was every player's dream, and so few were able to achieve it.

But we were the ones here now, and we had to make the most of this chance.

Unfortunately, in Game 5, we couldn't quite find our groove, and a few bad penalties were the difference between a win and a loss. While it sucked that we wouldn't be traveling home with the trophy, it would be even sweeter to win it on home ice.

So, that's where we placed our focus.

It was time to seal the deal.

Evie gave me a hug and kiss before I left for Game 6, wishing me good luck. My heart threatened to burst when I saw she'd dressed Hope in the custom Daddy jersey Maddox had gifted us at Christmas.

Crouching down, I pulled her from her swing and cradled her against my chest. "Well, aren't you the cutest little Speed fan I've ever seen?"

She was becoming more vocal by the day and let out a tiny squeal.

I bounced her. "Can you say, 'Go Speed'?"

Hope's response was incoherent babble, and drool drenched the fabric of my white dress shirt.

"Close enough." I pressed a kiss to the top of her head. "Be good for Mama, you hear?"

My mom moved toward us with outstretched arms. "Better get going, or you're gonna be late."

Rolling my eyes playfully, I replied, "Yes, Mom," and handed over my daughter.

Mom placed a hand on my forearm and squeezed. "Do you remember what I always told you going into a big game when you were growing up?"

How could I forget?

A smile touched my lips as I repeated her advice from my youth hockey days. "Play the game like you love it, and the rest will fall into place."

Brown eyes that matched mine grew glassy. "No matter what happens out there tonight, just know that everyone is so very proud of you—me, your dad, your siblings, and most of all, your beautiful wife and daughter."

Fuck, I had to get out of here before I let emotions take hold. I couldn't afford to be anything less than one-hundred-and-ten percent focused going into this game.

"Love you, Mom." I squeezed her from the side, making sure not to crush Hope.

Another quick kiss to Evie, and I was out the door.

Tonight was our night. It had to be.

The crowd was already on their feet screaming, and we'd barely taken the ice for warm-ups. If they could keep this up, maybe it would be enough to throw Chicago off their game.

As a team, we took turns shooting on Goose, warming him up. Then, we broke off into smaller groups to stretch and work on individual skills, such as passing or puck handling.

Asher and I had always paired up for this part, so he was right beside me when I dropped to my knees, spread them wide, and pressed my hips toward the ice to stretch out my hip flexors.

For some reason, women always went wild for this move. I mean, yeah, it did look like we were humping the ice, but it was an important stretch, one we couldn't very well stop doing because female fans made lewd signs or dedicated social media posts about how much it turned them on.

"Feeling loose?" Asher called out over the raucous crowd.

"Yeah."

The talk with my mom before leaving the house had helped me. This was a game I'd been playing my entire life. The stakes were higher than when I'd been a child, but the game itself hadn't changed. If we focused on fundamentals and team play, we should have an edge.

But there was still one thing weighing on my mind.

"Just sucks that if we do manage to pull this off, Evie and Hope won't be here to share it with me."

Raising an eyebrow, Asher's gaze shifted toward the curved glass in the corner where the players' kids usually hung out pre-game. "You sure about that?"

"What?" My head whipped around so fast I could have sworn I heard a crack.

There, pressed against the glass, was my tiny redheaded cutie, held up by her mother, the love of my life.

Asher nudged me with a shoulder. "It's Baby Girl's first hockey game. You should go over and say hello."

I let out a disbelieving laugh as I pushed off the ice and skated over.

A few of my teammates were hanging out there, making silly faces at their kids or tossing warm-up pucks over the glass for them.

I couldn't be sure who it belonged to, but a voice called out, "Make way for Cap! He came to see his girls!"

They all shifted, allowing me the perfect view of my little girl dressed in my jersey, a pair of oversized headphones gracing her tiny head. When her blue eyes landed on me, they lit up, and she flapped her arms, chubby hands making contact with the thick glass.

I waved a gloved hand in her direction as I approached, "Hey, little one." I knew she couldn't hear me, but the way her rosebud lips curved into a wide smile, it was almost as if she knew what I was saying.

Stopping at the glass separating us, I swallowed back the emotions at seeing my family on such a big night.

"I'm so glad you're here," I whispered. "Daddy's gonna go out there and win this one for you."

Dropping my forehead to the glass, I closed my eyes and took a deep breath, trying to center myself. My heart squeezed when I skated back and locked eyes with Evie. She knew how big this night was for me, for the team, and she'd made sure to be here with our daughter. I couldn't love her any more if I tried.

"I love you." I knew she could read the words on my lips.

Her smile brightened, and a touch of pink graced her cheeks as she said those three little words back to me.

Blowing them both a kiss, I skated away, more confident than ever that tonight was the night the Indy Speed would become champions.

Maddox made his pre-game speech, the emphasis on not getting ahead of ourselves.

Yes, the prospect of winning it all on home ice was exciting, but we couldn't get so focused on it that we forgot how to play the game. He stressed how important it was to take the game one shift at a time and make each one of them count. But he also cautioned that the Crush would be hungry. They were the ones with their backs against a wall, knowing if they didn't win, their season was over, so they were going to play tough. We would have to match their intensity if we had any chance at success in closing out this series and becoming champions.

We clapped in unison when he read the starting lineup. Then, he left the locker room.

Next, I stood, pouring my heart out to my teammates about the crushing blow of defeat we'd suffered three years ago. Those on the team at that time nodded along in agreement; that wound was still fresh in many of our minds. This was our chance for redemption—to show the hockey world that we were the best and to cement our legacy for generations to come.

Energized, the guys headed toward the tunnel in preparation for the pre-game hype video and our entrance before the anthem.

Maddox grabbed my elbow and pulled me aside before I could take my spot in our pre-determined lineup.

Usually, he and the rest of the coaching staff were on the bench before the players hit the ice, so I looked at him in question, wondering what he was still doing back here.

With his green gaze boring into me, he spoke, "The lights are bright, and the stage is set. It has always been our dream to do this together." Maddox let out a wry laugh. "We might not have pictured it in this dynamic, but I think we've both been on the receiving end of life's curveballs as of late." He took a deep breath, closing his eyes before reopening them. "A year ago, you were alone. Now, you've got the family you always wanted with the woman who has always held your heart. It's time to go out there and make your wife and kids proud."

I gave him a tight nod. "That's the plan."

"Good. Let's kick some Crush ass."

With a hearty slap on the back, he pushed through the players and disappeared down the tunnel toward where it opened up to the bench.

My best friend was right. There was no more powerful motivator than having my family in attendance and making them proud.

And that's exactly what I intended to do.

We couldn't say Maddox hadn't warned us. The Crush were feisty, not ready to go down without a fight.

Having been in their shoes, I knew the will to win wasn't always enough. The team that played harder and tallied more shots didn't automatically achieve victory.

Sometimes, it all boiled down to luck.

And that's what happened for the Speed tonight.

Tied 2-2 in the third, we were dragging, trying to keep up. If we went to overtime, I wasn't sure we'd be able to squeak out a win. And returning to Chicago for a winner-take-all Game 7 could be a death sentence after an incredible run.

With the seconds ticking down on the final period of regulation, we managed to get the puck deep into our offensive zone. Braxton chased, beating the Crush defender to the boards and shooting it up to Wyatt at the point.

Our D-man pulled his stick back, sending the puck hurtling toward the net. The Crush goalie blocked it, sending it toward where Asher skated below the circles. I hustled my ass to the net, knowing if I could create some mayhem out front, it would distract the goalie.

Asher was at a bad angle but knew he had support that could cash in on a quick rebound, so he shot toward the net.

It all happened so fast.

One second, I was confused about the sharp jolt to my skate, and the next, the crowd went wild.

Stunned, I stared back at my teammates, who were all pointing in my direction, arms thrown up in celebration.

Braxton rushed me from behind. "They don't ask how. They ask how many!"

"What?"

I spun around as Asher joined us, the big man grinning from ear to ear. "Nothing like a perfectly placed boot, my man."

It finally hit me.

Asher's shot must've deflected off my skate and into the net, scoring with—I checked the scoreboard—fifteen seconds left.

Barring a disaster of epic proportions, we were going to win the championship!

Hopped-up on a mix of adrenaline and disbelief, I skated with my teammates to celebrate what could very well be the game-winner.

But, of course, what would life be if not for a little drama?

The Crush's coach barked at one of the refs, accusing me of kicking the puck into the net. While it was legal for the puck to glance off any piece of player equipment on the way to scoring a goal, you couldn't actively kick it in.

Since it was the final minute of the period, he couldn't challenge it, but the delay was enough for the review booth to call down and ask to take a closer look. If this was what a championship boiled down to, they needed to be sure.

It was a good thing I was already drenched down to my base layer, so a little additional bit of sweat while I awaited their decision was barely noticeable. My heart beat in triple time as the nerves crept in the longer the refs were bent over their tablets, headphones on with a direct line to the control room, scanning the play from every angle.

I stopped breathing when they removed those headphones, and the head referee skated to center ice to address the crowd.

He pressed the button on his mic pack, and his words echoed throughout the deathly silent arena.

"After review, it was determined there was no kicking motion. We have a good goal."

Air rushed into my lungs as the roar of the crowd rivaled the buzzing in my ears. Black spots danced along my vision, and I bent over, placing my head between my knees.

A hand patted me on the back, and a voice I knew well said, "Sometimes, it boils down to being in the right place at the right time. Hell of a lucky break on that one, Knight."

Focusing on my breathing until I was no longer in danger of passing out, I straightened, turning around to survey my best friend behind the bench.

His smile said it all. He knew what we all did but were afraid to say out loud.

We were champions. And I was the lucky son of a bitch who'd made it happen in the eleventh hour.

Maddox inclined his head toward center ice. "You're the hero, Jenner. Take the face-off and enjoy it when the bench clears."

Fuck. I still couldn't believe this was really happening.

My skates moved on their own as Braxton winked, taking up a position on the right wing where I usually stood, allowing me to glide toward where the ref waited to drop the puck.

Squaring up against the Crush's center, Newson, I recognized the defeat in his eyes. A pang of empathy shot through me, knowing exactly how he felt. But there wasn't time to dwell on it as the puck dropped, and instead of trying to win it and risk losing it, I tied up Newson, allowing Braxton to swoop in and chip the puck back to Wyatt. He made a D-to-D pass to Ford, and the buzzer sounded.

Sticks and gloves and helmets flew into the air, and the noise level rose so high inside the arena that it was a wonder anyone would leave without permanent hearing damage.

But none of that mattered because, in this moment, my brothers and I had finally reached the top of the mountain. We had clawed our way back from a crushing loss only a few years back, letting it fuel us and lead us right here.

The Indy Speed were motherfucking champions.

We were a mass of bodies piled up behind the net, hugging anyone within reach. Some guys were openly weeping; others let out cheers as it finally sank in.

It took a while before we calmed down enough to line up at center ice to shake the hands of our opponents. I had to hand it to them. They'd played a tough series and could have easily won tonight if it weren't for a perfectly placed skate. It was a difficult pill to swallow, knowing that that was the difference between forcing a Game 7 and the end of their season.

Either way, I couldn't wipe the giant grin from my face while making exchanges with each of the players on the Crush, as I was the first through the line, being our team's captain. I stopped briefly to hug a few guys who'd been former teammates of mine throughout the years, and they graciously congratulated me and my team on our victory.

A member of the Speed staff was handing out branded championship ballcaps and towels, and I snagged a set for myself. Tossing the cap over my sweaty hair, I wiped my face with the towel before slinging it around my neck.

The pomp and circumstance demanded our attention next, but the only thing I wanted to do was celebrate with my girls.

Chapter 34
Evie

Win or lose, it had been the right call to attend the game tonight.

Etched in my memory for all time would be the image of Jenner and Hope when they shared their first warm-up interaction through the glass. It had been such a special moment, and I knew it had bolstered his spirits prior to the game.

Now, I couldn't be more proud of the man who'd always accepted me as I was—flaws and all—the father of my children, skating across the scratched-up ice surface, that gleaming silver chalice he'd always dreamed of winning hoisted high above his head as he let out a cheer.

The joy on his face, shown close up on the giant screen over center ice, was infectious.

Laughter bubbled up from my chest as I bounced Hope. "Look, there's Daddy."

I didn't know about him, but I'd been about ready to throw up when they reviewed his goal. Technically, Asher had shot it, but as the last player to touch the puck, it was credited to Jenner.

I was so mesmerized by the images of Jenner that it took a minute to process the rumble of voices inside the family suite. Peeking around, I noticed some of the women pointing down toward ice level, a few with hands pressed against their chests.

Turning my head to see what they were looking at, I saw it.

Jenner had accepted the trophy as the Speed's captain and was the first to take it for a spin. There were no hard and fast rules about the order past that. From what I understood, it was a personal choice, someone the current handler felt deserved the next turn.

But in all my years with Jenner, it always went from the captain to another player and so forth until each member of the team got their turn. What I'd never seen, and why everyone was staring, was that Jenner skated right up to Maddox, dressed in his head coach attire of a gameday suit. They exchanged a few words, and Jenner offered the trophy to his best friend.

The emotion etched on Maddox's face when it came into view was enough to tug on anyone's heartstrings. I'd heard about his injury in detail from both Dakota and Bristol over this past season—how it had come during their last run at the Finals. And I'd also learned that it still weighed on him. He felt personally responsible for their loss, that had he been able to take the ice, they would have won. So, to see him now, unable to hold back the tears at the gesture from his best friend, it was truly something special.

Unfinished business had been laid to rest.

A hand touched my arm, and I turned to find Dakota, her blue eyes glassy. "We're going to head down. Can I help with Hope?"

I nodded. "Sure, that would be great."

Dakota eased Hope from my arms, and we joined the rest of the friends and family headed down to ice level.

Long periods of standing or walking weren't my favorite these days, and the minute Jerry saw me at the gate tonight, he'd arranged with someone inside to help me around the lower levels in a golf cart. I'd used it earlier when I brought Hope down for warmups, and the same staff member had it waiting for me the minute the elevator doors opened beneath the arena. The blow to my pride hurt less than the waves of pain radiating around my hips to my lower back, so I'd accepted the offer of a mobile escort.

For years—when it was all I could think about—I'd waxed poetic about the beauty of pregnancy. I had built it up in my mind as this serene time when you counted kicks and constantly marveled at the life you had created.

As much as I already loved these babies, I was decidedly *not* having a blissful experience. Pregnancy was not at all glamorous when your skin had stretched to the point of splitting, you had to pee every five minutes and couldn't sleep, and most of the time, it felt like your kids were in the middle of a pay-per-view wrestling match inside the tight confines of your uterus.

I was over it. Plain and simple.

July 5th couldn't come soon enough. Only twenty-two more days to go, not that I was counting or anything.

With Dakota holding Hope, Pam, Jenner's mom, joined us on the cart that moved through the concrete tunnels until they narrowed between the locker room and bench access. I thanked the man for helping us out, and he said he'd hang around in case I needed a ride back after the celebrations wound down.

When we cleared the overhang that opened into the benches, my eyes went wide. The arena was still packed, every person in attendance on their feet and screaming just as they had when the buzzer sounded.

"Holy crap," Dakota breathed beside me.

Several of the WAGs had already made their way out to celebrate with their men, several with legs thrown around their significant others' waists. A few kids were riding on their dads' shoulders. It was a total party atmosphere; the undercurrent of elation could be felt from where we stood.

Knowing Jenner would have my head if I stepped onto that ice, I took a seat on the hard bench, grabbing Hope from Dakota before she took a tentative first step onto the slick surface herself in street shoes.

Braxton skated over immediately, spinning her around in his arms, and I couldn't help but smile at her squeal. When he finally set her down, the kiss they shared was so passionate my face flamed, and I covered Hope's eyes. I was willing to bet Dakota would have enough book inspiration to last her a while after tonight.

When they finally broke apart, Dakota clung to him, burying her face in his chest, but Braxton turned to me, placing two fingers into his mouth. I winced at the sharp sound of his whistle, but if he was going for attention, he'd gotten it. Several of his teammates turned to see what he needed.

Tilting his head in our direction, Braxton yelled, "Go fetch the captain! His girls are waiting."

Ducking my head in gratitude, it was only a few seconds later that I heard the cry of, "Evie!"

My eyes searched the crowd, trying to find Jenner, but there were too many people. But suddenly, hands shoved two players out of the way, and there he was. In all his sweaty, happy glory.

It was a good thing I was already sitting down because the expression of love etched on his face would have been enough to knock me over.

Skating to where we sat, he extended one arm to take Hope before offering the other to help me up. Leaning over opposite sides of the boards, he palmed the back of my head before stealing a kiss. His tongue swept inside my mouth, and damn if I didn't want to jump his bones. Sweat seasoned the taste of his lips, and even the smell of nasty hockey gear wasn't enough to tamp down my arousal. My husband was hot, and he was riding high as the hero of the hour. Pressing my thighs together wasn't nearly enough to quell the ache from the mental imagery of what he would do to me on a night like tonight if I weren't huge and knocked up and not allowed to act on the adrenaline rush of the win.

Kids. They wreaked havoc on your sex life.

Pulling back when we were both panting, he gave my neck a little squeeze before turning to our daughter. "Hey, beautiful! Are you having fun?"

That girl had moon eyes for her dad, even this late at night with all the bright lights and noise. I had to hand it to Pam; ordering those noise-canceling headphones had been a genius idea.

The gummy smile Hope gave Jenner melted my heart, and almost as if they realized they were missing out on the excitement, the boys started rolling around, making their presence known.

I placed a hand against my bump. Tonight was truly a family affair.

Jenner tracked the move and smirked. "They having a dance party?"

"Something like that." I twisted my lips when a particularly sharp joint jabbed me from the inside.

Bending down, he spoke to my belly. "Boys, you're never gonna believe this, but your old dad did a thing tonight. Someday, you'll see pictures and know you were almost there, but I promise to work hard to do it again for you." He straightened, bouncing Hope. "We'll get some pics of her tonight propped up inside the trophy, and I'll pull rank to make sure we get our day with it after the boys are born. Maybe late August. Can you imagine how cute it would be to smush them both in there together?"

Running my hand over his jaw and the overgrown playoff beard resting there, the excitement in his tone had me smiling. "The cutest."

"Hey, Casey!" Jenner called over to a passing staff member. They stopped immediately to see what he needed. "Can we get a carpet over here so my wife can step out from behind the bench?"

Casey nodded. "You got it, Jenner. Coming right up."

I gave an impressed laugh. "Wow, you're really running the show down here these days."

"Nah. That's Maddox. But scoring the game-winner has everyone treating me extra nice tonight."

Laughter floated from my lips. "Gotta cash in on those perks."

"You know it." He winked.

Casey returned with another member of the Speed staff, and they rolled out a red carpet along the boards. With one hand holding mine, Jenner helped me step down from the bench to the covered ice. Pulling me into his side, he signaled for Asher to have whomever had the trophy bring it over.

"Looking for this?" Wyatt Banks skated over, the sparkling silver trophy held in both hands horizontally across his waist.

"Yeah, set it down right here on the carpet for me, will you?" Jenner instructed, to which Wyatt immediately obeyed.

Resting at our feet, it came up to about my hip. Chewing my lower lip, I asked, "Is it okay to touch it? I know you guys are all superstitious about this stuff."

Jenner beamed at me. "Baby, what's mine is yours. Have at it."

With tentative fingers, I reached out to touch the cool metal. I would have expected it to be warmer with how many hands had been on it in the past half hour or so, but I guess the chill of the ice couldn't be completely outweighed.

Staring at the trophy my husband had worked his entire career to win, I whispered, "Jenner, they're gonna stamp your name on this."

"Still can't believe it," he breathed out beside me.

"You earned it, babe." I peeked up to find his chocolate eyes filling with tears.

Pressing a kiss to my temple, he said, "I'm so fucking glad you're here. Wouldn't have been the same without you."

There was an unspoken meaning to his words, and only I knew what he was really saying. Even though he'd be torn to shreds by the press and his teammates if he ever uttered it aloud, he was telling me that he was glad they hadn't won it during the years of my absence because it wouldn't have meant as much without someone to share this joy with.

It was almost as if the stars had aligned, and suddenly, both of us achieved our dreams at the same time.

Chapter 35
Evie

Forget pregnancy exhaustion. Championship fatigue was kicking my ass.

The events were endless. The entire city was celebrating.

Jenner had begged me to stay home from the parade, and it hadn't taken much convincing to agree. As much as I wanted to support him, the idea of sitting in the hot June sun for hours in the back of a pickup truck sounded like torture in my current condition. But even watching it on TV, my skin broke out in goosebumps. The sheer volume of people who packed the streets of downtown Indianapolis was mind-blowing. I couldn't have been more proud of my husband and his teammates for bestowing upon their loyal fans the chance to celebrate with them.

Even outside of Speed-organized celebrations, fireworks were being set off nightly. It grated on my already frayed nerves, not only for waking Hope but for making it impossible for me to sleep as well. As soon as I would drift off, a sharp crack or bang would sound, and I'd be jolted from a restless slumber.

I certainly hadn't been ready for the attention winning a championship would bring to the players. Sure, Jenner was often recognized in public, but fans were generally respectful of our privacy. Now that the Speed had won and Jenner, in particular, was the one who'd scored the winning goal, all boundaries had vanished.

I was still shaken from how we'd practically been mobbed at the medical center when we'd arrived for our most recent appointment to check on the twins.

While we were stuck in Indy for the summer, most of Jenner's teammates would be splitting off to various locations around the globe. That meant tonight was their last hurrah, and maybe we could find some peace before our lives descended into chaos with three babies on our hands.

Jenner could tell I was worn down and offered to let me stay home, but I wanted a chance to say goodbye to our friends. It would be months before we saw them again, and by then, everything would be different.

I'd watched Tessa struggle to get her two little ones to games, and they were a little less than two years apart. I wasn't sure when I'd be comfortable leaving the house with all three alone for playdates, let alone attending Jenner's games to catch up with the ladies.

While I'd insisted we attend the massive blowout party for the team and their families, my ass was parked on an outdoor couch under an umbrella. The pool looked cool and inviting as I sweated like a pig on the humid summer day, but there was no way I was attempting a dip. Not only were there too many kids splashing around, I wasn't sure I'd be able to get back out on my own.

My overly attentive husband never left my side for more than a few minutes, only long enough to fetch me cold water and food. Third-trimester heartburn was a bitch, and I could only manage a few bites here and there without aggravating it.

Thankfully, the ladies were content to hang out in the shade with me. While I could blame my exhaustion on pregnancy, theirs stemmed from being hungover.

Lucky bitches. What I wouldn't give for an ice-cold margarita right about now.

The guys decided to take the kids for a dip in the pool, and I couldn't put my phone down, snapping pic after pic of Hope in a big floppy hat strapped beneath her chin as she swam for the first time with her daddy.

"Ugh," Bristol groaned beside me. "Watching men with babies should be illegal. My ovaries are about to explode."

"Sure, it looks cute now"—I gestured to my gigantic belly—"but remember, sacrifices must be made."

Tessa reached forward to squeeze my hand. "How you hanging in there?"

Groaning, I shifted on the cushion, trying to find a spot that gave me any kind of relief. "Ready to be done, that's for sure."

She gave me a sympathetic smile. "Pretty soon, this will all be a memory, trust me. The end feels like it takes forever when you're in it, but when you look back, it went by in a flash."

I'd just found a position that was mildly comfortable when whichever little rascal was at the top shoved down on his brother, pressing his head directly into my bladder. I felt the tiniest gush and cringed. Bladder control this late in the game was becoming a real problem.

Wincing, I scooched forward to the end of the couch. "Sorry, guys, gotta pee."

Tessa and Dakota stood, each offering a hand to help me up.

Jenner's voice reached me from a few feet away. "You okay, babe?"

I waved a dismissive hand, rolling my eyes. "Bathroom."

He nodded, knowing the drill. Shifting his gaze to Tessa, he asked, "Mind going with her?"

"My pleasure." Tessa linked her arm with mine, leading me into the massive house of the team's owner, who was throwing our farewell bash.

When the air conditioning hit me square in the face, I sighed. "Damn, it feels good in here."

Tessa offered, "I can be a lookout if you wanna crash in here for a bit."

"As amazing as that sounds, it wouldn't last long. Jenner will panic if I don't come right back." I tried to keep the annoyance from my tone. I knew he was on edge as we inched closer to the boys' arrival, and he wanted to make sure all of us were safe and well cared for.

"He loves you." My friend bumped me with her shoulder. "He's just dealing with that expectant father anxiety. Asher was a total mess before Ollie was born. Trust me."

"Yeah . . ."

We reached the door designated for the powder room, and Tessa pushed it open.

"Need me to come in with you in case you need help getting up?"

She was only half teasing, and it made me laugh. "Appreciate the offer, but I think I can handle it on my own."

Nodding, she stepped aside. "Sounds good. I'll hang here till you get out."

Entering the bathroom, I closed and locked the door behind me. A peek at my reflection in the mirror had my nose wrinkling. My ponytail was a mess, sweaty pieces of blonde hair now framed my face, and half of my makeup had damn near melted off. I could fix that when I was done, but right now, I couldn't ignore that I really needed to pee.

Sighing in relief when my bladder emptied, I flushed and moved to the sink. After washing my hands with soap, I used them to cup water before leaning down to wash my face. No makeup at all was better than the look I had going on now.

As I straightened up, I felt another gush.

Aggravated, I groaned.

Seriously? My bladder is freaking empty. Where the hell is this coming from?

Shaking my head, I blamed it on the ridiculous amount of water Jenner was forcing on me. He'd upped my intake by fifty percent, claiming that heat-inducing sweating required more fluid replacement.

A light knock sounded on the door. "You okay in there?"

Drying my hands on the hand towel, I opened the door. "Yep. Better get back out there before they organize a search party."

Back beneath the umbrella, the girls were telling me about their summer homes.

Dakota and Braxton had a brand-new lake house in Minnesota, a wedding gift from Braxton's brother and sister-in-law. I gawked at her when she told me that, but I suppose a man who made an eight-figure annual salary had nothing better to do with his money than spend it on the people he loved.

Tessa and Asher, and two of my favorite little munchkins, would be off to San Diego. I couldn't wait to see those babies all bronzed up when they returned in the fall.

Then, there was Bristol and Maddox. I already knew Maddox summered in Seattle, but the couple would be spending some time in Hartford this offseason, as Bristol wanted to get married near her family.

A tiny pang of regret hit me in the chest that we wouldn't be able to attend, especially after the large role Maddox had played in our wedding—technically, wedding*s*.

When they asked where Jenner and I usually summered, I was just about to open my mouth to tell them that, typically, we split time between his family in Boston and mine in Oklahoma when another small gush happened between my thighs.

My disgust must've been evident on my face because each woman noticed instantly, leaning forward with concerned expressions as they all spoke at the same time.

"What's wrong?"

"Is it the babies?"

"Should we go get Jenner?"

I shook my head, palming my belly. "I'm fine. Apparently, these babies are using my bladder as a trampoline."

"Totally normal but super annoying," Tessa remarked as the only other mother amongst us.

Bristol hopped up. "I've gotta go too." She extended her arms. "Up you go, Momma."

Once I was on my feet, a quick peek at the pool confirmed Jenner was tracking my movement. One of his auburn eyebrows arched high enough that it almost disappeared beneath his backward-facing ballcap.

Again? he mouthed.

I shrugged. I wasn't the one calling the shots right now.

Alone in the bathroom, I ditched the wet panties. Continuing to wear them would only add to my growing list of ailments.

This time, I didn't even make it off the toilet before another gush happened.

"Fucking hell!" I yelled in frustration. This was getting old fast.

Bristol's panicked voice called through the thick wood door. "Evie?"

"I'm fine," I called back.

Quickly washing my hands, I flung the door open, plastering a bright smile on my face. "See?"

Blue eyes full of doubt scanned me from head to toe. Twisting her lips to the side, she nodded. "Okay."

"You go ahead. I'm gonna head back out."

Bristol stepped past me and into the bathroom as I made my way back to the patio. Jenner had a towel wrapped around his waist, and another threatened to swallow Hope whole in his arms.

I reached out to take my bundled-up baby, not caring one bit that her wet body made my clothing damp. "Did you have fun, baby girl?"

"She's a natural," Asher remarked. "Big smiles the whole time."

Cuddling Hope close, I rocked from side to side. "Maybe you'll be a swimmer like Auntie Blake." Jenner's older sister had been a competitive swimmer in her younger days, earning multiple gold medals in the International Games. That family was good at breeding athletes.

Jenner dipped his head beside my ear. "You okay?"

Turning, I kept my voice low, not wanting to share my embarrassing situation with the group. "I'm leaking, and it's driving me insane."

Rearing back, his eyebrows rose. "What do you mean you're leaking?"

Widening my eyes so he understood I didn't want to have this conversation publicly, I whispered, "I keep peeing myself."

Gaze dipping to my belly, he asked, "Are you sure that's all it is?"

That's when my frustration finally boiled over, and I yelled, "What do you want me to tell you, Jenner? Your big ass babies are wreaking havoc on my bladder!"

Several heads turned in our direction, and Asher snickered only to have Tessa elbow him in the ribs. He held his hands up. "Sorry. Just been there and realizing it's a lot more amusing from this side."

Folding both arms over his chest, Jenner challenged, "Has it happened like this before?"

Through gritted teeth, I uttered, "I'd prefer not to have this conversation in public."

Not backing down, my infuriating husband said, "Only trying to determine if we need to head to the hospital."

I stumbled back, bumping into Maddox, who gripped my biceps to keep me steady. Muttering a quick thank you to the man behind me, I gaped at Jenner.

"Not everything is an emergency," I shot back.

He raised an eyebrow in challenge. "You still haven't answered my question from earlier. Have you experienced leaking like this before?" Brown eyes narrowed. "And don't you dare lie to me, Evie Knight."

I tilted my face skyward, letting out a heavy breath. "Fine. No, I haven't."

"You can yell at me later for being overbearing if it turns out to be a false alarm, but we're going to get you checked out. Dr. Roberts said if even the tiniest thing felt off, we were to come straight in."

"Fine. Whatever." I huffed.

Bristol had returned at some point during this battle of wills and jumped up and down, clapping her hands. "Oooh! Is it baby time?"

"No," I said at the same time Jenner said, "Maybe."

I shot him a glare, but he was already grabbing our stuff, looking around at his best friends and teammates. "Okay, I wasn't drinking, but who else is sober enough to get Hope home and stay with her for at least a few hours?"

Everyone glanced around nervously. Of course, they'd all been drinking. We were at a celebration expected to last several more hours, and they still had plenty of time to sober up before driving home.

"Wait, I got it!" Dakota shouted, running off.

Staring at her retreating form, Jenner groaned. "I'm almost afraid to ask."

"Someone need a ride?" A voice came from behind us.

Okay, Dakota was kinda brilliant.

Goose came into view, a giant smile splitting his face. The loveable lug never drank, and we could trust that he would get Hope home safely.

Jenner tossed him the keys to our van. "You're on Hope duty." To the rest of the group, he explained, "We're gonna need a car. Goose's sports car is way too low for Evie."

Maddox stepped up, placing a keyfob in Jenner's hand. "Take mine. Bristol will go with Goose and Hope. I'll take his car to your house as soon as I'm good to drive, and we'll wait for your call."

Bristol squealed, "This is so exciting!"

Everyone would be so disappointed when Jenner's overreaction turned out to be nothing.

"It's a good thing you came in," Dr. Roberts remarked, tossing a pair of latex gloves into the trash. "Most people expect their water breaking to be this dramatic event, but if the membranes rupture higher up, it can be more of a slow leak and easy to miss."

Oh, I wanted nothing more than to punch the smug look off Jenner's face where he stood beside my hospital bed in the labor and delivery unit.

Folding her arms over navy blue scrubs, she offered me a bright smile. "Looks like these little guys are ready to make their grand entrance."

My anxiety shot sky-high at the thought.

This was it. After months of planning and preparation, it sank in that today was the day.

And God help me, I wasn't ready. I wasn't sure if I ever would be.

"You have a couple of options. The first is we get you prepped for a C-section, and you can meet these babies within the next few hours. Or, since Baby A is head down, you can opt to give natural delivery a try."

This was all too much, and it was happening too fast. Panicked, I turned to Jenner with wide eyes.

He held his hands up. "Don't look at me. I'm a smart enough man to know that I can't tell you what to do with your body."

Stupid, respectful man.

"Hey." Jenner gripped my hand, his brown eyes softening. "Whatever you want to do, I'm on board."

I'd spent almost my entire adult life waiting for this moment. With Hope already at home and the absolute miracle that gifted us these twin boys, I knew this might be my only chance.

So, scared out of my fucking mind, I turned back to Dr. Roberts. "I'd like to try a natural delivery."

She nodded. "Fine by me. And don't feel like if you want to change your mind at any time, you can't. I'm here to support you and get those boys here safely. If that means laboring for a while and deciding it's not for you, there's no shame in that. Got it?"

I swallowed past the lump in my throat. "Thank you."

"My pleasure. I'll be back in a few hours to check on you. Hit the call button on your remote if you need anything in the meantime."

With that, she left the room.

Jenner stood, pressing a kiss to my forehead. "You're amazing, you know that?"

I snorted. "Yeah, okay."

"No, I mean it. You kept our boys safe and sound for so long. I'm so proud of you."

When I dared peek at him, nothing but love and adoration shone in his dark brown eyes. That was enough to give me the tiny boost of courage I needed to face this challenge head-on.

Stroking my cheek with his thumb, he asked, "How are you feeling?"

Taking a mental inventory of the current state of my body, I shrugged. "A little crampy. It's not too bad."

Paige had told me labor felt like bad period cramps, so if that's all I was up against, I was sure I could handle it.

"This was a terrible idea," I panted, dropping back onto the sweat-soaked pillow behind my head.

Letting me squeeze the hell out of his hand through another contraction, Jenner said, "At the risk of losing my balls, I have to point out that this was *your* idea."

Head whipping to the side, the death glare I shot him was enough to have him rearing back with terror in his eyes.

He nodded. "You're right. Should've kept that one to myself."

I blew out a heavy breath as the vise grip around my belly loosened. It was only a temporary reprieve, but I relished those brief moments of relief.

"Yeah, well. That was *before* I was a tired, hot, sweaty mess whose entire body feels like a massive ball of pain." I sucked in a few shallow breaths, which was all my massive belly would allow.

"I know, baby." Jenner used his free hand to brush the sweaty strands of hair away from my face. "But you're getting there, and I'm in awe of your strength."

I huffed. Strength, my ass. I was barely surviving.

The hospital gown had gone by the wayside hours ago because I was in danger of overheating. Currently, all that covered me was a sports bra and the multiple monitors strapped to my bare belly. Even the thin blanket covering my hips and legs was too much, and I kept kicking it further down the bed.

Jenner grasped the edge to bring it back up, and my voice took on an almost demon-like quality when I threatened, "Do it one more time. I fucking dare you."

Shocked, wide eyes shifted to peek at me, and he dropped the material but couldn't let the subject go. "I'm trying to keep you covered." Gesturing to my lower half, he explained, "You're not wearing any underwear."

Did he think I didn't know that? Because *believe me*, I did.

"What are you worried about?" I challenged. "This whole thing doesn't happen without everyone who has or will walk through that door being all up in my business. So, what's the point of modesty? They're gonna see it at some point anyway, and half the staff has had their arm shoved so far inside me I swear it tickled my eyeballs."

Grimacing, Jenner backed off. "Got it."

I opened my mouth for another snarky remark, knowing full well that I wasn't in my right mind at the moment, but another contraction ramping up stole my attention.

Not gonna lie; this was way worse than period cramps. I was being squeezed tighter than that one time I'd tried shapewear. It had only taken once to learn my lesson that I never wanted to put myself through that torture ever again. It was uncomfortable as fuck, and I could barely breathe.

Only this was worse. I couldn't escape it, and the vise tightened at a faster and stronger clip each time.

"Fuck," I hissed, jaw clenched tight.

"You've got this, baby. Keep breathing. Mind over matter." Jenner's soothing words only served to set me further on edge.

"Shut up," I gritted out. "You're not helping."

A sigh slipped past my lips as I was released from the evil clutches of my traitorous uterus when Dr. Roberts walked in. "How's everything going in here?"

"I want the drugs. All of the drugs. Like, yesterday. Please help me," I begged.

Coming closer, she patted my leg. "I'm honestly surprised you've lasted this long without them. Let's see where you're at, and we can decide where to go from there."

I fought the urge to scream during her internal exam.

"You've made great progress, Evie." She beamed at me while removing her hand from between my legs. "You're sitting just shy of six centimeters, so I'd like to get you moved to the OR, where they can place your epidural, and the anesthesiologist will remain with us until you deliver."

"The OR?" Jenner's voice rose in pitch as he went rigid beside me.

Dr. Roberts nodded, addressing him. "We've been over this, Jenner. It's only a precaution. And it also provides more space. While my team will be focused on Evie, there will be a dedicated team for each baby."

"Right." He nodded, squeezing my hand tighter.

I couldn't help but smirk, coaxing, "Breathe, baby."

Jenner's jaw tightened, but he didn't say a word.

Yeah, not so funny now, is it?

"As long as I get the best drugs money can buy, I don't care which room we do this in."

Chuckling, Dr. Roberts replied, "Sounds about right. I'll get to work setting all of that up now. Jenner, a nurse will bring you scrubs to change into when we're ready to move Evie, and once we're all set up, they'll bring you to where she is."

"Wait." He held up a hand. "I can't go with her?"

"As soon as she's settled, they'll bring you in. It's standard procedure. I promise."

Jenner grudgingly agreed, though I could feel the tension vibrating off his body by my side. He didn't want to be separated from me, and I could appreciate that, but we had to let the team of doctors do their jobs.

"Hey," I said softly, and he dropped his gaze to where I lay in bed. "It's just for a few minutes. I'll be fine."

Dusting his lips over my knuckles, he let out a heavy exhale. "Okay. Just for a few minutes," he agreed.

Chapter 36
Jenner

"A few minutes, my ass," I grumbled under my breath, pacing the room in pale blue scrubs. It felt like hours since they'd wheeled Evie out.

I was right back to where I was when Hope was born, feeling out of control and out of the loop, and I hated it.

I'd done a bang-up job of staying calm in front of Evie, but the truth was that I was fucking terrified. So many things could go wrong, and my anxiety shot through the roof as I ran through all the possible complications.

"Mr. Knight?" My head popped up to find a young nurse standing in the doorway. "They're ready for you."

"Thank fucking God," I breathed out, rushing across the room to follow the nurse through the maze of tunnels before we pushed through double doors that led to the wing containing the operating rooms.

"We're right through here," she said, gesturing to Operating Room 2.

Stepping inside, I stopped short. Holy shit, there were a lot of people in here.

My chest tightened, making it hard to breathe. I pressed a palm against my sternum and rubbed, hoping it would loosen it, to no avail.

"How about you come over here and hold my hand before you have a panic attack," Evie's voice broke through the darkness coming in from all sides, and I was able to suck in a large lungful of air.

My wife was propped up on a bed in the center of the room, and I walked over, pressing a kiss to her temple, instantly calmed by her presence.

"And you didn't want to come to the hospital." My lips grazed her skin as I spoke.

"Yeah, yeah. I'm sure you'll be telling that story for years to come," she grumbled.

It was easy to smile when she gave me a little bit of her signature sass. "How can I not?" I teased right back. "I'm the hero in that story."

Evie's eye roll was audible. "You call a guy a hero *one time*, and suddenly, he has a complex."

I barked out a laugh, pulling back and scanning her form. They'd covered her with a blanket to move her, but she was back to being indecently exposed. Yes, I knew that was required for this to work, but that didn't mean I had to like it.

"Feeling any better?" I squeezed her hand.

"No more pain," she confirmed. "Just a lot of pressure."

Dr. Roberts, wearing a surgical gown over her scrubs, stepped up to the foot of the bed. "That's what we like to hear. Pressure means it's time to push."

My eyes bulged. "Already?"

She nodded. "Every mom progresses differently, but an epidural often helps in terms of letting the body relax and do its job. Seems that was the case today with Evie."

Stunned, I turned to my wife. "Oh my God."

Shifting on the bed, she eyed me. "You gonna be okay?"

"Yeah." In a daze, I nodded slowly. "Just wasn't ready for it to be *go time* the minute I stepped into the room."

"Lucky for you, big guy, you get to stand by and watch."

"Hey." I pressed my forehead to hers. "You know I'd do this for you if I could."

"Yeah," Evie breathed out. "I know."

"You're the strongest woman I've ever met. Everything we've been through led us right here. And now, we're at the finish line. Our sons are ready to join our perfect family, and you're the one who's gonna make it happen. Trust me when I say I will *never* be able to thank you for all you've given me, Evie."

A tear leaked from the corner of her eye. "I love you."

"I love you, too. So fucking much it hurts."

"Evie, are you ready?" Dr. Roberts's voice cut into our private moment.

My amazingly strong wife nodded with determination glittering in her violet eyes. "Yes."

"Jenner?" Dr. Roberts spoke to me next. "You're good where you are right now, but I need you to listen to me very carefully. I know it's going to go against every instinct you have, but when Baby A is out, you go with him." All my muscles tensed at the idea of leaving Evie. "And I will tell you why it's extremely important." Swallowing, I waited for her to explain. "With Baby A out of the way, there's going to be a lot of extra space for Baby B to do some gymnastics. My team needs to ensure not only that Baby B winds up head down but that Evie's uterus clamps down enough to get him out. Understand?"

Fucking logic. I understood, but I didn't like it.

"How long is that going to take? Between the two of them?" I asked.

"It varies. But usually, the average is half an hour."

I hummed. "Thought it would be faster."

Dr. Roberts let out a light laugh. "Most people are used to seeing the birth times of twins only being minutes apart because a good majority are born via C-section. Going this route requires a bit more time and the cooperation of both the baby and mom's body."

"Okay," I agreed. "I'll go with the baby."

She winked. "I knew I could count on you, Dad."

A set of nurses came over and removed the lower half of the bed before taking it away. When they returned, they pulled stirrups up from underneath the remaining portion, helping maneuver Evie's legs into them.

"Evie, the next time you feel a wave of pressure, I want you to grip the back of your knees and bear down while I count to ten, take a few deep breaths, then repeat until the pressure wanes," Dr. Roberts instructed. "You've got Jenner on one side to help with your leg and Jana on the other."

Right. I was on leg-holding duty. I could do this.

After a peek at the monitor, Dr. Roberts asked, "Do you feel it coming?"

Evie nodded.

"Good. Let's do this."

Wrapping my arm around the back of Evie's thigh, I held it back as she pressed her chin to her chest and pushed while the doctor counted.

"Perfect. Just like that," she encouraged. "And again."

Only the softest grunting noises escaped past my wife's lips as she worked on bringing our first son into the world.

Collapsing back on the bed, Evie sucked in air.

I was quick to move with her, pressing soft kisses to her forehead, whispering, "You're doing so great, baby. I'm so proud of you."

Resting between contractions, her eyes were closed, but she nodded, letting me know she'd heard me.

"Deep breath, Evie, and then let's go again," Dr. Roberts said.

Focused on my wife and her incredible strength, my eyes widened when Dr. Roberts remarked, "He's right there, Evie. Keep going."

I shifted to peek at my son making his grand entrance when Evie barked, "No!"

Stunned, my head whipped to her. "What?"

Tension marred her pretty face, flushed by the effort used to push. "I don't want you to look. I watched Hope come out. It's not pretty."

Scoffing, I countered, "Evie, I think I deserve to watch our son being born."

Eyes narrowing, she gritted out, "So help me God, Jenner Knight. You peek down there, and I will divorce your ass so fast your head will spin."

That was enough to have me straightening instantly and my eyes avoiding the area between her spread-open legs.

The nurse opposite me, Jana, chuckled, giving me a sympathetic smile. "Don't worry, they all say that."

I gave her a tight smile and a nod. "Uh-huh." It might be an idle threat to most, and I was fairly certain it was in this case, but I wasn't about to press my luck.

"The head is out," Dr. Roberts declared.

Evie's eyes popped open, and her lips parted. "Really?"

"Give me your hand, and you can feel for yourself."

Sinking her teeth into her lower lip, Evie slid a hand around her belly and between her thighs. "Oh my God," she breathed out.

"He's almost here," I whispered against her temple. "You've got this, babe."

She nodded, and after another few pushes, a garbled wail pierced the air.

Tears leaked from Evie's eyes as a relieved sob flew past her lips.

"You did it," I said, in awe of my wife and her sheer force of will that had made us into a family.

Those tiny cries continued, and I shifted my gaze to catch the first glimpse of our son.

Overwhelming love crashed over me when laying eyes on the little person we'd created. He was squirming in Dr. Roberts's hold as she suctioned his mouth, and another set of nurses clamped and cut his cord before he was handed off and carried to one of the waiting warmers across the room.

Her eyes met mine, and she tilted her head in the direction they'd taken the baby. "Go, Jenner. We've got Mom and will call you over when it's Baby B's turn."

With one last kiss pressed to Evie's forehead, I gave her hand a squeeze and forced my feet to move.

"Take pictures," my wife called to my back.

When I stepped closer, several people were surrounding the warmer, but when the two nurses from earlier saw me, they made room for me to approach where my son lay.

Emotion clogged my throat as I stared at the perfect baby boy. My hand twitched, and apprehension stole through me.

"Can—Can I touch him?"

"Of course," one of the nurses replied.

I skimmed the skin of his clenched fist, stroking the tiny knuckles softly until his fingers spread wide before closing over my much larger digit.

Tears burned behind my eyes, and I swallowed thickly. "Hey, buddy. Happy birthday."

A groan from across the room stole my attention, and I turned to peek at Evie.

Several people were pressing on her significantly smaller belly as she lay there, eyes shut, grimacing.

Almost like she could sense my eyes on her, she muttered, "I'm fine. And I know you're not taking those pictures."

She knew me too well. I had been so caught up in marveling at our son that I couldn't focus on much else.

With my free hand, I reached into the pocket of the scrubs pants and produced my phone. Swiping to open the camera, I snapped a few shots of our boy as his mama had instructed.

Viewing him through the screen, I said mostly to myself, "He's so pink."

A doctor with a stethoscope pressed to the baby's chest replied, "That's a good sign. For being a thirty-four-weeker, he's looking healthy and strong. Bigger than we'd expect at this gestational age for a multiple, too, at five pounds, four ounces."

My heart swelled. For all my worrying, he was here, safe and sound and thriving.

"Do we have a name for this little guy?" the nurse beside me asked.

Evie and I had nailed down names a few weeks ago, so there was no hesitation when I declared, "Hunter."

"I love it," she gushed.

I smiled to myself, knowing his twin brother's name and how adorable it would be every time we introduced all three of our children together.

They put a diaper on Hunter and placed him inside a clear plastic incubator atop a wheeled cart.

The doctor explained, "He looks good, but we're gonna make a pit stop at the NICU as a precaution for further evaluation since he is a preemie. My colleagues will assess Baby B after delivery and join us there. At that time, we can discuss whether they can be moved to the main nursery in L&D or if they need a longer stay in the NICU. Either way, you should be able to bring Mom to visit once she's in recovery."

I followed as they wheeled Hunter toward the door. Placing a hand through the circular opening on the side of the incubator and onto his chest, I whispered, "I'll come down to see you soon, bud. Gotta meet your little brother first."

Mesmerized, I watched from the doorway as a piece of my heart went with the team dedicated to his care.

Alarms blared behind me, and I spun around. There was a flurry of motion, and my heart dropped into my stomach.

Evie.

My gaze locked on her, and I stopped breathing.

Her eyes were closed like the last time I'd peeked at her. But any semblance of an expression, even one of pain, was gone. Her features had gone lax; her head lolled to the side. It took a minute for me to process what I was looking at.

Evie was unconscious.

Then, I saw the blood. So much fucking blood.

Coating the doctor's arms up to the elbow.

Streaked along Evie's thighs.

Pooling beneath the bed, the crimson stain growing larger by the second.

"What's going on?" I rasped as fear gripped me in a chokehold.

Barely sparing me a glance, Dr. Roberts commanded in an authoritative tone, "Get him out of here! Now!"

"What? No!" I cried when two members of Baby B's waiting team approached me. "I'm not leaving!"

The look of pity on their faces had my knees threatening to buckle.

That's when I realized this was bad—life or death bad.

The blood and alarms should have tipped me off to the severity of the situation, but shock had severely diminished my powers of deduction.

"Listen," one said softly like I was a horse about to spook. "They're gonna do everything they can for your wife and your baby, but they can't do that unless you let them do their jobs."

I tried to peek around him, but there were too many people surrounding Evie for me to see her.

"Come on." He clapped a hand on my shoulder, gently urging me from the room as I dragged my feet.

The terrifying thought crossed my mind that if I left, it might be the last time I ever saw my wife.

The male nurse eased me into a chair in a small waiting room and explained that someone would come to update me as soon as there was any news.

I was numb.

I couldn't feel anything. Not when I'd left half of my soul in that operating room.

If Evie didn't make it, I wasn't sure how much of me would be left to give my children. This whole thing didn't work without her at the center of it. This was her dream, what we'd fought so hard for, and now it might very well be the thing that killed her.

A vibration in my hand had me jolting. Until that moment, I hadn't realized I was still clutching my phone after taking pictures of Hunter.

Glancing down, the lock screen showed a text from Maddox asking for an update.

I couldn't do this alone, and my best friend had never let me down in his constant support over the years, so I swiped a finger across the screen, pressing the button to place the call.

My trembling hand could barely bring the phone to my ear. By the time I did, I heard Maddox's cheerful voice, seeming so out of place when my world was crumbling around me.

"Hey! Is Hope a big sister yet? Ready for us to bring her to visit?"

A strangled noise clawed its way up my throat.

Concern filtered into Maddox's tone. "Jenner? What's wrong?"

Everything. Everything was wrong.

But instead of voicing those words, I couldn't hold back anymore and began to sob loudly.

"Fuck," Maddox cursed. "I'm on my way."

It didn't matter. Nothing mattered. Not without Evie.

Time stood still as I stared unblinkingly at the double doors that led to the operating rooms, waiting for someone to emerge to let me know if my wife was dead or alive.

I nearly jumped out of my skin when a massive body dropped into the seat beside me.

"Talk to me, Jenner." Gone was my friend's usual gruffness as he sat forward to rest his forearms on his knees so he could see my face.

My gaze flicked away from the door for a split second to find Bristol standing beside where Maddox sat. Her sad blue eyes were more than I could handle right now. Not when my life—and Evie's—hung in the balance.

Voice hoarse from crying, I managed to ask, "Who's got Hope?" Even if the unimaginable came to pass, I was still a father and had at least two kids who would be depending on me.

"Emmy came by," Bristol whispered.

"That's good." I nodded, eyes fixed back on the double doors.

"What happened, Jenner?" Maddox tried again to get answers out of me.

Taking in a shaky breath, I said aloud the thought rolling around in my brain since they forced me from that room. "I killed her."

"What?" they cried in unison.

Fresh tears threatened to break free. "Everything was fine. Hunter came out perfect. Then there were alarms and blood and . . ." My words trailed off. "I did this to her. We had everything. Hope would have been enough. We would have been happy raising her as our one and only. But then I had to go and knock Evie up, and now she's going to die. Because of me."

My friends were silent for a minute, processing that massive information dump.

Maddox gripped my knee. "This isn't your fault, Jenner."

"It is!" I yelled. "If she never got pregnant, this wouldn't have happened."

Sighing, Maddox replied, "I know you're scared—fuck, I'm terrified for you, and she isn't even my wife—and it's easier to blame yourself than accept that, sometimes, life is outside of our control. But I need you to understand that you did nothing wrong. You gave Evie what she always wanted, and I saw how happy that made the two of you. She's your life; I get it. More now than I ever did before." His eyes shifted to his fiancée. "We are here for you, no matter what happens, okay? You and Evie and the kids are our family."

Done with words, I simply nodded.

Bristol couldn't hold back a moment longer and threw her arms around my neck, hugging me tight.

I knew these two loved my wife, and there was the tiniest bit of comfort that they were by my side as I waited to hear if I would be forced to live the rest of my life without the only person who'd ever given it meaning.

"Knight?"

A strange sense of déjà vu washed over me at hearing my name called in a hospital waiting room. I'd been just as scared that day, waiting for news of Evie's condition, but today, there was so much more at stake.

But my brows drew down when I realized that whoever was looking for me hadn't come from the double doors where my gaze had been glued for what felt like hours.

"Over here," Maddox replied for me.

A man in scrubs wearing a white coat over them—signifying his status as a doctor—stepped into my line of sight.

I stood instantly. "Is she—?"

The pity flickering across his features had me reaching blindly to grip Maddox's forearm for support.

Shaking his head sadly, the doctor replied, "Unfortunately, I don't have any details about your wife's condition."

Confused, I asked, "Then what are you doing here?"

"My name is Dr. Morris, and I was the one heading up the team designated for Baby B."

I sucked in a sharp breath. I wasn't sure I could handle learning I'd lost both of them today.

"I wanted to come down here and tell you myself that he's doing well after being delivered via emergency C-section."

"Emergency C-section," I repeated those words in a daze. They'd been forced to slice my wife open to save the baby.

"Four pounds, eleven ounces. A little smaller than his twin but just as feisty. Both boys are breathing on their own, regulating their body temperatures without help, and showing good sucking reflexes. We feel confident in our decision to have them moved to the main nursery. The team there will monitor them for signs of jaundice, which is extremely common, and if at any point they feel the babies need additional interventions, the nurses have a direct line to my team, and we can reassess."

"Okay." I didn't know what else he wanted me to say. I wanted to be overjoyed that my son had been safely delivered, but my mind was firmly rooted on Evie.

"If you'd like, I can take you to them now."

"Um." I tugged on the back of my neck, my gaze shifting to those double doors that hadn't been pushed open once in all this time. "I'm not sure . . ."

Turning his head, Dr. Morris acknowledged my concern. "We'll make sure your wife's team knows where to find you."

Maddox's voice finally broke through my panic at the idea of leaving this spot. "Come on, Jenner. Let's go meet your boys."

Swallowing, I nodded. "All right."

I pressed a hand against the glass door to the nursery, almost afraid to step inside. It felt wrong meeting our second son without Evie.

"Hey, we're right here," Maddox said in reassurance, noticing my hesitation. "Whatever you need."

Taking a deep breath that did nothing to loosen the tightness in my chest, I asked, "Come in with me? I don't want to do this alone."

Placing a hand on my shoulder, my best friend vowed, "You're never alone, Jenner. I've always got your back."

Bristol gave my hand a gentle squeeze before stepping toward the giant glass wall that showcased the rows of newborns nestled in glass bassinets. She was gracious enough to give Maddox and me this moment.

With the support of the man who'd always gone to battle beside me, I pushed through the door.

Dr. Morris had placed two hospital bracelets around my wrist that linked me to my sons. When I showed them to the nurse, her face lit up with a bright smile. "Oooh. The twins! Simply precious little guys."

We followed her to two bassinets side by side near the back.

I stared down at my sleeping sons, blissfully unaware that their entry into this world might coincide with the worst day of my life.

Maddox bumped my shoulder. "Surprisingly good-looking kids considering who their father is," he teased, trying to lighten the mood.

Without hesitation, I replied, "That's because they look like their mom."

The nurse remarked, "We didn't get a name on Baby B."

"Hendrix." The word was said on a whisper as I stroked a finger over his soft cheek.

"Oh, I love that," she chirped. "Hunter and Hendrix."

Maddox chimed in. "And don't forget about big sister, Hope."

She placed a hand to her chest. "Stop it right now. I love when parents give siblings matching names like that." Gesturing to the babies, she said, "Feel free to cuddle with your little guys. We can try feeding in a little bit if you'd like." With that, she walked away.

This was wrong. All of it was wrong.

I shouldn't be the first one to hold them or feed them. Evie had earned those experiences, a reward for her perseverance in making this dream a reality.

"Come on, Dad. Show me how it's done." My head whipped to the side to find Maddox smiling at my boys, dipping his chin toward them.

My jaw dropped. "You—you want to hold one?"

He shrugged. "Might as well log some practice hours for when it's my turn someday. And there happens to be two of them and two of us. Only makes sense we share in the cuddles."

A surprised chuckle flew past my lips. The sound was foreign, given the circumstances that I was sharing this moment with my best friend and not my wife.

"Yeah. Okay." I nodded. "Let's do this."

I reached into one of the bassinets, and Maddox mirrored my actions. I chose to hold Hendrix first, since Hunter and I had already had a moment in the delivery room.

I'd thought Hope was feather-light the first time I held her, but if I hadn't had my eyes on this little guy in my arms, I wouldn't have been able to believe he was even there. I was certain the blanket he was wrapped in weighed more than he did.

"This is wild, man," Maddox said in awe.

Hunter was smaller than that man's bicep, and I shook my head in wonder that these two tiny humans were half me and half Evie.

I could stare at these beautiful babies all day.

"Jenner?" a familiar feminine voice broke through my trance, and I spun around to find Dr. Roberts.

My throat closed up, and I struggled to draw in air. I couldn't bear to ask the question that had been burning at the back of my brain for hours now.

Was my wife alive?

She must have seen it in my eyes because she nodded, answering, "Evie's okay."

"Fuck." I sagged against the nearest wall, clutching my infant son to my chest. Willing my racing heart to settle, I asked softly, "What happened?"

Dr. Roberts took a deep breath. "Long story short, after Baby A was delivered, the placenta he and Baby B shared decided its job was done and began to detach too soon. The sudden and extreme bleeding caused Evie's blood pressure to tank, and she lost consciousness."

I shuddered. I would never be able to remove the image of Evie lying lifeless and covered in blood from my memory.

"Thankfully, we were already in the operating room and were able to take action quickly. Evie was placed under general anesthesia, and we delivered Baby B via emergency C-section. The hemorrhaging was extensive and took time and several transfusions to get under control. She's going to have a difficult recovery once she wakes up, but the important thing to remember is that she *will* recover. We were able to save her uterus, but after the trauma it went through today, I would strongly recommend against future pregnancies."

Stroking the back of the tiny infant in my arms, I nodded. "I think we've got our hands full enough."

She smiled warmly. "That you do."

"When can I see her?"

"I can have someone take you to her now."

Placing a kiss on Hendrix's forehead, I whispered, "Mommy's gonna be okay."

Chapter 37
Evie

Pain.

Pain everywhere.

And crying?

I think that's what that sound is.

That was enough to trigger my brain, and even though my eyes were closed—or so I assumed—the memories came rushing back.

The operating room.

Hunter being born and the overwhelming relief that came with it.

Painful pushing on my belly as multiple hands poked and prodded, trying to maneuver the baby still inside me into the correct position.

My hearing dropping out.

My vision closing in on me.

Opening my mouth to tell the doctors that something wasn't right, but nothing coming out.

Then darkness.

That's the last thing I could remember.

What had happened after that? Had Hendrix made it out safe? Where was I? Why was every cell in my body screaming in agony?

And most importantly, who was crying?

My eyelids felt weighted down, but I used all my strength to crack them open.

Immediately, I grew frustrated that I was still in the dark. What the fuck?

Eventually, my eyes adjusted to the dim room, and I found the source of the crying.

Jenner was hunched over in a chair by my bedside, head dropped into his hands as he openly wept.

My stomach bottomed out. In my mind, there could only be one reason for him to be crying. And as gut-wrenching as the prospect of losing a child was, I needed to know.

I licked my lips, my mouth feeling like it was stuffed with cotton, but I managed to croak out, "Did he make it?"

Jenner's head popped up, his sad brown eyes rimmed with red. In a flash, he was leaning over me, cupping my face.

"Evie," he breathed out, tears falling freely from his eyes and onto my skin. "Fuck, baby. I was so scared I'd lost you."

Terrified to utter his name aloud, I forced myself to ask the question again. "Hendrix. Did he make it?"

Pressing his forehead to mine, Jenner's shaky breaths fanned my face. "He's okay. Healthy and strong, just like his big brother."

My lower lip trembled, and my chest heaved.

"Thank God." The words were a garbled mess as emotions took over. They were both safe.

That sudden rush of relief was almost enough to make me forget the fire burning through my veins. Almost.

"It hurts," I whispered.

Pulling back, Jenner jumped right into action. "I'll find a nurse now. Once your pain is under control, it's time for you to meet our boys."

Our boys. Nothing had ever sounded so sweet.

It was almost a full week before the twins and I were discharged from the hospital.

I was one of the lucky few who got the pleasure of trying to recover from both a vaginal and surgical delivery simultaneously. And I definitely wouldn't recommend it. I had stitches and staples. Yay, me.

Jenner made me wait in the car until he'd taken both boys nestled inside their carriers into the house one by one. Then, he opened the passenger door and held my hand as I gingerly stepped out.

Pain was expected to be my constant companion for a while, and I just had to suck it up and deal with it. Sure, I'd been given medications, but they only took the edge off.

I learned pretty quickly that trying to breastfeed the boys only made it worse, and crying the entire time they nursed didn't exactly provide the serene bonding experience I'd hoped for. So, formula it was. The important thing was that they were getting fed, and I clung to that when thoughts of failing to feed my babies with my body crept in.

I'd barely made it a few feet into the house before I realized how busy it was. Excited chatter leaked into the mudroom from the common areas.

Gripping Jenner's hand tighter, I asked, "Why's everyone here?"

"Our families, both biological and found, wanted to be there for us," he replied.

Turning the corner into the kitchen, my mama caught sight of me first. Rushing forward, she pulled me into her arms. "Gave us quite a fright, darlin'. You always did have a flair for the dramatic, though."

I gave her a tight smile, biting my tongue about how almost dying during childbirth hadn't exactly been done for attention.

The noises layering over one another put me on sensory overload. I knew it wasn't polite and that our friends and family were only trying to help, but I couldn't deal with this right now.

"I want to go lie down," I said to Jenner.

There was no hesitation on my husband's part. "Of course. Let me help you get upstairs."

Climbing steps was one of those things on the list to avoid, but I gritted my teeth and pushed through the pain. I wanted to be in my bed, and once I reached the top, I planned to stay on the second floor for a while.

Jenner eased my shoes off as I sat on the edge of the bed and helped move the pillows around until I was in a comfortable enough position.

"I want Hope."

Emmy had brought her by the hospital once, but I was missing my baby girl something fierce.

"I'll bring her right up." Jenner pressed a kiss to my forehead. "We did it, babe. Our little family is finally complete."

It wasn't until after he'd brought me our daughter and went to check on the boys that I let the first tear fall.

I'd gotten everything I ever wanted. Why wasn't I happier about it?

"Okay, which one do you want?" Jenner walked into our bedroom with both boys cradled in one of his arms—they were that teeny tiny.

"Hunter."

My handsome husband shot me a look that told me he'd noticed how I gravitated toward Hunter. He knew me better than anyone else and could tell I was struggling, but he was afraid to bring it up.

Given my history of letting my emotions overrule reason, I couldn't say I blamed him for being apprehensive.

With a barely audible sigh, Jenner brought me Hunter, and I cradled his warm form to my chest. Next, Jenner handed me a prepared bottle from the pocket of his joggers.

Our moms and Emmy were around to help with all three kids during the day, but in the middle of the night, it was only the two of us against all three kids. Thankfully, Hope slept longer stretches, but the twins were up every two hours. Their tiny tummies needed constant filling.

Settling beside me in bed, Jenner popped a bottle into Hendrix's mouth, and the sounds of the boys' greedy sucking filled the quiet room.

I was hanging on, but just barely. I wasn't sure how much longer I'd be able to keep it together for my new family, even though I knew how much they needed me.

"Evie, are you crying?" Jenner's groggy voice reached my ears, and I froze.

Wiping a hand beneath my runny nose, I cursed my watery voice in my reply. "No."

"Evie." He sighed. "Why are you trying to hide from me? Why won't you let me help you?"

"I'm not allowed to complain," I whispered my confession.

"What?" The mattress dipped behind me before Jenner tugged on my shoulder, forcing me to roll over and face him.

Looking into his eyes only made me realize how much I'd failed him—failed all of them.

A sob burst free from my chest.

"Fuck, Evie." Jenner pulled me close. "I hate seeing you like this. Talk to me. *Please.*"

Muffled against the fabric of his T-shirt, I said, "I got everything I wanted and don't want to seem ungrateful."

"No one would ever think that," he vowed.

"But they will," I argued. "Because instead of enjoying my beautiful babies, I can't stop thinking about how I almost let them grow up without a mother."

"Babe—"

"No." I sat up, and he let me scoot out of his hold, sensing that I needed distance in this moment. "I almost died, Jenner!" I cried, saying the words aloud for the first time.

His Adam's apple bobbed on a hard swallow. "I know."

I lifted my shirt. "And I'm always going to have this jagged scar to remind me that what was supposed to be the best day of my life was actually the worst."

Jenner opened his mouth to respond, but I didn't let him.

"It hurts to even look at Hendrix knowing how I failed him."

Slowly, my husband scooched closer, taking my hand. "How did you fail him?"

"I wasn't even conscious when he was born. My choices robbed us of what was supposed to be this memory I carried forever."

"Choices." I could see the gears turning in his head. "What choices?"

"I turned down the elective C-section offered when I was admitted. All because I wanted an experience I'd longed for for so many years. I would have still left with a scar, but I wouldn't have all these negative feelings tied to it. I would have gotten to hear his first cries, kiss his tiny face, and tell him how much I loved him. Instead, I almost bled out on an operating table."

After that final admission, I burst into tears, the emotional pain tied to that day hitting me in full force.

Jenner wasted no time in pulling me onto his lap as gently as possible to avoid hurting me. I buried my face in his neck, my sobs growing louder by the minute.

He didn't try to tell me my feelings weren't valid or that I shouldn't blame myself because everything had turned out fine in the end. He didn't point out that he hadn't been witness to Hendrix's birth, either—or Hope's, for that matter. My husband simply held me, letting me release everything I'd been holding inside for weeks.

When I finally calmed down to the point where only the occasional hiccup remained, he kissed the top of my head and said, "I think we both need to talk to someone about our PTSD from that day."

When I reared back to look at him, there wasn't a trace of judgment in his eyes. Instead, I only found empathy.

"Because I almost died?" I asked.

"No. Because we both blame ourselves for what happened."

I shook my head in disbelief. "How could you be to blame?"

"While I sat there in a state of shock waiting for news of whether you'd made it, I realized that if I'd never gotten you pregnant, none of it would have ever happened."

My jaw dropped. All this time, I'd been punishing myself, and he'd been struggling, too.

"Seeing you like that..." Jenner's voice broke, emotion taking over, and my heart twisted.

"Baby." I ran my hand through his hair and along his jaw, and his eyes slid closed. "I'm so sorry."

"Me, too." He banded his arms tighter around me, like if he let go, I might disappear.

Holding each other close, we made promises to work through our individual experiences of the trauma of that day, both together and with the help of a professional. Because if there was one thing we'd learned after all this time, it was that we were stronger together.

Chapter 38

Evie

"I'm gonna eat this belly!" I declared before bringing my lips to Hendrix's tummy and blowing raspberries on his bare skin.

My baby boy's squeals made my heart swell, even when he brought both fists up to tangle in my hair.

"Hold on; don't move. I've got you," Paige's voice called over when she realized my three-month-old son wasn't about to release me, and I was stuck.

Her fingers pried his fists open, and I pulled back, chiding Hendrix playfully, "Naughty boy, pulling Mama's hair."

He gave me a gummy grin in response, not the least bit sorry.

Months of targeted trauma therapy had helped me create a bond with this incredibly sweet baby I was beyond blessed to call my own. He, along with his brother and sister, were my reason for living, and though it was exhausting having three infants, I'd never been happier.

Paige had been hesitant about increasing her role in Hope's life beyond the initial minimum ask of her birthday and Christmas. But over the summer, she'd gotten some much-needed counseling herself, and now that she was back in Indy for the fall semester, she popped over whenever she had a free afternoon.

I loved having her around. Not just for the extra set of hands, which were always welcome, but because she adored all three of our babies. I knew they would grow up viewing her as they would Jenner's teammates and spouses—an extension of our family.

Currently, we were on the living room floor, which had been cleared of the coffee table, so there was more room for the babies to spread out.

The boys were days from rolling over, and Hope was sitting up at six months old. I was afraid to blink most days for fear that time was slipping by too fast. The next thing we knew, they'd be crawling, then walking, then headed off to school.

Hunter whined from where he was lying on his belly, so Paige picked him up for a cuddle. Nuzzling the top of his downy-soft copper hair, she sighed. "Don't tell the others, but you might be my favorite. You're such a little love bug."

Hope took offense, a tiny scowl gracing her beautiful cherub face, and she reached both hands out for her birth mom.

Paige leaned over to press a kiss to her cheek. "I was just kidding, sweet girl. I love all three of you exactly the same."

Hope used the opportunity to grab Paige's free hand and brought it to her mouth. I was about to warn Paige, but I wasn't fast enough.

"Oh!" Widened blue eyes stared at me from across the room. "She bit me!"

Having been a victim of our resident piranha baby, I couldn't stifle a laugh. "Yeah, she does that. Teething toys work best, but she's not picky."

Shaking her head in wonder, first at Hope and then the boys, she remarked, "I don't know how you do it."

I wasn't going to downplay that having three babies so close in age was difficult. "Coffee's pretty much the only thing keeping me going at this point. That, and accepting help when it's offered. We wouldn't be anywhere without our Speed family and Emmy."

Paige squeezed Hunter tighter. "I know I say it all the time, but I'm so happy I picked you guys."

My nose tingled, and my vision grew blurry.

It didn't matter that after years of trying, we'd achieved our goal of conceiving on our own, bringing the twins into our lives. We would have been missing a piece without Hope. She made our family complete.

A tear slipped down my cheek, and I whispered back, "We'll never be able to repay you for the gift you've given us, Paige."

Her eyes grew glassy, and she pushed onto her knees so she could shuffle closer. She threw her free arm around me and hugged me tight, with Hunter squished between us.

"Thank you." Her watery words were right beside my ear.

When she pulled away, a shy smile graced her lips, and her eyes dipped to the floor. "I thought my life was over when I saw those two pink lines. But now I realize that Hope led me to some of the most incredible people I'll ever meet. Watching you and Jenner become parents, seeing your love for each other... You guys set the standard in my mind. And I don't want to settle for anything less."

Hendrix whined at being left out, so I scooped him up, bouncing him as I spoke to Paige. "Life isn't without its challenges. For being so young, you've faced more than most. But you remained calm and made a plan. You did what was best for Hope. She's going to grow up knowing you put her before yourself and that you cared enough to continue being a part of her life—even if it isn't as her primary parent. And someday, you're gonna meet a great guy who deserves you, and I'm honored that Jenner can provide you with an example of what a steadfast, supportive partner looks like.

"I didn't feel like I deserved him in my darkest days. He was too good, and I thought I was dragging him down. But even through all our time spent apart, we never stopped loving each other, which is a testament to our bond. He's my person, and I'm his. I've had to take a hard look in the mirror and accept that sometimes I need help because I struggle with inner demons, but I'm able to do so knowing that he'll always have my back, will always put me first, and he's never going to let me run away again."

Paige tangled her free hand with mine and squeezed. "You two have an amazing love story, and I'm so lucky to hold even the tiniest part of it."

"You're stuck with us, kid." I threw her a wink.

Our lives had been messy before the babies, but now they were crazy and loud and so full of love my heart threatened to burst, and I wouldn't change it for the world.

"All three are down for the count." The words were said with a sigh of relief as Jenner latched our bedroom door after stepping inside.

I set the book I was reading—Dakota's latest release—down on the nightstand. Having put Hope to bed while Jenner wrangled the boys, which took a bit longer, I'd been afforded a few precious minutes to read. Time for myself was a thing of the past with three babies under seven months.

Padding across the room on bare feet, Jenner cocked an eyebrow when he saw my choice of reading material. Then, a sexy smirk curved on his lips.

"Anything good?"

"Oh, you know. Guy meets girl, girl won't give him the time of day, but he pursues her anyway. She can't resist his charm, and they fall helplessly in love. Honestly, I don't know why I bother reading romance anymore. Seems like the same story on repeat."

His chuckle warmed my insides as he caged me in with one hand pressed to the headboard. Voice dropping low, he rasped, "Oh, come on, Evie. We both know you skim the storyline and head straight for the spice."

My face flamed because he was absolutely correct.

"I bet"—Jenner's lips ghosted over mine—"if I slipped my hand between your thighs, I'd find you soaking wet. Isn't that right, baby?"

Mouth suddenly dry, I found it hard to swallow as his hand skimmed over my waist, dipping beneath the hem of my sleep shirt. My gasp mixed with his groan as his fingers brushed against my core, which was indeed slick with my arousal.

It had been so long. Since the boys were born. I was fully recovered, but we were just too damn busy. When the chaos settled at night, sleep pulled at us before there was time to have a conscious thought about being intimate.

But I'd missed him—missed the way he made me feel.

"This okay?" Jenner murmured, his fingers sinking deeper through my slit.

My head dropped back on a moan. "God, yes."

Slowly, he pressed two fingers inside me and hissed. "Fuck, Evie."

"More," I begged.

Withdrawing slightly, he shoved back in, setting a slow and steady pace that allowed the heel of his palm to grind against my clit with every pass.

His mouth pressed hot, messy kisses along my exposed neck as he fucked me with his fingers. When he curled those digits, pressing on that magic spot, my back arched, and my thighs began to tremble.

Out of words, I could only moan as pleasure threatened to drag me under, but I would happily drown if it meant Jenner was the one to take me down.

"I know, baby. You're right there, aren't you?"

A whimper flew past my lips.

"Your pussy is gripping me so tight." His breath was hot in my ear. "Let go. I promise to catch you when you fall."

That was all it took. His words didn't just send me over the edge; they threw me over violently. Stars burst behind my eyes, and my lungs seized as all my muscles convulsed in unison. Jenner's hand followed my body's cues, only slowing when he was confident I was coming down from the intense high of my orgasm.

My stuttered breaths sounded in the air, my chest heaving with the effort. "Oh. My. God."

Humming against my skin, Jenner mused, "Not sure it'll ever get old, watching you come. It's beyond breathtaking."

"I need you, Jenner," I breathed out, the pulsing between my thighs still insistent.

"Look at me." The command was firm yet soft as he gripped my chin.

I forced my eyes open as a rush of heat pooled at my core at the sight of his hungry gaze.

"You want my mouth first? Or do you need my cock right now, baby?"

"Uh-huh." I managed a nod.

His husky laugh had my nipples hardening painfully. "Words, sweetheart. I know you have them."

Fuck. I didn't want to think right now; I only wanted to feel. Why was he making this so hard?

Hard.

That thought had my hand snaking down to grip his length tenting his boxers. His resulting groan was music to my ears, and I fought back a satisfied smile.

"This," I said, hoping it was enough to get the message across.

"You always did have good taste." He placed a kiss at the base of my throat before pulling away.

His cock slipped from my grasp as he stood, stripping down until he was naked before me.

My teeth sunk into my lower lip. Holy hell, my husband was hot. If I weren't so desperate for him to be inside me, I would have taken my time to lick across every hard line of muscle on his toned body.

And when he reached down to stroke his shaft, staring at me with hooded eyes, I almost came on the spot. The vision of him working his cock with his hand, the way his forearm tensed with each tug, was better than anything I could ever read in a book.

Closing the gap between us, he fisted the hair at the back of my neck and tugged, making it so I couldn't escape when his lips crashed down onto mine. His tongue swept inside, making my toes curl as he commanded this kiss, reminding me how good it could be between us, how much he desired me.

I felt cool air rush over the heated skin of my upper thighs, but when my shirt was tugged over my belly, I pushed at his chest.

I might have fifty pounds on the man, but he was a wall of solid muscle. Even if I used every ounce of strength I possessed, I knew I wouldn't be able to move him. So, when he drew back, it was only because he allowed it, not because I'd successfully pushed him away.

"No," I whispered.

With that single word, Jenner put more space between us. "You want to stop? Is it too soon?"

Squeezing my eyes shut, I shook my head. "It's not that."

A warm hand caressed my face, the rough pad of his thumb smoothing over my cheekbone. "Talk to me, Evie."

"I—" I swallowed. "I don't want you to see me like this." I tugged the hem of my T-shirt back down for emphasis.

I could hear the confusion in his voice. "Babe. I'm the one who took care of you. I've seen it all."

Blowing out a breath, I forced my eyes open. "That was different."

Jenner cocked his head. "How?"

Insecurity crept in at me from all sides, but I knew better than to hide my feelings from my husband. Therapy, combined with learning from past mistakes, had taught me that communication was vital.

With my heart in my throat, I confessed, "Because it's not sexy. And for as turned on as I am right now, I can't stand the thought of your dick going limp because of what my body looks like now."

His mouth dropped open, and he let out a disbelieving huff. "Not sexy?"

I shook my head. "Not even a little bit."

Blazing eyes bore into mine, seemingly searching my soul as he asked, "Do you trust me?"

Dammit. He was playing dirty. He knew that I did.

Jenner's gaze held mine as he awaited my answer.

I couldn't lie to him. "Yes."

Not saying another word, my husband urged me to sit up against the pillows lining the headboard and tugged the shirt over my head.

My first instinct was to band my arms across my waist, but it wouldn't be enough. I couldn't hide from him.

"Do you know what I see when I look at this body?" Jenner's soft voice had me peeking up at him.

I sucked in a sharp breath when he took a fingertip and traced the purple stretch marks lining the loose skin of my deflated belly. Next, he followed the line of my C-section scar.

Reverently, he said, "I see a fucking warrior. A strong woman who sacrificed her body to bring our sons into this world. More than that, I see a survivor. You fought hard for what you wanted and won. And as far as I'm concerned, I've never seen anything more beautiful in my entire life."

Hot tears burned behind my eyes, and I blinked furiously.

Classic Jenner. Taking what I saw as flaws and flipping them upside down into assets.

I was so goddamn lucky that, one day, he'd taken one look at me and decided that I was his future.

Leaning in to cup my face, he vowed, "I love you, Evie. You're my everything. Always and forever. Got it?"

I nodded, tears spilling over onto my cheeks.

He brushed them away, a tender expression crossing his handsome face. "Now, if it's okay with you, I'd like to make love to my wife—my warrior."

Letting out a watery laugh, I whispered, "Please."

He took my hand and brought it to wrap around his stiff cock. "See? No problems here, baby."

I gave it a firm tug, relishing how his eyes rolled back into his head.

"Fuuuuuck." His moan had me trying to press my thighs together, which was impossible with him kneeling between them.

Swallowing, he shook his head, chiding, "No. No more hiding. I want to be able to see every perfect inch of this incredible body, and that includes your pretty pink pussy."

With that, he spread my legs wider, holding me open as he gazed at where I glistened, so ready for him.

"Put me in, baby."

Jenner moved his hips closer so that I could line him up with my entrance. A shift of my hips, and he sank in the first inch.

Having been cautioned against the risks of having more children, Jenner had taken action and gotten a vasectomy. When I'd told him it wasn't necessary, he'd looked me dead in the eye and declared that nothing was going to come between him and his wife ever again. And that had been that.

So, there wasn't a second thought when he bottomed out inside me bare—skin to skin, the merging of souls.

Jenner's grip tightened on my hips. "Fuck, you feel so good." His eyes remained locked on where our bodies were joined as he began to thrust. "A perfect fit. Like you were made for me."

The way I was positioned, almost sitting up, each pass of his cock rubbed against my clit, and I was panting, reaching for him, trying to draw him closer.

"Look at us," he commanded. "Look at how well you take all of me."

My gaze dropped as instructed. My lower lips were stretched around his cock as it slid in and out, in and out. The erotic sight had my pussy gripping him tighter as a fresh wave of arousal slammed into me.

Jaw hanging slack, my husband looked like a Greek god with his abs tensed, his rhythm increasing with each snap of his hips.

I dug my nails into the tight flesh of his ass, urging him on. "Harder."

He braced one hand on the headboard, his control snapping, and he finally let me have it.

Writhing beneath him, I gasped when he hit the perfect spot. "Right there. Don't stop."

"Never, baby. I'll never stop," he gritted out.

A familiar tingling sensation gathered between my legs, coiling tighter and tighter, getting ready to explode.

"Come with me."

I shattered instantly, moaning as I clawed at him, trying to hang on and extend the feeling of pure bliss coursing through my veins. Jenner dropped his head to the crook of my neck, thrusting twice more before stilling, grunting as he came, filling me.

Sticky with sweat, I held my husband close, stroking his damp hair.

Our love story had been one hell of a rollercoaster, fraught with heartbreak and drama, but I couldn't be sorry if that was how we'd gotten here—with Jenner and me wrapped up in each other, our children sleeping peacefully down the hall, and a beautiful future ahead of us.

Epilogue

Jenner

One Year Later

It had been a long time since I'd set foot on the campus of Glendale State University, but even longer since I'd been inside the hockey arena.

Today, the university would be retiring my number. It was surreal that they would single me out for that honor. From this day forward, no player for Glendale State would be able to wear the number seventy-five, with my name being raised into the rafters as its permanent owner.

Even more mind-blowing was that they'd filled this five-thousand-seat arena for the ceremony.

I wasn't a local kid, and I hadn't played there in over a decade, but the stands were overflowing with students, Glendale State alumni, and those from the community who had tracked my career even after I'd left the desert. There was a split amongst the attendees, with some wearing my old college jersey, but most wore Indy Speed red and black with the name Knight stitched across the back.

Seated beside Evie, I listened to the remarks of the University's President, the Athletic Director, and finally, my old college coach before I was asked to make a speech to those gathered.

Evie gently squeezed my knee, and I rose, walking across the carpeted area over the ice surface toward a podium stand with a microphone. Adjusting it to the proper height, I smoothed my typed speech over the wood surface.

Clearing my throat, I began, "First, I'd like to thank Glendale State University and the Athletic Department for this incredible honor. It was my absolute privilege to have played for this outstanding program.

"I came to Glendale State sixteen years ago with something to prove. Not only to the team that drafted me but to myself—that I could compete, that I had what it took to play at the highest levels and win.

"Never in my wildest dreams did I expect that my biggest accomplishment during my time on campus would be meeting my wife, Evie."

I darted a glance to where my family sat. Evie had Hope in one arm, Hendrix in the other, while Paige sat beside her, holding Hunter.

"Some of my teammates warned that being tied down by a girl would be a distraction and that I should focus on the game to further my future career. But what they didn't understand was that she became my driving force. I pushed myself to be better for her. I wanted her to be proud of me.

"So, I'll thank you again because raising my name into the rafters will go a long way in impressing the girl I like."

That got a chuckle from the crowd, and Evie's cheeks pinkened.

"But all kidding aside, hockey has given me so much—intangible things that have helped me not just in my career, but in life. Skills like teamwork, resilience, discipline, and communication. And that's not to mention the lifelong brotherhood I have with every single guy I've had the pleasure of stepping onto the ice with since I was a kid.

"I've been fortunate to have a career playing the game I love. And my time at Glendale State played a major role in preparing me for the professional stage. I am thankful to each and every one of my teammates, coaches, and trainers for making me better along the way.

"I want all of the current Glendale State players to remember to enjoy their time here. Work hard and have some fun along the way. Because at the end of the day, win or lose, it is just a game. Whether you end up pursuing a future in hockey or other endeavors, you'll always look back on your days here as some of the best of your life. Those friendships with your brothers will last forever.

"I'm incredibly grateful that today I'm able to share this moment with my family, not only my beautiful wife but our three children—Hope, Hunter, and Hendrix. I know they're too little to remember it, but it's my wish that someday they'll look back on pictures and videos of this day and be proud of all their dad has achieved.

"Thank you again from the bottom of my heart. And go, Scorpions!"

The cheers grew in volume as I stepped back from the podium to find my family on approach. I grabbed Hope from Evie's arms. Our little girl's big blue eyes scanned the crowd in awe.

All of this was nice, but my legacy wasn't my name stamped into the silver of a trophy or lifted into the rafters inside arenas. No, it lived on through the three little gingers who would one day take on the world with as much wisdom as I could impart on them.

My life would forever revolve around them and their mama, but at the end of the day, our story had started right here.

Our messy, beautiful life began the day I worked up the nerve to ask a stunning, sassy blonde to come watch me play. The rest was history.

For a bonus scene from Hope's second birthday, you can find it under the Bonus Scenes tab at https://sienatrapbooks.com/

Our favorite golden retriever goalie, Goose, is up next when the Indy Speed series continues with *Goalie Goal*.

Missed out on Maddox and Bristol's story? You can catch up now with *A Bunny for the Bench Boss*.

Enjoyed your quick stop in Evie's hometown of Rust Canyon, Oklahoma? The Rust Canyon series kicks off with *Festive Faking*.

Acknowledgements

A huge thank you goes out to my husband for his incredible support throughout this entire journey. I know it's been a crazy ride, but you've been riding shotgun since before I even decided to start writing. So, thank you for believing in me before I believed in myself.

To my kids, especially my oldest. You are the one who made me a mom when it's what I wanted more than anything in this world. Though your entry into it was anything but uncomplicated, I would do it all over again in a heartbeat, even if that meant you were earthside while I was not.

To Katie, my editor. This was a story I worried might be too much for you. Thank you for sticking with me through it and for declaring that the emotion of it had you so invested that you barely noticed the spice.

To Nina, my proofreader. Thank you for your tireless efforts to comb through every word to make sure my work is perfect before going to print.

To Sam D. I couldn't do this without you. Your work behind the scenes makes my life so much easier and gives me more time to focus on what's truly important: the writing. Your creativity blows me away on the daily, and I know when I'm stuck, you're right there to lend an ear or offer feedback.

Thank you to Happily Booked PR for their support in launching this book.

Thank you to my Spicy Sidekicks. It's the highlight of my day chatting with you about our mutual love of books, and watching as those who are newer to the Siena-verse go back to the beginning.

The biggest thank you goes out to my incredible readers. Thank you for your constant support, often shouting from the rooftops how much you love my books. Most days it doesn't seem real. I might write the words, but you bring them to life. I am forever grateful that you've chosen to invest your time in this world that I've created.

About the Author

SIENA IS ORIGINALLY FROM Pittsburgh, Pennsylvania, where a love of sports is bred into a girl's DNA. Her love of romance novels came early as well. She would often accompany her romance reviewer mom to book lovers' and romance writer's conventions, where she sat in on workshops and met numerous best-selling authors. It wasn't long before she was filling notebooks with her own stories, which often starred herself and a certain real-life prince.

As luck would have it, she met and married a handsome athlete instead. After several temporary residencies in multiple states and Germany, they finally settled in Michigan, the land where youth hockey reigns supreme.

Her stories no longer feature herself, but draw from her past experiences as an educator, businesswoman, fashion consultant, and world traveler when creating her strong heroines. "Oh yes," she says with a wink and a smile, "There are bits of me in all of them." Now, she spends her days writing happily ever afters for fictional characters and her evenings at the local hockey arenas cheering for her three children.

Siena loves to hear from her readers. You can email her at: siena.trap.books@gmail.com

Or find her on social media (FB, IG, and TT): @siena.trap.books

More Books by Siena Trap

Remington Royals Series
Scoring the Princess
Playing Pretend with the Prince
Feuding with the Fashion Princess

Connecticut Comets (Hockey) Series
Bagging the Blueliner
Surprise for the Sniper
Second-Rate Superstar

Indy Speed (Hockey) Series
A Bunny for the Bench Boss
Frozen Heart Face-Off
Goalie Goal

Rust Canyon Series
Festive Faking
Coming Home Country
Crashing the Altar
Before You Can Blink

Made in the USA
Monee, IL
28 November 2024